RHAPSODY
FOR A
UNICORN

Oscar Cappelli

CHRISTOFFEL & LE CORDIER

Published by Christoffel & Le Cordier Ltd
401 Langham House
302 Regent Street, London W1B 3HH
www.christoffel.co.uk

ISBN 0-9542138-0-7 (e-book)
ISBN 0-9542138-1-5 (trade paperback)

Acknowledgments and Thanks

I acknowledge with gratitude the wise counsel of the people who read and edited the manuscript at various stages during preparation: Bryn Brooks, Brian Collins, Sally Hinwood, Ann Kritzinger, Michael McIrvin, and Jane Rafal.

A Special Thank-you to a Dear Friend

I am especially grateful to Junior, my Siamese cat. For over three years, he crouched on top of my PC and his ice-blue eyes helped me to overcome the moments of discouragement.

*"... A cry from the sea,
a voice in the woods."*

(From *Kaleidoscope,* by Paul Verlaine)

1

Guichard crossed Boulevard Saint Germain and walked past the Café de Flore. He glanced at the cafés and old bookshops, with unseeing eyes. As he was passing the La Fontaine & Mikaelian art gallery, the name "Bodin" caught his eye. Place de Furstenberg was nearby; he had time. He stopped to look in the window. They were holding a private exhibition of Impressionist paintings.

He peered through the glass, trying to catch sight of the Bodin, but there were too many people inside. He caught a glimpse of a woman's profile: the same smile, vaguely insolent, with dimples in her cheeks, and the same long, black hair.

It had been at a dinner party. He'd been sitting across from a professor of astrophysics, and she only a few places farther down the table. Their eyes had met more than once. When they'd been introduced, he had the feeling he'd seen her somewhere before. Who did those gray-green eyes remind him of?

"Haven't we met before?" he had asked.

After a moment's hesitation, she'd replied: "No, I don't think so. At least...."

At one point he thought he'd heard her mention a cardinal of the Church, but he'd managed only to catch a few random words.

As he entered the gallery, people turned to look at him. His height and long hair never failed to attract attention. The spotlights shot beams onto the ceiling, and the murmur typical of museums and churches rippled through the room. The Bodin hung on the far wall. As he walked towards it, he glanced at her again; she was immersed in conversation with another woman and was pointing out a painting. She appeared confident, as though she felt at home there. She wore a long, black skirt and a cream-colored, silk blouse buttoned to the neck, and a string of pearls. She had style. For a moment their eyes met. She recognized him.

"I'm Françoise Mikaelian. Can I be of assistance?"

Guichard shook her hand. "Guichard de Saint Clair. Do you remember me?"

"You were at the Seigneurs' dinner party, weren't you? You spent the whole evening talking to the astrophysicist," Françoise said, a hint of reproach in her voice.

"I wanted to talk to you, but thought you were with someone." Guichard glanced at her left hand. No wedding ring. An amused look crossed her face.

"I see you're interested in the Bodin."

"Bodin was a master of light. No one has ever managed to capture the Normandy countryside quite like him."

He questioned her about the picture on display in front of them, more to hear her speak than for any other reason; he already knew all about the painting. While she described its background and character, he kept wondering where he'd seen her before; it had nothing to do with their brief encounter at the dinner party. Something else intrigued him as well, not simply the way she acted. But the way she acted was gripping his attention now. Reserved? Not really. It was more like an invisible barrier that she wouldn't let anyone cross.

He'd never liked things to be too easy. It was the pathos of 'becoming' that gave life meaning, even with women. When the pathos was gone, what was left?

Françoise didn't trust handsome men; they were usually vacuous. But the man who was looking at the Bodin painting seemed somehow different. He looked like someone out of the *Three Musketeers*. He was tall, his hair long and starting to turn gray at the temples. But what struck her most was his face: determined, almost hard, perhaps because of the resolute line of his jaw and his Grecian nose. Yet his expression didn't suggest a rigid character, but rather a basic skepticism towards life in general. He gave the impression of someone who didn't belong to this world and, if it hadn't been for his perfectly cut dark-blue suit, she could almost imagine him in a cloak, wielding a sword.

As soon as she saw him enter the gallery, she experienced a feeling of déjà vu. She didn't want to give the impression of pouncing on a possible client, so at first she didn't approach him. When she eventually did, she remembered where she'd seen him before; it had been at a dinner party at the Seigneurs'. She'd noticed him and had been sorry that he'd not made any attempt to get to know her.

When they began to speak about the Bodin, Françoise realized immediately that he knew what he was talking about. They didn't speak for long, because he had an appointment. When he left the gallery, Françoise followed him with her eyes, until she lost sight of him in the crowd.

Two days later, he came back to the gallery and asked her if the owner of the collection might be interested in exchanging the Bodin for an Utrillo from his own collection. She looked at his business card. *Guichard de Saint Clair.* That name reminded her of something or someone, but for the moment she couldn't quite place what it was.

That evening she mentioned him to Jules, her senior partner at the gallery.

Jules's eyes widened as he looked at the card over the glasses resting halfway down his nose. "Don't tell me that this name doesn't mean anything to you. You're supposed to be the gallery's expert on Impressionism."

"The de Saint Clair collection?"

"Of course, the de Saint Clair collection. If it's *the* Guichard de Saint Clair, then you're dealing with the only living descendant of one of the oldest families in France, *les Comtes* de Saint Clair from Normandy."

"Do you know anything about him?"

"He runs an investment bank that handles large transactions," Jules said. "They say he owns a fortune, but I really don't know much about him. He has the reputation of being a reserved man." Then he added, his eyes gleaming: "Oh, I read somewhere that he's been seen playing the organ at St. Sulpice's. Am I to conclude that you've suddenly become fond of organ music?"

"Oh c'mon, Jules."

When Françoise called de Saint Clair to tell him that the owner of the collection had declined his proposal, he didn't seem too disappointed. So perhaps it hadn't been the picture that had led him into the gallery, after all. And Françoise wasn't surprised when he phoned her, the day after, to ask her out to dinner.

The dinner with Guichard de Saint Clair was a new experience for Françoise. For the first time, she found herself in the company of a successful man who not only didn't talk about himself, but who actually seemed annoyed when the conversation touched on anything personal. He deftly avoided subjects such as his family, his work, his hobbies, whereas he willingly discussed painting and music. If she had to sum him up in a single word, that word would be "elusive."

"... How does one feel bearing a thousand-year-old name?" she said.

"I was born with it, so it's hard to answer your question." Guichard took a menu and looked through it. "One thing I became aware of very soon, though. Bearing a name like mine meant feeling lonely, both at school and home."

"Lonely?"

"People expect you to be different, and that makes you different."

"In what respect?"

"In many respects, but it would be a long story. By the way, the Bodin painting, did you sell it?"

That dinner was followed by a second and then a third date, but Guichard de Saint Clair remained a mystery. The fact that he hadn't asked her to sleep with him—and Françoise had been somehow glad he hadn't—only added to the curiosity she felt about him, though maybe "curiosity" wasn't the right word any more.

"... What are the most important elements involved, when you decide to launch an unknown painter?" Guichard asked.

"Now it's me doing all the talking," Françoise said. "You promised me you would tell me about your playing the organ."

"What do you want to know? If I have one at home?"

"Why the organ? It seems so... exacting. It makes me think of someone from the 17th century, wearing a powdered wig."

"It was my father who initially encouraged me—I never figured out why—Soon, though, I started to like it."

"Why?"

"When I play the organ, I forget about everything else." Guichard seemed to be looking through her, as if she weren't there. "Space and time merge."

"What do you mean?"

"The notion of time stops, and I have the impression of seeing worlds I've been to before, yet in another dimension."

"Is it true that you play the St. Sulpice organ in the middle of the night?"

He smiled and raised a hand. "I confess it, Your Honor."

"I feel sorry for the poor sexton."

"He suffers from insomnia, like me, so he doesn't mind. He tells me it's like having a concert all to himself."

"And you play at night because of the insomnia?"

"It's at night that I feel like playing...."

Françoise stopped doodling and put her pen down. She caught herself thinking about Guichard again. This had recently been happening to her in the most unusual moments, like during a business meeting, or while shopping at the supermarket.... She sighed. She'd split up with her husband only three months before. The thought of Jean-Pierre no longer caused her anger or fear, just the need to forget and move on. She wasn't ready to start a new relationship—not a demanding one, at any rate. After all, she'd known Guichard for only a month; she was attracted to him, certainly, but wasn't it too early to say how she really felt about him?

A framed photograph, standing on her desk, caught her gaze. It had been taken at her ninth birthday party, at the house of her grandparents on her father's side, in Armenia. Her father was standing in front of her, encouraging her to blow out the candles. A mental picture of an exploding plane flashed through her mind. As usual, she tried not to think of how her father must have felt at that moment. She'd always tried to convince herself that it must have happened so quickly that he wouldn't have had time to react. At the time, she was only ten years old. One evening, tucked in bed, she heard her mother's muffled cry and the murmured words of comfort from her relatives, who'd rushed in from Yerevan and Innsbruck. The investigation had confirmed that the explosion had been caused by a bomb on the El Al plane. Terrorism was suspected, but no one had ever been brought to justice.

In spite of that, mysteries had fascinated her ever since childhood, and it wasn't by chance that detective novels had become her favorite reading. Maybe it was also for that reason that, after getting her diploma from art school, she'd specialized in combating art forgery, gradually earning a reputation in the field. The La Fontaine & Mikaelian art gallery was a consultant not only for the Ministère de la Justice, but also for museums like the Louvre, and for several private art collectors.

Françoise looked at her watch. It was eight o'clock. From her desk, through the open door, she could see the other side of the corridor. The lights in Jules's office were out. She liked working late, in the silence of the deserted gallery. Her office overlooked the church of Saint Germain des Près. The bell tower was lit up and the scents of a summer that refused to die drifted in through the window. The thought of Guichard stirred a feeling of longing in her.

As she was getting up to leave, the phone rang. It was Guichard.

"I'm off to Scotland for three days," he said. Then, after a pause: "Would you like to come with me?"

Cardinal Rolf Wolfenberg went over to the window of his office on the second floor of the Palace of the Holy Office. He looked at the right wing of the Bernini colonnade, the Baroque statues of saints on the balustrades, and the Apostolic Palace above. For a moment his eyes came to rest on the second to last window of the third floor.

After having served an early mass in his private chapel, His Holiness must already be busy in the daily meeting he held at 8:00 a.m. with the cardinal secretary of state. At the thought of Cardinal Missiroli—the secretary of state—his hands clenched behind his back. He lifted his eyes to the dome of St. Peter's and took a deep breath. That view always had the same effect on him; the dome and everything around it testified to the greatness of the Catholic Church. Instinctively, his hand reached for the gold cross suspended from his neck.

The thought that the Church was everywhere, keeping a sharp watch on society, gave him a sense of security. The Church went on being the conscience of all Catholics, even for those who never went to church and railed at priests. Just like the rest, they had absorbed those same morals in childhood, and would never be free of them. It was a conscience manipulated by the constant hammering of thousands and thousands of parish priests nestled in every corner of the earth. Through practices such as Confession and Holy Communion, the Church delved into the very soul of the people and was able to keep a tight rein on any social change. The secret? Make everyone feel guilty about something, starting with Original Sin. Besides, what did people know about things such as good and evil? Let God—and the Church—take care of it.

"Your Eminence, the members of the Commission are all here. They're waiting for you," said Monsignor Feliciani, poking his head round the door.

"Please tell them I'm coming, *Monsignore.*"

When would these blessed theologians learn that all that thinking could be dangerous? He sighed. Too much arrogance and too little faith, that was the problem. He went back to his desk and picked up the file on Father Fairchild, the latest troublemaker. His stomach knotted when he recalled names such as Küng, Boff, Curran, names against which his predecessor, quite rightly, had launched a holy crusade. He leafed through the first pages of the file. Oh yes, Fairchild was that young Franciscan who taught theology at the Ecumenical University of Washington. He rubbed his hands together. The problem shouldn't take long.

The friar seemed even younger than his twenty-nine years. The cowl he wore and those blue eyes of his gave him a defenseless air.

"Father Fairchild, your writings do not conform to the doctrine of the Catholic faith," concluded the cardinal. "This Commission therefore orders you to silence for a period of two years. You know what this means: no writing and no teaching."

The friar's pallor increased, and he stared for a moment at the cardinal, as if he hadn't understood. Eventually he lowered his head.

The cardinal was aware that his expression struck fear in people, and he used it to his best advantage. It was because of his jowls, bulging outwards towards his lower jaw. They quivered, making him seem like a mastiff, which gave people the impression he was biting into something. When he was angry, his cheeks turned purple and his jowls shook more than ever; this was the image the cardinal loved to portray to the theologians interrogated by the tribunal of the CDF—the Congregation for the Doctrine of the Faith, formerly known as the Holy Office.

Father Fairchild suddenly raised his head and looked Cardinal Wolfenberg squarely in the face, his eyes burning with indignation.

"You haven't even given me a chance to defend myself!" Father Fairchild said. "You are violating my rights."

"Here the only law is Canon Law!" the cardinal said.

"What am I being accused of, Your Eminence?"

"I'm amazed you should ask." The cardinal grabbed a newspaper from the file in front of him. "Just consider your last article on the problems of overpopulation, in which you wrote—I quote your exact words: 'the Roman Catholic Church will have to reconsider its attitude to artificial methods of birth control.'"

"Yes, I wrote that, and I'd write it again. My conscience tells me that the Church can't continue shutting its eyes in the face of such a reality. In twenty years, almost half of the world population will risk dying of starvation."

"Who are you to oppose the encyclical *Humanae Vitae*? Life is sacred. *That is blasphemy.*"

"Your Eminence, have you ever been to places such as Bangladesh or Zimbabwe? God would never want that."

The cardinal's face turned violet and his jowls quivered. "How do you know what God wants? If we started accepting a thesis like yours, we could soon be accepting even abortion, or homosexuality. Can you imagine something like that happening?"

"Your Eminence, neither you nor I know God's Will. But He gave us a conscience and a brain, to enable us to understand what is right and what is wrong."

The Dominican theologian sitting next to Cardinal Wolfenberg jumped to his feet. "This is heresy! Good and evil in the Christian sense cannot be separated from the Faith."

"No, Father, it's not heresy. Heresy is committed by those who insist on interpreting the Bible literally, by those who fail to realize that today's Christian morals can't be those of two thousand years ago, by those who condemn whole populations to starve to death on the basis of anachronistic dissertations—"

"That's enough," the cardinal said. "We made our views on this matter perfectly clear at the New Delhi Conference on overpopulation, in 2004. So why persist? If your beliefs are so inflexible, you should consider other options."

Father Fairchild withdrew his gaze from the cardinal, and for a few seconds his thoughts seemed to be far away. Finally he got up, removed his chain and put it on the table, right in front of the cardinal. For a moment his hand clutched the cross, and his knuckles whitened. Then he turned and left the room without saying a word.

At that same moment the Palace of the Holy Office was filled with the echoes of the bells of St. Peter's.

2

A bleak, northerly wind blew in from the Sound of Jura and swept across the jagged coastline and overhanging cliffs. The outline of the island was barely visible through the mists that hung over the far side of the Sound. The wind whistled through the church ruins and blew among the gravestones in the abandoned churchyard of Kilmory Chapel.

Guichard, his hands in his raincoat pockets, shivered and turned up his raincoat collar.

Françoise stopped in front of a rough stone slab. "Don't you think it's odd that there's no inscription on it?" She took a green silk scarf from her bag and tied it around her hair. "No name, no date, just the outline of a sword. What does it mean?"

"These are the graves of the Knights Templar. When a knight died, they would lay his sword on the gravestone and chip its profile around it."

"But why no names? Was that one of their customs?"

"No, it's only in Scotland that you find graves like these."

"I seem to have read somewhere that no one has ever found out where the survivors went after fleeing France."

Guichard didn't reply immediately. He gazed into the mist, and went back to that morning of seven centuries before, when the galleys set off in full sail for the Great Ocean.

"Some of them came ashore here, in 1307," he said at last, pointing to the Sound. "But all the others went on to North America.

Françoise was perplexed. "You seem very sure."

Guichard didn't bother to reply and strode off towards the church. Françoise followed him.

The roof was missing and only parts of the three walls were still standing. A pile of rubble was all that remained of the fourth wall. They stepped over what remained of the threshold. A Templar cross was engraved on a slab sticking up from the floor. Despite the weeds and brambles, one could still see the outline of other gravestones on the floor of the church.

"That cross confirms that this was once a Templar chapel," Guichard said.

He remained near the entrance, but his eyes were fixed on the stone slab in the center. Françoise took a few steps forward, picked up a pebble, and started to scrape the earth off the gravestone. Guichard clenched his teeth and tried not to look.

"Look, there's something on this one," she said. "What an incredible coincidence, the name's de Saint Clair! I can't read the first name, but the last two letters look like *r* and ...*d*."

"It's just a coincidence." Guichard tried to sound casual.

"Come here a minute. What's this symbol? The stone's all worn away."

"That's a set-square, and the symbol above is a compass."

"Why are they here?"

"In esoteric symbolism, they represent the rational mind and the creative mind."

"Are you telling me that the Templars already practiced Freemasonry?"

"No, Freemasonry started much later, at the beginning of the eighteenth century. The Templars came across the esoteric mysteries in the Holy Land, at the time of the Crusades."

"Esoteric mysteries in the Holy Land?"

"Certainly. Judaism and Islam were way ahead of Christianity in the mysteries of the spirit." As they were in many other things too, he thought. "It was as if a new, free world had opened up for the Templars, if you think of what an incredible madhouse Christian Europe was at the time."

"How do you know so much about all this?"

"Oh, medieval history has always intrigued me. Don't ask me why."

Françoise gave him a puzzled look.

To avoid further questions, Guichard made his way back to the car; out of the corner of his eye he saw that she was following him, even if unwillingly.

The first drops of rain started to fall. Dark clouds hid the island of Jura, and one could no longer see where the sea ended and the sky began. They got into the car and drove in silence along Loch Sween, until they reached the ruins of Castle Sween. A heron swooped down over the waters of the lake, then turned its neck towards the sky and disappeared into the mist.

The rain started to beat hard against the windshield. Guichard switched on the headlights, and glanced sideways at Françoise. He felt guilty about his vague answer when she'd asked him about the name on that gravestone, but she was asking too many questions. His link with the Templars had to remain a secret, and his personal life couldn't interfere with the Lodge's plan. The plan came first, before anything else: for the Templars, for the Lodge... and for him too. He'd be free, afterwards, and he'd be able to carry on with his life, if there was still a life left.

Guichard braked suddenly, almost blinded by the headlights of an oncoming car. Not far off he could see the steeple of Tarbert church. After a few more miles the outline of their hotel—an old, Scottish, baronial mansion—loomed into sight.

The driving rain pounded against the windowpanes in the dining room. A few dim lights flickered along the coast in the distance. Inside, a big, log fire was burning in the stone fireplace, and Guichard cursed inwardly. Making the excuse that he preferred a quieter area, he asked for a table at the far end of the half-empty dining-room. Françoise didn't say anything. As they drew closer to look at the menu, Guichard gave a start and jerked his head away.

"Oh, I'm sorry if I startled you, sir," the waitress said. "I was just going to light the candle."

"It's my fault. I was lost in thought," Guichard said.

Faces contorted in agony amidst the flames of Porte St. Antoine flashed before his eyes, anguished screams throbbed in his head, and the smell of burning flesh stung his nostrils. Then Arno's disfigured face, his charred body, and those bloodthirsty vultures, with their damned cowls and crucifixes....

"Guichard, what's the matter? Are you all right?"

"I... I'm fine. Do you mind if we put out the candle?"

Before she had time to answer, he blew it out, keeping his head well away. He reached for the water jug, his hand shaking. He forced himself to speak, trying to appear normal, but at that moment Françoise seemed like a floating figure behind a screen of flames, lost somewhere in a time yet to come. Gradually the images faded away, but his hands were still gripping the arms of his chair.

When they went back to their suite, the rain was still beating against the windows. Françoise hadn't spoken for a while, but Guichard exchanged her silence for embarrassment. Her nightdress had been laid on the four poster bed. Guichard drew the curtains. In the semi-darkness, he went over to her and took her in his arms, but Françoise pushed him gently away.

"Why?"

"Maybe I'm not ready for this yet."

"Is something wrong?"

"For me making love isn't something mechanical, Guichard."

"Thanks for the clarification."

"Don't be like that. I didn't mean to hurt you, but don't you feel there's something not quite right? We've known each other for a month now, but all I know about you is what I've read in newspaper clippings."

"Feelings are what matters, not résumés."

"Yes, feelings are what matters," she repeated, looking him squarely in the eyes. "But feelings are made up of little things, things from everyday life, from being together, even from sharing thoughts. But that's not possible with you. You seem to live in your own world, to the exclusion of everyone else."

"Those are just words. Like everyone else, you ask the questions and come up with the answers that suit you the best. You think it's my choice?"

"Whose choice is it then, if not yours?" She paused. "What is it, Guichard? What are you hiding?"

Françoise was perched on the edge of the bed. Guichard sat down next to her and took her hand.

"It's something that happened a long, long time ago, ages before you or I were even born."

"Why don't you talk to me about it?"

"I can't talk about it to anyone, don't ask me why." He pressed her hand to his lips. *"Please."*

For a moment they could hear only the roaring of the rain, then Françoise leaned towards him and her lips brushed his cheek.

§

Françoise awoke suddenly in the middle of the night. For a moment she couldn't make out where she was, then she realized that Guichard was tossing and turning in his sleep. She groped for the light switch and turned towards him. He was uttering strange, incomprehensible phrases. She held her breath. He was lying on his back, his head jerking from side to side, his forehead damp with sweat. She reached out to touch him, but hesitated. Then she leaned over him and stroked his face.

"Guichard, wake up, Guichard!"

The thrashing stopped and the moaning eased. Françoise carried on stroking his face, whispering his name. At last his eyes opened.

"You must have been having a nightmare. Are you all right?"

"Yes, I'm fine… I'm sorry if I frightened you. I feel ridiculous."

"Don't be silly. We all have bad dreams."

Guichard looked at her, alarmed. "Did I say anything in my sleep?"

"Just a few odd words that didn't make much sense."

"What words?"

"Things like 'help', 'fire', 'God'."

Guichard grabbed her arm. "Are you telling me the truth? I didn't say anything else?"

"Why would I lie to you?"

"Sorry, forget what I said."

"Tell me something, though. This has happened before, hasn't it?"

Guichard looked away. "Once or twice, but it's nothing important."

Françoise reached out and turned his face towards her again. "That's not true and you know it. Can't you see I'm only trying to help?"

Guichard sat up and propped the pillow behind him. "Do you think I don't know that?" he said in a somber tone. "It's just that there are things in my life I can't discuss, at least not at the moment. I've already told you that."

"So what does being a couple mean to you, then? Just someone to go to bed with?"

"You know it's not like that."

"What then?"

Guichard's jaw stiffened. "Please, let me be, Françoise. This is something I've got to sort out for myself. By myself, don't you understand?"

Françoise took his hand in hers. "Then I'll wait until you're ready."

But she wasn't prepared to wait forever. She had learned at her expense that in life you had to fight to safeguard what you treasured. And at that very moment, she realized something she hadn't been prepared to acknowledge until a few hours earlier: Guichard had come into her life to stay.

She had to do something.

As soon as he returned to his office, Cardinal Wolfenberg went straight to the small cupboard behind his desk, poured himself a brandy and swallowed half of it in one gulp. *That blasted Fairchild!* As the liquor warmed his stomach, he began to feel better. He went over to the window and looked out towards St. Peter's.

He thought about the protests organized by the theologians in Germany, France, and the United States, as well as in Italy, against the decisions of the tribunal of the CDF. What had happened to the mysteries of the spirit and the mystic vision of life?

The Church's vast umbrella seemed to welcome widely different groups, yet dissenting voices invariably ended up like St. Simon — preaching in the desert. Pluralism? The cardinal shook his head. Nonsense! What had Henry Ford told Americans? "People can have the Model T in any color — as long as it's black." Henry Ford would have made an enlightened pope, no doubt about that.

The cardinal clasped his pectoral cross. Manus Domini was the answer. He thought about the years of internal struggle he had spent blocking the Jesuits' underhanded power; in the end he'd succeeded, and now all of the conservative factions of the Church identified themselves with Manus Domini. Certainly, the fact that the pope firmly believed in Manus Domini was important. And besides, why not admit it? That forceful temperament of his, typical of the Russian people, had helped.

The cardinal turned and walked over to the suit of Templar armor standing near his desk, as if keeping guard over it. He ran his hand slowly over the helmet, while his gaze moved along the antique prints hanging on the walls. They portrayed battle scenes between the Templars and the Saracens at the time of the Crusades. He could almost hear the clash of swords and the cries of the wounded as the warrior monks' blood-red crosses moved forward on the battlefield, imposing God's will.

Manus Domini was one with the spirit of the Templars, and this was the reason for its success. Just like the Templars in the Crusades, Manus Domini had taken up the sword again. The 'Hand of God' would strike Marxist materialism, nihilism, and wanton sexuality, and in the end would win back secular power.

Yes, there were groups like the moderate wing of the Roman Curia [the papal court at the Vatican] who thought the power of the Church should be limited to the spiritual realm. The "right-thinking" moderates claimed that, even without secular power, the Church ruled the lives of over a billion people. The cardinal's mouth curved into a sardonic smile. How naive!

Manus Domini could count on 95,000 laymen who had sworn blind obedience to its cause. At least 50,000 of them—the *initiati*—held key positions in the economy of five continents. A veritable army.

The cardinal sat down at his desk, and glanced through the letter he had received a month earlier from Manaus, capital of the Amazon. *Hoc est signum Dei*—This is a sign of God, he thought. It had been written by Dr. Ignacio Escobar, president of SARN—Sociedade Amazonica do Recursos Naturais—a company founded only three years earlier, but backed by a respectable, fully paid-in capital of 230 million reais.

Escobar had written that Recursos Naturais had started an ambitious program aimed at exploiting the resources of the Amazon rain forests. They intended to carry out the project with the collaboration of cooperatives, whose members would be the Amazon Indian tribes. Escobar ended his letter inviting the Holy See to underwrite a large bond issue of the Manaus-based company.

The cardinal skimmed through the reference letters from the Amazon region's governor, and FUNAI—the Brazilian governing body responsible for the Amazon Indians. He nodded with satisfaction. More than comforting indeed.

Escobar's proposal fitted in perfectly with Manus Domini's plans, and with *his* plans. The cardinal refolded the letter and began to fiddle again with his cross. The contacts he'd made in the past few weeks with the bishops and cardinals who sided with him showed that it could be done.

Quite unwittingly, Ignacio Escobar had indicated the way. The cardinal emptied his glass in a single gulp.

3

"Mr. Kovacs, the report on the budget for the fourth quarter has arrived," Louise said.

"And about time too," Laszlo Kovacs said.

Kovacs went through the report. He grunted, closed the report and slammed it on his desk. For Chrissake, he'd expected a loss, but nothing like this. It would mean a substantial loss for him too, being Allied Petroleum's major shareholder. But this wasn't the problem. He pressed his finger down hard on the intercom.

"Louise, tell O'Neill I want to see him."

"I think Mr. O'Neill is in a meeting at the moment, Mr. Kovacs."

"I don't care where he is. Tell him I want to see him."

Kovacs stood up and limped over to the large windows, on the top floor of the Allied Petroleum Tower overlooking San Francisco Bay. In the early morning mist seagulls circled incessantly over the jetty, swooping down to skim the surface of the water.

"Good morning, Laszlo." Phil O'Neill made his way over to the table in the corner, as usual.

"I saw the year-end budget. I didn't expect a loss like this."

"Blame the presence of vinyl chloride in many of our fine chemicals. A lot of countries have passed laws prohibiting their use and there's just nothing we can do about it. The drop in the prices of petrochemicals has done the rest."

"Nowadays everyone pretends to be playing the ecology game, but they don't fool me. What the hell should we have done?"

"I didn't mean to criticize. The acquisitions made in fine chemicals are sound. The loss is the price we have to pay for moving into a richer market."

"So it's only a temporary problem."

"A loss of $350 million is no joke, even for a company the size of ours. Wall Street will make us pay dearly for this. You can bet on that."

Kovacs frowned. "How much?"

"It's too soon to tell."

Kovacs thought of the consequences the loss would have on the takeover of Overseas Chemicals, a $2 billion project that he and the Overseas boss had been working on for months. That acquisition would make it possible for Allied to reduce its presence in the oil industry to below fifty percent of sales, and that would make him feel much safer. He'd planned to finance the take-over with a stock issue. But Jesus, that was the idea *before* this loss.

"The Overseas deal can't wait," Kovacs said. "How much?"

"The price of our shares could drop by as much as twenty percent, perhaps more."

"And the effect on the Overseas takeover?"

"Wall Street will turn down our stock issue."

"What the hell's Gladstone up to? *Are they our investment bank or not?* Damn spongers, it's up to them to underwrite the placement!"

"Those guys aren't idiots. Come on, Laszlo, wouldn't you do the same?"

"How about just facing the market on our own?"

"I wouldn't suggest anything of the sort," O'Neill said.

Kovacs slowly unscrewed the cap of his pen. He wasn't going to let this opportunity pass by. His thoughts went back to the communist guard who shot at him from the bridge, as he fled Hungary fifty years before. He could still feel the pain as the bullet shattered the bone in his leg, just below the knee. Life soon taught you a ground rule: it was either shoot or be shot at. He jotted down a few lines. "Let's meet again at eleven o'clock."

As O'Neill left, Louise poked her head round the door, a notepad in her hand. "There are several calls waiting, Mr. Kovacs. The most important one—"

"Keep them on hold, and get me the number of de Saint Clair in Paris. D'you remember? The Iranian deal.... Some three years ago."

Seated at the conference table in Kovacs's office, O'Neill was flipping through his notes. When Kovacs entered the room, he rose to his feet. The coffee-pot steamed.

"The takeover of Overseas must go through at all costs." Kovacs reached for the coffee-pot. "All we have to do is prevent Allied from showing a loss."

"But we're talking about a loss of $350 million, with only four months until the end of the year."

"We need $350 million of additional profits. Right?"

"So far."

"Well, I think I've found a solution," Kovacs said. "An asset disposal, to put into effect by the end of December."

O'Neill gave Kovacs a questioning look.

"A joint venture with another petrochemical group, with the obvious condition that the partner comes in with the cash," Kovacs said with a grin, "while we contribute the fixed assets."

"Which fixed assets?"

"Our Kentucky coal."

"But those mines are carried on our books at only $150 million," O'Neill said, "and at current prices they aren't worth more than $270 million."

Kovacs looked at O'Neill, unmoved.

O'Neill jotted down a few quick figures and turned his notepad toward Kovacs. "$270 million worth of coal for $500 million in cash? Why not? A little present of $230 million. I'm sure our partner won't mind."

"Is that all?"

O'Neill's right eye twitched. "No, that's not all. There'd be immediate talk of 'window dressing,' and the result would still be a drop in our shares."

"And you think I'm going to give up just because of some stupid accounting rule?"

"I wouldn't dismiss the issue like that."

"Who's going to stop us from declaring that the deal stems from strategic reasons?"

"And account for the capital gain as normal operating revenue? Forget it. To start with, our auditors would declare war on us and include a negative comment in their report."

"Then they'd have to start looking for another client."

"But a profit and loss statement like that would be misleading for thousands of minority shareholders. Don't you realize that?"

Kovacs shrugged. "Minor details."

"Well, then, remember that the SEC and the Wall Street regulators might also want a say in the matter. For what you call 'minor details,' we'd risk federal charges."

"Do you think the other listed companies all abide by the book?"

"I have to worry about Allied's accounts, not about the others."

"Well, try not to worry too much, then."

O'Neill didn't reply.

"I think that'll be all." Kovacs stood up. "But I'd like to make one thing clear. We're not selling the mines. We're *contributing* them to a joint venture, to obtain strategic advantages. Is that understood?"

O'Neill, lips tightened, got up slowly without saying a word.

Left on his own, Kovacs sat down at his desk and stared out beyond the bay. Less than four months until the end of the year.... There was no other way. He turned on his laptop, keyed in the password, and typed in a name. He reached for the phone, then stopped. Better call later from the Hyatt Regency.

"*Anima tua requiescat in pace,*" the priest said, giving his blessing with the aspergillum.

Surrounded by a roof of black umbrellas, four men wearing gray aprons lowered the ropes holding the casket into the grave. A dull thud broke the silence, followed by the rustle of the ropes falling onto the casket.

An umbrella held above him by a young priest of the arch-diocese of Innsbruck, Cardinal Wolfenberg swiftly crossed him-self. His eyes rested a moment on the headstone of the grave in which his mother had just been buried, then moved over to the headstone on its left — that of Helmut Wolfenberg, his father.

The photograph on the headstone portrayed a man with the bearing of a general of the Austro-Hungarian army, his face ex-pressionless. He must have been one of the last Austrians to wear a waxed moustache; he took meticulous care of it with the aid of a special wax that a farmer from St. Anton got for him. He had been a professor of Greek and Latin at the University of Innsbruck, where his expectations of a brilliant career had soon clashed with reality. So dear old Helmut had ended up channel-ing half his frustration into useless linguistic perfectionism, and the other half into his favorite pastime: corporal punishment in-flicted on his son Rolf.

What offences? Late homework, a low grade, a presumed lack of respect.... No doubt trifles for the rest of the world, but not for dear Helmut, the inflexible perfectionist, for whom eve-rything ended up being "a matter of principle": a tragically empty cliché, just like the soul and brain of the waxed puppet he was.

"Rolf, you know it hurts me more than it hurts you, don't you?" his father would invariably say.

Helmut unbuttoned his vest, rolled up his sleeves, and fi-nally took off his black leather belt. He did it with slow meas-ured movements, with the solemnity of a high priest about to officiate at a secret rite.

"Yes, father," would be his reply, since he had learned at his expense that the old man's "Don't you?" was no rhetorical question. His affirmative answer, prompt and convinced, was an essential part of the rite, so that it was Rolf who had to feel guilty for forcing his father to punish him.

"Moral pain is far worse than that of the flesh. Are you con-vinced, Rolf?"

"Yes, father."

"Then why do you persist in hurting me? Do you repent, at least?"

"Yes, father."

His father folded the belt—Rolf had to give him credit for always holding it by the metal buckle—and then he cut the air with two hissing lashes.

"Pants down," was the next ritual phrase.

The procedure required that he should bend at right angles. Rolf's mind focused on the bronze bust of Cicero displayed on the desk. Through the window framed by baroque curtains, his gaze wandered beyond the copper roofs of Fürstenburg Castle and followed the snow-covered contour of the Eastern Alps.

"One," Helmut said, as the first lash struck Rolf's buttocks.

He clenched his teeth and his nails dug into his knees. He would rather drop dead than give that son of a bitch the satisfaction of letting out even one moan. Waiting for "ten", his eyes studied Cicero's face, the face of an insipid man who had produced insipid prose, loved only by insipid people.

At the count of ten, Rolf never knew which hurt more, his buttocks or his bladder, which always seemed on the point of bursting. He had long grown used to the blood trickling down his thighs.

His mother and his sister Inge lived terrorized by Helmut. In her own way, his mother must have loved him, but fear had been stronger than love.

When at nineteen he entered the seminar of Sankt Poellen, he did not do so out of calling, but as a rational choice based on two considerations. First, taking vows was the only sure way he'd found to get away from home at last. The second was more a long-term reflection. He'd realized that in life either you belonged to those bending their ass at a ninety-degree angle, or to the ones holding the belt.

Why the Church?

Inexplicably, the dogmatic side of Catholicism had always fascinated him. He had an inquisitive mind and the dialectics of a consummate criminal lawyer, so right up to the last minute he had been torn between the lawyer's gown and the cassock. But eventually, between haranguing a jury in a courtroom or the whole world, he had chosen the second alternative, and therefore the Church.

Celibacy hadn't been a sacrifice. Women didn't interest him, less than ever after what he was to hear through the grille of the confessional at the church of St. John the Baptist. He felt mild sexual stimuli, which he'd learnt to satisfy not autonomously — masturbation was disgusting to a man of his caliber — but by resorting to the discreet services of professional prostitutes. He'd got hold of a dark suit and a gray scarf to hide his clerical collar, and had set up careful schedules and routes, with the meticulousness of a chess player.

The absence of family "joys" had enabled him to devote himself fully to his studies, motivated by an inflexible determination aimed at one goal: to excel. He got his doctorate in theology magna cum laude from the University of Vienna. He turned down a number of tempting proposals that had been put to him, and instead he decided to join the church of St. John the Baptist in Jena for two years, as simple parish priest. What he heard at the oak confessional of that church persuaded him that he had made the right choice: infinitely better the afterlife hell of the Church than the earthly hell of a family. A lightning-swift career had followed: at 29, assistant professor of Dogmatic Theology at Mainz University; at 33, coadjutor to the Archbishop of Cologne; at 37, professor of Dogmatic Theology at the Pontifical Gregorian University in Rome and advisor of the influential International Theological Commission. In 1990, when he was only 48, the Slavic Pope had elevated him to the College of Cardinals, and in 2003, Pope Sergius I had appointed him prefect of the CDF, the most sought-after position in the Holy See.

He had never seen his father again since he was nineteen. When Helmut had been hospitalized at Innsbruck University Hospital for three months, where he had died of lung cancer, Rolf had never gone to see him. On hearing about his death, he had felt nothing inside. In spite of the insistent request of both his mother and sister, he hadn't gone to the funeral.

Remembering the pain of the lashes, he was reminded also of the bust of Cicero and the promise he'd made to himself. No one would ever touch him again, because people would be afraid of him.

After he'd entered the seminary, he'd decided that dialectic virtuosity pushed beyond that of the Jesuits themselves would be his weapon, infinitely more effective than the stakes of the Inquisition. He would concentrate it, though, on Man's most important instinct: the instinct of self-preservation, and the related fear of death.

The rest had been child's play. And that was just the beginning.

"Forgive me, Your Eminence," said the young priest looking at his watch," but it's already 4:40 and your flight to Rome leaves at 5:30."

"Certainly, Father. Just a moment and we'll be on our way."

The cardinal stepped to the grave, bent down and picked up a handful of earth, which he dropped onto the casket. Then he turned and walked briskly towards the exit gate, the priest scurrying after him, his umbrella up.

After visiting the castle and the cemetery in Kilmartin, Guichard and Françoise took the southbound road again. Françoise's eyes scanned the horizon. The mid-Argyll region, with its medieval ruins, its solitude, and its contrasts, gave the impression of hovering between history and legend. Rugged hills and glens dotted with secret lochs followed one another on the mainland, while across the Sound of Jura an archipelago of islands, amidst sea lochs and a maze of channels, flashed past. On the coast, rocky bays alternated between raised beaches backed by caves. The blue morning sky had turned a leaden gray, and now streaks of black and gray furrowed the sea.

Guichard drove in silence. Françoise studied his profile. In the abandoned graveyard at Kilmartin's church, he'd stopped in front of one of those anonymous graves bearing only the outline of a sword. Françoise had gone over to him to say something, but he'd looked at her as if she weren't there, lost in a world of his own. She thought back to the words he'd uttered in his sleep... "God... Fire... Help."... Maybe "Inquisition." *Inquisi-*

tion? Could that be? Although she'd tried to discuss what had happened two nights before, he'd avoided the subject.

Françoise realized that if she wanted any answers, she'd have to find them herself. As they got out of the car, she thought of her friend Corinne, who ran the Saint Germain branch of the Gibert bookshops. Of course! Corinne.

As they were leaving their room to go down to the hotel pub, she told Guichard she needed to make a phone call and that she would join him shortly.

"You probably think I'm crazy calling you from Scotland just to ask you something like this, but I couldn't wait," Françoise concluded.

"Is there a man involved?" At the other end, Corinne sounded surprised.

"Maybe."

"First thing tomorrow I'll go through our database."

"I'll try to stop by around one o'clock."

"I'll do my best to have something by then." Corinne chuckled. "You're really in deep, aren't you? I'm really curious to meet him."

§

"Your Hennessy, sir." The waitress put a glass on the terrace table in front of Guichard.

He glanced at his watch. Quite a long phone call, he thought, looking around to see if there was any sign of Françoise. He took a sip of brandy. From the terrace, his eyes followed the track winding its way down to the loch. Evening shadows darkened the waters of the lake, and clouds of mist were gathering in the glen between the two hills.

He could still smell her scent, feel her body against his, hear their murmured words in the dark.... Then that cursed nightmare. What if he'd said something else in his sleep? She'd realized that it was more than just an isolated incident. He looked down at his hand: it clenched and unclenched, rhythmically. He'd never quite understood why stress always manifested itself in that sort of conditioned reflex.

He shook his head. She might have some vague ideas, but she'd never be able to string them together. She wasn't a woman to underestimate, though. She could be tender and loving one moment, and a moment later trap you with that hammering rationality of hers, without you even becoming aware of it. This contrast was what most attracted him to her, but it was also what he feared most.

That first night there had been a moment when he'd been tempted, for just a moment, to let himself go and tell her everything, which showed just how dangerous their relationship was becoming. Besides, even if he told her the truth, she'd probably think he was out of his mind. Seeking revenge for something that had happened seven centuries before, traveling back in time, overcoming the human boundaries of space and time.... Who would believe him?

After seven centuries, only a heap of bones was left in that grave, yet capable of challenging any scientific knowledge. A strange thing, genetic memory; it was like an imprint that you carried in your genes, which enabled hate to go on burning, regardless of time. What had caused that hate? What else, if not the lust for power? Since the dawn of time that's how it had always been, and that's how it would always be.

The instinct to dominate was as old as humankind itself. Everyone pursued power: the state, the Church, the business world, men, women, whites, blacks.... Power enabled people to control everyone else's destiny, and for power people were prepared to sacrifice everything. It wasn't simply a matter of money, but a lust for power itself: insidious, creeping, evil. It was the same power that burnt you at the stake a thousand years ago, accusing you of heresy, and that nowadays killed you day by day, depriving you of justice in the courts, of a way to make your voice heard, of the hope for a better future. It was the same power that stole your most precious possession, dignity, and forced you to sit up and beg like a dog, just to have your rights respected.

The de Saint Clairs had always suffered from that kind of power, paying with their own blood, until finally one day one

of them had said "that's enough." Any means was justified—
even violence—in order not to submit to the power of others.

But didn't power also touch the relationship between a man
and a woman? So wasn't it better to limit oneself to superficial
relationships, ending them as quickly as they had begun? Relationships broken off during their 'becoming,' before being stifled by the unbearable brutality of everyday mediocrity.

A voice rose in his head.

*By the dragon of St. George, thinkest thou this to be the right mo-
ment to lose thy head over a wench?* said the Voice.

Guichard did not reply.

Thou must not see her again, dost thou hear me? said the Voice
in a commanding tone.

You're right—as always—he had to admit, waving the
Voice away.

Then the moonlit roofs of Jerusalem, and the reflections of
the minarets and of the Dome of the Rock flashed before his
eyes, and he perceived a moment, a thousand years before,
when he would have liked time to stop. To hell with the Voice!

Thou knave! Thou forgettest I can read thy thoughts.

Guichard felt a sharp pain between his shoulder blades. He
gasped for breath.

You, who seem to know everything, Guichard said, tell me
something: how is it that the right things always take the pleasure out of life?

*If thou wilt not refrain from thy enfeebling fantasies, I will make
thee rue it,* said the Voice.

A heavy silence fell.

Guichard felt hands on his shoulders, and Françoise's voice
came from behind him.

"Tell me the truth. Deep down you hoped I wouldn't come
back, didn't you?"

For a moment Guichard felt as if he were being dashed to
his doom. He scrabbled for an answer, like a mountain climber
slipping and searching frantically for a grip on a rock face.

Darkness mingled with the black waters of the loch. Just a
few lights filtered through the mist, but they were far away,
and seemed to belong to another world. The flickering light of

an oil lamp in a passage below heavy beams.... A red cross on a white tunic.... A woman's stifled cry.... Shadows crossing the barrier of time, like echoes of an endless dream that carried the regret of something he'd lost forever.

"Mr. de Saint Clair, there's a call for you from the United States," said the girl from the bar, handing him a note. "Will you take it from the booth?"

Guichard read the note: *Allied Petroleum, Mr. Kovacs.* He looked up, aware of Françoise's stare. "I'm sorry, I'll try not to be long."

Laszlo Kovacs wasn't someone you could easily forget. Guichard remembered the Iranian operation two, maybe three years back. There'd been moments when the deal seemed to be falling through, because neither of them was willing to yield.

"Good afternoon, de Saint Clair. This is Laszlo Kovacs, of Allied Petroleum. I'm sure you remember me, just as I remember you, so let's skip the preliminaries. I've got a problem and, in light of the Iran deal, I think you might be just the man I'm looking for."

"Please go on."

Kovacs outlined his plan. "Any questions?" he asked in the end.

"Better forget it, it wouldn't work. It would make Allied show a profit, but it would be a 'non-operating profit.' The stock analysts wouldn't let you get away with it."

Kovacs grunted. "From someone like you I would have expected something more substantial."

"I'm really afraid I can't be of any help to you, Mr. Kovacs."

"Oh, but you can, you can. I want you to find me a joint venture partner. Don't think your presence in Tripoli last May went unnoticed. The market knows well you're tight with OPEC—even if the reasons why are beyond me."

"Even if that is the case, I don't see how I could fill a $230 million gap."

"Let's not get lost in minor details. Allied's gratitude will fill that gap."

Only someone like Kovacs could refer to $230 million as "minor details." Guichard's gut feeling was to decline; at the moment he had much more important things to worry about. He was on the point of telling Kovacs no, when a name flashed through his mind, and an idea started to take shape. Why not check into it? He could always turn the offer down later.

"You know how I do business," Guichard said. "I rarely negotiate my conditions."

"Neither do I."

Guichard rubbed the bridge of his nose slowly. "Can you meet me on Friday?"

"Where?"

"My London office."

"Fine."

Guichard leaned against the side of the booth, his hand still on the phone. It would have to be a company prepared to accept Kovacs' price for the coal-mines, and Kovacs's "gratitude" would cover the rough spots. For that kind of maneuver he needed a state-owned company, no doubt about it. He thought of a number of Middle-Eastern oil companies.... No, all they did was extract the crude without processing it. The name of the company he'd first thought of kept returning to mind. The political scenario of that country was a disaster, though, and a direct contact wouldn't stand any chance of success. Suddenly he smelled the scent of lemon tree blossoms, and a dazzling sun blinded him. He straightened up, clicked the button on the receiver and dialed a number.

"*No, non è qui al momento, signor de Saint Clair,*" said a voice with a strong Sicilian accent. "But I can try and get him for you."

A few moments later, Guichard recognized the voice of Tano Franzese at the other end.

4

The metro began to slow down, and Françoise fought her way towards the exit door. The train finally creaked to a halt at the station of Place de l'Odéon.

As she was making her way towards St. Sulpice's Church, the silence and open spaces of the Highlands seemed light years away, and it seemed almost impossible to imagine that she and Guichard had boarded the plane in Glasgow only a few hours earlier. When they said goodbye, she had a presentiment that there was something final about it. She forced herself to drive the thought away, and her mind went back to their first night together.

When he took her hand and pressed it to his lips, his touch seemed to tell her all the things she wanted to hear him say, and she felt something inside her change. She thought of his tenderness, of his hands as they ran lightly over her body, and of the words he'd murmured to her as they made love. A flush spread over her face. Then those odd words muttered in the dark, his awakening and that anguished look in his eyes.

"Do you think I don't realize that? It's just that there are things in my life I can't discuss, at least not at the moment."

"Then I'll wait till you're ready," she had told him.

She remembered what Jules had told her about Guichard and his family. Wasn't it logical to suppose that the gravestone bearing the name "de Saint Clair" may have belonged to one of Guichard's ancestors? But what about his terror of fire?

"I seem to have read somewhere that no one ever found out where the survivors fled to, after escaping from France," she had said.

"Some of them came ashore here, in 1307," Guichard had re-plied, pointing to the Sound in front of them. *"But most of them went on to North America."*

How could he be so sure about the Templars' whereabouts after their escape from France? She'd heard stories about people who suddenly "remembered" incidents that had happened to someone else centuries before. In spite of her European heritage and Catholic upbringing, she'd believed in reincarnation for many years. It made no sense to discard something automati-cally, just because there was no scientific evidence to back it up. Call it mind, or soul, or whatever. What did science have to do with things like that? Our spirit came before matter, and it didn't make sense to try to reach our spirit starting from matter. Even physicists had been forced to acknowledge that Buddhist mysticism had known things like this for over twenty-five cen-turies. Zen meditation didn't need Einstein in order to think in terms of space-time and of the energy-matter duality…. Could it be that behind Guichard's mystery actually lay a case of reincarnation?

At Gibert's, Françoise took the escalator and stepped off on the third floor. From a distance she caught Corinne's eye. Corinne, seated at her desk, pointed at a pile of books in front of her.

Barely an hour later, Françoise left the bookshop carrying a bulging bag.

For a moment, a doubt assailed her. Wasn't she embarking on something bigger than herself? Yet a thought gave her back her self-confidence. If in those books she didn't find the clues she was looking for, she could always turn to her Uncle Rolf in Rome for help. Who better than a cardinal could help her shed light on a mystery linked with the Knights Templar?

As Françoise crossed Place de St. Sulpice, the bells struck the hour and a deafening clanging filled the square, drowning the babbling of the fountain. She stopped near the Fontaine des Quatre Evêques and looked up at the twin-towers. The black figures of two priests passed by.

Following her instinct, she went inside the church. The smell of incense hung in the air. Someone coughed, and the noise echoed through the naves. All churches were like that;

even the slightest sound seemed to reverberate, yet never enough to interfere with your inner thoughts.

Passing through the patterns of the stained-glass windows, the sunrays struck the floor and the walls of the basilica; the ensuing play of light created reflections of mystical luminosity.

Françoise paused by a large shell-shaped stoup and, without thinking, she dipped her fingers into the holy water. She was about to make the sign of the cross, a habit inculcated in her when she was a child, when she stopped. Why stick to gestures that had lost any meaning?

She slipped into one of the back pews, assumed a Zen posture, and concentrated in order to reach the awareness of her breathing.

During the ensuing hour, a ray of sunshine rose gradually from the transept until it struck the end of the nave where Françoise was sitting, enveloping the back rows in an aura of bluish light.

A taxi stopped in front of a stately-looking mansion at the intersection of Rue de l'hôtel Colbert and Quai de Montebello. Guichard climbed out. A distinguished man in his shirtsleeves, wearing a green apron, hurried out of the entrance. He gave a slight bow, shook hands with Guichard, and took his suitcase. Guichard raised his eyes to the building.

The de Saint Clair *hôtel particulier* [an old, private French mansion, a symbol of status and power] had been the de Saint Clairs' town residence ever since the time of the kings of France, and dated back to the fifteenth century. The building — with its cream stucco façade, wrought iron gratings and lamps, and slate-covered roof with its garrets — was surrounded by a yard with walls and iron railings. The third and fourth floors were used as a penthouse, Guichard's home, whereas the remaining floors accommodated the Paris offices of Compagnie Financière d'Arcadie, Guichard's investment bank. The east side of the mansion overlooked the Seine; on the far side of the river, Notre Dame Cathedral's soaring structure stood out against the sky.

Bach's *Toccata and Fugue* echoed through the penthouse. Music was one of the passions of André, Guichard's butler. As Guichard passed in front of the French windows, a barge glided on the Seine. He closed the sliding door behind him, and a musty smell of books took him back to his childhood in the de Saint Clair castle. Just like then, he felt the same excitement that arose from the discovery of mysteries and from the awakening of distant memories.

He walked across the library, the carpet muffling the sound of his footsteps. He climbed the spiral staircase, went along the gallery to the end wall, and reached out his hand towards a wall lamp, turning it downwards. Silently the end section of the bookshelves began to rotate, and he heard the familiar hum of the humidifier. He felt for the light switch. Beams from the spotlights hit the vaulted ceiling.

He looked at the paintings on the walls. The de Saint Clair collection. His gaze rested on the painting hanging directly in front of him: *Road and Cypress on a Starry Night.* The painting displayed an unpretentious signature: *Vincent.*

The short, nervous, multicolored brush-strokes took Guichard beneath the sky of a Provençal night, and he found himself astonished and his eyes turned heavenwards, staring at those yellow auras and whirls of color spinning like Catherine-wheels possessed. Van Gogh's sunflowers, his stars, his cypress trees, were the creation of a man obsessed by the questions that humankind had been asking since the beginning of time. Looking at that painting was like looking inside oneself and reaching out towards the ultimate frontier of the unexplored, where the unconscious listens to the eternal silence of infinite spaces.

Guichard stared at a writing desk, his eyes following the pattern of its inlay. A Louis XVI. Even the most knowledgeable of thieves would have said it was just an antique, and nothing more. Guichard went over to the secretaire and pressed a button under the base. *Click.* He took hold of the two side knobs, and slowly pulled out the drawer. He'd done this a thousand times, yet each time he had that same feeling he'd first felt at the castle at Les Andelys, when he'd seen them for the first time. But he hadn't realized, then, what he was looking at.

He passed his fingers over the parchment scrolls, and the characters in Aramaic took him back in time, to the fires, the tortures, the remnants of blood-soaked clothing with the red Templar cross still visible. Who would have thought, looking at them, that a few mere scrolls could have caused all that? Deep down the Church had always known. Not with certainty, but they'd always suspected it. It was this suspicion that had unleashed their bestiality.

The plan is ready. Why shouldst thou tarry? asked the Voice.

One thing is still missing.

What? Thou hast the scrolls. Reveal thou to the populace their gloomy secret, and of the Roman Church not a vestige will remain. Nine centuries is a long time. My soul is weary.

You're too impatient. The Church must pay off its debt in full.

I begin to ask myself whether thou knowest what thou contrivest.

More than you think.

I trust it be thus. For thine own sake.

Guichard pointed a finger to the ceiling. Don't you threaten me!

I can tell thou hast inherited not only the escutcheon, but also all the haughtiness of the de Saint Clairs.

Again a sharp pain stabbed Guichard in the back. He gasped, and had to lean against a wall.

Take heed, Guichard de Saint Clair, said the Voice. *Thou puttest my patience to a severe test.*

Guichard pushed the drawer in until he heard the click. He returned to the platform and turned the wall lamp upwards again. As the panel began to rotate, something pressed against his right leg. Even before looking down, he knew it was Julius.

The Siamese cat was gazing at him with its ice-blue eyes. When Guichard leaned down and stroked him, Julius started to purr, and continued staring at him. Whenever Guichard felt his urgent need to look at the scrolls, Julius always materialized out of nowhere, and waited in the gallery for Guichard to come out.

It had happened first during a visit to the castle. Julius had suddenly appeared in front of Guichard and had trotted after him. Ever since he was a child, cats had always fascinated him.

They seemed to possess a mysterious magnetism, rooted in time. No wonder the ancient Egyptians, an enlightened people, held cats as sacred. It wasn't true that people chose their cats. On the contrary. It was cats who chose their "masters," even if the masters didn't realize it. For this reason, when Julius had appeared in front of him and followed him, Guichard had decided to adopt him right away.

Guichard left the penthouse and went down the marble staircase, not even seeing the friezes and frescoes covering the walls. He stopped on the second floor landing. A large glass door bore the name Compagnie Financière d'Arcadie. The words ran across a red shield, with a white unicorn prancing in its center. Guichard entered the reception room, where a spotlight shone upon a secretaire Louis XVI, and returned the receptionist's deferential greeting.

He stopped in front of a door marked *Entrée Reservée*-Private, and poked his head into the foreign exchange dealing room. Feverish buzz engulfed him, made even more frantic by the ticking of teleprinters and blinking screens. At one end of the room, an array of digital clocks showed the time in the world's major financial markets. The dealing room was the financial heart of the company and the major contributor to its profits, together with Mergers & Acquisitions, the sector he headed.

That never-ending noise meant money, and pure neurosis: the frantic search for a lightning profit exploiting currency movements by outguessing the system. One felt in charge of one's destiny: an inebriating feeling.

Traders, sleeves rolled up and hair disheveled, sat at their desks, their eyes glued to their PCs. The continually changing currency prices blinked in green and red on the computer screens. Many of the traders spoke alternately between two phones, and they closed transactions worth millions of dollars by simply pressing a button on their keyboards. Guichard expected them to make a multiple of five times their remuneration, and this was the reason why one could smell adrenaline in the air.

"OK, at 1.71 my 14. Citibank New York for me and Deutsche Bank Frankfurt for you." ... "At 123 your 100. Sanwa Bank Tokyo for me and Chase Manhattan New York for you."

Guichard stepped over a tangle of computer cables, and paused near the chief dealer's hexagonal trading desk. He scribbled "Singapore?" on a scrap of paper, and held it in front of Jean-Paul's eyes. Jean-Paul, his face sandwiched between two telephones, glanced first at him and then at the scrap of paper, put one handset on his shoulder, and signaled him an OK.

Guichard entered his office and went over to the window. It took up the entire wall and looked out over Notre Dame whose gargoyles and chimeras, seen from the side, dominated Paris with their sinister glares. Horned vampires, demons devouring suppliant souls, and winged monsters guarded Paris as a sadistic executioner guards a prisoner sentenced to death.

It was a corner office with modern, black lacquered furniture and an L-shaped desk. On the walls there were bookshelves stacked with books on quantum physics. Table lamps, scattered here and there, emitted a diffuse light, and a large kilim carpet covered most of the parquet. Behind Guichard's desk hung Dali's *The Persistence of Memory*. The other paintings were all surrealist: Magritte, Tanguy, Motta — sinister shadows, metaphysical shapes, delirious associations. It was an explosion of amorphous objects, floating in spectral dream-spaces produced by the unconscious mind. Those images seemed to testify to the supremacy of the unconscious over the conscious, the need to cancel the boundaries of time and space.

Guichard sat down at his desk, and pressed the intercom. "Marie Claire, can I see you a moment?"

"... Cancel all my appointments and book me a flight to Palermo," Guichard said.

"No hotel in Palermo, right?" his secretary asked after a moment's hesitation.

Guichard shook his head. For a long time there'd been an unspoken pact between them. His trips to Sicily were a thing apart, and she never asked questions.

"Ask Paulette to come here a minute, please."

Paulette Janviers sat in front of his desk. She wore a string of pearls over a black sweater. Her glasses gave her an intellectual look, which somehow seemed to enhance her femininity, but the picture was misleading. She was capable of making sense of even the most obscure balance sheets, and was stubbornness personified. Paulette would be perfect for the project he had in mind.

"So, thanks to the joint venture, Kovacs thinks he can avoid the losses," concluded Guichard. "Any questions?"

"Where does Kovacs think he can find a partner like that? In Fairyland?" Paulette asked with a skeptical smile.

"In Rome."

"Why Rome?"

"CIP, Italy's national hydrocarbons agency, would be an ideal partner for Kovacs's project."

"*CIP*? But they're losing a lot of money, and they have politicians in the way all the time," said Paulette. "How can they —" She stopped. "Oh, I see. That's the whole point, isn't it?"

"Exactly." Then Guichard assumed an air of indifference. "By the way, I'd need an analysis of CIP's petrochemical division."

"By when?"

"Let's see, today's Tuesday.... By Friday morning."

"*You must be joking.*"

"Do you think I'd ask you, if I didn't know you never give up?"

"Do you think it's fair to ask me in a way I can't refuse?"

The clock on Guichard's desk read three o'clock in the afternoon, which meant nine in the morning in New York. At that time Eugene Miller, his partner in charge of the New York branch of Financière d'Arcadie, would already be in the office, swearing as usual at the Grand Central Station chaos. He dialed his direct number.

"I also need the latest stock exchange comments on Allied Petroleum," Guichard said.

"I seem to have heard someone say — maybe I read it somewhere — that they're having problems," Eugene said.

"Find out as much as possible, and try to fax me your report to our London office by Friday morning," said Guichard. After a pause, he added: "I think I have to leave for Italy."

A moment's silence followed at the other end. "Palermo?"

"I don't see any other way. Do you?"

In spite of all his resolutions not to see her again, Guichard couldn't stop thinking about her. He reached for the phone, but his hand froze in mid-air. Why not? There wouldn't be anymore mistakes, like the one in Scotland. He dialed the number of the art gallery.

"Saturday evening then, about eight?" Guichard said.

There was a pause on the other end of the line. "I had a feeling you weren't going to call me again," Françoise said.

Guichard's first instinct was to deny it, but he'd learnt not to underestimate her. Better ignore her question. "Will you come then?"

"Of course I will. You haven't said where, though. "

"You wanted to see my collection, didn't you?"

A pause. "At your house?"

After hanging up, he found himself counting the days until Saturday.

By all the hounds of Hades, thou art truly a numskull! said the Voice. *At times I ask myself if it's the de Saint Clairs' blood that flows in thy veins.*

Stop meddling in my life! Guichard said, slamming his hand on the desk.

While Guichard was opening his mail in the library, André came in.

"How is business on the stock exchange, André?".

"I can't complain, Monsieur le Comte," André said. "I've had a certain satisfaction from my investments in the Hong Kong hotel industry."

Guichard told him of the dinner invitation. Silence fell.

"A business dinner, Monsieur le Comte?"

"Not exactly. It's something more... personal."

"I understand." André stroked his grizzled moustache. "The only reason I asked was to find out in advance what sort of ambiance Monsieur le Comte would like."

"What's the problem?"

"Do I have Monsieur le Comte's permission to speak frankly?"

"We've been together a long time."

"Does Monsieur le Comte not think that an invitation to dinner here — addressed to a single woman — could prove... dangerous?"

"I can assure you that the lady I have invited is of a much milder temperament than Josephine," replied Guichard, hinting at their authoritarian housekeeper, with whom André had been fighting a losing battle for years.

Guichard knew that André, however much of a misogynist he might be, didn't disdain the occasional company of a woman. But no one could get it out of his head that there was no place for women in the de Saint Clair household. He was convinced that the three of them—including Julius—got along perfectly well on their own.

"Monsieur le Comte, a woman who accepts such an invitation is only after one thing."

"And what's that?"

"She's thinking of marriage, *Mon Dieu!*" André said with terror in his eyes.

"I'm a confirmed bachelor."

André gave Guichard a stern look. "I had always thought so, but invitations like this have never been made before, unless it was for business."

"There is no reason to worry."

"Monsieur le Comte, our lives follow a safe, orderly path, with no hitches—apart from Josephine, of course—and I'm sure you wouldn't want anything irreparable to happen." He cast an allusive glance towards the library. "Women aren't happy until they've found everything out about a man, down to his last secret." Then André put a finger to his lips. "Shh…. Did you hear that?"

"What?"

"That noise. *Scratch, scratch, scratch.* It's the women, digging away day and night. They never give up."

Guichard made a superhuman effort to contain his laughter, for André was very touchy, even more than Julius. Then, suddenly, he had the feeling that André's words were, unintentionally, a premonition of impending danger.

Julius, as enigmatic as the Sphinx, was watching them from atop one of the bookshelves.

5

"Your Eminence, I have Monsignor Dyakonov on the line. Will you take it?" asked Monsignor Feliciani over the intercom.

"Is that you, Markus?" the cardinal said. "... No, I need to get out. I'll meet you there."

A few minutes later, Cardinal Wolfenberg was walking under the busy Arco delle Campane and into St. Peter's Square. Oblivious to the stares of the onlookers, he walked briskly across the square, all the way to the southernmost corner. As he made his way through the Bronze Door, the two Swiss guards in full blue-and-orange striped uniform sprang to attention. The cardinal took the elevator to the third floor, which housed the offices of the secretariat of state and the pope's private apartment.

"Come in, Rolf," said Archbishop Dyakonov. "Please excuse me, but I'm having a problem with the archdiocese of New Orleans. I'll be back in just a few minutes."

While he was waiting, the cardinal took a thin aluminum tube from the folds of his robe, and extracted a Romeo y Julieta. He ran it under his nose, then carefully lit it. Dyakonov was a key pawn in Manus Domini's strategy — and in his too. And furthermore, he was a faithful member of Manus Domini. As the substitute of the Vatican secretariat of state, Dyakonov was in charge of the *Ufficio Primo* of the secretariat, the office that dealt with general administration. This meant dealing with all the pope's incoming and outgoing correspondence, which involved eight linguistic sections, divided by country. The cardinal grinned: an invaluable secret agent, indeed.

Although Archbishop Dyakonov was directly responsible to the secretary of state and to the pope, his main contact was actually with the Holy Father, whom he met with every day at 6:30 p.m. Dyakonov had gradually become one of the people in whom Sergius I confided most, sharing this position with the pope's personal secretary, Monsignor Petrov, also a member of Manus Domini.

The thought of the secretary of state, Cardinal Missiroli, made the cardinal's jaw tighten. Missiroli had gathered around him all the moderates in the Curia who backed the Second Vatican Council. The Council had promised a more liberal attitude on the part of the Church. The cardinal knew well that Sergius I had strong reservations regarding the results of the Council. This was one of the reasons His Holiness had favored the growth of Manus Domini and the CDF. The "distinguished" cardinal secretary of state would now have to reckon with him — and with Manus Domini.

The cardinal exhaled slowly, watching the whirls of smoke waft upwards. The moment had finally come to launch the project that would show the Church and the Christian world Manus Domini's power, once and for all. The loan to Escobar's Brazilian company would provide the right opportunity. Thanks to that plan, not only would Cardinal Missiroli and his followers be relegated to the background, but so would Father Cafiero, the father general at the top of Manus Domini. The Russian Pope was old and sick: he wouldn't stand much longer in the shoes of the Fisherman.

"Sorry for the delay." Dyakonov sat himself in the chair next to the cardinal's. "I wanted to warn you that Cardinal Missiroli is furious with you."

"And just what has wounded the susceptibility of our esteemed secretary of state?"

"Everyone at the secretariat of state knows what happened this morning with Father Fairchild."

"As usual, gossip in the Vatican travels faster than the Holy Ghost."

"As soon as he heard about it, Missiroli rushed into His Holiness' study. Just be prepared to have to discuss the matter, that's all."

"Thank you for telling me, but you know only too well that in these matters His Holiness feels exactly as I do." Cardinal Wolfenberg rubbed his hands together, and pulled his chair closer to the substitute's. "Let's move on to more serious things. Brazil."

"I would have raised the subject myself. Rolf, I need to know more about it."

"Just think. A big loan underwritten by the Holy See, for the utilization of the Amazon forest's natural resources. To help the Indian tribes!" The cardinal leaned towards Dyakonov, gave him a sly look and patted his knee. "I can already see the newspaper headlines."

"Doesn't it seem risky? If anything were to go wrong, we could compromise years of hard work."

"What's worrying you?"

"Well, you mentioned a colossal sum of money."

"I've seen three popes come and go, and I've still got my head above water. It's understood that we'll underwrite the bonds only if we have the Brazilian government's guarantee — a perfectly acceptable risk nowadays, according to Monsignor Griffith, head of the APSA [the Vatican portfolio management unit] portfolio managers."

"But you're talking about a figure of between 5,000 and 10,000 billion lire! The Holy See would be forced to sell all the Vatican Museum's works of art to meet a similar commitment, and even that probably wouldn't be enough."

"That's not what I mean. APSA would underwrite the loan thanks to funds provided by Manus Domini. It wouldn't be the first time we'd be financing the Vatican."

"I still don't see how we could rake together such an enormous sum," Dyakonov said. "We couldn't reach that figure even if we were to put together all the assets of the Manus Domini foundations."

The cardinal shook his head. "O ye of little faith." He smiled mockingly. "Manus Domini does its charity work with other people's money, not its own. We'll simply ask for an extra contribution from our *initiati,* as usual."

"If we start asking for money again so soon, many of them might back out."

"I wouldn't be so sure. You seem to underestimate the psychological impact of this deal." The cardinal's eyes twinkled. "Think what it's for. *To help the poor Amazon Indians.*"

Dyakonov's mouth twisted. "The Boff affair should have taught us something about the attitude towards social justice in Brazil."

"You're wrong. The Brazilian *initiati* and their companies will make the most of an occasion like this. They'll see their participation as a way to improve their country's image." The cardinal assumed an air of studied indifference. "Besides... any good chess player always thinks at least two moves ahead."

"Which means?"

"It won't be hard to convince Brasilia to grant a tax deduction for those companies underwriting the Amazon loan."

Dyakonov studied the cardinal. "You've already sounded things out, haven't you?"

The cardinal's smile summed up a life of lobbying in the Vatican's dark meanders.

"All right. I'll speak to Monsignor Petrov, and we'll start getting His Holiness used to the idea."

"Excellent." The cardinal slapped his knee. "Excellent." He thought of Jacinto Vallanco-Torres, the layman in charge of the Holy See's Press Office. "Now we need to tell Vallanco-Torres to set things in motion."

"Would you mind doing that yourself?" the substitute asked. "It's easier to be allowed to speak to His Holiness than to *Dr.* Jacinto Vallanco-Torres. Downstairs on the first floor is like being at NASA. All that technology scares me."

"I know what you mean. But he's one of us, and it's thanks to him that the Holy Father's trips have brought us the benefits we all know."

"I suppose I'm just an old-fashioned Catholic. I didn't know that Jesus Christ had traveled round the world or talked on television."

"My dear Markus, the leadership of CDF has taught me to be pragmatic. If CNN had existed at the time of Jesus Christ, well, probably He wouldn't have ended up on the cross."

The archbishop turned pale. "If these words hadn't come from a man like you, they'd sound like blasphemy."

"No, it's just proof that times have changed. And that's why the Vallanco-Torres are important pawns." The cardinal put a hand on the substitute's shoulder. "*Nunc est bibendum*—This calls for a toast—as our friend Horace used to say. Why don't you offer me a glass of that Kentucky bourbon you keep hidden away?"

They raised their glasses. There was no need for either of them to say anything. The cardinal knew that Dyakonov wanted to sit on St. Peter's throne. And the substitute knew that *his* secret ambition was to take Father Cafiero's place.

The cardinal was convinced that it was money that controlled politics—especially in the Vatican. And it was Manus Domini who held the purse strings.

§

The following evening Cardinal Wolfenberg returned to the third floor of the Apostolic Palace. In the semi-darkness of the corridor in the secretariat of state, he recognized Dyakonov's unmistakable profile against the light shining through the glass doors of the transmission room. The clock read eleven-thirty. Apart from two lay clerks who sat chatting, the transmission room was deserted.

The cardinal opened his folder and took out six encoded messages that he had had prepared by a faithful *alumnus* at the Manus Domini office. He showed the messages to Dyakonov. Three of the six messages were for the dioceses of São Paolo, Rio and Brasilia. The other three were addressed to the foundations that Manus Domini controlled in Geneva, London and Madrid.

In just a few minutes the transmitters of the Vatican's telecommunications center in Santa Maria di Galeria, eleven miles outside Rome, had relayed the messages to their destinations.

The center, ten times bigger than the Vatican City, was located in a secluded area that enjoyed diplomatic immunity.

But outer space does not recognize diplomatic immunity.

Within seconds, one of the satellite dishes at the NSA [the National Security Agency] communications station in Menwith Hill, England, intercepted five of the six messages. Also the sixth one, addressed to the Oppenheimer Foundation in Geneva, did not manage to escape detection, and was intercepted by the six-meter dish of the NSA satellite station in Bad Aibling, Germany.

The VAX computers in the two stations started to process the data, before sending them on to Fort Meade, Maryland.

Samuel Abramson's Falcon 2000 landed at Baltimore airport at four o'clock in the afternoon. A few minutes later the president of the Joint Affairs Commission — the ultra-secret commission that represented the major economic interests of three continents — got into the NSA limo idling on the runway. The car sped along Route 295 towards Fort Meade. Abramson, his face grim, opened his briefcase and leafed through the papers from the last meeting of the USCIB, the NSA Security Council. It was entitled: *Interception of Messages Regarding Manus Domini.*

"In the period from 8 August to 30 August of this year, our satellite stations at Menwith Hill in England and Bad Aibling in Germany, using the Echelon system, have intercepted the fourteen messages enclosed herewith. These communications refer to faxes and telephone calls all found to have been made between offices and people linked with the Catholic association known as Manus Domini...

What is Manus Domini?

Manus Domini is a lay order at the far right of the fundamentalist movements within the Roman Catholic Church.

Manus Domini and Power

Since the Russian Pope's nomination, Manus Domini has driven a real campaign for power in many of the Catholic countries in South America, the United Nations and the EC.

High-ranking prelates belonging to Manus Domini hold a number of key positions both within the Roman Curia and within Sergius I's immediate 'entourage'. Cardinal Rolf Wolfenberg, the powerful prefect of the CDF — the Congregation for the Doctrine of the Faith (formerly the Holy Office, heir of the Inquisition) — is a member of Manus Domini. Archbishop Markus Dyakonov, the substitute, and Monsignor Petrov, the pope's personal secretary, are also members of Manus Domini.

Despite the disagreement of quite a few bishops of moderate views, in 2003 Sergius I raised Manus Domini to the status of "personal prelature". Consequently Manus Domini is now under the pope's direct control, rather than of the bishops' congregations.

Sergius I's decision to raise Manus Domini's status was a clear confirmation that the extremist right-wing of the Vatican had taken over...

Manus Domini's Plans

The fundamentalist attitude of the Russian Pope and of the Church are signs of a gradual decline of the papacy as an institution, to the extent that in the not-too-distant future we may see it disintegrate. Is it possible that Manus Domini fails to be aware of the danger? Unlikely. Manus Domini is probably the real puppet-master behind it. It cannot, therefore, be ruled out that Manus Domini's strategy consists in encouraging a progressive weakening of the papacy with the aim of reducing the pope's authority and replacing it with its own....

Members of Manus Domini

It was not until 2003, shortly after Pope Sergius I's nomination, that Manus Domini came into the limelight. Various sources give us an estimated membership of

100,000, distributed over five continents. The members of Manus Domini are divided into *alumni* and *initiati*. The *alumni* (about forty-five percent of the total number) are young graduate intellectuals who take a vow of chastity and poverty and live in residential centers belonging to Manus Domini. The *initiati* (about fifty percent of the total number), are married laymen who, apart from the vow of celibacy, have similar obligations to those of the *alumni*, but they are expected to make periodic "voluntary" contributions. One discriminating criterion is that they have to hold top positions in business, finance or politics. Priests make up less than five percent of the overall membership, but occupy all the managerial posts....

Secrecy

Manus Domini does not issue financial statements, nor does it release lists of its members. Officially Manus Domini and the Vatican have always denied this aspect, and have spoken of a "comprehensible confidentiality linked to charity work"....

Foundations and Money

In 1985 Manus Domini established the Oppenheimer Foundation in Geneva, today linked with an impressive network of foundations and financial institutions operating in various countries. These foundations have educational or equivalent ends, so they are exempt from income tax. There are no formal or legal links between these foundations and Manus Domini, but in reality the members of the Board of Governors are controlled by Manus Domini....

Signed: Lt. Gen. Christopher J. Stone, NSA director."

The satellite recordings and a name, Cardinal Wolfenberg, got Abramson's full attention. The car slowed down and left the Baltimore-Washington Parkway at the Fort Meade exit. A few miles further on it stopped outside the main entrance of the Fort George G. Meade military base.

The marine on duty looked inside the car, checked his list, and waved the driver on. A few minutes later the limousine stopped in front of the NSA headquarters. Abramson slammed his folder shut.

Abramson burst into General Stone's office. The NSA director was standing, waiting for him. After a nervous handshake, the two men sat in front of Stone's desk.

"The president has informed me of the result of your latest security committee meeting. I don't like it, and I'll say even more. *It stinks!*" exploded Abramson.

"I don't think that's a fair comment," General Stone said in a conciliatory tone. "We've decided to keep Manus Domini's movements under control, which means monitoring their communications round-the-clock."

"And you call *that* a decision? Don't you have any idea of the weight of our interests in Italy?" Abramson shook the report at the general. "Doesn't the fact that your European stations have picked up fourteen messages like this in only three weeks, tell you anything?"

"And what does it tell *you*?"

"You need to ask? Something big's going on in the Vatican, big enough to get Manus Domini moving."

"What's the link between something happening in the Catholic Church and our interests in Italy? Isn't that their own business?"

"Their own business? One acquires power by controlling the flow of money, and this is exactly Manus Domini's strategy."

"Meaning what?"

"Damn it! You yourself have written that Manus Domini has an army of 50,000 *initiati* who hold key positions in the economy of ninety countries. Do you think Italy ranks last on the list?"

"What do you know about their members in Italy?"

"They have five thousand *initiati* in top positions." Abramson took another report from his briefcase and leafed through it. "Up to now we've identified three hundred of them. Banks, insurance companies, the main industrial groups, the media, Catholic finance.... They're everywhere. They operate in secrecy and have sworn 'blind obedience' to the father general guiding them, who in turn 'blindly' obeys the pope. Want to know more?"

"One actually gets the impression there are a lot of people in Manus Domini who need a guide dog to get around," General Stone said, serious. "Still, any other move, at the moment, would be premature."

"It's incredible how Joint Affairs allows national security to be left in the hands of types like you!"

"What would *you* have done, in our place?"

"Oh Lord, forgive them, for they know not what they do. All you have to do is cross the Tiber and stop in St. Peter's Square."

"We're already on Manus Domini's back. What else should we do?"

"We have to propose an alliance, that's what. Taking care, though, to do things via the Manus Domini birettas who have a foot in the other camp too, at the top of the Roman Curia."

"The man in question must be Cardinal Wolfenberg, then, if we are to judge by the tone of the messages," General Stone said.

"His Eminence is indeed our man."

"Even if we help them in their plans, when they no longer need us they'll simply kick us out."

"You still haven't grasped the key point: it's economy that rules world affairs. Manus Domini and we in Joint Affairs speak the same language, with the only difference being that they hide their true faces behind a mask of Catholic hypocrisy."

"But they don't need us in Italy."

"Christ! You just don't want to understand!" Abramson banged his fist on the table. "Don't you realize that we live in a global economy? If Wall Street sneezes, Italy catches pneumonia."

"I'm not sure I'm with you."

"Even if it's true that Manus Domini can do without us in Italy, they have *initiati* even in the middle of the Amazon. There are a lot of countries where they badly need us. That's why, in Italy, they're going to have to squeeze together a bit and make an extra place for the guest."

General Stone stared pensively at a world map covering an entire wall. "What should I do?"

"Keep a round-the-clock check on all communications, incoming and outgoing, of the key places of the Vatican City, starting with the Apostolic Palace. If need be, stick a microphone in Wolfenberg's toilet too and point your damn satellite at his cock."

The general huffed. "We'll need the backing of the CIA station in Rome."

They both knew it. Despite the NSA being in charge of espionage and counter-espionage in matters of telecommunications and computerized security, often boundaries overlapped with the CIA. Echelon, NSA's global electronic surveillance system capable of listening to billions of phone calls round the globe, had aggravated conflicts between the two agencies.

"I've already spoken to the White House. At Langley they know what to do."

"The next move?"

"The president has already talked to Fox, our ambassador in Rome. I believe that in the next few days our friend Fox will be knocking on a certain door in St. Peter's," Abramson said, with a mocking look. "And I'll be there, making sure things go in the right direction."

The beating of the rain against the windowpanes grew louder, and for a moment it drowned their words.

6

After a few miles Guichard lost his sense of direction. The Mercedes had started off up a steep hill, the road flanked by Mediterranean pines. The scent of fruit trees and tropical flowers wafted in through the open window. The only sound was the chirping of the crickets, which seemed to sing in unison. Every so often faded old houses emerged from the trees, with an air of having many a tale to tell.

When the car reached the top, that sliver of Sicily jutted out before him in all its splendor. Under the radiance of a flawless sky, olive and orange groves stretched as far as the eye could see. On a hill to the left, sheep grazed among the ruins of a Norman castle, in fields filled with lemon-flowers. Guichard looked down towards the road that wound its way through the valley; a donkey laden with bales of hay plodded along in the hot sun. The peasant walking beside it stopped, took off his *coppola*, and wiped his forehead with a white handkerchief.

The car stopped in front of a high wrought-iron gate. A man armed with a rifle leaned out from his security post at the side of the gate. He touched his cap and went on munching an Indian fig. The automatic gate opened, and the car drove through. A man was raking one of the flowerbeds, a gun sticking out of his belt.

Leaning against one of the stone lions in front of the entrance, Rosario Astarita raised his hand in a sign of welcome. His glasses gleamed in the sunshine.

Guichard got out of the car, and they shook hands.

"Tano is waiting for you," Astarita said, leading the way. Baroque, gilt-framed paintings were hanging on the white-washed walls. When they reached the reception room, Astarita shut the door behind Guichard.

Tano Franzese stood in front of the airy French-styled windows, gazing out over the park. He was wearing an impeccable dark suit, as usual. When Guichard walked in, Franzese turned round. Aquiline nose, bushy moustache, still-black eyebrows—a common sort of face in that part of the world. Yet people remembered him, even those who didn't know him. People remembered him because of his eyes—black, piercing, commanding. They were the eyes of the Boss of the Organization—Guichard knew that Franzese avoided using the word "Mafia," as if it were somehow disrespectful.

Franzese was nothing like a conventional Sicilian boss. He was cultured and professional, and his decisions were unaffected by emotion. Even before being appointed head of the Organization, barely six months before, he hadn't had a *famiglia* or a *caporegime* or "soldiers" under him. He had gained general respect because he had shown he knew how to handle money, and it was thanks to him that the Organization had almost unlimited access to bank credit now. In the dominant philosophy of violence, Franzese was different from the other *capifamiglia*. It wasn't a question of ethics, just business. Killings simply didn't pay, he used to say. Early in his career, Astarita had told Guichard, one day someone had addressed Franzese as "the banker." Franzese had crushed the man with his glare, and no one had ever dared call him that again.

"Ciao, Guichard. The Highlands of Scotland must have beautiful colors at this time of the year. It's a real pity leaving a place like that." Franzese reached for his watch in his vest pocket. "What can I do for you?"

The park that surrounded the villa was enclosed by a low stone wall with Graeco-Roman statues along it. At the far end, across from the villa, stood an oval stone fountain, with a statue of Neptune in the middle, holding his trident aloft. A stream of water spouted from the god's mouth, cascading down to the water below and rocking the water lilies back and forth. That evening a warm breeze blew in from the valley and the sound of the crickets mingled with the babbling of the water.

"So I've come to the conclusion that Compagnia Italiana Petroli would be our best bet." Guichard leaned against the low wall behind the fountain.

Sitting on a garden chair with his legs crossed, Franzese lit a cigarette. "December would be too late."

"Why?"

Franzese made an evasive gesture and looked towards Astarita, who was sitting on the edge of the fountain.

"CIP seems tailor-made for a deal like this," Astarita said. "The directors are just a bunch of *pupi*—puppets— manipulated by the politicians."

"Which party is in charge?" Guichard asked.

"The Labor Party, a minority party."

Astarita reminded Guichard that in Italy they had a multi-party system, with unstable majorities. The instability was such that since the end of the Second World War there had been some seventy administrations, in over half a century of Republican governments. Very little escaped political patron-age: banks, insurance companies, state-run firms.

"Leo Accardo, the prime minister, has been the historical leader of the Coalition Party, the majority party, ever since I can remember," Astarita said. "For a deal like this, CIP, as a state-owned company, will need government backing. We've been in league with the Coalition for a long time."

"Then all we have to do is talk to Accardo," Guichard said.

Astarita snickered. "Not so fast."

"What do you mean?"

"The reason is Accardo himself. With him, it's not just a matter of money."

"I'm not following you."

"Accardo has the air of someone you might see in the pub and not even notice...." Astarita said.

Guichard's mind went back to the photos circulating in the newspapers. They portrayed a thin man with a bony face and big, dark eyes, made even bigger by thick lenses. His thin,

white hair was carefully combed back. He was the most powerful man in Italy, Astarita continued. His power had become
something endemic, rooted in the political rationale of the
country. Through the years, Accardo had woven such an intricate web of alliances and complicity that no one would ever
dare attack him, because he knew everyone's secrets. The
Church was Accardo's traditional ally, partly because he was a
practicing Catholic. His second ally was the Organization.
Many knew this, but pretended not to know. Accardo was like
a drifting mine, to which everyone gave a wide berth.

"If it's not just a matter of money, what else is at stake?"
asked Guichard.

"Power. Accardo must be persuaded that the Allied affair
will be politically advantageous."

"But it is."

"We'll still have to convince him," Astarita said. "You'll
have to meet him."

"In person?"

"Sure. He doesn't trust anyone, starting with his own allies — and he is right."

"What do you suggest?"

"Tomorrow you'll be flying to Rome. When you get to
your hotel, you'll find a message from a certain Lucchese. He's
our man in the capital. He'll arrange the meeting."

Guichard could see that Franzese was lost in thought. During the phone call from Scotland, Franzese had given him the
impression of being in even more of a hurry than Guichard
himself to meet.

Now Franzese took the floor. The Coalition and Accardo
considered themselves irremovable, he said, and that had become a problem. Franzese had worked out a plan, based on an
alliance with Manus Domini, the fundamentalist wing at the
extreme right of the Catholic Church, to overthrow Accardo's
government and seize power.

His plan was centered on a raid of unprecedented boldness
on the foreign exchange market.

At the thought of an alliance with Manus Domini, Guichard's jaw tightened. "Is that why you said before that the Allied-CIP agreement had to be made before December?"

"Of course. In December there will be a change of government, which means a lot of new faces around," Franzese said. "The agreement must be made by the end of October."

Guichard detected a note of deception in Franzese's voice. It was too detached, and the evasive look in his eyes proved it. Franzese was no fool. He'd just become boss of the Organization, and would never waste his time on minor matters. So why would he care about an oil deal that seemingly had nothing to do with his own plan? And why did he want to close the Allied-CIP deal shortly before overthrowing Accardo's government?... *A bait.* Franzese wanted to use the joint venture as bait, cause a scandal, and make much more money out of it. Brilliant, and worthy of Franzese.

"Any comments?" Franzese asked, stroking his moustache.

"It will work," Guichard said.

"Any suggestions?"

"Why that figure of 100,000 billion lire?"

"The Bank of Italy's current reserves amount to 80,000 billion lire."

"Why is your figure higher than their reserves?" asked Guichard.

"Even if it's been three years since the Euro system fell through — of which I was certain from the very outset, because this will always be *l'Europe des patries* [the Europe of motherlands] as our friend General De Gaulle used to say, and no euro will ever be able to unite what two thousand years of history have divided — we still have a grid of fixed parities to deal with."

"So?"

"The other European Community central banks will come to the Bank of Italy's rescue: you can bet on that. I need a safety margin."

"The end of October's not far off. How long will it take you to get a sum like that together?" Guichard said.

"I can already count on 70,000 billion lire, and I'll soon be signing 'stand-by' lines for another 30,000 billion."

A cool breeze picked up, and the spray from the Neptune fountain stung Guichard's face. An idea sprang to his mind, vague at first, then sharper and sharper.... *Perfect.* It was the idea he'd been waiting for from the very start, to trigger off the Lodge's plan. His anger vanished, blown away by the breeze. *"Any suggestions?"* Franzese had asked. Yes, indeed. Now he was ready to take the bait and contribute to Franzese's plan with a little touch of financial engineering.

"I'd use that 30,000 billion differently," Guichard said. "There's a way to invest less and make a much larger profit."

Franzese uncrossed his legs and straightened up. "How?"

"All you have to do is buy six-month call options on dollars and D-marks against lire."

There was a full moon. A gleam in Franzese's eyes told Guichard that no further explanation was needed. Franzese was a man of finance.

"You still haven't told me what you expect from me, though," said Guichard who, on the contrary, knew perfectly well.

"Why should I explain the obvious? You'll organize the whole thing."

The tone of Franzese's voice told Guichard he wouldn't accept "no" for an answer.

"Will the Vatican come in on the operation with its own funds?" Guichard asked with studied indifference.

"Not directly."

"Not directly?"

"Well, they'll be our allies, after all. I've got to whisper something in their ear when the moment comes. If I know them well, I doubt they'll limit themselves to saying three *Paternosters* and one *Ave Maria*." Franzese frowned. "Why do you ask?"

At that point Guichard had found out what he needed to know. He must give Franzese the reply he expected, making a show of it. "You know why. I don't want to have anything to do with the Church."

"Forget your grudges. It's only business. Everything's at stake for the Organization—and for me too." Franzese's voice grew cold. "If anything goes wrong, our friendship won't count for anything. *Non te lo scordare*—Keep that in mind."

Franzese didn't have to worry. What he had in mind wouldn't interfere in any way with the Organization's plan. "No need to remind me of that."

"*Bene. Allora l'affare è concluso*—Good. We can call it a deal, then."

After a while, Guichard managed to stifle a yawn. "And now if you'll excuse me, I've got an early plane tomorrow morning."

As Guichard walked toward the portico, he felt their eyes full of silence following him.

§

"Why didn't you tell him what we've got in mind?" Astarita asked after Guichard had left.

"I couldn't ask him to betray Allied Petroleum. You know Guichard; he's got his own code of honor. That's why we trust him, after all."

"Then what are we going to do, when the time comes?"

Franzese threw his cigarette butt over the low wall. "The Allied-CIP affair will explode in his hands and set off our plan. What's important is that he must never get to know who lit the fuse."

The two men walked towards the portico of the villa. Only their footsteps on the gravel and the splashing of the fountain were left to break the silence of the night.

§

Guichard stepped away from the lemon trees, a few yards below the low wall and on the slope of the hill overlooking the valley. The cigarette stub was still glowing in the dark. He waited in the shadow till the footsteps died away, then he followed the narrow path surrounding the low wall, and went up the stone steps. When he reached the top, he looked up at the starry sky.

There was nothing more intoxicating than the scent of a Sicilian night. The statue of Neptune gleamed in the moonlight, and it seemed as if the god of the sea was preparing to hurl his trident at the stars. Guichard took a deep breath.

The way becomes hard, said the Voice. *Art thou armed with a sword?*

I am wearing a breastplate, and my crest is straight, Guichard said, unsheathing an imaginary sword.

Darest thou mock at me?

Guichard did not utter a word.

The wicked brigand has a sullen look. He is leading thee unto a gloomy forest.

Thank you for telling me.

Silence! *I see a fierce fight approaching. Raise thy horn! We must dig ditches, and defend our walls.*

Better buy options at the Stock Exchange.

Thy language is arcane, and thy ways are bizarre.

I'm not *thy* squire.

My eye shall follow thee like a falcon a dove. And brandishing my bare blade.

The following morning, while waiting for the car, Guichard took a walk down to the fountain. A blanket of mist still covered the woods in the valley. The sun was creeping from behind the mountains, and the first golden rays were just touching the sides of the hill. He sat down on one of the garden seats and leaned back. The cacti cast long shadows on the pathways through the park. He gazed out beyond the valley.

The morgue attendant had slid the drawer out of the refrigerator. A pale blue sheet covered the body, leaving just the feet sticking out. An identity tag hung from one of the toes. The attendant pulled back the sheet just enough to uncover the head. Véronique's face and neck were covered in bruises and her broken jaw was held in place by a strip of gauze wound under her chin and over her head. She had been raped and killed on her return to the castle, after visiting a friend. A policeman approached his father who was standing next to him, and started to ask him questions. His uniform contrasted with the whiteness and the stainless steel of the morgue. Guichard could not take his eyes away from the scar on Véronique's chin; she had got it from falling down in the park while chasing a ball. The smell of formaldehyde stung his throat and his mouth turned dry.

Guichard's stomach contracted as he listened with his father to the judge reading the sentence. They declared that animal partially insane, and sentenced him to ten years in a high-security mental hospital. But the sentence included probation after three years, subject to the psychiatrists' approval. The man, a disdainful smile stamped on his face, looked at them defiantly, then exchanged a satisfied handshake with his attorney.

When the verdict was read out loud, his father didn't say a word. He didn't appeal. Shortly afterwards, Guichard began to notice strange people wandering about the house, especially a man dressed in black, wearing a dark hat and a high-necked sweater. Guichard's father would spend hours with that man, shut away in the library. Four months after the sentence, his sister's killer was found dead in his cell, hanging from a pipe. The whole incident presented many unclear aspects, but in the end the police had been forced to dismiss the case as suicide.

Guichard had been seventeen at the time, but he'd understood, even though his father hadn't told him anything, either then or later. His father had sought justice elsewhere when he saw it was not forthcoming from the courts. As Guichard was to find out many years later—when he realized who was hiding behind the mysterious "Falcon Trust"—it was just during this period that his father had begun to do business with the Organization. It was then that he himself had started to act differently towards state authority, and any other form of authority.

As he grew older, he came to hate all those worthless men, whatever their political views, who played God and speculated on other people's lives, hiding behind the screen of a "higher authority."

But was the power of the Church any different? Or the power of the media, of the business world, of hospitals, of schools? Power in all its forms, from the most blatant to the most deceitful, was the heart of a society where everyone strove to control everyone else's life. But not his. He'd understood this at his expense, and was no longer willing to play the game. In order to resist, everything was justified: lying, deceiving, even killing.

Astarita was beckoning to him. Beyond the mountains the sun painted red and orange streaks in the sky. A flock of birds circled above the villa. One of them flew down and perched on Neptune's head. Guichard rose and walked towards the villa. The babbling of the fountain faded away into the distance.

Kovacs pushed his way through the rotating doors and crossed the main lobby of the Hyatt Regency toward the phone booths. He stood, waiting for one of them to become free. After a while, he shifted the weight of his body to his sound leg, looked at his watch and figured out the time in Washington, D.C.

He thought of Ackerman's drooping moustache and of those eyes behind magnifier-like glasses. Officially, International Security, Ackerman's company, followed cases of industrial espionage. However, for a narrow circle of clients, Allied Petroleum among them, Ackerman took on "special" assignments, so special that they could have landed him in a federal jail for a good twenty years

"I need to see you," Kovacs said. "Tomorrow, in San Francisco."

On the other end, Ackerman looked at his date book, sighed, and crossed out a series of appointments. "I'll be there, Mr. Kovacs."

"Good. In the lobby of the Hyatt Regency, on North Point Street at 2:00 p.m."

At 2:00 p.m., Kovacs entered the lobby of the Hyatt Regency, stopped in the doorway, and looked around. His eyes met Ackerman's, and he went over to the detective and shook

his hand. Ackerman reminded him of a big walrus, maybe because of the moustache. Kovacs spotted two armchairs in a
corner, where no one would notice them.

"Is everything clear?" said Kovacs in the end.

"Where do I come into it?"

"Let's just say I need a 'statement', bearing the signature of
a top coal expert."

"A statement?"

"A declaration that our coal-mines have a market value of
$500 million."

"Well, it'll sure take a lot of persuasion to convince an expert that $270 million of coal is worth $500 million."

"I thought that 'persuasion' was your specialty." Saying
this, Kovacs took a folded sheet of paper out of his wallet, unfolded it and passed it to Ackerman.

> *Dr. Helmut Meiner, Kohl Zentral-Institut, Cologne, Germany*
> *Dr. Paul Kramer, Coal Research Center, Louisville, Kentucky*
> *Prof. Jorg Svantesson, Karolinska Institut, Stockholm, Sweden.*

Ackerman read it and looked at Kovacs blankly.

"These are acknowledged coal experts. PhDs, plenty of articles in international journals... Big stuff," Kovacs said. "If
you're with me on this, I'll arrange for an advance of 500
grand to be paid into whatever bank account you wish, and I'll
credit a further 500 when I get the declaration I need."

Ackerman stroked his moustache. "OK, I'll do it."

"But there's one condition. I need the statement no later
than four weeks from today." It was a tight schedule, but
Ackerman must have known that one didn't get paid that kind
of money for nothing.

"OK," replied Ackerman. "One thing, though, to avoid any
problems later. I want to make it clear, here and now, that I
can't guarantee the result."

"You *can't guarantee* the result? Sure, after all it's only a
million bucks."

"Maybe none of these guys have anything worth hiding,
Mr. Kovacs. In that case I'll hang on to the first $500,000, as
due compensation for my trouble."

Kovacs looked at the detective straight in the eye. It was a calculated risk. Ackerman had to satisfy his clients, if he wanted them to continue doing business with him.

"It's a deal. But don't forget. If there are any surprises, this will be the last you see of me."

Once back in his office, Kovacs sat down at his desk and leaned back in his chair. Ackerman would delve into the very souls of the three men. In the end he'd pin the most rotten one against a wall and pry the damn signature out of him. Because everyone on this planet had some deep, dark secret. This thought gave him a sense of security, a kind of security founded on the fundamentally rotten nature of humankind.

He was sure he would come out on top once again and was overcome by a wave of euphoria. He felt a sudden desire for a woman's body and thought of Martha. Whenever he was in her arms, he felt young again. He would call his wife and make up the usual story about a business dinner. He reached for the phone.

§

When he left the arrival hall of the Washington National Airport, Ackerman took a cab straight to his office, a two-story brownstone in Georgetown.

Ackerman sat down at his desk, and for a while he stared at the three names written on the sheet of paper Kovacs had given him. He began to flick through the card index, and extracted three cards. The first call he made was to Hans Hübner in Berlin. As soon as the detective came on the line, he began to speak with him about Dr. Meiner of the Kohl Zentral Institut in Cologne. Then he made a second phone call to Igor Svensson in Stockholm. Eventually he dialed a number in Louisville, Kentucky. Receiving no reply, he left a message on the answering machine, asking to be called back.

Ackerman had asked the two private detectives to delve into the lives of the two mining experts, leaving nothing to chance. Sexual habits, tax declarations, professional ethics.... They had one month to do their job, not a day more. October 8 was now only twenty-nine days away.

The detective stretched his arms behind his head, then loosened the knot of his tie and called his banker's home number in Grand Cayman.

7

"Your Eminence, I have Mr. Fox, the US Ambassador, on line one," Monsignor Feliciani said over the intercom.

The cardinal picked up the phone.

"Would tomorrow morning be too early, Your Eminence?" concluded Fox.

The cardinal glanced at his diary. "Unfortunately tomorrow is a busy day, Mr. Ambassador."

"I'm sorry it's such short notice, but it's rather urgent. Mr. Samuel Abramson, president of the Joint Affairs Commission, will also be present."

The cardinal straightened his back and drummed for a moment on his pectoral cross. "I'll arrange to alter my appointments. When and where?"

Half an hour later, Archbishop Dyakonov was sitting in front of Cardinal Wolfenberg's desk, holding a thick folder.

"What do we know about them?" asked the cardinal.

Dyakonov said that for over thirty years the Joint Affairs Commission had been the secret pivot of international political and economic balance. Although the list of its members was secret, as was the agenda of its meetings, Joint Affairs counted only people of international standing among its ranks: presidents of multinationals, bankers, politicians. The Commission was structured in three regional headquarters — New York, Paris and Tokyo — supervising respectively the Americas, Europe, and the Far East. The Vatican secretariat of state was convinced that the last five US presidents had been elected thanks to Joint Affairs' support, and that every one of them, once elected, had appointed members of Joint Affairs to key administrative posts.

Dyakonov looked through his file. "You'll certainly recall the state visit that the king of Saudi Arabia paid to the US a month ago. Well, before flying to Washington, the king stopped in New York for half a day. Can you guess who he met there?"

"Abramson?"

"Abramson in person, the president of Joint Affairs." He shut his folder. "And they speak of democracy!"

The cardinal looked heavenwards, exhaled slowly and watched the bluish cigar smoke whirling towards the ceiling. A shrewd smile appeared on his face.

"What is on your mind?" Dyakonov said.

"I think that Joint Affairs — the name speaks for itself — and Manus Domini are quite alike. *Pecuniae obediunt omnia* — money governs everything."

"I nourish the hope that Manus Domini is also driven by ideals, and not just by power and money."

"Democracy, ideals, equality...." The cardinal made a fatalistic gesture. "Meaningless words."

"Don't you think you are being a little bit too... disenchanted, to say the least?"

"Just pragmatic. Democracy is a luxury item that most people can't afford. So why promise it to them? Unless it's during an election campaign, of course."

"This would mean that everything is hopeless, then."

"The older I grow, the more I am convinced that it's not true that all men are created equal. Power, both spiritual and secular, should not be diluted among the crowd, but shared only among a few chosen spirits."

"A peculiar idea."

"What can you expect from all those people out there?" The cardinal waved his hand in the direction of the windows. "Power must be concentrated in the right hands, hands that know where to draw the line between good and evil. Believe me, this is *precisely* what people want, because all of them are terrified of decisions."

"And who will guard the guardians?"

The cardinal raised a finger. "*Est deus in* nobis — A god dwells in us."

Dyakonov stared at him in silence.

Jules didn't seem surprised when Françoise called him to say she intended to take the rest of the week off.

"Do I know him, Françoise?" Jules asked.

"You're a nosy parker. You won't believe this, but I've got some books I need to read, away from the phone."

"That's such a ridiculous excuse it just has to be true."

Françoise sat down in front of the terrace coffee table. The bell tower of Saint Germain des Près stood out against a clear sky. In the distance, the Jardins de Luxembourg glowed with a thousand hues. On the street corner, the cream awnings of the Café de Flore, where Sartre and Hemingway used to be regulars, shaded the customers sitting outside from the sun. More than a Paris quarter, Saint Germain des Près was still a way of life.

Her eyes fell on the pile of books she had bought from Gibert's and she had a feeling of uneasiness, almost of fear. All of a sudden the carefree atmosphere of Saint Germain faded away. The thought of that mysterious gravestone and Guichard's disconnected words, murmured in the dark, flashed through her mind. Then she thought of him, closed her eyes, and felt her breath quickening. He was a tender and passionate lover, and in his arms she'd forgotten everything.

Then, little by little, a disconcerting feeling had grown in her, so disconcerting that she'd tried to smother it, but in vain. Guichard had let a few words slip that she hadn't understood, but she was sure it was medieval French. It was as if he was making love to someone else, but not simply to another woman, but rather to something immaterial, like a ghost or a memory from the past. Was it just her imagination?

She checked the titles of the books and chose one. After a few pages she found herself taken back centuries, to the times of the Crusades and the Templars. Why had the Church persecuted the most powerful religious order of that period with such ruthlessness? From 1118 to 1127, even before the foundation of the order, nine knights had started making excavations in Jerusalem, under the ruins of what had once been Solomon's Temple. What were they looking for? The Holy Grail? A treasure? The Bible said in the Book of Exodus that the biggest treasure of all had been hidden in the Temple: the Ark of the Covenant. And the Ark must hold the two Tables of Testimony that God had given to Moses on Mount Sinai. Was this the treasure that had led the nine knights to Jerusalem?

A flock of birds circled around the bell tower and their piercing shrieks filled the sky.

According to the written account by Abbot Bernard de Fontaine, their mission was crowned with success, but neither the abbot nor the Church had ever revealed what this success consisted of. However, historians seemed to agree on one point. In the Holy of Holies the knights found the Ark and the two Tables, some scrolls in ancient Hebrew and an inestimable treasure. But a number of historians believed that the knights had found something more, something that must have struck terror in someone in power. Despite the lack of evidence, these historians linked the Church's persecution of the Templars with that mysterious discovery. If that correlation was correct, what had the Templars discovered that was so overwhelming?

Françoise lifted her eyes from the book. The bell tower of Saint Germain was now casting a long shadow across the boulevard.

Françoise turned the page. The discovery of the apocryphal Gospels of Nag Hammadi drew her attention. In 1945, an Arab boy working in the fields near the village of Nag Hammadi, in Egypt, dug up an earthenware jar. He broke it open and found thirteen big papyrus manuscripts. The boy had discovered the Apocrypha inspired by Gnostic Christianity. The manuscripts had remained buried in that jar for 1,600 years. They were copies; the originals dated back to the first century. The Apocrypha had given a picture of Christ as a man, of His background, of His family, and the Apostles, which widely contradicted the Books of the New Testament.

Two years later, in 1947, a Bedouin shepherd found some earthenware jars in a cave in Qumran, on the shores of the Dead Sea. The archaeologists who arrived on the scene found over 500 manuscripts. They had discovered the Dead Sea Scrolls, the oldest collection of Old Testament writings in the world, and also writings regarding Jesus and the early years of Christianity. Those scrolls provided documentation from well before the Gospels of the New Testament. The latter dated back to the second half of the first century and were written by men who had not actually known Jesus. The scrolls, on the other hand, were written by the Essenes, a community of religious ascetics who had settled in Qumran in the third century B.C. The Scrolls had been written using an allegorical code. It was not until 1956 that Manchester University researchers finished deciphering the Qumran Copper Scroll. In that scroll, they found proof that an "indeterminable treasure" had been buried underneath the Temple.

The more Françoise read, the more a different interpretation seemed to take shape, compared with what the Church had been telling the world for two thousand years. Why had the Church taken no stand on this?

A gust of wind raised a whirl of dust, and a clatter of broken tableware came from the outside tables of the Café de Flore.

The New Testament appeared to her in a different light: a light tinged with doubts. The Nag Hammadi manuscripts spoke of Jesus' family, of his wife Mary Magdalene, of a brother known as Joseph the Just, of a misogynous Peter—a complainer who was always arguing with Mary Magdalene and asking Jesus why he loved that woman more than the apostles.

Philip's Gospel spoke of a "resurrection" very different from that of the New Testament. It spoke of the resurrection of the Gnostic Christians, who ridiculed the Christians who had taken the word literally. According to the Gnostics, the resurrection of the soul occurred during life, not at death. The soul only became immortal at death if during life one had reached a state of gnosis—that is, cognition—which was in contrast with the "faith" demanded by the Roman Catholic Church. The picture of Jesus that emerged from the Apocrypha was that of a great initiate, but yet a man.

The Essenes wrote using a code based on allegories, symbols and metaphors. Their symbolism was very close to that of the teachings of Jesus Christ. Was it possible that Jesus was an

Essene? If so, could it be that Jesus himself used the term "resurrection" in a figurative sense? Had the Church really misinterpreted things, or had they known the truth all along? The initiation rites of the Essenes were similar to those of the Order of the Templars, and later, of Freemasonry.

Françoise opened a heraldic guide to France to the pages referring to *les Comtes de Saint Clair* and began going back through their family tree. She stared at the final page, puzzled. In the period that interested her most, 1100-1320, there was a blank space. *Why?* It was unthinkable that the Saint Clairs didn't know the identity of their ancestors in so crucial a period of their family history.

A light, cold breeze brushed Françoise's arms. She shivered.

Perhaps there was a way to find out. She checked her watch. She walked into the living room, grabbed the phone book and found the number of the Bibliothèque Nationale de France.

Ten minutes later she got into a taxi, and told the driver to take her to the Bibliothèque Nationale in Rue Richelieu.

Rows of vines heavy with black grapes flashed past on either side of the road, intermittently revealing stretches of a blue, shimmering sea. Guichard rolled down the window and his lungs filled with country air.

A smell of wax wafted in. The driver told him it came from a wax factory they had just passed. It was the same smell that filled the air when the cleaning women did the polishing at the castle. It came from a thick, yellowish wax that they spread on the terracotta floors. It was strange how certain smells would remain imprinted on one's mind and trigger memories dating back to long before.

The bookshelves full of old books and the worn leather armchairs came to his mind. His father would shut himself away in the library for hours on end, talking business with long-faced people.

One day his father told him that the de Saint Clair family belonged to the European "black nobility," a term that frightened Guichard. The black nobility, his father said, was a group of ancient European families of nobles, dating back to the Holy Roman Empire. But at the age of eight he didn't understand much. His confusion turned to bewilderment whenever he stood before the pictures hanging on the walls of the castle, which depicted bearded knights armed with swords and dressed in suits of armor. That bewilderment changed to fear when he began looking at the old, musty books in the library, and when bloody battles between the Templars and the Saracens started to haunt his nights. In those dreams, the red of the blood mingled with that of the crosses blazing on the white surcoats the knights wore over their armor.

His father told him that their ancestors had taken part in the Crusades, as knights of the Order of the Temple. At the time he thought that those stern-faced men he saw every so often in his father's library must have belonged to that sect of knights, and that their forefathers had also fought in the Crusades.

Suddenly, overnight, clanging machinery appeared on the castle grounds, and people he'd never seen before started digging big holes first all round the walls of the castle and then in the underground vaults. He and Véronique—she was five at the time—crept stealthily down the stairs leading to the cellars, clutching each other's hands, to watch the men at work. Meanwhile, his father was rushing about everywhere as well as back and forth from the library, holding what looked like old papers.

Then one day it all stopped, as suddenly as it had begun. The holes were filled in and the workmen disappeared, taking their machinery with them.

New faces started to appear in and out of the library. He remembered one man in particular, who was dressed in black and wore a tall hat that he never seemed to remove. He had a long, white beard, with strange curls. His father told him he was a rabbi, but at the time Guichard wasn't quite sure what a rabbi was.

He would never forget the moment when, taking advantage of the absence of his father and the rabbi, he first saw the parchment scrolls; they lay open on the desk in the library. Outside it was pouring with rain and the branches of the old oak were beating against the windows. Although he was only nine, he realized that the scrolls must hide something mysterious. With his heart pounding, he moved the lamp nearer. He stared at the elongated characters that sloped backwards, and remembered having seen them in the books in the library; his father had told him it was Hebrew writing, from the time of Jesus.

He was about to touch the parchments, when Véronique pulled him back by his arm.

"Don't, Guichard," she said. "What if daddy comes back? I'm frightened."

"Don't be such a coward. Let's just have a look."

He was showing off, for he was frightened too. But he was feeling more intrigued than frightened. He glanced towards the library door to make sure no one was coming. He reached out for the scrolls, but before touching them he hesitated, his hand hovering in mid-air, not so much for fear of his father, but because he had the feeling he was doing something he would regret. In awe, he slid his hand across the top scroll, then lowered his head in order to better sniff that odor of mystery.

He turned the scrolls over, one by one, until he reached the bottom one. It was different from all the others. The writing appeared to be in some kind of old French, but he could understand only a few of the words: some of them, like *graal* and *sang real*, were repeated several times. Then he saw *it*, and stood motionless.

"What is it, Guichard? What have you seen?" Véronique grabbed his arm.

"Ssh! Be quiet. It's nothing!"

But it wasn't true. He stared at the signature at the bottom of the scroll: *Guichard de Saint Clair* – his own name! And next to the signature there was a date: October 20, in the year of our Lord 1308!

Guichard reached out his hand and touched the signature. A flash of lightning lit up the library and the windows burst open with a great crash.

"Ouch!" Guichard jerked back his hand and rubbed his arm where he'd felt the shock. For a moment he thought he'd seen strange images dart in front of his eyes.

"Well it serves you right! I'm not coming here with you again." Véronique ran out.

That very night, in his sleep, he'd started seeing the images and hearing the Voice. It was as if the spirit of something or someone from centuries before had reawakened and taken over his body. At first it was all confused, like clips from a film still to be edited. And yet his immediate feeling was that he'd lived through it all before, in a far distant past.

A few weeks after the work had finished, his father began to change. He became depressed and more and more taciturn. Until then, he had been a practicing Catholic and wanted Véronique and Guichard to have a strict Catholic upbringing. To their great joy, he suddenly stopped taking them to church on Sundays. Then one day the headmaster summoned Guichard to his office, and told him that in the future he wouldn't have to stay with the rest of the class for religion. He left the headmaster's study, doing his best to hide his joy at that godsend. As he ran down the stairs, he caught a glimpse of his father's austere figure walking away across the courtyard.

With this respite from catechism, Guichard stopped being afraid of the dark. All his nightmares vanished, and with them vanished the images of all those saints burning alive on apocalyptic nights, thunder and lightning showing all the wrath of a vindictive God. Life began smiling on him again.

But that period of peace was not to last.

His father's gloom reminded Guichard of five years earlier, when his mother had died giving birth to Véronique. It was as if his father had plunged into the same grief once again.

It had been a difficult labor, and complications had arisen. The doctor presented his father with a choice: the mother or the child. His father made the only choice compatible with the conscience of a convinced Roman Catholic: Véronique had been born and Guichard's mother had died.

It was not until many years later, on the eve of his father's death, that Guichard had come to understand the link between his father's change of mood when the scrolls were discovered and his mother's death. On his deathbed, his father revealed to him the contents of the scrolls and confessed him that if he had known the secret contained in the scrolls at the time his wife was in labor, he would have been able to make a choice with the conscience of a free man, and not according to the dogmas dictated by a cruel religion.

Men who had nothing whatsoever to do with God had deprived Guichard of his mother's love. For two thousand years, those same men had imposed arbitrary rules of moral behavior, preaching from a pulpit they had no right to, and inflicting suffering of every kind on humanity. They had always lied to the entire world, and those scrolls were the living proof of it.

After his father's death, Guichard read the translation of the Hebrew scrolls. The scroll signed by his ancestor was a faithful account of what really happened to the Templars after they had fled from France. It disclosed the secret of their "treasure" and told where they had hidden it: a secret that went far beyond anyone's wildest imagination.

But the late Guichard de Saint Clair also spoke of the tortures inflicted on the Templars by the Inquisition and of the death of his brother Arno, who had also been a Knight Templar. *"Noses and ears were lopped off, eyes were gouged out, and lips were torn off. Marcel de Lisleferme, Roger d'Avignon, and Pascal de Tissier ... Many had had one or more limbs hacked off, and all that had been left were stumps blackened with pitch ... Arno was reduced to a skeleton and bent at the knees, supported by the chains that held him to the pole...."*

Those words, written seven centuries earlier, expressed a contagious, implacable hatred, a hatred stronger than time.

The need for revenge matured slowly inside Guichard, eventually exploding like the bursting of a dam that had held back centuries of anger and hatred. His memories turned more and more into nightmares, and through those nightmares Guichard de Saint Clair started to seek revenge from his grave in Kilmory Chapel.

Guichard had refused to think of reincarnation—wandering souls that a law of karma attracted to prospective parents, in order to deal with unfinished business in a previous life. To him reincarnation and regression had always been some obscure phenomenon belonging to Oriental mysticism.

Jung spoke of a 'collective unconscious' — a sort of collection of archetypal images responsible for the instinctive aspects of our personality — that all of us inherit from previous generations and share with the rest of humankind. Jung also spoke of a 'personal unconscious', which he defined as repressed memories derived from personal experience, something our mind is unaware of and that we experience only in dreams or fantasies.

What if this personal unconscious also contained the memory of episodes that had happened during our ancestors' lives? But how? The unconscious dies when we die. So how could the memory of events that happened before birth be explained?

Perhaps genetic memory was the answer. After all, wasn't that double helix like a computer program? Perhaps the brain wasn't the only seat of mental activity. Perhaps DNA was mentally accessible and all cells contribute something to mental processes. Jung's collective unconscious could only be imprinted into an individual's DNA. Couldn't it be that our genes contained a sort of hereditary unconscious, accessible to the brain, coming from previous generations, with each generation adding a link to a chain that went back to the day of creation?

But even if this were true, what would trigger this ancestral unconscious? *The thunderbolt.* The very moment he had touched the scroll, lightning had struck very close to the castle, and he'd felt the electric shock. Could a strong electromagnetic field be the cause?

The car braked sharply. The driver swore as a dog dashed across the road. A road sign said it was three more miles to Punta Raisi Airport. Guichard recalled what Franzese had said the night before regarding the role the Vatican would play in the plan of the Organization.

"... I don't want to have anything to do with the Church."

"Forget your grudges. It's only business. If anything goes wrong, our friendship won't count for anything."

Guichard's fist started to clench and unclench, as if responding to a remote command.

8

"Damn, I've done it again!" Tancredi de Santis turned the platen of his typewriter to correct his mistake. He'd once tried to use a word processor, but had given it up and gone back to his old Olivetti. He had to be the only journalist in Rome, and possibly in all of Italy, still clinging to a typewriter. He retrieved his cigarette from an overflowing ashtray and took a last drag. The typewriter was just an excuse, he knew that. He was no longer sure where he was going with those articles on the petrochemical industry. He felt like a huntsman who hears a noise behind a bush and takes a blind shot, hoping that will be the one to hit the mark.

He got up, and making his way through the piles of newspapers heaped up against the walls, he went into the next room—a cubbyhole he used as a kitchen. He squeezed between the sink and the wall, and put some coffee powder into his old *napolitana*. He refused to use the automatic machine: apart from the taste, how the hell could anyone drink coffee from a machine? As he drank his coffee, he leaned on the window sill and gazed towards Trastevere. He loved Rome; he loved its climate, the food, the kasbah-like chaos in the streets, the impression of being at a crossroads between the West and the Middle East.

He thought of all the research he'd done to put together some convincing data. He'd had to go back twenty-five years, but in the end it had been worth it. The Italian government had thrown away a fortune building plants in the South, and with disastrous results. The figures involved gave rise to a load of questions. Who had gained from all this?

His articles had left their mark; the newspaper had received several anonymous phone calls and letters threatening to make him pay for it if he carried on. But what news-paper didn't receive threats? He was attached to that news-paper. *La Voce Independente* was the only truly independent Italian daily; they didn't take money from anyone. For the first time in his life he felt he was doing some serious journalism, the kind of journalism that didn't make compromises and that gave the public the chance to make up its own mind. The phone rang in his office.

"What's eating you?" asked Sergio Morganti.

"Nothing," Tancredi said. "It's just one of those days."

"How about a sandwich?"

From his voice, Tancredi understood that there must be something in the air. "At *Bar Nazionale*?"

"OK, see you there at 12:30."

He and Sergio had always been friends. It was one of those friendships that start at school and carry on through life. Sergio held a position of responsibility in the anti-Mafia department of the Ministry of the Interior. Tancredi had asked him for help with his articles, and Sergio had passed him confidential infor-mation whenever he could. He would never have asked him if he hadn't known that Sergio, deep down, was a left-winger.

Sergio's phone call reminded him of the anonymous letters. He'd never mentioned them to Carla. He thought for a moment about Simona, who'd celebrated her tenth birthday just the day before. For a moment he felt a sense of guilt, but tried not to think about it.

Tancredi made his way through the crowded café. Sergio was already there, sitting at a table in the rear, looking the eter-nal undergraduate. He beckoned to him.

"Hello, sorry I'm late," Tancredi said.

"Ever since you embarked on those articles, I don't see much of you." Sergio looked around cautiously. "I haven't got long. I've got a meeting at two o'clock."

"I'm listening."

"Rome, as you know, is full of busybodies who live in the shadow of the ministries." Sergio stopped while the waiter laid the tray on the table. "Most of them are just small fry. Some of them, though, are into the really juicy stuff and make big money."

"The usual connections, no doubt."

"Sure, the ingredients are always the same: political cover, a corrupt big-wig in one of the ministries, and, of course, an unscrupulous company ready to pay to get around the law."

"I've got the picture."

"One of the middlemen we've been keeping an eye on is named Lucchese."

Lucchese was Sicilian, said Sergio. He had started up his company some ten years before, after leaving the management of the overseas department of a Palermo-based bank. He kept a low profile, but he handled big deals, too big for a small company like his. The Ministry of the Interior was convinced that Lucchese was linked to the Mafia, but they'd never succeeded in catching him out.

Sergio told him that just that morning, at six o'clock, they'd recorded a suspicious phone call Lucchese had made to Zergas, the administrative manager of the Coalition Party. Lucchese had requested an urgent appointment with Prime Minister Accardo for a Frenchman, a certain Guichard de Saint Clair. The Ministry of the Interior had immediately asked the Italian Embassy in Paris for information. De Saint Clair controlled an investment bank, with its main offices in Paris, and among the deals his bank had closed in the past, there were a number of production agreements within the oil industry.

"Why do you think it's the prime minister himself this de Saint Clair wants to contact?" asked Tancredi.

"He might want to discuss an oil deal with him."

Tancredi put down his glass of beer. "Don't tell me you're thinking of CIP."

"Who else?"

"Wasn't there anything else in the phone call between Lucchese and Zergas that could give me a clue? Think hard. Even some seemingly unimportant detail."

"The call was short.... Wait, though. At a certain point Lucchese said that de Saint Clair would be arriving at the Leonardo da Vinci airport this morning at... 10:30. Yes, 10:30."

Tancredi thought for a moment. "I'd give anything to know if de Saint Clair was already in Italy and if so, where and with whom."

"Oh God, I can see the Red Baron look already." Sergio rolled his eyes, then got up from the table.

The waiter waved the bill. "Hey, Mister, who's going to pay? You or the Red Baron here?"

The runway of Punta Raisi Airport in Palermo flashed by below him as the jet took off for Rome. Guichard found himself thinking of the dinner at the Seigneurs a few months earlier when he'd met Françoise. He had been sitting across from an astrophysicist.

"I've read that, in principle, quantum physics admits the concept of time travel," Guichard said.

"Surprisingly enough, there is nothing in Einstein's theory of relativity to prevent it," Professor Bieri said. "Einstein's equations, however, show that nothing can travel faster than light, and that at the speed of light time stops."

Guichard listened attentively.

"That's where black holes come into play," added the professor. "Time travel, though, would require the technology to manipulate black holes, hardly something you'd find in your back yard."

"What's a black hole, exactly?"

"It's basically a black void in space, formed by the implosion of a large star. The star shrinks until it reaches a point of infinite density, when the gravitational pull becomes so intense that nothing can escape, not even light."

"A sort of gigantic vacuum cleaner in space?"

For a moment the professor looked puzzled. "Why not? I suppose you could look at it that way."

"You were saying that not even light can escape," Guichard said, pouring the professor a second glass of Bordeaux.

"That's right, and that's why you can't see black holes. Nevertheless, several have been detected using powerful radio telescopes."

"But why does a black hole make time travel possible? What would you have to do? Jump into it?"

The professor burst out laughing. "In the unlikely event that you ever come across one, keep away from it. For your own good."

The professor went on to explain that, at its center, a black hole contains a *singularity*, a point of infinite density where time-space is bent and ceases to exist and where the laws of quantum physics no longer apply. If you were swallowed up in there, he said, you'd be literally annihilated, squeezed to infinite density.

"Which would mean losing any hope of traveling in time," Guichard said.

"Not necessarily. You shouldn't imagine a stationary, non-rotating, spherical black hole, sitting somewhere in space and sucking in anything that comes close to it. Start thinking in terms of rotating black holes."

Rotating black holes, the professor said, were voids in space that later manipulations of Einstein's relativity equations had proved existed. Imagine a black hole rotating on its axis faster and faster, until a hole is formed, like in a doughnut. The singularity still exists, but in the shape of a ring. Diving through it, you would avoid coming to a bad end. Mathematics had shown that rotating black holes always have two ends, and in fact physicists speak of *wormholes* — time tunnels crossing time and space. Think of Gruyère cheese, he said. Wormholes are like gateways to otherwise disconnected regions of the four-dimensional universe. However, the professor added, no scientific or empirical evidence had yet been found to prove the existence of wormholes.

"If you went through the tunnel, what would you find at the other end?" Guichard asked.

"A difference of thousands or even millions of years, forwards or backwards, depending on the distance between the two ends of the tunnel and their relative positions."

"It all sounds like science fiction."

"Not at all. It was Einstein himself who showed, back in 1935, that the theory of relativity allows wormholes. All you need to do is place the wormhole in an anti-gravitational field, in other words a field exerting reverse pressure on it, to keep the tunnel open."

"Antigravity isn't something one can produce in one's garage, though."

"Ordinary matter around us is plunged into a four-dimensional space-time with a positive curvature. Just think of a sphere. We can't either see or imagine space-time, because our senses deceive us and we think in terms of linear time. But in a universe of galaxies these limitations don't apply. Up there, space-time can be warped inwards and this would enable us, through a wormhole, to travel into the past. Time would be negative."

So, in principle, quantum physics acknowledged that traveling back in time was possible. While the professor went on talking, little by little an idea crept into Guichard's mind. To explain genetic memory, wasn't it possible that our biology and our brain, under certain conditions, might follow quantum physics? Couldn't it be that a strong electromagnetic field, like the one produced by lightning, might make forgotten ancestral memories imprinted in our DNA accessible to our brain? The DNA strands turned into a sort of biological wormhole enabling our brain to reach the unreachable. The human brain as a quantum system.

The seat-belt signs went off. Guichard reclined his chair, breathed deeply, and his muscles relaxed. He could feel himself falling down... further and further down, swallowed up by a whirlpool rotating fast, too fast. It was as if time didn't exist any longer. All around him just silence, and the indescribable mystery of infinite worlds.

♣

The valley of Bannockburn, Scotland. June 24, in the year of our Lord 1314.

On the horizon a timid sun filtered through the banks of mist and reflected on the knights' armor. A horse neighed, an archer drew his bow, a foot soldier brandished his axe.

Two Scottish priests shook the bells they were holding in their hands and thousands of Scottish foot soldiers and knights knelt down. Maurice, the blind Abbot of Inchaffray, raised his arms to heaven. *"Comfort ye, comfort ye my people, saith your God. Speak ye comfortably to Jerusalem, and cry unto her, that her warfare is ended, that her iniquity is pardoned..."* The abbot intoned the words of Isaiah loudly, holding his crosier aloft.

From the top of Coxet Hill, hidden in a thicket, Guichard de Saint Clair observed the English gathering in the marshes on the south side of Bannock Burn, the brook that crossed the plain. He looked to his right. In Gillies Hill wood, about two hundred yards away, King Robert the Bruce was waiting at the head of five hundred Scottish knights. The Scottish army — eleven thousand men armed only with axes, maces and spears — was concentrated between the two sections of woodland. Bruce had learnt many things from Wallace and he had chosen a battlefield that would favor the Scots: a reduced front and a narrow gorge that, down at the foot of the hill, divided the two armies.

Men armed with twelve-foot spikes protected the two-hundred-yard front. What the English didn't know was that, in the past few days, the Scots had dug hundreds of pits in the strip of land in front of the lancers and had covered them with branches and grass, turning them into lethal traps. Guichard looked back again at the English army. Through their informers, they knew that King Edward's forces amounted to 32,000 foot soldiers and 2,500 archers. Edward could also rely on 3,000 mounted knights. The English outnumbered them three to one.

To make up for the disparity on the battlefield, Guichard and Bruce had to count on surprise. Guichard's hundred and fifty Knights Templar were hiding in the thick of the wood. From time to time, the white of their cloaks and of their black-and-white-striped banners flashed in the semi-darkness. Silence crept into his bones, a silence broken every so often by the stifled neighing of a horse and the dull thudding of hooves on damp turf. Soon, on his orders, his knights would be charging down the hill shouting the Templars' battle cry *Beau Séant!*

amidst the thunder of hoofs and the glint of armor. The memory of the Templars on the battlefield still struck terror in people, but this was all that was left of the Templars' army. Would they be enough?

Guichard stared at his hand clenching and unclenching. Only seven years had passed since that ill-fated dawn on October 13, 1307. Now, the clash with the English was imminent.

Guichard's mind went back to the day it had all started, almost two hundred years before.

♣

Clairvaux Abbey, France. January 17, in the year of our Lord 1117.

The horse neighed. Steamy breath rose from the animal's nostrils, mixing with falling snowflakes. Geoffroy shivered and pulled his cloak more tightly round his shoulders. He rubbed his numb hands briskly together. The track leading up to the abbey was steep at this point, and the horse picked its way forward slowly. Geoffroy felt his chest: the leather scrip was still there. He shook his head and huffed. If it hadn't been for Hugues' insistence, he would never have ventured as far as the abbey in the depths of winter.

From time to time, the horse's hooves struck a stone beneath the snow and the slush covering the track, and that was the only sound that broke the silence of dawn. He looked out over the valley of Langres. Snow-capped woods emerged through the morning mist, and the waters of the Aube wound their way through the trees.

Here the path curved to the right. Geoffroy looked up and shivered again. But this time it wasn't from the cold. At the edge of a sharp drop to the valley below, in a gorge enclosed between mountains covered with forests, Clairvaux Abbey stood on the crest of the hill.

A blanket of snow wrapped the abbey in deep silence. Geoffroy tightened the reins. That silence aroused respect, awe, but also an indefinable feeling of uneasiness. The sound of the muffled chants of the monks of the abbey did nothing but sharpen the feeling of solitude of that place. A high wall, broken only by dark, narrow slits, surrounded it. The church tower and three rough stone buildings were barely visible above the walls.

Geoffroy dug his heels into his horse's flanks.

His horse's hooves resounded on the wooden slats of the bridge. Geoffroy dismounted and walked to the gate. He raised the iron knocker and let it fall with a dull thud. Nothing happened. He was about to knock again when he heard a creak. A peephole opened in the door, and two eyes peered at him through the crack.

"Who are you? What do you want?"

"Count Geoffroy de Saint Clair. I'm here to see Abbot Bernard. Didn't they inform you?"

The wicket closed again. After a few long minutes, the massive door began to rise amidst a cranking and rattling of chains. Geoffroy remounted his horse and rode through the entrance.

Damn boor, he thought, as he passed the hooded monk. If he hadn't been wearing that habit, he'd have had his serfs tan the man's hide.

There was no fire in the grate, and Geoffroy's teeth started to chatter, even though he was still wearing his cloak. A muffled chorus of chanted prayers broke the silence and made him shiver even more. He put a hand on the straw mattress: it was as hard as iron. A shuffling of feet, mingled with the caws of ravens, came from outside, and Geoffroy went over to the slit that served as a window. Two monks were crossing the courtyard, following a pathway cut out in the snow, as a flock of ravens circled above them, the birds' shrill cries resounding among the walls of the yard. The monks were carrying wooden pails full of pieces of bloody meat, wearing only sandals on their bare feet.

One certainly couldn't say that the Cistercians didn't obey the Benedictines' rules to the letter. Geoffroy slammed his fist against the icy stone wall. How silly of him to give in to Hugues! How long would he be segregated in this cell? Somebody knocked at the door.

A monk entered. Probably about twenty-five, with ash-blond hair and deathly pale skin, his eyes seemed to shine with an intense light, which made him look older. He was wearing the white cowl of the Cistercians, a black scapular, and a leather belt round his waist. An uncanny magnetism emanated from his person.

"I am Abbot Bernard. My cousin, Count de Payens, has often spoken of you, Count de Saint Clair."

"Father," Geoffroy said, bowing his head.

"Have you got the scroll with you?"

"I have it here." Geoffroy pointed to the leather scrip hanging round his neck.

"Please follow me, Sir Geoffroy."

It took only that brief meeting for Geoffroy to realize why this man had become prior of the abbey, and head of the Order of the Cistercians, at such an early age. Not by chance had he been nicknamed the Second Pope. It was said of Abbot Bernard that his faith was so contagious he made instant converts wherever he went. Many men abandoned everything simply to follow him. He'd heard that women were terrified of the abbot. Mothers, wives and fiancées did their best to ensure their men never met up with him, for fear they might disappear forever. Bernard had even persuaded thirty of his relatives to join him in the Order, including his father and five of his brothers.

In the library, a dozen monks were busy reading and writing. The only sound was the turning of pages. A pungent smell of ink and paint filled the air. On the left, an arched doorway decorated with octagonal pieces of stained glass separated the library from the scriptorium, where the illuminators were at work on their scrolls, hunched over their workbenches in two long rows.

The abbot approached a monk who was standing in front of a reading desk. The man was all skin and bones, with a bald head and a long, white beard. Abbot Bernard whispered something to him, and the monk looked over at Geoffroy.

"Brother Abelard is in charge of the library. He speaks and writes fluent Greek, Latin, and ancient Hebrew," the abbot said. "None of the illuminators can compete with him."

"Will you show me the scroll?" Brother Abelard spoke in a cavernous voice, and stretched out his skeletal hand.

Geoffroy had never seen eyes like these. His pupils were so pale that they merged into the whites. Geoffroy hoped he would never come across him at night. He undid the drawstring closing the scrip and handed the scroll to the monk, who unrolled it slowly. After a few moments, Abelard widened his eyes and murmured something in Abbot Bernard's ear. The abbot frowned.

"Who gave you this scroll?" Abelard asked.

Geoffroy felt his eyes piercing his very soul. "I found it among my father's papers, after his death."

"And whom did he get it from?"

"He found it in the Al-Aqsa Mosque, when he entered Jerusalem with the other crusaders, in the summer of 1099."

The monk's eyes narrowed with suspicion. "In all these years it's never been shown to anyone?"

"At the beginning my father showed it to some Benedictines, but he soon gave up because nobody was able to make any sense of it."

"So you have no idea of what's written here?"

Geoffroy had had more than enough, but made an effort to keep calm. "No, of course not. But why all these questions?"

Abelard whispered something else in the abbot's ear.

"Brother Abelard suggests we meet again tomorrow. By then the scroll will have been translated," Abbot Bernard said.

A monk ushered Geoffroy into a bare, vaulted room adjacent to the library. Geoffroy could still feel the cold of the night in his bones, and hear the muffled prayers in the dark and a succession of sharp thwacks and stifled moans, as if someone were scourging himself. He grabbed a stool, went over to the fireplace and sat down. Abbot Bernard walked in.

"You'll find it hard to believe what I'm about to tell you," the abbot said, sitting down by the fireplace.

The expression on the abbot's face left no room for doubt. Brother Abelard must have succeeded in translating the scroll.

"What's written in the scroll?"

"It indicates where the Holy of Holies from Solomon's Temple is to be found." The abbot's eyes were gleaming.

Geoffroy's eyes widened in surprise. *"The Holy of Holies?* From the Old Testament?"

The abbot nodded. "Brother Abelard has no doubts regarding the authenticity of the scroll. It's written in Aramaic and dates back to A.D. 70, the year in which Titus and his legionaries destroyed the Temple of Jerusalem."

"Do we know who wrote it?"

"No, unfortunately not. The signature is illegible," the abbot said, shaking his head. "We can only make out the first letter, an *F.* It might have been the Jewish historian Flavius Josephus. Who knows?"

"Does the scroll tell how to get to the Holy of Holies?"

"In some places the script is so faded that nothing at all can be read. What is clear, however, is that the Temple stood exactly where the Al-Aqsa Mosque now stands."

"Does the scroll say what was inside the Holy of Holies?"

"It gives a detailed list of everything. The treasure consisted of twenty-four separate items."

Geoffroy, dumbfounded, stared at the abbot.

"But that's not the real treasure," said the abbot, with an enigmatic smile.

"What do you mean?"

"The Ark of the Covenant, with the Tables of Testimony. *That's the real treasure."* The abbot got up and stood in front of the fire, rubbing his hands. "This morning I sent a messenger to Rome; I want the Holy Father to hear the news right away. But in the meantime I have a proposal for you."

"What sort of proposal?" Geoffroy asked, a little uneasy.

When the abbot had finished explaining, Geoffroy felt bewildered. He'd never thought of such a possibility.

"You look perplexed, Sir Geoffroy. You wouldn't be thinking of refusing such an honor, would you?"

"No, any knight in my place would be attracted by such a challenging undertaking," Geoffroy said with conviction. "What surprises me is your plan for an order of warrior monks. Why?"

"Imagine! The Order of the Knights of the Temple, an order that will defend the routes of the Holy Land, sword in hand. I will go to Rome myself to discuss the matter with Pope Pascal."

Just then, Brother Abelard appeared in the doorway, holding the scroll. Damnation! Those eyes made Geoffroy feel guilty for sins he'd never committed. Geoffroy's hand began to clench and unclench....

"Sir, please wake up, sir!"

"What?... What's the matter? Who is it?"

Guichard felt a tug at his arm, and was swallowed back into the whirlpool. The tunnel spun round him faster and faster....

"I'm the air hostess, sir," said the woman, leaning over him. "Please wake up, sir. We're about to land in Rome."

9

An official black Lancia Flaminia with Vatican City plates drew up in front of the United States embassy on Via Veneto, in the center of Rome. A military policeman approached the driver's window, checked the visitors' identities, and waved them on. The car drove up the sycamore-lined drive that ran through the park, and stopped in front of Palazzo Margherita — the neo-Renaissance, pink-colored palace that was now the premises of the embassy. Ambassador Fox was waiting between the columns of the entrance. He was wearing a dark, pin-stripe suit, with matching silk handkerchief and tie. Cardinal Wolfenberg got out of the car.

Abramson was standing in Fox's study. After a brief introduction, Fox called upon Abramson to speak.

"Your Eminence, some dramatic changes are likely to take place, very soon, in Italy's political scenario, and I'm not just referring to one of the recurrent political crises."

Abramson said that Joint Affairs could no longer accept a state of instability in Italy that threatened its own primary interests. The men of the Coalition Party, along with the other politicians of the majority, had become not only useless, but even dangerous. Enough was enough.

The ticking of the pendulum clock filled the room.

"Continue, I pray you," said the cardinal.

"Italy's too important to us. Joint Affairs doesn't want to run the risk of a *coup d'état*."

"No one wants that."

"We of Joint Affairs have been following the silent rise of Manus Domini's *initiati* to this country's top positions with great interest." Abramson opened his briefcase, took out his report and skimmed though it. "Banks, large corporations, big dailies, ministries.... My congratulations, Eminence."

"I don't see what your point is."

Abramson, impassive, kept leafing through the report. "If I'm not mistaken, the same holds true within the Church. According to our data, almost half of the present one hundred and twenty *cardinali elettori*—voting cardinals—belong to your ranks." Then he raised his eyes, a serious expression on his face. "By the way, how is His Holiness' health these days? Not so good, they tell me."

The cardinal's eyes had narrowed to two thin slits.

"You see, Your Eminence, Joint Affairs reached the conclusion many years ago that politics is too serious a matter to be left to politicians."

"A peculiar statement."

"We too want a place at your table."

"Why on earth should we lay an extra place, to stick to your colorful image?"

"Joint Affairs, starting with the States, has learned to put its resources at the disposal of deserving men and worthy causes. And the results are more than satisfactory," Abramson said. "We've already elected five presidents."

"Rome's alleys can be much more treacherous than Washington's boulevards."

"You still have problems in South America. Joint Affairs might make a little extra room and throw Manus Domini some juicy T-bone steaks."

"I see."

"Eminence, the time has come to get rid of Accardo."

"Get rid of Accardo?" the cardinal said, his voice skeptical. "How?"

"Eminence, your words amaze me," said Abramson. He showed all his thirty-two teeth, leaned towards the cardinal and whispered: "With democracy."

"*Timeo Danaos et dona* ferentes—I am wary of the Greeks, even when they are bearing gifts—wrote Virgil, over two thousand years ago."

"Would you mind explaining, for the benefit of the man in the street?"

"When someone must resort to words like 'democracy,' my first instinct is to start telling my beads. Is the translation clearer now?"

Abramson grinned, visibly pleased, and slapped his knee. "I knew it, I knew it even before meeting you, that the two of us were made to understand each other. Yessir."

"You think so?" The cardinal lit a Romeo y Julieta. "What do you expect from the Holy See?"

"From Manus Domini, Your Eminence. *Not* from the Holy See."

The cardinal kept silent.

"Let's face it, Eminence. Manus Domini's ways and ours overlap. That's why I've come to you. To offer an alliance."

"An alliance? What kind of alliance?"

"An alliance to form a government in which key positions go to reliable people."

"What do you mean by 'key positions'?"

"Posts such as the head of Banca d'Italia, the Treasury, the Ministry of Finance.... In other words, the state's whole technocratic structure."

"And what about the political appointments?"

"The prime minister and the other top politicians would be elected with Joint Affairs' support, which includes financial backing. Even so, the politicians would still do only what we tell them to do."

"And if they didn't?"

A disdainful smile flashed across Abramson's face. "In that case they wouldn't last long."

"How are you thinking of getting rid of Accardo, then?"

"It's a question we've asked ourselves, and we've come to the conclusion you're the only ones who can come up with an answer."

"We?"

Abramson gave the cardinal a smile of complicity. "Your Eminence, let's be frank. Imagine for a moment that I'm your confessor."

"A highly unlikely assumption, Mr. Abramson."

"For over fifty years you've been this government's time-honored ally, and besides, I know only too well that the government has a third ally, too."

"I don't follow you."

"Come on, Eminence! You have good friends in Sicily—and you know very well to whom I'm referring. We've been wondering if perhaps your friends in Palermo might like to join us."

The cardinal looked at Abramson with icy eyes. "You have just insinuated that there's a collaboration between the Holy See and the nation's organized crime syndicate."

Cardinal Wolfenberg knew well how to strike terror in someone, because the CDF Tribunal kept him in constant training. Moreover, he'd been schooled by the Jesuits, unparalleled masters in making plain treachery sound like the Holy Scriptures. And, last but not least, no one in the Vatican had ever managed to beat him at a game of chess.

"You have just dared to ask a cardinal of the Curia to form an alliance with the Mafia, against a country that has always been near and dear to us."

Abramson tried to back down. He assured the cardinal that he'd had no intention of making insinuations damaging to the Holy See's reputation. His references to contacts in Palermo were only a hint that it would be advisable that the move be made by someone other than the CIA or the Holy See. The cardinal said how surprised he was to hear that the US Government and the CIA would have to ask anyone else for help in contacting "the friends in Palermo." He said that the United States and the CIA needed no introduction because history, from Lucky Luciano right up to the present, confirmed that the United States government had always been on excellent terms with the Italian Mafia.

"Your Eminence, that's only a legend," Fox snapped, his face scarlet. "I'm surprised a man of your intelligence gives credit to such stories."

"Mr. Ambassador, this intelligence is the product of two thousand years of experience." The cardinal's look crushed Fox. "It would be an unforgivable mistake to underestimate that, especially coming from a diplomat."

The cardinal advised Fox not to forget that he was in a Catholic country, where Confession was a sacred practice. Even in the smallest village, tucked away in the remotest corner of Sicily, there was a Catholic church with a Catholic priest who missed nothing of what went on in his parish.

"You have the CIA, but we have the capacity of delving into the minds and souls of the people," the cardinal said. "Believe me, Mr. Ambassador, I would never exchange my secret service for yours, because it would be to my loss. And *I* am not used to being on the losing side."

The ticking of the pendulum clock became deafening.

It took Fox a few moments to recover from the shock. "I refuse to listen to innuendoes that are damaging to my government's reputation and—"

"No bullshit, Martin," said Abramson.

The cardinal had heard enough. "It's a fascinating problem, gentlemen, a bit like a game of chess. Mind you, I'm talking merely as a spectator."

"And, as a chess player, what move would you suggest?" Abramson said.

"It's the opening that always determines the outcome of the game. Remember that, Mr. Abramson."

"Your favorite opening?"

The cardinal gave Abramson a shrewd look. "I'll contact Ambassador Fox, if I find an acceptable move. Rest assured of that." The cardinal got to his feet and headed for the door, followed by the two men.

Fox and Abramson stared at one another in silence.

Fox wiped his forehead. "I'm not ashamed to admit that I'd feel a lot safer if I knew that Wolfenberg was in charge of the US secret services."

"In comparison, Langley's boys look like kids still pissing in their pants," Abramson said. "I'm now beginning to understand the reasons behind the Church's spiritual monopoly. Instead of Harvard, I should have attended the Gregorian Pontifical University."

"What do you think of it, Samuel?"

"Something tells me that in the next few days you'll be having coffee at the Vatican."

"You know what? I was thinking exactly the same thing."

§

From the second floor window of the Embassy, Steve Zaslow, head of the CIA station in Rome, watched Fox and Abramson shake hands with Cardinal Wolfenberg.

"Talk of the devil," he said, beckoning to his deputy.

"Abramson must have a hell of a lot of sins to confess," said his deputy, as he watched the scene over Zaslow's shoulder.

Zaslow unfolded the sheet he was holding and looked down at the coded message he'd received from Langley the night before.

As soon as he got back to his office, Tancredi went straight to see Rodolfo Quilici, the publisher. *La Voce Independente* had been started up two years before from an idea of Rodolfo's, and thanks to some capital he'd managed to secure.

Quilici was on the phone, standing by his desk. Tancredi knocked on the glass and indicated to him to cut the call short. In jeans and with his shirtsleeves rolled up, Quilici could have been anything but a newspaper publisher. Looking at him, with that heavy beard and the thick, black hair bursting from his sleeves and collar, one couldn't but agree with Darwin.

"... The de Saint Clair affair could be the chance we've been waiting for," Tancredi said. "We only have to prove that there's a link between the Frenchman and the Mafia."

"That's easy to say," Quilici said.

"We know de Saint Clair arrived in Rome this morning at 10:30. Let's check if he came in on a domestic flight. And, if so, where from."

"Hmm, that would give us a clue. If it's the place we're both thinking of."

Quilici looked up a number in the phone book, then reached for the phone. "Hello, is that Gulliver Viaggi? It's Quilici from *La Voce Independente*. May I speak to Stella, please?...Hello, Stella, it's Rodolfo. Can you do me a favor? Can you check what domestic flights were due to arrive at Leonardo da Vinci airport at 10:30 a.m. today?... You can? Great, I'll hold on." There were a few moments of silence. "Only two flights with that arrival time. Where from?... One from Bologna ... Yes... and the other from Palermo. Could you give me the number of the flight from Palermo, please?... AZ 257." Quilici gave Tancredi a confirming glance. "I don't know how to thank you, Stella sweetheart. How about dinner tonight? ... What? ... A dirty bastard? If you only gave me half a chance... Bye, Stella."

"We know Bonfanti, at the Alitalia Reservations Office," Tancredi said. " Why don't we try asking him if the Frenchman was on that flight?"

"You know what airlines are like about giving away that sort of information."

"No harm in trying. Bonfanti owes us a favor or two."

Tancredi dialed the number and switched on the phone.

When Tancredi told him what he wanted, Bonfanti was immovable. In the end Tancredi thought of a roundabout solution.

"How about if I count to ten?" Tancredi said. "If the name I've given you wasn't on the AZ 257 flight, you hang up before I've reached ten. But if it was, then you wait till after I've reached ten. How does that sound?"

"You journalists are really a pain in the ass."

"... seven... eight... nine... ten."

Bonfanti hung up.

Quilici's teeth gleamed through the dark forest of his beard.

"One thing is certain. De Saint Clair didn't go to Sicily to visit the Greek ruins," Tancredi said.

Quilici reached for a file and his face grew serious. "There's something else we have to talk about." He pushed a few sheets of paper across his desk to Tancredi. "It's the end-of-year budget. Not very encouraging, as you can see."

Tancredi glanced through the report. "There's nothing here we aren't already aware of. Besides, ever since we started, administration has been saying that we won't last more than another six months."

"This time it's different. It's an ultimatum. Either December's figures break even or we shut down."

Tancredi sank down into a chair. "I hadn't realized it had gone that far."

"This seems to be a difficult time for our shareholders. Unless they can see things taking a turn for the better, they don't intend to go on funding the newspaper."

"Did you contact our banks?"

"*Banks!* Are you kidding? I wouldn't be surprised if they cancelled our overdrafts."

"Then we're left with only one option," Tancredi said.

"What? Sell ice-cream in front of the Colosseum?"

"We bet all we've got on the Frenchman. It's either him, and the prime minister, or us."

Tancredi sat down at his typewriter. The de Saint Clair affair seemed now as dark as the cave of hell. Sure, if their suspicions were sound, by the end of December their circulation would be booming. *If.* The calendar-clock hanging on the wall attracted his attention. Only three and an half months until the end of the year.

The blue shades shone in the semi-darkness of the reading room of the Bibliothèque Nationale. Françoise slammed shut the last of the books on heraldry. Missing! It was as if the Saint Clairs wanted to conceal those two hundred years. But why?

Françoise pulled out the drawer in the catalogue section, and looked up 'Templars' in the index cards. She sighed. More than 200 cards. Eventually she resorted to filling in six request forms. Who knows? She might be lucky.

Twenty minutes later the librarian called her name in a toneless voice.

She didn't find anything in the subject index of the first three books. Without much hope, she opened the fourth book and ran her finger down the index. She stared at a name...
Guichard de Saint Clair!

Guichard de Saint Clair, born in 1270, had entered the Order of the Templars on an unknown date. He had escaped capture by fleeing France on October 13, 1307. From then on, all traces of him had been lost. How could she be sure he was the right de Saint Clair? Couldn't it be just a namesake? Unfortunately the book didn't mention the birthplace.

It was at this point that an idea started to form in her head, a thought that had been coming and going for days. She picked up the last book, looked in the index and found the page that referred to the excavations in Jerusalem. On the third page she found what she was looking for: the names of the nine Knights who went to Jerusalem in 1118.

It was there, in black and white: Hugues de Payens, Victor de Mauriac, Bertrand de Blanchefort, Archambaud de Saint-Amand, Gondemare de Saint-Omer, *Geoffroy de Saint Clair*…. She turned the pages looking for Geoffroy de Saint Clair's birthplace. Nothing. If she were able to prove it was the same family, then it might be possible that Guichard knew something about the scrolls the Templars had found under Solomon's Temple.

Françoise raised her eyes from the page and stared at the blue shade…. What Guichard knew might not be limited to the scrolls.

As the taxi drove towards Saint Germain des Près, Françoise realized there was only one way to find out: her Uncle Rolf. If he, a cardinal, couldn't answer her questions, then no one could.

The sound of car horns startled her. The taxi had now stopped, held up in the usual rush-hour traffic jam. In two days she'd be seeing Guichard again. She laid her head on the seat and thought about a heron disappearing off into the mist…. Guichard's hands began to stroke her body.

Once more she heard the words in medieval French that Guichard had let slip while they were making love, and a thought froze her. Were those caresses really meant for her? The frantic whirling of a thousand lights enveloped her and she could hear the lonely notes of a strange musical instrument, a sort of mandolin. Its tone was loud and harsh, somewhat like a woman's voice. There was a sudden jolt and Françoise opened her eyes. The taxi had restarted. Her heart was beating fast and a sort of anguish grabbed her by the throat. It was as if something had suddenly surfaced from her subconscious, from time immemorial.

As soon as she had shut the door of her apartment, she went straight to the study. She looked under the letter *W* for her uncle's private number in her address book and reached for the phone. While she was dialing the number, she stopped: a draft of cold air was turning the pages of her address book.

The notes of the same mandolin echoed in the room.

10

A limo carrying the Venezuelan flag pulled up under the projecting roof of the Raffaele Hotel, in Piazza della Pilotta. One of the two liveried doormen rushed forward to open the rear door. Almost immediately, an Aston Martin came to a stop behind the limo. The waiting reporters clustered round the car, the flash-bulbs of their cameras bombarding the man in a striped double-breasted suit getting out, while the second doorman was trying to step between the man and the journalists.

Franzese told his driver to stop the car some two hundred yards from the hotel, got out, and continued on foot, the car slowly following him. When he entered the conference room he had booked at the Raffaele, followed by two bodyguards' discreet yet attentive eyes, Prime Minister Accardo had already arrived. Franzese had in mind a precise plan to convince him to support the joint venture with the Americans. He knew only too well that Accardo would make that move if persuaded by sound political reasoning, and not just by money.

"I realize that the deal may seem of marginal interest," said Franzese eventually. "It's really a rip-off for the country, offset by the cut for your party."

"Besides, it's certainly not the right moment," Accardo said.

"But for that very reason, why not take this opportunity to palm off those plants in the South on the Americans? CIP is losing a lot of money down there and the press gives you no respite." Franzese gave the prime minister a meaningful look. "Why not make this a condition for accepting their proposal?"

The prime minister did not answer immediately. He took off his glasses and polished the lenses carefully with the edge of his vest. Franzese had known him for more than twenty years and knew that Accardo never showed his emotions. At that moment, though, behind that expressionless mask the prime minister was weighing the political advantages of his proposal.

"Kovacs is no altar boy," Accardo said. "If we ask for something like that, he will understand right away, and negotiations will fall through even before they start."

"I wouldn't be so sure."

The prime minister tilted his head slightly with a questioning look.

"Allied's financials this year are going to close with a big loss. Kovacs wants to avoid that at all costs. The coal-mine deal would enable him to get rid of the loss."

"I can't see how, if we force him to take over a heap of scrap iron."

"A logical objection, but irrelevant." Franzese looked at the date on his watch. "As long as we convince Kovacs to take over the plants within — say four months — from the signing of the joint venture contract."

The prime minister, who was sitting with his legs crossed, seemed intent on studying his left shoe. "Which would take us up to the beginning of next year."

"*Exactly*. So Allied can account for those losses in the next financial year, and show a break-even this year."

"This would mean finalizing the agreement by the end of the year."

"Kovacs wants it by the end of October," lied Franzese, careful not to betray his thoughts. "This way he'll have all the time he needs for the Allied stock to go up."

The prime minister made no comment.

Franzese looked at Accardo and knew he'd won. It was a shame, though, that his friend Leo didn't realize one thing: those coal-mines would mark the end of his political career.

Although Guichard found the message from Lucchese waiting for him at the hotel reception desk, he already knew his first phone call wouldn't be to the Mafia middleman. He remembered what Franzese had said to Astarita the night before near

the fountain, when he was hiding below the low wall: *"The Allied-CIP affair will explode in his hands and set off our plan."*

As soon as he got to his room, he picked up the phone. A
few seconds later he heard Gilbert de Molay's voice on the
other end.

§

On his return to Palazzo Chigi, Prime Minister Accardo sat
down at the Empire desk in his office, and found the information that Zergas, the Coalition's finance manager, had promised
him. The fax came from the investigation agency Cauvin et Fils
in Paris:

> Compagnie Financière d'Arcadie SA has a staff of
> about one hundred people, distributed among Paris,
> London, New York, and Hong Kong. The company is
> managed by four senior partners. Guichard de Saint
> Clair is one of them, as well as being the managing di-
> rector and president of the company. In his turn,
> through a trust, de Saint Clair is the major shareholder
> of Financière d'Arcadie's holding company, Trafalgar
> Investments Ltd.
>
> Trafalgar is an Irish non-resident company, whose
> shareholders are two trusts on the Isle of Man. Finan-
> cière d'Arcadie's four partners are behind one of these
> trusts, but the identity of the beneficiaries of the second
> one, the Falcon Trust, remains unclear. However, it se-
> ems that somebody with large financial resources lies
> behind it....
>
> Guichard de Saint Clair graduated in Business Admini-
> stration from the Haute École d'Études Commerciales in
> Fontainebleau. He formed the Compagnie Financière
> d'Arcadie as soon as he completed his studies, while his
> father, Count Etienne de Saint Clair, was still alive....
>
> Very little is known about his private life, except that
> he is unmarried, interested in art, and owns an excep-
> tional collection of Impressionist paintings. He has a pas-
> sion for organ music....

The prime minister stirred his coffee slowly, then drank it in a couple of gulps, his eyes glued to the fax. He took a red pen, circled *Falcon Trust*, and put a question mark in the margin.

He looked up at the Murano glass chandelier hanging in the center of the lacunar, as he drew the stem of his pipe back and forth along his lower lip.

§

When Guichard had finished speaking, there was a moment's silence in Accardo's office. The prime minister, eyes half-closed behind his round glasses, leaned back in his chair with his elbows on the armrests. He held his hands upright, his fingertips barely touching.

"Why CIP?" asked the prime minister. He took off his glasses and held them up to the light to inspect the lenses. "Why not a private group?"

"I concentrated on petrochemical companies in trouble," Guichard said.

"Thanks for the compliment."

"Allied also deals in fine chemicals, which would enable the joint venture to supply them with intermediates. This would improve CIP's profits—and don't tell me you don't need it."

"We're not the only ones losing money in petrochemicals," Accardo said. "The over-production of ethylene has hit all oil companies. So why us?"

"Your losses are by far the worst, not to mention all the taxpayers' money your Government has squandered in the petrochemical plants in the south."

The prime minister filled his briar pipe, pressed the tobacco, and lit it using a Zippo. Guichard stared at the glowing pipe bowl, his hands gripping the arms of his chair. A spicy tobacco aroma filled the air.

"Why come to me?" Accardo puffed repeatedly on his pipe. "Why didn't you speak to the secretary of the Labor Party? Or to the chairman of CIP?"

"For a deal of this nature, they would need the government's authorization. Which means yours."

Accardo looked upwards, as if seeking inspiration from the Almighty.

"Let's suppose that CIP agrees to put $500 million in cash into this deal, against those old coal-mines. They are valued in Allied's books at $150 million, right?"

"Right."

"Well, your client, Mr. Kovacs, will have to come up with some fairly convincing arguments to bridge a gap of $350 million." Accardo rekindled his pipe. "I wasn't put in this chair to make gifts to Mr. Kovacs."

"Let's assume for a moment that this difference does exist — just as a hypothesis — and amounts to $230 million."

"Only as a hypothesis, it goes without saying. What then?"

"Kovacs will have a $500 million market value of Allied's mines confirmed by a top-notch expert," said Guichard. "What would you do, then?"

"CIP would appoint its own expert, of course. "

"You know what experts are like. At times they hear voices."

"Hmm. Voices, you say? That might well be so. And if a voice were to whisper the right words, how much would Allied be willing to pay?"

"Two percent."

"Huh, so we're talking about $20 million." Accardo began thoughtfully biting his pipe mouthpiece. Eventually he sighed, pursing his lips in a doubtful expression. "Without committing myself in any way, I'll find out if the deal interests us and let you know."

"That's not good enough. I need a reply by tomorrow. CIP's not the only company I've been talking with."

The prime minister's dark eyes scanned Guichard.

"But this would imply obtaining everyone's *placet* in less than twenty-four hours," Accardo said. "*Impossibile.*"

"It's a billion-dollar deal.... Furthermore, people say that only one *placet* is required here in Italy: yours."

The prime minister emptied his pipe by tapping the bowl on a crystal ashtray. "How much longer are you going to be in Italy?"

"I leave for London tomorrow at 6:00 p.m."

"Okay. Tomorrow at two, then. Here." Accardo got up.

As Guichard started towards the door, the prime minister's parting words hit him like a lash.

"By the way, I was forgetting. Say hello to those friends of yours at the Falcon Trust."

Guichard turned and studied the subtle smile on Accardo's face. "If I happen to meet them in the pub, I'll certainly pay them your respects."

The elevator descended.... What would Franzese think up to sink the deal and set off a scandal? The Organization would find a way, no doubt about that. And by that time the Lodge would be ready.

In my time, brigands were hanged from a tree, said the Voice.

In this world there wouldn't be enough trees, Guichard said.

I long for vengeance against the Roman Church, and thou knowest it, but I never asked thee to become like the Church.

Do you want vengeance? This is the way.

Machinations, lies, betrayals? the Voice said.

When you deal with thieves and crooks, you have to outsmart them.

The de Saint Clairs and the Knights Templar had a code of honour, Guichard de Saint Clair.

Honor, nowadays, is too expensive.

Thinkest thou so?

The door of the elevator opened. He had to do something to keep Allied, his client, from being caught in the midst. Allied, *not* Kovacs. Yes, a code of honor existed, which had to be respected, but not out of respect for people like that, though — commoners lacking any dignity — but because of the code itself. Let CIP, Accardo, and all the others go to the dogs. Who cared?

Standing on the terrace of his hotel room, Guichard checked his watch, worked out the time difference with Brazil, and dialed a number on his cell phone.

"The moment's crucial," concluded Guichard. "I've phoned Gilbert and —"

"I know," said Philippe de Mauriac at the other end. "He's already called me and told me about this Sunday's meeting."

"Something tells me that you'll soon be paying a visit to the upper floors of the Vatican. Watch out for all those violet skirts."

Philippe chuckled. "Just for once I'll keep my hands to myself." A pause. "What makes you so sure, anyway? All I've got from them, so far, is a fax requesting the memorandum."

"I'll tell you on Sunday. In the meanwhile, talk to the press and make yourself heard everywhere. I want to see your face in all the Brazilian papers...."

Guichard leaned on the railing of the balcony. Red and orange streaks crisscrossed the sky and the sun was sinking below the horizon.

Uniting the descendants of the first Templars had been easy. The brethren hadn't neglected the slightest detail, no matter how insignificant, in order to create an image of absolute trustworthiness for the Brazilian company. The brethren were rich, very rich. They controlled vast fortunes, with financial and industrial interests spread everywhere. Each of them contributed equally, providing the company with a fully paid up capital of 230 million reais. They channeled their stakes in the company through operating holdings; the link between these holdings and the Templar descendants was lost in a long chain of interwoven shareholdings, protected by the filter of a trust.

Guichard fabricated false identities for all five board directors. For this, he got help from the Organization. Via friends, pressure, exchanges of favors, and even blackmail, they built up controllable curricula for each of the five people. They organized everything to perfection, from college certificates to work experience, from memberships in prestigious private clubs to bank references. Of course, the management and clerical staff were unaware of what really lay behind the company. His temperament and physical appearance had made Philippe a natural for the position of chairperson.

The contrasts in the sky had grown violent. A bank of clouds had turned a leaden gray, and a halo of white light traced their outlines. They reminded him of two armed knights on horseback, in battle array. The clouds seemed to move in synchrony with the horses' muscles, as if to emphasize their efforts.

Sweep away the Roman Church, said the Voice. *That is the ultimate aim.*

Do you doubt me, by any chance?

Thy thoughts have grown muddled of late, like the clouds thou art watching.

Guichard did not answer.

A treacherous design is crawling though thy mind, nesting in it, like a viper in a shady bush.

Guichard shrugged his shoulders.

Take heed, Guichard de Saint Clair. Tighten the bit to thy reveries, before misfortune should o'ertake thee.

Another threat?

Naught but a warning. For the nonce.

At first it had been only revenge. But now? The Voice was right. Now it was something much more intricate and indistinct, like the memory of a dream. It was something that had to do with his own mind and that stemmed from a restlessness he'd been feeling for a long time. A restlessness provoked by a sort of malaise, buried deep down in his subconscious—a marine abyss where he could see a tangle of monstrous figures, dark and blurred, wandering ceaselessly around, with serpent-like sinuosity. At times, suddenly and for a fleeting instant, that abyss was lightened by a bluish, opalescent brightness, allowing a scent, an emotion, an image to surface.

It was a fixed, recurrent, delirious idea. It had started when he'd seen Françoise again at the gallery, even if at that moment he hadn't been aware of it. Getting even with the Church was no longer the ultimate aim; yes, he had to do it, but now revenge had become the means to… to what? It was all so insane that he couldn't even admit it to himself.

Voices, clouds of sand, the muffled clatter of horses' hooves…. And in the background the music of a rebec.

Françoise stopped for a moment in front of a green-framed glass door, faded with time. The sign, written in gilt, Gothic characters, said Eustace Séverin, Master Lutanist and Restorer.

The echo of a bell accompanied her entrance into the deserted shop plunged in semi-darkness. An odor of wood and resins hung in the air. Glass cases covered the bare stone walls, and two semi-circular display counters towered in the middle of the shop. The place looked like a cross between a museum and a wine cellar.

A muffled tapping attracted Françoise's attention. On one side of the entrance, an arched doorway opened onto a workshop, its walls covered with hand tools, where three craftsmen wearing gray aprons and black oversleeves, were hunched over their workbenches. They were working on stringed instruments under the light of flexible lamps.

One of them, with ruffled white hair and wearing a pince-nez, raised his eyes, laid a violin delicately on the bench, and came over to her.

"Can I help you, *madame*? I'm Monsieur Séverin."

"I'd just like to take a look around. May I?"

"Of course." Séverin pressed a switch and went back to his bench.

The glass cases lit up. Violins, violas, cellos, and lutes gleamed in their ancient varnishes amidst a whirling of soundboards, strings, and peg boxes.

Françoise browsed around the showroom, stopping from time to time to read the metal tags describing this or that instrument, the type of wood it was made of, its history.

An unusual instrument attracted her attention. She had an odd feeling of familiarity.

The three-stringed soundboard was pear-shaped. Its neck derived from the gradual tapering of the soundboard itself, and ended in a diamond-shaped peg box, surmounted by the carved head of a faun. It was a short instrument, about two-feet long. The bow, which lay in front of it, was curved. There was no tag. Françoise's breath grew quicker. Obeying an uncontrollable instinct, she opened the glass case, held the instrument resting its curved end between her chin and her collar-bone, and picked up the bow.

For an instant she felt ridiculous. She didn't read music and had never played any musical instrument. What was she thinking of doing? Giving a concert? Yet her hand seemed to obey a silent command. The bow dipped, and Françoise's arm slid it across the strings with skill and grace. A slow melody, almost a lament, rose in the showroom, its notes having a sharp, piercing tone. Anguish and sorrow alternated deep within her. That music sounded like a love cry, laden with longing, surfacing from an ancient past. She saw herself in a candlelit room, and for an instant the profile of a veiled woman flashed before her mind's eye.

Françoise opened her eyes and became aware that she wasn't alone. Monsieur Séverin and his two craftsmen were staring at her, wide-eyed.

"I... I don't know how to apologize," Françoise said. "It must be a very valuable instrument...."

"*Madame*, may I ask where you learned to play like that?" Séverin said.

Françoise shook her head with a dazed expression, her eyes staring at the instrument. "How can I explain? It all seems so absurd... unbelievable. If I told you I've never played before, you wouldn't believe me, would you?"

"My family, *madame*, have been making stringed instruments for six generations, and I'm an acknowledged expert in medieval musical instruments, like the rebec you've just been playing. I've never heard *anyone* play a rebec like that."

"You must believe me. I'm even more amazed than you, unbelievable as it may seem.... But please, tell me, what is it that struck you so much?"

Séverin studied Françoise with perplexity. "It was your style of playing. It's hard to say, but I'm certain of one thing. It's just the way the *troubadours* must have played the rebec in the twelfth century."

"In the *twelfth century*?"

"Don't you think this joke has gone on long enough? Only a great virtuoso can play like that, not to mention the piece you've just played."

Françoise said nothing, but a question could be read in her eyes.

"Now don't tell me you don't know what you've just played."

"It's the truth. Won't you tell me the name of that piece? *Please.*"

Séverin sighed and looked heavenwards. "It's a *chanson* written in Provençal French of the twelfth century, by an unknown author. The title must have been something like *A vous, Amors, plus qu'a nule autre gent*—To you, Love, More than Anyone Else."

"So the troubadours used to play it in France, at that time?"

"Well, not only in France. That particular song became popular in the Holy Land after the first Crusade, because of the French knights fighting there. It's a love song."

Françoise held her breath. "Do you know what the song says?"

Séverin stroked his chin with a gouge chisel. "Hmm, I only remember the beginning. It goes something like this… "*A vous, Amors, plus qu'a nule autre gent, est bien raisons que ma dolour conplaigne. Quant il m'estuet partir outrement et dessevrer de ma leaul compaigne*—To you, Love, more than to anyone else, it's only right that I should sing my sorrow, for I must go away, and leave my faithful companion."

Françoise felt that cold draft again, and the shop seemed to be whirling all around her.

"Madame, aren't you feeling well?" Séverin grabbed Françoise by her arm.

"No, no, thank you, I'm feeling all right." Françoise leaned on the display counter. Then she gazed at the rebec, still clutched in her hand. "Monsieur Séverin, is this rebec for sale?"

11

The hotel was located in the heart of an old quarter of the city, and the roof-garden restaurant overlooked the Roman ruins. The evening breeze brought with it the scent of Mediterranean pines.

"I'll help myself, thank you," said Guichard to the waitress, who then left the bottle of Hennessy on the table.

Guichard poured himself a glass of cognac and took a sip.

However hard he tried to banish thoughts of her from his mind, he just couldn't. He'd always been one for short-term relationships. Now that he thought about it, he'd always been the one to break things off. He'd often found himself already wondering how to go about it, even just a few days into a relationship. All too often he'd awakened in the middle of the very first night with a sense of uneasiness, almost of oppression, thinking of the least painful way of calling it off the following morning, before it really got started.

Perhaps it was due to fear. Fear that the expectation of the 'becoming' would be followed by disappointment, and then by the usual feeling of emptiness. With Françoise it was different. At the Seigneurs' he'd had the feeling he'd seen her somewhere before, and at Saint Germain, when he'd made out her profile through the window, he'd entered the gallery following an instinct. Was it imagination or reality?

It never happens twice, said the Voice. *Resign thyself.*

Never! Why didn't you go back? *Why?* Guichard said.

It's as if a hydra nested in our hearts, taking an evil delight in devouring the best things of our lives.

How could you?

I was bewitched by the vain dream of a glorious deed. Ambition, glory, vanity.... A cry of rage and grief rent the air. *Man himself is the cause of his unhappiness,* said the Voice.

I would have wanted time to stop, Guichard said.

How canst thou stop perfection? said the Voice, its voice broken by regret.

Guichard held the glass of cognac up to eye-level, and the lights illuminating the Colosseum glowed through the amber-colored liquid. The image refracted by the crystal multiplied. He slowly turned the glass, and an infinite succession of Colosseums and distorted faces appeared. Illusion or reality? One day lightning strikes, a child feels a shock run up his arm, and suddenly something inexplicable happens to him. He starts to remember facts from his ancestors' lives. And not only that. He starts to dream of strange worlds, and in each of them he sees a replica of himself—each time in a different space-time—rather like the sequence of images in the glass.

The pianist started to play an old Neapolitan song. Some people got up and began to dance.

At times he saw himself as Geoffroy, and at times as the late Guichard, with identical physical traits, as if they were all the same person. At other times he saw them with their own faces, much as a spectator off-stage would see them. But, as a spectator, something strange happened to him. There were moments in which he wasn't aware of his own identity. Ancestral memories, buried in the depths of his DNA? But there were other times when he was fully aware of himself. *He was* there.

There were times when it was as if holes suddenly opened up in space—strange holes, black, enormous, swirling frantically. He would be swallowed up inside them and projected into a completely different dimension, and he would wonder whether he would ever return to his own world, and, if he did, what he might find—or not find—on his return. Come back? Why? She would be there, and time would stop.

Thou thief of thoughts, said the Voice in a sharp tone. *She was my woman.*

Mine too.

Thou art mistaken, Sir Knight. Thou hast come late—just nine centuries.

You're forgetting a small detail. You can travel in the future, but I can travel back in time.

Thou thief, felon, traitor! *Unsheathe thy sword, so that I can pierce thy ungrateful heart.*

This time the pain in his back seemed unending. Guichard took a few deep breaths, and wiped the sweat off his forehead. The breeze lifted the edges of the tablecloth.

Did an outside world really exist, or was it only the product of subjective thought? Did the mind shape what was around us, or was it the opposite? At school those questions had seemed meaningless abstractions. Parmenides had said that anything rationally conceivable had to exist. *What a genius!* Guichard remembered having thought at the time. So what? Parmenides must have been the village idiot. No, anything but. That Greek from five centuries before Christ had intuited the most disconcerting aspect of modern physics, discovering a truth that cancelled out the boundaries between philosophy and science, and that forced one to question one's own sanity.

Near the orchestra some floodlights came on, and red and green beams of light cut across the dark. Tired clapping marked the end of the music.

Twenty-five centuries after Parmenides, Einstein had reached the conclusion that $E=mc^2$ and the world had ceased to be the same. Those lights in the sky: waves or particles? Both the one and the other. Probability waves a moment ago when you weren't looking, and particles a moment later: you only had to raise your eyes for one of those probability functions to collapse and become tangible matter. With just the flicker of an eyelid you could influence the reality around you. *The observer effects the reality he observes*, modern physics had discovered. Everything around us was just an illusion. But then, if our own senses deceived us, what was reality? Where? How could one reach it?

Waves, particles, infinite worlds, said the Voice. *Art thou insane?*

How can I explain to someone from the Middle Ages the consequences of $E=mc^2$?

What dost thou prate about? The de Saints Clairs have never been paragons of virtue, true. In 1395, Gaston de Saint Clair stole fifteen cows from his neighbor, branding them in the night with his mark. In 1548, Audric de Saint Clair, dressed as a brigand, attacked and robbed one of the king's couriers. In 1690, Sauville de Saint Clair died of a heart attack at the age of seventy-eight, in a Toulouse brothel. In short, all sorts of things have happened, but I can recall no cases of insanity.

Insanity? We'll see about that. And, in any case, my thoughts are my own business.

We have an agreement, thou knave, and it's because of that agreement that thy thoughts are also *my affair. Revenge comes before thy daydreams. She can't come back. Forget her!*

Have you?

Silence.

You always speak as if you were the repository of revealed truth, Guichard said. Besides yours, there are other ways of doing things.

If something goes wrong, I swear by the dragon of St. George that thou wilt rue the day thou saw the light.

Guichard poured himself another glass of brandy, then stopped, the bottle held in mid air. He could have poured out some more, and then more still, thus obtaining an infinite series of possibilities.

There was no limit to the number of possible worlds, no boundaries, except those imposed by the limits of our mind and our senses. Any one of us, ideally, could glance into each of those worlds and see a carbon copy of ourselves, different in each world according to the specific choice made. But no link could exist between them, science said.

And yet what would happen if a time traveler coming out of a time tunnel interfered with the reality of a space-time from the past, bringing with him the knowledge of the future?

The music of a rebec arose in his mind and the scented breeze blowing from the hills around Jerusalem on summer nights caressed his skin. An awning flapped, a pounding of horses' hooves faded in the night, and the sing-song of a prayer arose from the white roof of a house nearby. He heard the swish of her robe, inhaled her perfume of lavender, felt the touch of her hands.... He tried to grab her hand, but felt only something cold. He opened his eyes. His hand was gripping his glass of cognac.

He breathed deeply and ran his hand through his hair.

Being able to conceive with one's mind what lay beyond the furthermost limits of the world, and at the same time being trapped in a body incapable of seeing and hearing: this was Man's true curse.

The wind blew stronger. Lightning lit the sky and a gust of rain shook the awning above his table.

Lufhansa flight LH 786 from Washington landed at Düsseldorf airport at eleven p.m. on Wednesday. At the exit Carl Ackerman, Kovacs's detective, spotted Hans Hübner, his German associate, waiting for him.

As they drove along the *Autobahn* A52 towards Cologne, Hübner updated him about times and alarm systems. He'd arranged a meeting between Ackerman and Dr. Meiner for nine o'clock the following morning. Ackerman would introduce himself as Leonard Collins, manager of Mineral Resources Investments, Washington DC. Hübner handed Ackerman a pack of business cards.

"*Herr...* Collins," Dr. Meiner said, glancing at the business card. "I'm not quite clear what your company deals in."

"Mineral Resources is a holding company with its head office in Washington," Ackerman said. "We hold stakes in mineral research projects in various parts of the world."

"I'd never heard of you before. Do you specialize in coal?"

"No, but at present we're interested in a coal project with a state-run company in the Chinese People's Republic."

"In what part of China?"

"In the Shaoxing Province."

Meiner made no comment.

"Before signing the contract, however, we want to check the quantity and quality of the coal," Ackerman explained. "That's why I'm here."

While Meiner was giving him a run-down on the Kohl Institut, Ackerman made a mental note of all the details of the office. He could see no wires or detectors that revealed the presence of hidden alarm systems.

"My company is very particular about data security," Ackerman said. "Can you guarantee this?"

"You must be joking." Meiner gave him a scornful look. "Come and see for yourself." He beckoned him to the window. "You see that turret with the yellow indicator on top of it? If anyone should try to get into the building, a siren will go off, causing a phone message to be relayed to a police station nearby."

Ackerman made a mental note of the tower and its position. He then pointed to the computer on Meiner's desk. "What about the secrecy of computer data?"

"They're more than safe. This is only a personal computer where I keep personal data and... other minor matters."

That pause didn't escape Ackerman's notice.

"So your PC is not linked to the main computer network?"

"There's no computer network here at the Institut. Confidential data are held on a central computer and you need to know the password to get access."

"Someone might get a hold of it."

"What do you take us for? Only three of us know it, and we change it every week."

Ackerman had all the information he needed. He told Meiner he would contact him again from Washington.

Before leaving the building, Ackerman went into the restroom. They still had the old type of flushing system, with a chain-operated cistern. He slid his hand behind one of the cisterns and nodded with satisfaction. There was all the room he needed.

Around eleven thirty that evening, a white van—displaying the name Johannes Elektrizität—pulled up beside the wall surrounding the Kohl Institut, in Pauliner Strasse. Three men in blue overalls got out. They unloaded some trestles of the type used to mark road works, and put them in the middle of the road, some twenty yards behind the van. They fixed a yellow flashing light to the barrier. One of them got back into the van. Shortly afterwards, an extension ladder started to rise slowly from the roof of the vehicle. The ladder stopped when it reached the level of a turret with what seemed to be a yellow mushroom on top. Two men climbed the ladder, jumped onto the top of the wall, and proceeded to tinker with the turret.

After about twenty minutes they signaled to the third man who was waiting at the foot of the wall. He swung a coil of rope round twice and threw it up towards them. They fixed the rope ladder to the top of the wall, let it down on the inside, and disappeared from sight. The man remaining outside quickly loaded the lamp and trestles back into the van, started the engine, and parked on the opposite side of the road.

After forcing the front door, they both stood motionless. Nothing. Ackerman shone his flashlight in front of him and went up the stairs, followed by Hübner. When they reached Meiner's office, Ackerman sat down at the desk and unscrewed the mouthpiece of the handset, while Hübner took a screwdriver out of his bag and started to remove the computer frame. It took Ackerman only a few minutes to insert the microphone into the mouthpiece. Then he went into the hallway and pointed his flashlight towards the restrooms.

He took a state-of-the-art radio-transmitter out of his pocket—a small box only about one third the size of a pack of cigarettes. He slipped it behind one of the cisterns and fixed it in place with adhesive tape.

When Ackerman returned to Meiner's office, Hübner was keying something into the PC.

"How's it going, Hans?" Ackerman said.

"*Es geht*, I am almost finished. *Herr Doktor* is *wirklich ein* beginner."

"Aren't the files coded?"

"*Nein*. He hass only gifen *fantastish* names to his personal files." Then Hübner took the floppy disk off the driver. "*Sehr gut,* ve can go. If the Kohl Institut security systems are anything like Meiner's, zen zeir clients had petter start praying."

As soon as they got back outside, Ackerman and Hübner scrambled up the rope ladder. From the top of the wall they signaled towards the van, which drew away from the sidewalk, did a *U*-turn and stopped next to the wall. The extension ladder started to rise and stopped when it was on a level with the two men. They let the rope ladder drop to the ground, and climbed down the extension ladder. When they got down, Ackerman picked up the rope, and the three men climbed back into the van.

That same night, similar scenes were re-enacted at the Karolinska Institut in Stockholm and the Coal Research Center in Louisville.

At six the following morning, a Johannes Elektrizität van, a long antenna swinging on its roof, parked in Pauliner Strasse, less than 400 yards from the Kohl Institut.

Inside the van, a man started fiddling with wires and reels.

When Guichard was ushered into the prime minister's office, Accardo was sitting at his desk, an Italian flag to his right and a cross hanging behind him. The prime minister appeared relaxed and sure of himself.

Guichard's gaze slid over the gilded mirrors, the paintings in their baroque frames, and the coffer ceiling. He had the unpleasant sensation of kneeling in a church confessional, awaiting his penance, and for a moment he could almost smell incense drifting in the air. He grimaced.

Accardo motioned Guichard to sit down. "I accept your proposal, de Saint Clair." He raised a finger: "On one condition."

"And what's that?"

"A little present for me," Accardo said. "As due recognition of all my efforts—it goes without saying."

"It's only fair," Guichard said dryly. "How much?"

"Oh, just one percent of the whole deal, that is $10 million." Then, with a serious face, Accardo added: "On top of the two percent for my party, of course."

"That goes without saying," said Guichard, just as serious.

Accardo looked at him with an ambiguous smile, half-challenging and half-mocking. One after another, questions arose in Guichard's mind, but without an answer. Why was Accardo so confident? Besides, everything was going too smoothly, and experience had taught him to be wary of situations that appeared too smooth. Accardo knew the coal mines were worth at least $200 million less than the price set by Kovacs. Why did the prime minister seem so ready to make such a gift to Allied? Even the three percent commission that Kovacs would have to pay to the Coalition Party and to Accardo, $30 million in all, didn't make the accounts balance.

"Oh, one last thing." Accardo scribbled something on a slip of paper and handed it to Guichard. "In our future dealings, use only this number. And only in the evening, after nine o'clock."

"The Allied-CIP agreement must be signed by the end of October. Don't forget."

"I never forget anything. If I did, I wouldn't be here." Accardo stared at Guichard. "Keep that in mind."

As Guichard went down in the elevator, he could still smell incense.

I once met a rascal of similar countenance, said the Voice. *A Saracen caliph; his name was Adil ibn Ruzzik. Canst thou divine what he used to do?*

Tell me.

In the night before a battle, he relished skinning prisoners alive. Their screams rent the darkness and reached our tents. I thought my head would burst.

Did he act like that just out of sheer wickedness? Guichard said.

No. He wanted to terrorize us, and convince us he was invincible, like this sullen prince.

What became of him?

I confronted him in a duel, in front of everyone. I unsaddled him with a lance thrust, and finally I cut his head off with a clean blow. I can still hear the hiss of my sword cleaving the air, the smell of his blood squirting all over my face, the dull rolling of his head on the ground. By a thousand gryphons, what celestial music!

Quite a victory. Guichard loosened the collar of his shirt.

'Victory' thou sayest? Aarrghh! What canst thou understand, thou who fightest hiding thyself in dark alleys? My chest was beating with fiery ardour, and the shouts of acclamation of the crusaders were for me the most intoxicating of all wines. I was a Norman knight, of

ancient lineage, and I believed in arms, honour and the cross. Until… —but the Voice could not continue.

Until?

Until one day the Church of Rome shattered my dreams, and no other glorious dawns lit Jerusalem any more.

The saints and biblical figures of the frescoes that decorated the cardinal's office glowed in the morning light. The Vatican's muffled noises seemed to penetrate that place almost on tiptoe. For a moment just the tinkling of teaspoons against coffee cups broke the silence.

"So what do you think?" asked Substitute Dyakonov.

"Abramson knows too much: our lists, veiled hints at Latin America, our moves…." Cardinal Wolfenberg thoughtfully stirred his coffee.

"Are you saying a spy is hiding among us?"

"I don't know… but in the future we'll have to be more cautious."

"I'm not convinced about this alliance," Dyakonov said. "They are the ones who are going to benefit most from it."

"You think so?"

"You know the kind of resources they can count on. If Joint Affairs joins the government, we'll never be able to get rid of them."

"You are forgetting that this is a *do ut des*," Cardinal Wolfenberg said.

"With Latin America as set-off?"

"Abramson's hints at the *cardinali elettori*—voting cardinals—and at the pope's health were by no means fortuitous."

"So?" said the substitute.

"Abramson knows only too well that we must focus on Latin America if we want to gain control of the majority of *cardinali elettori* at the next conclave."

"But what can they do for us down there?"

"Are you joking? Just think of the US multinationals, in sectors like food, mining and heavy industry, and think of their presence in South America. Do you realize what they could do for many of our local dioceses, afflicted by an atavistic hunger for money, if only Joint Affairs spoke the right word at the right time? The *cardinali elettori* of those dioceses, from Saõ Paulo to Santiago, would remember Manus Domini when the moment comes. You can rest assured about that."

"Italy plays a key role in our strategy," Dyakonov said. "I wouldn't want us to risk losing control in Rome, in order to strengthen our position in Saõ Paulo. Once they're in, who will budge them from Palazzo Chigi?"

"I wouldn't be so pessimistic."

"Pessimistic? They can count on the CIA, and you know well what the CIA did in Italy for over twenty years, blaming the Red Brigades."

"If they can count on the CIA, we can count on Palermo."

The substitute turned pale. "There are times when you scare me."

"Let's put it this way. I have no doubts about choosing between a Catholic Franzese and a Protestant or Jewish Abramson: I choose Franzese."

"You know what? It's your so-called 'pragmatism' that scares me most."

"A drop of brandy in your coffee?"

Françoise's eyes were fixed on the rebec lying on the couch. She stretched out her arm to pick it up, but stopped. Somewhat tremulously, she passed her finger over the edge of the sound box. That instrument seemed to have awakened something in her, like a memory dormant in her subconscious since time immemorial. But it wasn't just that. She had the uneasy feeling she was no longer alone. The night before she had lain awake for hours in the dark, thinking of a thousand phantoms and magnifying the slightest noise in her imagination.

She let out a deep sigh, her face buried in her hands. She'd always thought she had a strong character, but she'd never had to face anything like this.

"Our common friend Corinne has only mentioned your problem," said the psychoanalyst, a strong-chinned, white-haired woman, wearing frameless glasses. "I'll try to be of help, if I can."

"At the moment I don't feel ready for a session. I only need some information."

"No problem."

Françoise told her about the events of the last few days. "Do you think it could be a case of reincarnation?"

"It's too soon to tell."

"Do you believe in reincarnation?"

"Of course," the psychoanalyst said. "I've had several cases that I've been able to treat only by taking my patient back to a previous life through hypnotic regression."

"That surprises me."

"I know what you mean. Unfortunately, we westerners re- fuse everything we can't explain rationally. But we're wrong. However, the medical profession is broadening its views, even if very slowly."

"Do you believe that the soul is reincarnated in the body only at conception, or that it can also happen later on in life?"

"I've had cases of regression that started well past infancy."

"What can set it off when the body's already adult?"

"A lot of things: a place, a person.... Even a strong emo- tional experience."

"Even physical contact with an object?"

"Certainly. It's quite possible for a particular object to trig- ger off a regression."

For a moment, Françoise's mind seemed to wander else- where. "Is it true that, during regression, people can recognize the place they find themselves in, without anyone telling them anything about it?"

"That phenomenon's called 'extrasensory perception.'"

Once more, Françoise's thoughts went back to the blurred im- ages of a veiled woman, in a bedroom lit by a flickering candle.

"May I ask you what your religious beliefs are?" the psycho- analyst said.

"I grew up as a Catholic, but I've been a Buddhist for many years."

"That explains many things. However, reincarnation isn't the only answer."

"What do you mean?"

"A paranormal phenomenon."

"You mean... ghosts?"

The psychoanalyst smiled. "Don't say it like that."

"You, a psychoanalyst, believe in occultism?"

"Believe in it? My dear, allow me to correct you. It's no longer a matter of 'if,' but of 'how.'"

Françoise gave her a questioning look.

"You would be surprised to learn the amount of funds that the US Government itself allocates for espionage applications of psychic phenomena. We're not alone, my dear, just because the limitations of our senses prevent us from seeing and hearing."

Françoise tossed and turned in bed. Eventually she jumped to her feet, put on a robe and went out onto the terrace. The lights of the Café de Flore mitigated her anguish. Was it just her imagination? No, that bow gliding on the rebec was real.

"It's a chanson written in Provençal French of the twelfth century ... That song became popular in the Holy Land after the first Crusade..." the master lutanist had said. *"To you, Love, more than to anyone else...."*

A heavy thud came from the living-room. Françoise sprang to her feet, her fists clenched, and for a moment stood motionless. She edged up to the French window and peered into the room. Nothing. She walked a few steps, and her eyes fell on a few books lying on the floor. They had fallen from the bookcase for no apparent reason.... Maybe she had put them back carelessly.

Françoise went closer and knelt by the books. They were the books on the Knights Templar. One of them, the heraldic guide to France, lay open face down. Françoise picked it up and turned it over. She paled.

The page showed the family tree of *les Comtes* de Saint Clair.

12

Guichard left the subway at Bank Station and found himself being carried along by the crowd that poured into the City of London every day. A dull drizzle was falling, made even more unpleasant by the wind that swept the streets. Guichard turned up the collar of his raincoat and set off briskly towards Lombard Street, where Compagnie Financière d'Arcadie, his investment bank, had its City premises.

"Good morning, Carol," Guichard said at the reception desk. "Have any faxes arrived for me yet?"

The receptionist, a fair young girl with a ponytail and a Swiss convent-school style, hastened to put her cup of coffee down. "Yes, several, Mr. de Saint Clair. I put them on your desk."

Both Eugene's and Paulette's faxes had arrived. Guichard put his briefcase on the desk and, without taking off his raincoat, started to scan Eugene's fax.

In the past six months Allied's shares had lost nine percent, and stock analysts advised selling. The analysts were unanimous on one specific point: Allied needed to make a big takeover in fine chemicals, and quickly.

Paulette's report on CIP's petrochemical division left no room for doubt. Although petrochemicals accounted for only a minor portion of sales, they wiped out all the profits from the energy sector. Guichard leafed through the pages full of numbers and shook his head. The Coalition had strewn the whole of the south of Italy with petrochemical plants, telling the country that that was the way to fight unemployment.

Carol poked her head round the door of Guichard's office. "May I bring you a cup of coffee, Mr. de Saint Clair?"

"What? Oh, yes, thank you Carol. Black, no sugar."

"Um, sir?"

"What is it?"

"May I remind you that you've still got your wet raincoat on?"

Guichard took his Burberry off, and tossed it on the chair across the desk. The raincoat slid to the floor.

He recalled his meeting with Accardo and the uneasy feeling he had had the day before in Rome. He tilted his chair back and started to fiddle with his letter opener. That subtle smile.... "*I accept your proposal,*" Accardo had said. Guichard pulled the chair upright. The plants!

"*It's not just a matter of money ... Accardo must be persuaded that the Allied affair will be politically advantageous,*" Astarita had said during their meeting in Sicily. What political move could be more astute than palming off CIP's plants in the South on Allied?

Guichard grabbed Paulette's report again, read through it and stopped at the page with the financial forecasts. How much were those plants worth? He opened his briefcase and took out his pocket calculator. His fingertips ran over the keys. He stared at the display.... Could it be possible? He looked at his watch. Still four hours until Kovacs's arrival. He dialed Paulette's direct line in Paris.

"... Paulette, I need a reply by two o'clock." He slightly moved the receiver away from his ear.

"What munificence! Why not right away?" Paulette said. "After all, what are thirty-six plants?"

It was 1:45 p.m. when Carol entered Guichard's office, waving a long fax triumphantly. She spotted the raincoat lying on the floor, gave Guichard a reproachful look, and hung the raincoat in the closet.

It was Paulette's fax. Guichard skimmed quickly through it and focused on the numbers at the bottom. A malicious smile appeared on his lips, and his mind went back to Franzese's plan. He slowly rolled up the fax. Discuss the matter with Kovacs? Why? No, better to speak to him only if and when the problem cropped up. What mattered now was one thing only. His hand gripped the fax. It was those very plants that would

set off the trap for the Vatican, and no one must be aware of it—
starting with Franzese.

Kovacs limped in. "Well, de Saint Clair, have you come up
with a solution?" he asked, after a brief handshake.

Despite Kovacs's usual harsh manner, Guichard could sense
a note of apprehension in his voice. He told Kovacs why he'd
chosen CIP, Italy's hydrocarbon national agency, as partner,
then mentioned Accardo's conditions. As he expected, Kovacs
went straight to the key question.

"How will the Italians go about appraising the coal-mines?"

"… So their expert will confirm your appraisal," Guichard
said.

"This is what I wanted to hear," Kovacs said, visibly relieved. "Your fees?"

"Fifteen million dollars—1.5 percent."

"*Fifteen million dollars?* That's highway robbery!"

"You can always find someone else."

"Don't play the wise guy with me. Besides, what guarantee
have I got that the deal will come off?"

"Guarantee? I'm your guarantee."

"Oh, my apologies, 'Monsieur le Comte.' I was forgetting
the high opinion you have of yourself." Kovacs gave Guichard
a challenging look. "What's to prevent me from making a direct
proposal to that prime minister of yours?"

Guichard smiled, apparently amused. "You're welcome to
try. But I'm afraid that his reply, in the event you got one,
might not be to your liking."

Kovacs glared at Guichard and got up. "Send me a draft of
the mandate in San Francisco."

Kovacs reluctantly shook Guichard's hand and walked out.

*Not even all the devils of the Underworld would understand what
treacherous machinations dwell in thy mind,* said the Voice.

Trust me, Guichard said.

*Trust thee? A wizard of rogueries? Thou art even worse than
the malicious, limping knight who mixes black oils—the one who
comes from the land beyond the Great Ocean—not to mention the
sullen, white-haired prince, and the blazing-eyed brigand of Sic-*

ily. Thou hast forsooth procured worthy companions-in-arms, Guichard de Saint Clair!

Are you being fussy now, as well? This is not the Middle Ages, and I remind you that "arms, honour, and the cross" are somewhat outdated values around here. Moreover, don't come out pontificating about ideals. Ideals vanished at the very moment the first man set foot on earth—with Jehovah's blessing.

Sayest thou so? I used to confront the enemy with sword and spear, in single combat, as was fitting for a blue-blooded knight, and for a de Saint Clair. And I did not fight for a handful of silver dinars, but for an ideal.

An ideal? Guichard said. Ha, ha, ha! With the Roman Catholic Church as your sponsor?

Thy words are indeed sharper than the point of a spear. I will bear in mind thy merciful heart, have no doubt. However, I paid a dear price for my mistake.

Agreed, but the fact remains that you were mistaken: so don't think you can teach me how I should live in *this* world.

Art thou so convinced thou knowest it?

Guichard was groping for an answer, when the buzz of the intercom saved him.

As she left the international arrival lounge of Leonardo da Vinci Airport, Françoise stopped under the projecting roof and looked round. Her eyes met those of a young priest in his cassock, standing by a shiny car. A slender figure with glasses, and thin, fair hair, he looked uneasy, like a freshman on his first day of college. She smiled at him. He blushed, hesitated for a moment, and then came towards her with an embarrassed smile. He said he was Father Emilio and that "His Eminence Cardinal Wolfenberg" had sent him to meet her.

The car was a black Mercedes with Vatican plates. Many curious eyes watched the scene, probably trying to guess the identity of the attractive woman getting into an official limousine of the Holy See.

The car sped along the superhighway towards Rome, as the Roman hills rolled past. Françoise's gaze was lost in the distance, her hand fiddling with her purse buckle.

We live many times, until we reap what we sowed in a previous life and put right what went wrong. Karma was a law of nature. If reincarnation was the answer, in whose body had she lived before? What was pending? And why was it all coming out now?

"*... We're not alone, my dear, just because the limitations of our senses prevent us from seeing and hearing,*" the psychoanalyst had said. A ghost? This would mean admitting that *that* soul, before reaching its astral plane, had decided for some obscure motive to set things straight on its own, without being reincarnated into anyone's body.

In her mind's eye she saw the bow sliding across the strings of the rebec again. What was that force that had guided her arm? How? Those books couldn't have fallen from the bookcase like that for no apparent reason. And besides, that heraldic guide, falling open at *that* very page, the Saint Clairs' family tree. The same force? What did that being want from her?

"We've arrived, madam," Father Emilio said. The Mercedes crossed St. Peter's Square and drove through the Arco delle Campane.

"*Wie geht es dir, mein Liebchen?*—How are you, my dear?" asked the cardinal, welcoming her with open arms.

They'd always talked in German, since the Wolfenbergs were originally from Innsbruck—her mother was a Wolfenberg. Although Françoise had been brought up in France, from the time she was a child her mother had always talked to her in German at home, asserting herself over her father, who would have liked Françoise to speak Armenian instead.

"So, why this sudden rush to visit your old uncle?"

Françoise was careful not to mention Guichard, hinting merely at a person "who meant a lot to her."

"I want to find out if Geoffroy and Guichard de Saint Clair belonged to the same family, and what part of France they came from," Françoise said finally. "Uncle Rolf, please don't say no. I'm sure you must have something about the de Saint Clairs in your archives."

The cardinal's face darkened. "Why do you want to know about things that happened so long ago?"

"This person has a problem, and I want to help him," she said. "But it's not only that...." She hesitated, looking at her uncle's quivering jowls.

"What else is there?"

"There must be some dark secret hidden behind the Templars, and I feel this person's problem has something to do with it."

The quivering of the jowls became frantic and Françoise immediately regretted what she'd just said.

"I warn you, Françoise. You're getting involved in matters that are of no concern to you. *Dangerous* matters," the cardinal said. "Stop, before it's too late."

"Oh, come on, Uncle Rolf, we're talking about something that happened in the Middle Ages. How could it be dangerous?"

"Because *I* say so. *That's why!*" The cardinal slammed his hand hard on his knee.

Françoise gave a start.

A more easy-going expression appeared on the cardinal's face. "You realize I've reacted like this only because I care for you, don't you? I don't want anything to happen to you, that's all."

"I also realize that you don't want to help me."

"Be reasonable. Those facts date back to the time of the Crusades. What makes you think our archives go back that far?"

"Tsk tsk tsk." She waved a finger. "Uncle Rolf, I can tell when you're not telling the truth. Do you think it's right for a cardinal to tell lies?"

"All right, all right, I give in. You're stubborn like all the Wolfenbergs." He grunted and shook his head. "But I don't promise anything, mind you. I'll check in the archives and let you know."

"And the Templars' secret?"

The cardinal leaned towards Françoise with a threatening expression. "*Forget about that.*"

To Françoise, his reaction was the most eloquent of all answers. Something really mysterious must be hidden behind the Templars, something the Church seemed to be very much afraid of, even if seven centuries had gone by.

The phone rang.

"Yes Monsignore? ... At once? ... All right, please tell His Holiness I'm coming." The cardinal hung up. "My dear, His Holiness wishes to see me right away. Are you sure you want to go back to Paris this evening?" He took her hand and patted it. "We could have dined together...."

Françoise hugged him. "Don't forget, Uncle. I'll be waiting for your phone call."

As she went out, she noticed the picture hanging next to the doorway. Odd. It had to be a reproduction, since the original was in the Louvre. The Vatican was not in the habit of settling for reproductions. But what struck her most of all was the subject matter: it was pagan, while all the other paintings hanging in the study were masterpieces depicting Christian subjects.

That picture had a story behind it, but Françoise couldn't think just then what it was.

It was 6:30 p.m. when Cardinal Wolfenberg left the pope's private study. As he left the Bernini colonnade, he slowly set off for the Palace of the Holy Office, his hands clasped behind his back.

How ever did Françoise, of all people, come to be involved in that blessed mess? What if she knew more than she admitted? He shook his head. At the most Françoise might have some suspicions, nothing more. Anyway, what proof could she possibly have? The Church had been looking for proof for over eight hundred years and had never managed to find any.

What seemed to matter most to her was the information on those two Templars, the de Saint Clairs. Was there a man involved? There must be, otherwise she wouldn't have been so reticent. Who could it be? A descendant of the Saint Clairs? The cardinal's jowls twitched.

How stupid of him to lose his temper like that. His niece was no fool, and she must have guessed something was up. So what was he to do now? He stopped. Aha! Why not pretend to give in to her wishes? He would help her trace those de Saint Clairs. To begin with, this would persuade her that the Vatican had nothing to hide. But in the meantime, he'd keep an eye on her and... who knows? Perhaps his very niece, unaware of it, would succeed where they had failed.

He strode briskly towards the Arco delle Campane.

When he reached the Palace of the Holy Office, he did not take the elevator up to his office. Instead, he went down the flight of stone stairs leading to the underground vaults. The two Swiss guards sprang to attention. He stopped in front of a reinforced door, rang the bell and waited. The lens of a closed-circuit camera watched him from above.

The door opened and the skinny figure of Father Parisi appeared in the doorway. The Jesuit had been in charge of the archives for thirty years and they no longer held any secrets for him.

As soon as the priest closed the heavy door, the cardinal whispered something to him. Father Parisi looked at him with alarm in his eyes. The cardinal gave him a reassuring look.

They went through an endless number of large rooms enveloped in semi-darkness, with bare stone walls and high, vaulted ceilings, until they came to an iron door. Father Parisi searched in his robes and took out a bunch of clinking keys. He inserted one of them into the lock and the door creaked open. Inside, the air smelt musty. Massive, dusty cupboards, each secured with a solid padlock, covered the walls. Father Parisi led the cardinal to the reading-room, a bare cell. Silently he walked out.

Ten minutes later, the Jesuit returned, pushing a trolley stacked with voluminous dossiers.

"This one covers the years 1118–27 in Jerusalem, and it also includes a few parchment manuscripts handwritten by Abbot Bernard himself," he said, pointing to a black dossier bound up with a violet ribbon. "The other four cover the period from October 1307 to October 1314. Your Eminence, may I remind you that nothing can be removed from this section without written authorization from His Holiness?"

Bertrand de Blanchefort, Archambaud de Saint-Amand, Gondemare de Saint-Omer, Hugues de Payens, *Geoffroy de*

Saint Clair.... Geoffroy de Saint Clair was one of the nine knights that Abbot Bernard of Clairvaux had sent to Jerusalem in the summer of 1118, to search for the Ark of the Covenant. Where was he from? The cardinal went down the list... He was originally from Les Andelys, a village in Normandy.

Guichard de Saint Clair had been the preceptor of the Templar preceptory in Paris when Philip the Fair had attacked the Temple, but there was no record of where he came from.

The cardinal went through the manuscripts of the second half of 1308 and read the minutes of the interrogations of the Templars captured in the Temple of Paris on the dawn of October 13, 1307. There were two questions the Dominicans of the Inquisition kept on repeating: What was the destination of the knights who fled from Paris on the night of October 13? What had they taken with them?

In spite of the tortures, the Inquisition had managed to extort very little information, which showed beyond any doubt that the captured Templars knew nothing. A grimace of disgust distorted the cardinal's lips. He felt sick. Under that kind of torture, he himself would have confessed to anything, even the most infamous crime, if they'd just asked him.

Pope Honorius II had been a good judge. *Et in Arcadia ego!* That diabolic phrase had sprung to light then, and the interrogations made it clear that it originated with the first Templars. But the Inquisition failed to discover its true significance. Quite likely, only the Grand Master of the Templars and a few others knew it. He thought about the reproduction of the Poussin hanging in his study. How had Poussin come to know the secret? One fact had emerged from those interrogations and from the documents confiscated from the Templar preceptories: that phrase was linked to a secret—a terrible secret, no doubt about it— hidden somewhere on a mountainside. And ever since, the Church's suspicions had had a name: *Et in Arcadia ego,* a phrase that had the sound of a threat.

The cardinal leafed though the brittle, yellow pages. A few knights, probably forewarned of the impending danger, had managed to escape before dawn. Only they could have answered the Inquisition's questions. Three of the prisoners confessed that, on the night of October 13, a group of seventeen knights had left the Temple of Paris. They had taken four carts with them, loaded with precious items and documents from the underground coffers of the Temple.

The cardinal's eyes widened: *Guichard de Saint Clair*. According to these witnesses, the leader of that group of fugitives was Guichard de Saint Clair! He couldn't remove his eyes from the page. The flourishes on that *S*, traced by the diligent scribe of the Inquisition, appeared sinuous like a nest of vipers.

Where was that Guichard de Saint Clair from?

At 10:40 p.m., the cardinal shut the last of the dossiers covering the period 1307-1314 and heaved a deep sigh. Nothing. Guichard de Saint Clair had died in the battle of Bannockburn, on June 24, 1314, but there was no indication of his origins. The documents lying on the desk showed that "de Saint Clair" had been a fairly common family name at the time, so nothing proved that Geoffroy and Guichard originated from the same family. What should he do now? The cardinal tapped a finger on his lips, his eyes staring blankly at the bluish light bulb of the lamp hanging over the writing desk.... Hmm, Father Parisi?

"You wouldn't by chance know, Father, where I could find this information?" the cardinal asked.

"Why didn't you ask me right away, Your Eminence? I could have saved you a lot of trouble," Father Parisi said, a gleam of satisfaction flashing through his watery eyes. "Have the courtesy to follow me."

The Jesuit led Cardinal Wolfenberg into another dimly lit room, with a lamp illuminating a long desk placed against a wall. Geometric order reigned over the desk, on which two lit computer monitors, each placed at either end of the table, seemed to be keeping watch like two rottweilers. Father Parisi said that the Templars had always been his favorite research subject, and that years before he'd created a card-index file in which he'd recorded the names and main information about all the Knights Templar he'd found traces of in the Vatican libraries and archives. Two years before, he'd transferred all the data to a computer file.

"So the information could be in those computers?"

"Forgive my immodesty, Your Eminence, but I would be surprised if it weren't there."

Father Parisi sat at his desk and clicked on a mouse. A dialogue window appeared on the screen. He keyed in "de Saint Clair, Guichard," and pressed a key. The screen blinked.

Name: De Saint Clair, Guichard

Born : January 2, 1270

Died: June 24, 1314

Place of birth: Les Andelys, Normandy, France

The cardinal went on staring at the screen…. *Françoise was on the right track.*

"Father, you've rendered me a great service, as well as the Church. I shan't fail to duly point out to His Holiness the praiseworthy way in which you supervise our archives."

The Jesuit bowed. "I am honored, Your Eminence."

The steel door of the underground archives shut behind the cardinal. He took the elevator to his private apartment on the fourth floor. He went straight to his study, looked for the phone book of the Holy See, and flipped the pages over until he came to the name he was looking for: Cardinal Roger Blanchard, head of the archdiocese of Paris.

"*Roger? C'est Rolf Wolfenberg à l'appareil.* Sorry for calling you so late at night."

"*Rolf, mon cher ami, quel plaisir.* I'm delighted to hear your voice. No need to apologize. I was just torturing Chopin on my piano."

"In the interests of the Church, I have a big favor to ask. I know I can rely on your absolute discretion…."

§

Françoise was about to leave her apartment when the phone rang. She was tempted for a moment to let it continue ringing, because the taxi was about to arrive at any moment. With a sigh, she ran down the hallway and picked up the receiver…. *Uncle Rolf.* Françoise listened.

Her handbag dropped to the floor.

13

As Tancredi collected the pile of morning mail, his eyes fell on a manila envelope. He turned it over, but couldn't find the sender's name. Expecting another threatening letter, he opened it.

Mr. De Santis,

Like you, I too am persuaded that this country needs a change. However, your articles are not convincing, because up to now you have shown no proof. Corruption in the petrochemical industry is nothing new. Antigono Zergas, the Coalition Party's administration manager, owns a PC that would give you a much wider picture, and getting hold of those files is everything but impossible. As for me, I am ready to finance this undertaking. What part are you willing to play? I will call you on Tuesday night to discuss the matter. In the meanwhile, I would suggest that you start looking for a hacker.

Signed: A sympathizer

Tancredi kept on staring at the letter, his mind in turmoil. Perhaps someone was trying to put him off the petrochemical trail.... No, that didn't make sense. Why, then, was he giving him a clue like that? That guy seemed to be well informed. A hacker? Tancredi dialed Sergio's direct line.

§

When Tancredi walked into the bar, Sergio had not yet arrived. An old Frank Sinatra tune came softly from a jukebox, and the aroma of coffee filled the air. He sat down at a corner table lit by a shaft of sunlight filtering through the lace curtains. As the barman came to take his order, Sergio walked in. Tancredi took out his letter.

"At the Ministry of the Interior you pull all sorts of dirty tricks," Tancredi said. "Could you help me find a hacker?"

Sergio stared at him. He put his hand into his breast pocket, then pretended to look through an imaginary address book. "Let me see. Hacker... hacker.... Oh yes, here we are. Would you like them all, sir, or do you want only those with references? Anything else? A Muslim terrorist? Just ask. At the Ministry of the Interior we deal in a wide range of commodities."

"Are you here to help me or act stupid?"

"A touch of school spirit wouldn't hurt."

Tancredi reached over and slugged Sergio's shoulder. "I'm sorry. This story is starting to worry me. The newspaper under pressure, those letters, and now this...."

"Come on, Tancredi, college was just the same. You worried about everything, and in the end your grades always turned out to be the best. Why don't you start taking life as it comes?"

"Oh, thank you so much, Sergio Freud." Tancredi heaved a deep sigh of relief. "Now that you've shown me the light, I feel much better."

"You know what? I should have strangled you the first day I met you at school. I'd be out on parole by now," Sergio said. "Anyway, at the ministry I know someone who works in the 'dirty tricks and base deeds' section. I'll ask him."

"When will you have something?"

"I'll call you tonight at nine. Is that OK?"

"I'll be waiting for your call."

"Aw, no need to thank me."

"Thanks. Without you I'd be lost."

Sergio gave Tancredi a piercing look, laden with skepticism.

"I mean it," Tancredi said.

"That's the problem. One never knows if you mean it or not."

§

Carla sensed there was something important in the air. Tancredi always behaved like that, whenever he said he had to go down to the bar around the corner to make one of those mysterious phone calls. She drew back the window curtain casually and watched him leave through the main gate and turn the corner. She sat down in an armchair, staring blankly at the TV screen.

§

A military march resounded in the bar. Tancredi told Annibale, the owner, that he was expecting the usual phone call.

Annibale was a large man always in a good mood. He was totally bald, his scalp always shining with sweat, but he had bushy eyebrows. He was proud of his collection of miniature historical soldiers, which he kept in a glass cabinet near the counter. Tancredi knew that he nurtured a boundless admiration for Julius Caesar and secretly longed to be like him, so much that his deepest regret in life was not having become an army general. So now he cheered up listening to military marching and grand opera music, of which he owned an impressive set of CDs that he religiously stored behind the counter.

While he was waiting, Tancredi ordered a bourbon.

One could hear the cracking of pool balls coming from the end of the billiard room, and Tancredi went to watch. He liked observing people playing billiards, especially the way players studied the table before striking the ball. He liked the cue racks, the feel of the cloth of the table, those big, green lights hanging low from the ceiling and casting their circles of light on the table, leaving all the rest in semi-darkness. He sensed all around a comforting feeling of mystery, and was unconsciously engulfed by it, as in a reassuring mist, which gave him the illusion that he could shut the world out, with all its problems.

A phone rang in the distance, and a few moments later Annibale beckoned to Tancredi from the bar counter.

"The man you're looking for is called Gianni Carlomagno," Sergio said. "Have you got a pen?"

Tancredi wrote down the number and address on the back of a business card. "Is he someone I can trust?"

"The Ministry of the Interior trusts him."

"Quite a reference indeed."

"They also tell me he sings in the church choir." Sergio snickered.

"The final touch. Is he a good hacker, *at least?*"

"Carlomagno—and his name says it all [Carlomagno is the Italian name for King Charles the Great]—can crack any system. He's the man you want."

Tancredi hung up and immediately dialed the hacker's number.

Carlomagno was a surprise. He had a calm, reassuring voice, and spoke in a well-educated manner. They agreed to meet at Tancredi's office the following morning.

As Tancredi headed for the door, someone called his name. Annibale was pointing to his glass, still half full. Tancredi went back to the counter and drank the bourbon down in one gulp.

The feeling of warmth in his stomach was like the trail of a falling star crossing a starless sky.

§

Three days earlier, shortly after Guichard had left the villa, Astarita, a frown on his face, had gone into Franzese's office and had laid an open copy of *La Voce Indipendente* on his desk.

"Take a look at that." Astarita stabbed his finger at the front page.

Franzese looked away from a Reuters screen and glanced at the headline on the front page: "The Petrochemical Trail Leads from Rome to Palermo." He skimmed through the article, then put the paper down and kept silent for a moment.

"Just what we need," Franzese said eventually.

"Are you kidding? This guy isn't short of names. I say we should shut him up for good, and quickly."

"That would be a big mistake. The journalist's got guts."

"What are you getting at?"

"Our friend is an idealist. Not only should we not shut him up, but we should actually encourage him. Just think what'll happen if this De Santis finds out what CIP and Allied are up to. Once he's got proof, he won't think twice about slapping it all over on the front page of his paper. Can't you see? The journalist is just the fuse we've been waiting for."

Astarita stroked his chin. "An anonymous letter?"

Franzese's subtle smile was the response.

The man in the dark-gray suit seated in front of him didn't fit Tancredi's ideas of a hacker at all. He'd have expected to see someone in faded, ripped jeans, of the 'Silicon Valley nut' variety. On the contrary, Carlomagno, with his bow tie and gold-rimmed glasses, looked more like an intellectual or a research scientist.

"What if we don't succeed?" asked Tancredi at last.

"If we don't succeed, it'll be because the files are coded," Carlomagno said. "In that case, I'll have to make a copy of the hard disk and work on it in the lab."

"Zergas might have neglected to protect the data."

"If he had, Zergas would be an idiot, which I'm sure he is not."

"How long will it take you to find the decoding key?"

"How many millions, or billions, of combinations will I have to try?" Carlomagno said, with a fatalistic gesture. "It all depends on the coding string."

Tancredi thought of the stockholders' threat to shut down the paper. If he and Quilici wanted to break even by the end of the year, they had to publish the news by the beginning of December. That meant removing the files no later than mid November, giving them two months from then.

"By mid-November?" Tancredi asked.

Carlomagno shook his head. "I can't offer any guarantees. Why is timing so important?"

"To use a cliché, it's a question of life or death."

"You know what Mark Twain used to say?"

"Let's hear it."

"He used to say that people spend all their lives worrying about things that will never happen."

"Mark Twain played the philosopher because he didn't have a budget to struggle with."

He had to take the risk. Doing nothing would mean the end of the paper. Moreover, the *Voce Indipendente* would miss a unique opportunity to wipe out Accardo and his mob. Carlomagno would cost 250 million lire, and the paper couldn't afford it. Tancredi thought of the anonymous letter and of the "sympathizer's" offer to finance the project. If he didn't keep his promise, he and Quilici would manage to sort it out somehow, even if that meant using their own resources.

"You know, you don't look like a hacker."

"Why? What's a hacker supposed to look like?"

Tancredi told him. "No offence meant."

Carlomagno burst out laughing, until he had to take off his glasses and wipe his eyes.

"That would be like saying that all locksmiths are burglars," said Carlomagno, still trying to stifle his laughter. Then he turned serious and said: "No offence taken."

"Good. When can you start?"

§

When Carlomagno left Tancredi's office, he hailed a taxi and gave the driver an address in the fashionable Parioli district.

The taxi stopped in front of a stately building. Carlomagno crossed the hallway covered with sparkling marble, where a cleaning woman was running a floor polisher. The woman stopped, frowned at Carlomagno's footprints, and muttered something. Carlomagno went into the elevator and pushed a button.

When he was on the landing, he rang the buzzer next to an oak door. The brass plate on it read: *Tincani & Genovese, Agenzia Investigativa* [Private detectives].

The hall clock was striking eight when the penthouse doorbell rang. André placed the *canard à l'orange* on the kitchen table, looked at it with a clinical eye, and told Josephine—her sleeves rolled up over her wrestler-like forearms—to check the *quiche Lorraine*. He took off his apron and left the kitchen. As he walked past the hall oval mirror, he gave himself a critical glance and stroked his moustache.

"The de Saint Clair collection?" Guichard asked Françoise.

She wore a black, sleeveless dress. A silver necklace set with green amber hung around her neck, and her hair was tied back with a matching green silk ribbon.

"Why else do you think I'm here?" replied Françoise with a teasing smile.

"You certainly know how to flatter a man's vanity," Guichard said. "I'll lead the way."

Guichard flipped a switch. A row of spotlights came on, lighting up a long corridor adorned with paintings along both walls. The circular wrought-iron chandeliers hanging from the ceiling had come from the family castle, Guichard said. Half-way along the corridor, a massive wooden stairway led to the upper floor, and an arched, glass door opened onto the reception room.

As they went down the hall, looking at painting after painting, Guichard answered Françoise's questions. He could tell right away that Françoise's interest in art, more than her work, was an inborn passion. Pausing in front of a Cézanne painting, Françoise made a remark on his use of unmixed primary color and small strokes to simulate feeling. She seemed able to sense what had gone through the artist's mind while he was painting the picture. A rare sensitivity — dangerous, though.

As they started up the stairs, Guichard's eyes fell on the painting hanging on the landing wall. Cursed fool! But it was too late to do anything. A few seconds later, in fact, Françoise stopped in front of the picture and stared at it almost in disbelief, even more of a reaction than he'd expected. The painting was a reproduction of Nicolas Poussin's *Les Bergers d'Arcadie, II*. It showed three shepherds by a grave in a valley, and on the right stood a female figure. Two of the shepherds were leaning over and pointing at an inscription on the side of the tombstone. The third shepherd was looking at the female figure inquiringly. The expression on the woman's face was enigmatic.

"But, Guichard, I don't understand. What does this have to do with the others?"

"I know it's out of place," Guichard said. "But the myth of Arcadia has always intrigued me. Since the original painting is in the Louvre, I've had to make do with a reproduction."

Françoise stepped closer to the painting and stood on her tiptoes. "*Et in Arcadia ego*," she read. "That Latin inscription.... I seem to remember some controversy over its meaning."

"True, but the interpretation most widely accepted is that the verb is missing and that the word 'sum' is taken for granted."

"So the translation would be...."

"I too in Arcadia."

"*Ego* refers to Death, doesn't it?"

"Er... yes. Death exists even in the sort of paradise on earth that Arcadia represented in Greek mythology," Guichard said in a matter-of-fact tone. His hand clenched and unclenched. "That's what Poussin intended the inscription to mean."

Françoise followed the movement of Guichard's hand. "The painting certainly gives you the feeling of some Arcadian place: the colors, the pastoral setting, the clothing worn by the shepherds."

Guichard hoped that that was it and started to go up the second flight of stairs.

"Wait a minute," Françoise said without moving. "Have you had a good look at the expression on the woman's face?"

"Why?"

"Firstly, she's not looking directly at the shepherd. It's almost as if she didn't want to be part of what's happening in the picture, that is, the shepherds' desire to know. But it's not just that."

"What do you mean?"

"Well, it's her expression. Puzzled? No, that's not the right word."

Guichard kept silent.

"I can't think of the word, but I'm sure I'm right. That's the expression of someone who knows something, but isn't sure it would be a good thing for others to know it too." Françoise went closer to the painting. "On the other hand, it's right for a Greek muse—in an Arcadian setting like that the female figure can't be anything but a muse."

"You make me see aspects I wasn't aware of."

Françoise looked him square in the eye. "Do you know who that muse reminds me of?"

"Something tells me I already know the answer."

"Good. Then I'll spare you."

Towards the end of dinner, André approached the table. "Monsieur le Comte, the champagne is served on the terrace," he said, giving Guichard a warning look.

Behind Notre Dame, the night lights of Paris were twinkling in the distance, and the streetlights of the bridges and along the *quais* were reflected on the waters of the Seine. The breeze lifted Françoise's hair. Guichard filled the glasses, handed one to Françoise, and brushed her cheek with a kiss.

"I couldn't stop thinking about what happened in Scotland," Françoise said.

"I couldn't either."

A mischievous flash crossed her eyes. "I didn't mean *that*."

"Then what?"

"You know what."

Silence.

"I've done some research over the past few days."

Guichard took half a step backwards. "Research?"

"About your ancestors."

"Can I ask why?"

"Because I want to help you, don't you see?"

Guichard seized her arm. "I made it quite clear you were to keep out of this. Why are you trying to spoil what we have?"

Françoise pulled herself free. "Why can't you understand I *need* to help you? Why?"

"It'll all be over soon. Then I'll be able to tell you everything."

"The Guichard de Saint Clair buried in the graveyard of Kilmory Chapel is an ancestor of yours, isn't he?"

A flash of bewilderment crossed Guichard's eyes. "And even if that were so?"

"If the spirit of that Templar has in some way come back to life in you, you can get over it. Why don't you talk about it?"

"*Get over it*? Get over what? You speak as if I were out of my mind." Guichard snorted, turned sideways and looked towards Notre Dame.

"You make me feel so useless...."

Guichard sighed and pulled her towards him. "Just a few more months and it will all be over. Don't spoil everything. *Please*."

Françoise, her face earnest, stared at him, then put her arms round his neck. Guichard's hand ran over her side.

§

Françoise threw her pillow aside, curled up next to him, and whispered in the dark: "Tell me about your childhood. "

Guichard stroked her hair. "I... I don't want to."

"Why?"

"Because it hurts."

"If you let your problems stay buried, you'll never free yourself from them."

"Words, words, words..."

"The truth is that it's more convenient to ignore them, right?" Françoise stroked his cheek. "It's Véronique, isn't it? I've read the newspapers from that period, and I know what happened."

Guichard didn't say anything. He held her closer.

"Why don't you try and talk to me about her?"

Guichard swallowed hard. "They say that forgetting pain is man's biggest curse, because by forgetting it he continues to repeat the same mistakes over and over again. Unfortunately, I'm not affected by this curse, because not a day goes by in which I don't remember every minute I spent with her, and my pain grows more and more each time. The noise of her sandals down the hallway, when she came running to my room.... The way she used to get mad at me when we played hide-and-seek, because she said I'd spied on her — she was right.... Her hand clutching mine when she was afraid, like when we went down in the underground vaults.... "

"You've got to face such pain, Guichard. It could hide even deeper problems."

"Do me a favor! Let's not turn this night into a psycho-analysis session. Nothing can wipe out such pain. Besides, why forget?"

"What do you mean?"

"You must remember things like this every day and tell yourself: this is the world we've built. Only one thing differentiates Man from animals: intelligence. But intelligence makes Man evil, which in turn makes him much worse than the fiercest animal. And you know why?"

Françoise kept silent.

"When animals kill, they do so out of necessity, following their instincts, and not out of self-interest or for the sheer pleasure of doing it. We've lost the hair covering our body, but we're no different today from what we were when we learned to walk standing on two feet. Violence remains the only law, and the fear of violence remains its only deterrent. For each act of violence you suffer, strike back much harder, and without pity."

"Oh, c'mon, Guichard! Where would such 'morals' lead us?"

"Whoever commits an act of violence, either physical or moral, must know that sooner or later that violence will bounce back, even after a thousand years. It doesn't matter whether we're dealing with a rapist, or with an institutional criminal like the Catholic Church."

"You can't believe what you're saying. It's bitterness that makes you talk like that."

"Sorry to disappoint you, but this is what I am, and it's this world that made me what I am."

Guichard's tone and words revealed bitterness and hardness to an extent that Françoise had never suspected. She felt afraid, and pressed herself harder against him. That physical contact, though, only served to make her realize how distant he was. She felt close to tears.

Before he spoke, Françoise had been tempted to tell him about the rebec, her visions, and the episode of the falling books, but now something told her not to. Besides, what would she tell him? Reincarnation? Or, even worse, that a ghost had entered her life? Guichard would look at her with his air of skepticism and she'd feel like an hysterical fool. A convenient skepticism, which would make allow him to persist in his silence. No, she'd wait. But wait for what? The next move of the being, or whatever it was that had entered her life?

Françoise awoke in the middle of the night. She could sense Guichard was awake. A moment later he sat up. She was about to turn over and speak to him, when he slipped out of bed. He moved stealthily, so as not to wake her. He opened the door of the room and shut it quietly behind him.

He wasn't going to the bathroom, because the room had a bathroom en suite. Where was he going, then? Françoise climbed out of bed, put on the dressing-gown she found hanging in the bathroom, and opened the door silently.

The hallway was cloaked in darkness. At that very moment, a pendulum clock struck three. The echo of the strokes seemed to be endless. She tried hard to remember where the staircase was.

Fortunately, someone had had the foresight to carpet the wooden stairs. When she reached the bottom, she looked both ways down the hallway. Which way? When Guichard had taken her around the house, he'd shown a preference for the library. She went that way.

The sliding door was slightly ajar, and a dim light filtered out through the crack. She slid the door carefully back. She took a few steps inside, and only then did she realize that the light came from the far end of the library, up on the platform. What was there, up on the platform? When she'd put one foot on the spiral staircase the night before, letting Guichard understand that she wanted to go upstairs, he had walked past, pretending not to notice.

Françoise groped her way towards the end of the library and stopped in front of the spiral staircase. She started to climb the steps, her stomach muscles tightening at the slightest creak. Finally she reached the top.

When she was only a few feet away from the shaft of light, she understood. A panel in the library wall had moved, revolving on itself. *A secret room.* Even if she couldn't see him, she felt deep down that Guichard was in there. What could there possibly be, inside that room, to make him go there in the middle of the night?

Françoise's heart thumped. She leaned slowly towards the shaft of light and peered inside. Guichard, with his back towards her, was sitting at a desk, absorbed in reading something. They looked like old parchment scrolls. The desk was too far away for her to see properly, but she caught a glimpse of some strange characters. Suddenly it struck her. *The scrolls of the Essenes.* The scrolls that the Templars had found digging under Solomon's Temple!

§

The slanting Aramaic characters started to swirl ever faster in front of Guichard's eyes, until he could see them no longer....

♣

Jerusalem. July 12, in the year of our Lord 1118.

The clattering of the horses' hooves echoed through the passage leading to the Old City. The two crusaders on guard gave the riders an odd look. They were staring at their white *surcottes* [a loose, short cloak worn over armor] with the red cross on the front and back, the likes of which they'd never seen before. Geoffroy glanced at his fellow knights. Sweat streamed down their dust-caked faces and soaked into their ragged beards. The scorching sun made their suits of chain mail almost red-hot. Trapped inside the metal, his undergarment was sticking to his skin. He thought of their mission and forgot his exhaustion. He looked up at Mount Moriah rising high above him. He spurred his horse on.

The road started to climb up towards Temple Mount. The track was so narrow that they had to ride in single file, and yet they began riding at a gallop, yelling and digging their spurs in the flanks of the animals. The clattering of the horses' hooves on the cobbles was deafening; as they passed, people drew back against the walls and veiled women raised their arms as if in self-defense.

Suddenly they came to an esplanade full of light and enshrouded in an unusual stillness. The Dome of the Rock! The sunrays, reflecting off the bronze of the cupola, dazzled Geoffroy, and he tightened the reins. Down there, at his feet, lay Jerusalem, the Holy City. The white houses of the Holy City shone in the blinding midday sun. Geoffroy's eyes followed the slender profile of the minarets rising above the Al-Aqsa mosque. There was no need for words. How could you describe perfection?

Geoffroy turned his horse and rode over to Victor de Mauriac. Victor was leaning forward, his arm resting on the front of the saddle, his gaze lost among the hills. In an inspired tone, he uttered a few verses in Greek. Geoffroy was not surprised. Victor was the scholar of their group, which no one would ever have guessed by looking at the bulk of that bearded giant. Yet Victor had such a passion for the classics that he went as far as making up phrases in Greek or Latin, tailoring them to the circumstances.

"Is that one of yours?" Geoffroy asked.

"No, it's something Plutarch wrote." Victor sighed and added in a melancholy tone: "He's better known than I am, just because he was born ten centuries ago."

Geoffroy had realized from the start that Victor's modesty didn't match his literary talents. "What do those verses mean?"

Victor raised his arms in a theatrical gesture and gazed at the sky. "'It is said that when the Heavenly Host announced the Birth of Christ to the shepherds of Bethlehem, a great groan was heard throughout Greece: the god Pan was dead.'"

"Bethlehem is just over those hills, isn't it?"

Victor nodded, his eyes nostalgic.

They had removed their chain mail suits and were stretched out on the grass in front of the mosque. Geoffroy, lying on his back, was looking up at the sky, letting his thoughts wander. After all those hours in the saddle, he could almost feel the horse still moving under him. His hand ran over the grass. What would they find inside that mountain?

"His Majesty King Baldwin will see us in the afternoon to give us his royal blessing," said Hugues de Payens, sitting up.

"And tomorrow morning we'll be received by the patriarch of Jerusalem, in whose presence we have to take our solemn vows of poverty, chastity, and obedience."

André de Montbard said what everyone was thinking.

"Poverty, chastity, and obedience are fine, because this is what we agreed to with Abbot Bernard. But we have to find lodgings and we'll need some money, otherwise who'll pay the serfs to look after our horses and arms?"

"Don't worry, my friends," Hugues replied. "His Majesty's going to grant us his protection, which means we'll be given rooms in a wing of the palace and money to cover our expenses."

Cries of satisfaction met Hugues's words.

As the other knights walked towards the entrance to the mosque, Geoffroy grabbed Hugues's arm.

"What does the King know about our mission?" Geoffroy said.

"Officially nothing. Abbot Bernard told me that he and the pope told only the patriarch."

"Doesn't this kind of welcome make you wonder, then?"

"We can't rule out that the pope himself might have exchanged a few words with King Baldwin."

"So officially we're here just to defend the roads of the Holy Land and make them safe for the pilgrims."

"That's the official version and it's what the Knights of the Order of the Hospital of St. John have been told," replied Hugues. "King Baldwin told me, in confidence, that the Hospitallers made a real fuss when they heard about us."

"What did King Baldwin say about it?"

"'The hospitals and the welfare of the pilgrims are your business, whilst the safety of the roads will be the Templars!' That's what he said."

"Well said! Arrogant villains." Geoffroy scratched his beard. "Then, when do we start digging?"

Hugues pointed to the mosque. "Tomorrow morning we'll make a preliminary survey of King Solomon's Stables. Then we'll have to find someone willing to help us with the excavations."

Geoffroy told Hugues he'd join them shortly. He lay down again on the grass, shut his eyes and thought back to his first visit to Clairvaux Abbey. It had been in January of the previous year. That meeting with Abbot Bernard had changed his life. Geoffroy had donated his lands and money to the Order and had taken vows of poverty, chastity, and obedience. He himself could hardly believe what he'd done. Those vows went against everything he'd always stood for. As a knight, he'd never believed in obedience, nor in poverty — and least of all in chastity. Why, then?

The abbot's eloquence was unbelievable, but that couldn't be the reason. It took much more than an abbot's dialectics, even if the abbot's name was Bernard. This was the once-in-a-lifetime chance every knight hoped for, the chance to accomplish a true mission worthy of being handed down to posterity. He'd felt he belonged to a chosen few. He and his fellow knights would leave an indelible footprint in the history of Christianity. He had no regrets.

Some of them had had scruples about taking up the sword and killing in the name of Christ, but once again it had been the abbot who'd put their doubts to flight.

"*To kill non-believers is not homicide and is not a sin,*" Abbot Bernard had decreed.

"So be it," muttered Geoffroy, even if deep inside something felt wrong. The Church had tried to cover things up, but everyone knew what had happened when Godfrey de Boullion and his crusaders had entered Jerusalem on July 15, 1099. Not only had they set fire to the town and ransacked it, but they had slain men, women and children, to the cry of *God wills it!* The carnage had gone on for three days and three nights, until the town was awash with blood. Was that really God's will, or was it the will of the Church?

He then considered the three vows. He'd go for the poverty and obedience, but as for chastity... well, that was quite another matter.

That evening, making up an excuse, Geoffroy managed to get away from the mosque and walked down the road they'd ridden up on their arrival. Without his chain mail on, he felt like flying. In the moonlight, the white houses stood out against the blackness of the hills. Thousands of tiny lights flickered in the darkness, enfolding Jerusalem in an aura of mystery. Soon Geoffroy found himself outside the old city walls. He looked round, and walked along a cobblestone alley that wound down beneath a series of archways. The alley came out into a wide road lined with colonnaded arcades, under which merchant stalls and shops followed one another. This must be the Cardo, the thoroughfare that ran through Jerusalem from north to south, linking St. Stephen's Gate to the Gate of Sion.

The torches on the walls cast the long shadows of the columns across the road. A squad of crusaders galloped by, followed by the frowns of the rare passers-by.

Geoffroy crossed the Cardo and went down the Street of David, until he reached a maze of narrow alleys draped with awnings. To the left ran a roadway wider than the others, flanked with houses built from large blocks of stone. Moonlight illuminated a square tower with a double row of merlons and rhombic grating. From the indications a crusader had given him up at the mosque, that must be Patriarchate Road, where the Armenian quarter began.

Geoffroy followed the road, passing under the archway of the tower, accompanied by the echo of his steps. A beggar's hand stretched out from the darkness. The howling of a dog faded along the alleys.

The smell of freshly-baked bread filled the lanes. As he was passing a house with a thatched roof, Geoffroy caught a glimpse of flames from a stone oven. On the porch of the house across the road, a group of women sat spinning wool. They were using a foot-operated spinning wheel, of a kind he'd never seen in Normandy.

He turned down a narrow alley, and soon came in sight of an inn sign lit by a torch fixed in the wall. An eye over a seascape! From Archibald's description, this must be the place. Geoffroy banged on the knocker. No answer. He knocked again. A dull shuffling and, a few moments later, a vent opened in the door.

"What do you want?" asked a sullen voice. "The inn's full."

"I want to see *Madame* Miriam."

"Is she expecting you?"

"Certainly."

"Your name?"

"Geoffroy de Saint Clair."

A grunt came from the dark interior, and the door was flung open.

"Upstairs, first door on the right," the villain said, his back deformed by a large hump.

Geoffroy was about to go up, when the man took hold of his arm. "*Seignior*, haven't you forgotten something?" he demanded, holding out his hand.

Geoffroy shook his arm free and handed over a silver denier.

Customs in the Holy Land were not much different from those in the Ardennes or Borgogne. He felt his way up the dark, wooden staircase, until he reached the landing. An oil-lamp, hanging from a ring on the wall, lit the corridor with a faint glow. He stopped in front of the door referred to by the villain. From inside came the sound of a rebec. He knocked. The music ended.

"Who is it?" asked a woman's voice from inside.

"Geoffroy de Saint Clair, a Norman knight. Archibald de Thierry sends his regards."

The door opened. Even in the dim light of the oil lamp, he could see she was as beautiful as Archibald had described. She was wearing a long, loose robe of turquoise silk, closely fitted under her breasts. Her long, raven-black hair was covered by a purple headband secured by a diadem of small, enameled mail. Her eyes were of a peculiar gray-green. But what struck him was her gaze. A gaze that seemed to keep him at a distance.

Miriam looked him up and down. "Please come in, sir," she said, somewhat insolently. "Before leaving, Sir Archibald told me that soon you'd be arriving in Jerusalem."

Geoffroy sat down on the couch. She placed the rebec and the bow in a niche in the wall, and sat next to him. Her perfume made his head spin. For months he'd been in contact only with men and had almost forgotten what it was like to be in the company of a woman. He slid his hand under her robe. He felt the warmth of the velvety, smooth skin inside her thighs and his hand ventured further upwards.

Miriam stiffened, seized his arm and looked at him with eyes sharper than a spear.

"*How dare you*? You certainly don't waste time — *Sir Knight*."

"What's the matter? Am I not to your liking?"

"I have no knowledge of what Sir Archibald may have told you, but I feel you have been misled. I earn my living with my inn, not by bartering my body."

"When I see something so beautiful, I make it mine. It's as simple as that."

"With the well known arrogance of you Normans." Miriam's face hardened. "Everything is due to the *valiant* crusader conquerors, women included. Right?"

"You speak as if we were a mob of the worst sort."

"If you had been around here since the crusaders came, you would understand."

Geoffroy thought of the atrocities he'd heard about, and preferred to keep silent.

Miriam's expression softened, but at the same time she turned her nose up. "Excuse my frankness, sir, but you smell like a pigsty. Don't you ever wash?"

Geoffroy's hand began clenching and unclenching. "The rule of my Order forbids it. And who do you think you are, woman, to speak to me in that manner?"

"Why sir? Are you perhaps used to being treated differently?"

"My family rules over a land as large as half the Holy Land. I am a knight of noble stock."

"A knight of noble stock? I could hardly tell, from your manners."

"How dare you? In the Ardennes, females don't make so much fuss. Besides, I've never bothered about asking myself whether they enjoy it or not, even if — to be truthful — they usually have."

"Then I fear you have a few things to learn, and quickly, about women in Jerusalem, especially the Armenian ones like me."

"You are lucky you're a woman," Geoffroy said, his hand going wild.

She looked at him again with that insolent smile of hers, her eyes resting on the tunic and the sword. "When did you arrive in Jerusalem?"

"Today. Why do you ask?"

"Are you by chance one of the nine knights — the Templars? This is how you are called, isn't it? All Jerusalem is talking about you."

"And what if I were? Why all the curiosity?"

"We all thought the Hospitallers demented, until we heard of the things you Templars have done." Miriam shook her head. "And what about the vow of chastity?"

"Woman, do you want to drive me mad?"

"Well, my good knight, if one day you want to share a bed with a woman of Jerusalem — and you have a long road ahead of you — I'm afraid you will have to break the rule of your Order, together with your vow of chastity." Miriam got up. "And now, if you wish to stay for dinner, you are invited. For us Armenians hospitality is a duty, even when the guest doesn't deserve it."

Geoffroy turned purple. "How can one refuse an invitation made with such grace?"

"Good. First, though, I shall ask one of my serfs to prepare a tub. One cannot breathe in here."

Geoffroy grabbed her by the arm. "I am convinced I would know what to do, to change that proud look of yours into the eager look of a woman."

Miriam pulled herself free, her eyes full of challenge. "Be a good boy, Sir Knight. And who knows, someone might even come and scrub your back."

Geoffroy scratched his beard. By the dragon of St. George, what an intriguing woman. In sooth, he'd never met the likes of her before.

He undid his sword-belt.

§

Françoise wasn't quite sure how long she had been standing there. All of a sudden, something strange rubbed against her legs. She held her breath. Something was pressing against her right leg and was moving back and forth.... *Meow.*

She'd hardly had time to recover from the shock when a noise came from inside the room. The panel of the library suddenly swung open, and she found herself trapped between it and the wall. If Guichard were to find her there, he would think she'd been spying on him.

"André is that you?"

"*Meow.*"

"Julius! One of these days you'll make me die of a heart attack! Come here at once."

Guichard picked Julius up and disappeared inside.

Françoise went back the way she had come, hardly daring to breathe, and in no time at all was back in the safety of the bedroom. She took off the dressing-gown and snuggled back under the bedclothes.

Within a few minutes, the door of the bedroom opened again. Guichard lay down next to her. She pretended to be asleep.

Françoise thought of the Poussin painting. The same picture her uncle had in his study in the Vatican. Why? The solution to the mystery must be hidden in that picture.... *The muse's expression.*

§

The man in the blue Citroën glanced at the clock on the dashboard. It was 4:15 a.m. He looked up towards Rue de l'Hôtel Colbert. In the semi-darkness broken by street-lamps, the outline of the de Saint Clair *hotel particulier* was barely visible. He'd been there since eight o'clock the previous evening. He snorted with impatience. Another two hours before someone else took over.

For the umpteenth time, he reached over to the radio and pressed the tuner button to find something worth listening to.

14

A blue Volvo van drove slowly along a tree-lined road in the Parioli district in Rome. The first sun rays shone between the buildings and reflected off the windshield.

Giancana pulled down the sun visor. "Can you see the numbers?"

"Just about," said Intini. "Hang on. Slow down a bit.... Yes, this is it."

Giancana spotted a parking place in front of a bar on the other side of the road. A man in a white apron and a red and white striped T-shirt was pulling up the shutter. Giancana parked the van.

"Where's the envelope?" asked Giancana.

"On the back seat."

Giancana opened an envelope labeled Tincani & Genovese, Agenzia Investigativa, and took out a plastic folder and three photographs. He studied the photos, then flipped through the folder. Antigono Zergas had been in charge of the Coalition Party's financial department for seven years. Married, with a son working as an engineer in Paris, Zergas was described as Prime Minister Accardo's watchdog. Zergas's wife, Giovanna, worked as an art director in an advertising agency. The photo showed a youthful-looking woman with short, dark hair and a decisive air about her. The couple owned a house at San Severino Marche, two hours' drive from Rome, where they often spent the weekend. A humdrum routine, just like any other.

"Let's sit outside," Giancana said, "so we can keep an eye on the front gate. Coffee?"

The man with the striped T-shirt brought their coffees, his hand trying to smother a noisy yawn.

"What fun," Intini grunted. "A whole week like this, from six-thirty to midnight."

"Enjoy the sun and stop making all this fuss."

At 7:00 o'clock a superintendent opened the massive front gate of the building. Giancana mentally photographed the woman's thickset body.

"Let's go back in the van," he said, getting to his feet.

Seated sideways on the front seat, Giancana checked the front gate of the building through the back window. Intini was fiddling with the radio, occasionally glancing through the rear-view mirror.

Zergas was the first one to come out. Tall with white hair and wearing gold-rimmed glasses, he looked exactly the same as in the photo. Giancana signaled to Intini, who got out of the van. and followed Zergas from a distance.

Intini returned fifteen minutes later. "He's parked in a private parking lot about fifty yards away. The car's a metallic Alfa Romeo 2000. I took down the plate number."

People came and went for twenty minutes. Then a woman with short black hair strode out of the building. She was wearing a stylish gray suit.

"D'you think it's her?" Intini said.

"Hmm, hmm. Decisive, to say the least. Poor devil, I don't envy him. C'mon, move your ass. And don't lose her."

Half an hour later, Giancana threw his half-smoked cigarette from the window, got out, went to the back of the van and opened the doors. He glanced around him, then disappeared inside.

He reappeared ten minutes later wearing gray overalls and a blue cap, both bearing the words *Mariotti & Figlio – Consegne Urbane* [City Deliveries]. Under his arm he was holding a bright red, gift-wrapped package.

Giancana walked confidently through the main entrance and stopped in front of the superintendent's window. The woman finished sorting through the mail and gave him an indifferent look.

"Good morning," Giancana said with a broad smile. "This parcel is for Mr...." He looked at the delivery note. "Oh yes, Zergas. Which floor?"

"I'll take care of it."

"Thanks, but I have to deliver it in person. Company policy."

"The Zergases never get back before six-thirty p.m.," she said. "The cleaning girl is there. You can give it to her, if you like."

"All right. Which floor?"

"At the end of the garden on the left, third floor."

When Giancana reached the third floor, he checked the brass nameplate on each of the two doors. He rang the doorbell on the left and waited. A brunette with curious eyes opened the door.

"Good morning, I'm from Mariotti's. A package for Mr. Zergas."

"You can leave it with me."

"Just a signature, if you don't mind." Giancana took out a pad of receipts and made as if to take a pen out of his pocket. "Damn it! I must have dropped my pen in the van. You wouldn't have one to lend me, by any chance?"

"Sure. Come in a minute."

As soon as the girl left the front hall, Giancana took a quick look around. The door was equipped with several internal steel bars, which extended outwards into the door frame when the door was locked. He leaned down and examined the lock. He ran his hand along the top of the door. No electric circuitry.

A small picture hanging to the left of the door caught his attention. He moved it sideways, and a smile of satisfaction flickered across his face. A small, steel plate, with a keyhole in it, fitted into the wall. Giancana looked up at the ceiling. Up in the left-hand corner he saw what he was looking for: a little white box with a red LED in the center, pointed towards the front door. *An infrared detector.*

At that moment the brunette came back holding a ballpoint pen. She had just finished signing the receipt pad, when suddenly Giancana put his hand to his mouth and began coughing uncontrollably, his face purple.

"*Oh, my goodness!*" After another coughing fit, he said in a hoarse voice: "Could you get me a glass of water?"

"Sorry. Sure, I'll be right back." She ran off.

As soon as the girl disappeared, Giancana took a small, metal box out of his pocket, opened it, and extracted a block of plasticine. He moved the picture sideways, pushed the plasticine against the lock, and pressed on it with the palm of his hand. Then he pulled it off with care, looked at it, and nodded with satisfaction. He put it back into the metal box, cleaned the steel plate with his sleeve, and returned the picture to its place. He started coughing again.

"Okay, quick, drink this," said the girl, handing Giancana a glass of water.

Giancana emptied the glass. "Wow, I thought I was going to choke."

When Giancana said good-bye, the girl seemed almost sorry to see him go.

Cardinal Roger Blanchard, archbishop of Paris, stood in front of the window of his study on the first floor of the archbishop's palace. He seemed to be lost in thought, his hands behind his back. His aquiline nose, his Richelieu-like goatee, and his thin face made him look as if he'd jumped out of one of the paintings covering the walls of his study. The lamp standing on the Louis XVI desk cast the cardinal's long shadow on the wall. A knock at the door stirred him and he turned his head.

"Your guest is here, Your Eminence," said his secretary, poking his head around the door.

"Have him enter, Father."

The man—fat, thick-lensed glasses, his hair shining with brilliantine and parted down the center—sat down in front of the cardinal's desk. The chair on which he sat was low, which, combined with his short height, forced him to look up at the cardinal. He rummaged through his bulging briefcase and took out a manila folder. He half rose and passed it to the cardinal.

"Summarize the main points, please," Cardinal Blanchard said.

While the man was talking, Blanchard thoughtfully massaged his temples, his eyes half-closed.

"So you've no doubt whatsoever that it really was Madame Françoise Mikaelian," he said eventually.

"None at all, Your Eminence. One of my agents followed her from her home in Saint Germain des Près to Rue de l'Hôtel Colbert. Madame was seen entering the *hôtel particulier* de Saint Clair at 8:00 p.m. and leaving it at 8:10 a.m. the following day."

"Does the domestic staff consist only of a butler and a housekeeper?

"Yes."

Cardinal Blanchard leafed through the report. "One certainly can't say that de Saint Clair's whereabouts are easily foreseeable."

"Please, say no more, with all due respect, Your Eminence. One night—it was me on duty—he went out at 1:15 a.m. Can you guess where he went?

"Where?"

"To St. Sulpice's Church."

"*To St. Sulpice's*? At that time? What for?"

"To play the organ."

"An unusual man, that's for sure." The cardinal closely examined one of the photos attached to the report.

"Unusual? In my humble opinion, that man should be committed to the psychiatric ward of the Salpêtrière's."

"You haven't done any check on his family background."

"It wasn't requested, Your Eminence."

"I'm requesting it now."

"Excuse me, Your Eminence, may I ask you what it is you want to know, exactly?"

"I want you to delve into the life of that man and his family, by retracing the family tree of the de Saint Clairs as far back as the Crusades. Any questions?"

"One of our agents will have to go to Les Andelys to check the town records, and we'll also have to enlist the services of a firm specializing in heraldry. It will take time."

"I don't care how you do it, as long as you proceed with the utmost discretion. Is that clear?"

"You can count on me, Your Eminence."

"Three weeks. Not one day more," Cardinal Blanchard said, getting up. "Keep me informed. Oh, one last thing. Go on keeping a round-the-clock watch on the de Saint Clair mansion. I want details of times, habits, and comings and goings."

When the private detective was gone, Cardinal Blanchard looked up a number in the Holy See telephone directory, then reached for the phone.

"*Rolf, ç'est moi, Roger*. I've got the preliminary report," Cardinal Blanchard said.

"Tell me everything," Cardinal Wolfenberg said.

♣

Geoffroy wiped the sweat from his brow. His companions were wandering around among the arches of the stables, and the echo of their words faded away in that labyrinth of columns. The stifling heat was driving him mad, and he could feel his tunic sticking to his back. The air was heavy with the smell of horse dung, since the crusaders used King Solomon's stables for their mounts—it was said that up to two thousand horses could be accommodated there. Daylight penetrated the stables through small, square holes that opened in the east and south walls, tracing oblique, bright shafts through the air.

"How many feet below the esplanade are we?" Geoffroy asked, raising his eyes to the vaulted ceiling.

Hugues looked at his plan. "Forty-three, more or less."

Hugues was kneeling in front of the plan spread out on the ground. The stables dated back to the times of King Solomon, he said. King Herod had ordered massive works to double the size of the esplanade above. However, he had encountered many obstacles because of the conformation of the southeastern side of Temple Mount. Hugues turned and pointed to the south wall. On that side, he said, there was a sheer hundred-and-fifty-four-foot drop to the River Kidron. To solve this problem, Herod had built an embankment to a height of ninety-eight feet, supported by a wall sixteen feet thick. Archambaud de Saint Amand, who had worked as an architect, was observing the vaults with a critical eye.

"After which, in order to get to the top and support the esplanade, Herod was forced to build these columns and retaining arches," Archambaud said in his deep voice.

"Exactly," said Hugues. "By doing that, Herod raised the level of the southern part of the esplanade by a good forty feet. At that time the esplanade sloped downwards from north to south."

Payen de Montdidier shrugged and asked Hughes: "We only want to know one simple thing: where's the tunnel?"

"I wish I knew," Hugues said.

Eight pairs of eyes looked at him amid a chorus of surprised muttering.

Hugues said he'd spent hours checking and rechecking the measurements of the stables with King Baldwin's architect the day before. The ceiling was supported by eighty-eight columns in twelve parallel rows with thirteen 'aisles' in between. The arches were thirty feet high, and each side of the square columns measured over three feet. The two stables were a hundred and ninety-seven feet wide from north to south, and two hundred and seventy-two feet long from east to west.

"But that doesn't match the figures in my father's scroll," Geoffroy said.

"That's the problem." Hugues made a helpless gesture.

Geoffroy knelt down next to Hugues. "Where's the discrepancy?"

"Well, while the width of the stables is confirmed as a hundred and ninety-seven feet, the length is only two hundred and thirteen feet—instead of two hundred and seventy-two," Hugues said, pointing to the plan. "So there's a difference of fifty-nine feet in the length."

"If the scroll really dates back to A.D. 70, Herod had already finished his work some time before," Geoffroy said. "So, if you ask *me*, there can only be two explanations."

"Which are?" Hugues asked.

"Either whoever wrote the scroll was wrong, or the Moslems have made some changes. After all, they've been in Jerusalem for over five centuries."

"Well," broke in Archambaud, pointing to the walls and the vaults, "if they've made any alterations, they've done an expert job. You can't see any difference at all in style."

A deep silence met his words.

"And now, what do we do? Weep?" Geoffroy looked first at Hugues, then at Archambaud.

"*Spes, ultima Dea*—Hope, last Goddess," Victor said.

Geoffroy looked askance at him.

"I say follow Geoffroy's father's scrolls and go ahead as if the difference didn't exist," Hugues said, looking at Archambaud.

"The scroll tells us that the entrance to the tunnel is at a depth of twenty-three feet," said Archambaud. "Considering this difference of fifty-nine feet, the entrance could be at any point along these fifty-nine feet." He shrugged. "It really doesn't matter which end we start at."

"And what if we don't find anything, after digging the first hole?" Geoffroy said.

"What do you mean?" Archambaud said.

"We might be unlucky enough to have to dig holes over the whole fifty-nine feet, in the hope of coming across that tunnel, at some point."

"No, no. If we don't find anything with our first vertical shaft, once we're down there, we'll remain down there, just like moles. We'll dig an underground passage horizontally, until we come across the opening to the tunnel."

After a brief silence, a muttering of resigned consent rose from the group.

Hugues got up and, plan in hand, walked over to the northwest corner of the stables. Geoffroy and the others followed him, not overly convinced. Hugues measured eighteen paces from the west wall, hugging the north wall. Finally he unsheathed his sword and stuck it into the ground.

"This is the spot," Hugues said. "We start digging here."

Archambaud put his hands on his hips and looked round. "Geoffroy's scroll says the tunnel is three hundred and ninety-four feet long, at exactly forty-five degrees to the northwest."

Geoffroy pointed towards the eastern wall. "The sun rises over there."

"Tonight I'll check the position of the stars again," said Archambaud. "For the moment, though, one thing's certain: the tunnel runs in that direction."

Archambaud unsheathed his sword and traced a cross on the ground. Then he dug the point of his sword into the center of the cross and drew a straight line forty-five degrees to the north-west.

"Three hundred and ninety-four feet, *in that direction?*" Geoffroy said. "But the tunnel, then, would end up right under the Al Kas fountain! Why don't we just dig there?"

Hugues shook the plan at Geoffroy. "We can certainly thank the unknown author of the scroll. The whole area above the Holy of Holies — that is, right under the fountain — is protected by several layers of rocks and boulders, each sixteen feet thick. I defy the devil himself to go through there."

Hugues rolled up the plan. Geoffroy slapped himself on the neck, shooing off a fly.

§

"A fly, Monsieur le Comte?" André asked, rolling down the window of the Bentley.

"A fly? Oh, yes, there must be a fly," Guichard said. He undid the top button of his shirt. "It's hot in here, André. Please turn on the air conditioning."

"It's been on ever since we left Paris, Monsieur le Comte." André looked at Guichard in the rearview mirror.

Guichard ran his hand around his neck and withdrew it dripping with sweat.

André poked his head out of the car window. "Le Comte de Saint Clair," he said.

The guard greeted them by touching the peak of his cap. He checked the name on his list, bent down and looked inside. A few seconds later the wrought-iron gate swung open, and the man waved them on. As the car started to move up again, the guard went back into the guardroom and dialed a number.

The car sped along an oak-lined drive. Soon the branches intertwined thickly above the road, forming a shady canopy. André opened the sunroof. Guichard looked up, and his eyes followed the sunbeams filtering through the tangled mass of branches. The car crossed a bridge, rattling the wooden slats. The babbling of the brook alternated with the croaking of frogs. The road started to climb.

With its slate roofs and dark stone towers, the massive hulk of de Molay castle loomed on the top of the hill. A hawk flew across the sky and disappeared beyond the crest. The car proceeded slowly across the drawbridge, and stopped in front of the grating.

A butler ushered Guichard into the Arms Room and closed the heavy oak door behind him. The Arms Room had a rough stone floor and a high ceiling supported by massive wooden beams. French windows opened onto the parapet-walk. The maroon carpets were embroidered with the de Molay coat of arms—a gryphon clutching three arrows. Two rows of Templar suits of armor stood along the walls, which were covered with paintings, weapons, and the Templars' black and white striped banners. The paintings depicted several Grand Masters of the Knights Templar, battle scenes, and images of Jerusalem at the time of the Crusades.

Guichard's eyes wandered over the brethren of the Templar Lodge: Claude de Montbard, Yves de Saint Amand, Philippe de Mauriac.... Like him, they were descendants of the first nine Knights Templar. And like him, they too hadn't forgotten.

A set square, a compass, and a Bible were lying at one end of the oak table. Each place was marked by a sword lying on the table.

Guichard shook hands with the brethren, helped himself to a cognac from the buffet, and joined the others standing outside on the parapet-walk. His eyes met with Gilbert de Molay's. Gilbert took him aside to learn more about the meeting with Franzese.

Gilbert listened to Guichard, keeping one hand in his pocket, and holding a glass of whiskey in the other. He was wearing a blue blazer and, in place of a tie, a silk cravat with yellow and blue patterns over a light-blue shirt. He was a taciturn man, with a gaunt, deeply lined face, but it was his proud, piercing eyes that spoke for him. Guichard could not recall the last time he'd seen him smile. When they had set up the Lodge three years earlier, Gilbert's appointment as Grand Master had been unquestioned: that role was his by right.

Gilbert was standing in the doorway of the French window, looking out. His white hair and expression recalled a ghost from the past. Behind Gilbert, Guichard caught a glimpse of a portrait of Jacques de Molay, the last Grand Master of the Templars, hanging on a wall. After seven years of prison and unimaginable torture, De Molay had been burnt at the stake in front of Notre Dame Cathedral by the Inquisition, on March 14, 1314. Before dying, the Grand Master shouted out the Order's innocence and cursed Pope Clement and Philippe IV, King of France. With his last breath he summoned both of them to meet him twelve months hence, for the final judgment "in front of God's Throne." Clement V had died in April and Philippe IV in November of the same year.

"I believe everyone is here." Gilbert gazed around the room, then sat at the head of the table. "Let's get started." He looked towards Guichard. "The floor is yours."

Guichard told the brethren about the Organization's plan and the role the Church would play in it. Then he revealed his plan to them.

"In conclusion, Franzese is offering us the opportunity we've been awaiting for three years," Guichard said.

For a moment, silence fell. Then stifled chuckles spread round the table, until a Homeric guffaw worthy of Henry VIII burst out, swamping all the others. It was Philippe de Mauriac, his bearded bulk shaking and his head literally bent backwards.

Philippe drew on his cigar and banged his fist on the table. "You've said it, Guichard. *No discounts.* Just as they didn't give us any."

"Why are you so sure the Church will be taken in?" asked Gilbert.

"Because of the usual reasons. Power and money," Guichard said. "A killing on the foreign exchange market will be the perfect bait. And by the time the Vatican discovers what's behind it, it'll be too late."

"If we want to turn Franzese's plan against the Vatican, we need the guarantee from Brasilia—and fast," Gilbert said. "Is it too much to ask what you have in mind?"

"A mole," Guichard said.

"A mole at the *Ministry of Finance*? How?"

"Another three weeks, and everything will be ready. Don't worry."

"It's my job to worry. Through Franzese?"

"Yes."

"May I remind you of the amount of our investments in this project?"

"There is no need to."

Gilbert's eyes scanned Guichard for a few moments. "Under your responsibility?"

Everyone's eyes turned to Guichard.

"Under my responsibility."

The brethren raised their hands.

"Guichard's plan is approved," Gilbert said. He got up and grabbed his Templar sword from the table. The brethren followed suit. He raised his sword in front of him, and with the tip he touched first the set square, then the compass, and lastly the Bible.

"*Et in Arcadia ego*," Gilbert said.

"*Et in Arcadia ego*," echoed Guichard and the other brethren.

Their sword points barely touched above the symbols, dipped, and rested on the Bible—a strictly Hebrew Bible.

Guichard's sword, which had belonged first to Geoffroy and later to his namesake Guichard de Saint Clair, slashed the air of a thousand battles, and in that very moment a thousand copies of himself flashed in front of Guichard's eyes, like images in a kaleidoscope....

Why share with the brethren what he had in mind? They, like the Voice, would have considered him crazy, which would have only caused problems.

Thou perjurer! said the Voice. *Thou knowest not how much thou defiest the whims of fate.*

Fate? Nothing is written, Guichard said.

By a thousand gryphons! In sooth thy haughtiness knows no bounds.

15

Franzese bent over, took Cardinal Wolfenberg's hand and kissed his ring. The cardinal gave him a paternal hug, then pointed to a red velvet chair. On the wall behind them hung an oil painting of the Sermon on the Mount. A dove was flying over the crowd of followers gathered round Jesus; in place of the usual olive branch, the dove held a fluttering ribbon in its beak, with *Pax in terris* — Peace on Earth — written on it.

"Thank you for coming, Tano," Cardinal Wolfenberg said.

"A convocation from the Vatican is a particularly important event, Your Eminence."

"My dear friend, *Mala tempora currunt* — We live in hard times — We have important things to discuss."

"I'm listening, Your Eminence."

"The political situation has become intolerable." The cardinal lit a Romeo y Julieta, inhaled, and studied its tip. "Something has got to be done."

"Things have gotten out of hand."

"*That's precisely it.*" The cardinal pointed his cigar at Franzese. "Things have got out of hand."

The cardinal updated Franzese on the meeting he had attended the previous Friday at the American embassy.

"Joint Affairs is right," Franzese said when the cardinal had finished.

"In what respect?"

"Abramson spoke nothing but the truth when he said that politics is too important a matter to be left to the politicians. Nowadays it's finance that makes the world go 'round. Politicians simply act as its fan belt — and when the fan belt wears out, you change it."

"Around here we should have changed that fan belt ages ago," the cardinal said.

"It's not too late."

The cardinal stared at Franzese. "To do what?"

"Start from scratch."

"What about the tenant at Palazzo Chigi?" The cardinal gestured toward the Tiber.

Franzese looked at the cardinal with a sly smile. "It surprises me that Your Eminence should underestimate the Organization to such an extent."

"Well, well..." The cardinal leaned forward and patted Franzese's knee. "Tell me everything, Tano."

"Sorry, Your Eminence, but you have to take my word for it."

"By all means." The cardinal smiled and rubbed his hands together. "However, why not continue doing things together? True friendships are eternal, don't you think so?"

Franzese stroked his moustache thoughtfully. "Why not?"

"Well, well. It seems to me that our interests are linked once again, are they not?"

"Your Eminence, the Organization doesn't do anything for nothing, any more than the Holy See and Manus Domini do. Your reward—and Joint Affairs'—are clear. What do we get out of this deal?"

"What is it you want?"

Franzese drew some papers from his briefcase and handed them to the cardinal, who put on his glasses.

"It's a list of a hundred and seventy names, which we've subdivided according to their destinations. As Your Eminence can see, the most important posts are the law courts, the police, the Ministry of the Interior and the Department of Justice."

"And these names on the last page?"

"They're just people who are, shall we say, too zealous. So they deserve promotion and, of course, a move to a different position."

"*Promoveatur ut amoveatur*—You have to promote someone if you want to get rid of him."

"Synthesis: that's Latin's great merit. No wonder the ancient Romans conquered an empire."

"I don't see any problem in making this agreement, Tano—except, of course, for examining the list," the cardinal said. He drummed on his pectoral cross. "However, you *must* tell me something. How do you intend to do it?"

"Through the foreign exchange market."

"You're whetting my curiosity."

"I can only tell you that the foreign exchange market will remember it as a master coup. As you see, Your Eminence, next Sunday I'm going to have something to confess—the sin of vanity."

"Won't you give an old friend even a hint?"

"In a few weeks, the lira might cause some bad dreams to your APSA people. Just tell them this: to get a good night's sleep, the dollar will be the right remedy."

The cardinal's thoughts went back to the bond issue soon to be launched by Escobar's Brazilian company. *The loan was denominated in dollars.*

"So, can I tell Abramson that we've reached an agreement?" the cardinal said.

"That depends only on Abramson's reply." Franzese pointed to the list.

"Tano, what is it you want from me?"

"I expect Your Eminence to confirm that this list will become operative within ninety days from the next general election—the one after the Organization has thrown out Accardo, of course."

"Agreed. I will speak to Abramson about it, and I'll let you know." The cardinal got up. "In the heat of the discussion I've neglected my duties as host. How unforgivable." He took a bottle of Remy Martin and two brandy glasses out of a cocktail cabinet, filled the glasses, and handed one to Franzese. "I propose a toast to our alliance and the new course of events. Prosit."

"Cheers, Your Eminence."

A reflection of light bounced from the glasses and hit the helmet of the Templar armor.

The cardinal waited until Wednesday afternoon before phoning the American Embassy. He did not want either Fox, *or* Abramson, to think that Manus Domini was too anxious to reach an agreement, so he invited the US ambassador for coffee at 10:00 a.m. the following Monday at the Palace of the Holy Office.

As the cardinal hung up the phone, his mouth curved into a two-thousand-year-old smile. He turned towards his ivory chess set. The finely carved chessmen represented soldiers and medieval knights. He picked up the white queen and held it over the chessboard. Pensively, and with a light blow, he knocked over the black king.

Françoise awoke with a start and lay still in the dark. Her heart and her temples throbbed wildly. *It was the rebec.* It was playing! And the music was the same she had played in the master lutanist's workshop. *A vous, Amors, plus qu'a nule autre gent....*

She hoped that each note would be the last, but in vain. Perhaps it was just a dream, a bad dream. Certainly. It must be the tension that had been mounting inside her, and now suggestion was playing a nasty joke on her. She would soon wake up, and would laugh at herself. She dug her fingernails into the palms of her hands. It wasn't a dream.

She got out of bed, and for a few long moments she stood still near the bed, unable to connect.

"Reincarnation isn't the only answer," the psychoanalyst had said.

"What do you mean?"

"A paranormal phenomenon."

She thought of a weapon.... How stupid she was! What weapon? Against what? She walked cautiously toward the door.

The music came from the living-room. Françoise would have liked to disappear into a deep dark hole, but it would be of no use. That awareness did nothing but increase her anguish. The being wanted something from her, and there was no hole in the entire world deep enough to hide her. Françoise moved on along the hallway.

When she arrived at the doorway of the living-room, she stopped. It was pitch dark. However, the music went on: haunting, piercing, implacable. She stood still, trying with each cell of her body to see the unseeable.... The music was coming from the direction of the couch. She recalled well that she'd left the rebec on the coffee table in front of the couch. And now?

Françoise reached for the light switch.

As soon as the light flooded the room, the music stopped and a dull thud came from the couch, together with the sound of an untuned string instrument.

Françoise barely had time to catch the image of the rebec and the bow falling down on the couch. She sensed a slight cold draft. *The being was there.*

Françoise remained motionless. She felt paralyzed. Finally, she managed to swallow and took a deep breath, hoping that this would quiet the pounding of her heart.

"Who are you?"

Silence.

"What do you want from me?"

Silence.

"Do something! *I beg you.*"

The lights flickered repeatedly and the window curtains fluttered, like leaves stirring in the breeze. Something fell on the parquet floor, producing a sharp, metallic noise. Françoise looked down.

It was something dark and small, a few feet in front of her, but she couldn't make out what it was. She bent down, and stopped for a moment, her hand hovering in mid-air.... Finally she grasped it.

She couldn't take her eyes off the thing she was holding in her hand. It was a small metal chain darkened by time, made of links somewhat larger than those of the chains that people wear round their necks. At the center, the chain was divided by a sort of oval medallion, dark and worn, on which something was engraved. Françoise examined it closely in the lamplight: her hand clutched it tightly.

It was an emblem portraying a unicorn prancing in the center of a shield.

The coat of arms of the de Saint Clairs.

"Agreed, then," said Guichard.

"I'll call you when I get there," said Philippe on the other end. "Bye for now."

Guichard replaced the receiver, swiveled his chair around, and stared outside. A dreary drizzle was falling. A long line of cars crawled along the Quai de Montebello. He'd never liked autumn, because it meant the end of something good and the beginning of something bad. He watched the rain falling into the Seine.

Circles in the water.... A unicorn leapt out of the water and galloped skywards, along a shimmering path lined with pomegranate trees.

♣

The horses galloped to the east towards Qumran, on the northwestern shore of the Dead Sea, raising clouds of reddish dust. After their first visit, Geoffroy and Hugues had decided to return alone. Only the pounding of the horses' hooves and the thudding of their swords against the saddles broke the silence of the desert. The sun glinted off their chain mail.

Geoffroy scanned the crest of the hills: no trace of the Saracens, just rocks and desert. The land they were crossing was not in Christian hands; it was no-man's land. Despite it being a barren wilderness, strewn with reddish rocks and boulders, there was something uncanny about it: the magic of the desert.

Three hours later they reined up at the edge of a rocky valley. Below them, on a strip of land sloping down towards the northwestern shores of the Dead Sea and set in the midst of date-palm plantations, lay the village of the Essenes. Their white tents were dotted here and there between the lake and the foot of the mountain, columns of smoke rising from them. Pieces of linen lay on the ground in a long ribbon winding along the base of the mountain. They were laden with seeds and medicinal herbs left to dry in the sun. To north and south, the village bordered on terraced slopes covered with balsam plants. The shore gleamed white with the salt banks from the lake, like snow in the sunshine.

As Hugues spurred his horse down the slope, Geoffroy straightened up on his saddle and raised his gaze to the horizon. In the limpid air, his eyes followed the outline of the jagged hills of the land of Moab. The wind of the desert scorched his back and a swirl of sand swept over him. He flicked the reins and galloped after Hugues. As they rode down to the village, Geoffroy thought of their meeting a month earlier with Joash ben Uri, the Essenes' spiritual leader.

Joash had told them that the Essenes were ascetics who lived in strict adherence to the laws of the Old Testament and made their living from agriculture and medicinal herbs. They had always been known as healers of the body and of the mind. They had settled in the land of Qumran three hundred years before the birth of Christ, and there they founded a new sect.

They preached temperance, shunned wealth, and imposed celibacy. So women were strictly banned from their community. Hearing this, Geoffroy had muttered something. Victor, his eyes gleaming, had whispered to Geoffroy that Pliny the Elder, in his treatise *Natural History*, had called the Essenes *"gens aeterna est, in qua nemo nascitur* — an eternal race in which no one is born."

So it was only through the adoption of new members that the Essenes could assure themselves continuity. The rites of initiation into the mysteries of the Community passed through three stages. After three years of apprenticeship, the candidate became a novice and received a sword, an apron, and white robes — a symbol of purity. After three more years he went through the remaining two stages and became a disciple, a full member of the Community. In taking his oath, the new member pledged to preserve the sect's secrets.

The Essenes preached tolerance, and Geoffroy had been struck by this attitude. Tolerance was something he was unused to in the Christian world. In the shadow of the Church of Rome, "unbelievers" were called heretics and burnt at the stake.

Towards the end of their first meeting, Joash had made a strange reference to Jesus Christ, speaking about Him in a way that surprised them. It was for this very reason that he and Hugues had decided to come back.

Something mysterious was hovering above that lake.

The robes of the Essenes plowing the fields showed white against the clods of earth. When Geoffroy and Hugues rode past the outer tents of the village, two Essenes drew the reins of their draft horses and watched them riding by, their hands resting on the plow handle.

Looking up at the rugged crag above the lake, Geoffroy saw the bony figure of Joash, his loose, white robes blowing in the wind. They dismounted, hitched their horses, and started to climb up the mountain path.

"Peace unto you, Joash ben Uri," said Hugues, raising his arm.

"May God's countenance be upon you, brave Knights." The old man signaled them to sit down on the boulders facing the cave.

Joash was sitting on the ground at the foot of a thick, horizontal slab of stone on which seeds and medicinal herbs were neatly heaped. He was busy grinding them in a stone mortar.

"Joash, we've come back to hear more. We have a lot to learn," Hugues said.

"What do you wish to know?"

"Last time, when you talked about Jesus, you talked about Him as if Jesus were one of your Community. This can't be true."

"Why?"

"Because the Bible, the Christian Bible, doesn't say that."

"Perhaps you have never really read it."

"What do you mean?" asked Geoffroy in a tone he regretted.

Joash raised his hand. "Let me tell you a story."

He told them that one day a long time ago, on that very shore, in that very same village, a man had appeared. His name was Jesus. He had come from the north, from a village called Nazareth in the province of Galilee. He became one of them and always respected the oath he'd made. In his teachings Jesus often mentioned the Sadducees, the Pharisees, the Zealots and the other tribes and sects that populated Palestine at that time, but he never mentioned the Essenes, because this was a condition of initiation into the secrets of the Qumran Community.

Hugues's eyes widened. "Jesus was... an Essene?"

"He was indeed."

"Why did he leave the Community, then?" asked Geoffroy.

"He left when John, Teacher of Righteousness, died."

"*John... Teacher of Righteousness?*"

"When John was killed by order of Herod, in the thirty-second year of the Common Era, Jesus decided to go among the people, to preach the Word."

"The John you mention is John the Baptist, isn't he?" Geoffroy said.

"Who else?"

"So he must have been an Essene, too."

"The man you Christians call John the Baptist was a pillar of the Qumran Community, and Jesus was one of his disciples. What you know as the 'baptism of Jesus' in reality was the first stage of His initiation into our Community—no different from any other Essene's."

"*I can't believe it!*" Geoffroy said. "If this is true, then the Church must have made up the whole story."

"Today at sunset two new members will be taken through the initiation rites for the first stage of entry into the Community." Joash pointed to the shores of the lake below them. "Stay if you like, and you will see that their heads will be immersed in the waters, exactly as was done with Jesus over a thousand years ago."

"If Jesus really was an Essene, why is there no mention of it anywhere in the Gospels?" asked Geoffroy.

A smile crossed the old man's face. "That's what you say. We naturally do not recognize your Gospels, but I have read them, and I can assure you there's no page where our brother Jesus does not preach our Word."

"I just don't understand," said Geoffroy. "Where? When?"

"My good knight, it was a language for those 'who had ears to hear,'" Joash said. "The Church of Rome has never wanted to hear, nor has it ever allowed anyone to listen. It wasn't just by chance that, out of all the two hundred or so gospels in existence, the Church chose the four that served their purpose best."

"What do you mean?" asked Geoffroy.

"Jesus always spoke in our symbolic language."

Geoffroy and Hugues looked at Joash with inquiring eyes.

"It was a language in which a 'leper' was someone who had not yet been initiated into the mysteries of the Community, just as 'blind' meant someone who had not seen the light of knowledge, and 'risen from the Kingdom of the Dead' meant someone who had found the path leading to the Truth. 'Water' referred to those not yet initiated, and 'wine' were the disciples." Joash smiled shrewdly. "Do you understand, now?"

Geoffroy and Hugues stared at each other in silence. Geoffroy thought about that language, meant only for those "who had ears to hear." What if the things Joash had said were really true? Had he always been deaf himself? At first he was appalled, then he felt lost, and eventually anger started seething inside him.

He grabbed a stone, jumped to his feet, and hurled it as hard as he could into the waters of the lake.... He stood there, stunned, watching the ripples spreading out in ever-widening circles, glistening in the amber rays of the sun as it sank on the horizon.

From the very center of the circles leapt a unicorn, breaking the sheet of water with its spiraling horn. Its coat was a dazzling white, its eyes deep blue. Following a shimmering path lined with pomegranate trees, the unicorn galloped upwards to the highest mountain, where it reared up on a crag. From up there you could see a world without a tomorrow. The mountains crumbled, the sea flooded the land, the sun darkened. As the last lion roared and the last falcon hovered high in the sky, the crag split and the unicorn leapt into space.

The surface of the water was calm again, barely ruffled by the wind. It had only been a vision.

Circles in the water. Everything came to an end, but not the unicorn, because the unicorn was past, present, and future. To capture it had always been Man's dream, but the unicorn was beyond mortal reach, untamable and immortal, and only knights pure in heart could hope to see it. A unicorn was everything a knight could ever dream of: freedom, strength, virtue, magic....

Geoffroy raised his eyes to the sky, a feeling of uneasiness overcoming him. Someone was watching him from above, someone who, somehow, was part of him. And it was not the first time.

§

The whirling lights of starry firmaments spun around Guichard. A ray of sunlight dazzled him. Joash, Hugues, Geoffroy.... Where were they? Where was the Salt Lake? In his mind's eye, he saw Joash's white robes flapping in the wind, the fiery sun behind him and the glistening waters of the lake.

He looked around him. Where was he? What were those strange objects around him? And what peculiar clothes for a knight!

The early morning haze was starting to lift and the first rays of the sun were appearing over Notre Dame. He had to go back and tell him. *Tell him what*? Tell him to stop and run away, thus changing the course of history? Geoffroy belonged to a different dimension, and there was no way Guichard could convey to him the knowledge of the future. It was physically impossible, for it would mean going against the laws of Nature! Unless....

Unless he, Guichard, was prepared to pay the price. He tried to imagine a world with a Guichard physically identical to himself, but with a different subjective identity utterly oblivious of his former ego. He felt like a stranger left to his own resources in a foreign land, who knew he would never be able to go back home.

Was he ready to do that?

Guichard turned to the last page of the mandate for Kovacs. He got up and poked his head around the door separating his office from Marie Claire's. A flame flashed in front of his eyes. He held his breath, and flattened himself against the door.

"*For Chrissake, Marie Claire!* When are you going to stop smoking? Don't you know it's bad for you?"

Marie Claire turned pale. She put out her lighter and hid it behind her back, together with the cigarette.

"Yes, you're right, sir. I'm sorry. I... I shouldn't... I know."

16

Françoise closed the front door of the gallery behind the last customer of the day.

A shaft of light was cutting across the dark corridor. Françoise strode down the hall. Jules was sitting at his desk jotting down notes, Orff's *Carmina Burana* playing in the background. Françoise went in and sat down in front of him in silence.

Jules sighed, pushing his papers aside. "*Très bien*, I hear a storm coming."

Françoise told him about the dinner at Guichard's house and about the painting. She told him she'd also seen a reproduction of the same painting in her uncle's study in the Vatican.

"A strange coincidence, I must say. And why *Les Bergers d'Arcadie II*?" Jules said. He went over to the bookshelves and came back holding a thick book. "What struck you most about the painting?"

"The muse's expression."

"The Roman numeral after the title is not without significance. Did you know that Poussin had already painted another version of the same subject some ten years earlier, around 1630?"

"I seem to remember something from my art academy days."

Jules turned the book round for Françoise to see. The page showed both versions of the painting, one above the other.

"So I was right!" she said. "I wonder what happened to Poussin in the ten years between the two paintings."

In *Les Bergers d'Arcadie I*, the female figure was actively taking part with the shepherds in the discovery. She was wearing a dress that left one breast and her left leg bare. From her face you could see that, like the shepherds, she couldn't explain the mystery of the inscription.

"Between the two versions there's certainly an evolution in the female figure," said Jules. "An instinctive shepherdess in the first painting, and a composed muse in the second."

"But that's not all," Françoise said.

"What do you mean?"

"I mean the atmosphere of the two paintings. The setting of the first one is clearly pagan. It makes you think right away of a mythological Arcadia, lost in a golden age. But take a good look at the second painting. It's far more... composed. It seems to represents a less pagan Arcadia, more 'aware.' What do the experts say?"

"The mystery seems to be tied up with the interpretation of the Latin inscription *Et in Arcadia ego.*"

"But the translation is fairly straightforward," Françoise said.

"Which means...?"

"It means that death exists even in an earthly paradise like Arcadia. The muse has found out, but she's reluctant to tell the shepherds."

"A plausible explanation, but I doubt if it's the most credible," Jules said with a subtle smile.

"C'mon, Jules. What else do you know?"

"It seems that Poussin knew a secret—a terrible secret."

"*A terrible secret?*"

"It's mentioned in a letter sent from Rome by Abbot Louis Fouquet in 1656 to his brother Nicolas Fouquet, King Louis XIV's finance minister. Abbot Fouquet told his brother he'd met Poussin in Rome, and that Poussin was hiding a secret, a secret that could shatter the whole world."

"Is it known what he was referring to?"

"No," Jules replied. "But a series of facts—odd, to say the least—occurred during Louis XIV's reign, and they prove that the abbot wasn't making things up."

In 1661, at the court of Louis XIV, the Sun King, a shady intrigue led to the life imprisonment of Nicolas Fouquet by order of Louis XIV himself, on the basis of vague accusations of financial malpractice, Jules said. The king had all Fouquet's possessions confiscated, and personally went through all his correspondence. He had Fouquet confined in the citadel of Pignerol, where Fouquet rotted in total isolation for 19 years and was prevented from speaking to anyone at all until his death in 1680. The king went to great lengths to get hold of *Les Bergers d'Arcadie II*, and in 1685 he succeeded. Louis XIV locked the painting away and didn't allow anyone near it.

Françoise looked once more at the reproductions of the two paintings. "Then Poussin must have discovered the secret in the period between the two paintings."

Jules nodded. "This would explain not only the change in the female figure, but also a different interpretation of the Latin inscription."

"What interpretation?"

Jules went back to the bookshelves. He returned with a book, which he handed to Françoise. The title was *The Holy Blood and the Holy Grail*, by M. Baigent, R. Leigh, and H. Lincoln.

"The book's authors did some episodes for the BBC on the Rennes-le-Château mystery — you know, that village in the south everyone's talking about. With regard to the Latin inscription, a BBC viewer wrote to the authors suggesting a different translation, based on an anagram."

Françoise gave Jules a skeptical look.

"Wait. This viewer did an anagram of the inscription and made it *I tego arcana dei*, which translated from Latin means —"

Françoise blanched. "*Go, I hide the mysteries of God*," she said, more to herself than to Jules.

"A translation worthy of the niece of a cardinal." Jules suddenly slapped his forehead. "Guercino!"

"What has Guercino got to do with this?"

"A lot. He was the first painter to use that phrase."

Françoise stared at Jules with wide-open eyes. "Where?"

"Surely you must have seen the painting all over the place. Two shepherds coming out of a forest and looking at a skull perched on a stone slab."

"Yes, I remember it. But what's the link with the Latin phrase?"

"Guercino's painting's called *Et in Arcadia Ego*. Isn't that enough?"

Françoise stared at Jules in disbelief. Why had Guercino called his picture that? Did Poussin know about Guercino's picture?

"What do we know about Poussin's life?" Françoise asked.

"Wait a sec." Jules leafed once more through the book. "Oh, yes, here. He was born in 1594 in Normandy, but spent his entire life in Rome, where he died in 1665."

"In Normandy? Where?"

"Les Andelys."

The notes of the final fortissimo of *Carmina Burana* exploded in the air.

Les Andelys! *The hometown of the de Saint Clairs.* Guichard himself was born there. Françoise grabbed the first thing within reach on Jules's desk.

"Françoise, that statuette cost me nine thousand francs!" Jules snatched it from her and hugged it to his chest.

♣

When Geoffroy turned into the alley of the inn, it had been a while since the vesper-bell had rung. The shadows of the night had already descended on the city.

A man in a silver-hemmed cloak passed by, preceded by a serf lighting the way by means of an oil lantern, and followed by a second serf with his hand gripping the hilt of his sword.

Why that invitation to dinner? Over a year had gone by since his arrival in Jerusalem, and in spite of his many efforts, he doubted whether he'd made any progress at all with Miriam. That woman had bewitched him: those eyes, that gaze…. He would catch himself thinking of her at the oddest moments, cherishing thoughts that he would never confess to anyone: he, a Knight Templar, whose first aim in life had become a holy mission on behalf of the Church! Still, he couldn't do anything about it and, after all, he didn't care. He longed for her as a beardless pageboy longs for an unattainable châtelaine.

He went into the tavern of the inn. The big fire, together with the inviting aroma of food and the odor of damp straw, reminded him of the kitchen at the castle in Normandy, and of the stables where he used to hide and make love to one wench or another on heaps of hay.

At the far end of the tavern, a fire burned in a large stone hearth. A serf was turning a spit on which a lamb was roasting. Judging from the aroma, a vegetable soup must be cooking in a cauldron hanging over the fire on a hook and chain. The rest of the tavern was dimly lit by oil lamps and tallow candles, their smoky and pungent smell mingling with that of the food. On a wooden counter separating the tavern from the kitchen stood a large oak barrel, from which a serf was tapping wine into pitchers. There were few other customers at this late hour.

"Mistress Miriam has invited me to have dinner with her," Geoffroy said.

"I know, *Seignior.*" Krikor gave him a nasty look and muttered words in an unintelligible language. He made a rude gesture to follow him.

Krikor had made him feel uneasy ever since the first night. Despite being slightly taller than a dwarf, and in spite of that huge hump, there was something in him that aroused fear. He always wore a brown leather apron strapped tightly around his waist, and from his coarse canvas shirt, his arms jutted out unexpectedly brawny and hairy. From the way he carried around four full wine pitchers at a time, he must be fairly strong. What's more, Geoffroy had noticed that only a glance from Krikor was needed for the other serfs to obey him without uttering a word.

"You may be seated," Krikor said. "My lady will be here in a few minutes."

Geoffroy took off his cloak and his sword, put them on a bench, and sat down. He admired the lavish way the table had been set. Not far from the fire, places had been prepared for two, with round trenches of decorated wood facing each other. A white cloth with red embroidered edges covered the table, in the center of which towered a three-branched candelabrum, each branch forged in the form of Pegasus. Ceramic goblets replaced the usual wooden mazers, and Geoffroy could smell spiced water in the finger-bowls. Why such treatment?

A serf set up two trestles on one side of the table, and laid a board on them. Then he took a big, round loaf of bread, cut it in half, took out the crumb with a spoon, so that only the crust was left, and laid the crusts on the trenchers.

Miriam appeared at the bottom of the staircase. She was wearing a long, green, silk robe with loose dangling sleeves. Her hair was covered with a transparent veil held in place on top by a chaplet of colored beads. Geoffroy stood up, unable to take his eyes off her. When Miriam sat down in front of him, he thought he noticed a new light in her eyes.

"You must be wondering about the reason for all this, Sir Geoffroy," she said.

"Yes, indeed. I didn't get the impression I had entered into your good graces to such an extent."

"Today is exactly the first anniversary of your arrival in Jerusalem. Have you forgotten?" Miriam beckoned to a serf, who came over and poured wine into their goblets. Miriam raised her goblet. "To you, Sir Geoffroy, and to your mission, whatever it might be."

"I'm at a loss for words, Lady Miriam," he said.

"Then drink with me."

"Who is that fellow Krikor?" Geoffroy said, as a serf was putting a slice of roast lamb in his crust.

"Why do you ask?"

"I doubt whether I'm to his liking."

Miriam told Geoffroy that Krikor was Armenian, like her. He came from her same village, where he'd been in her family's service ever since she could remember, until her parents' death. He was very fond of her, almost like an elder brother, and felt it was his duty to protect her against everything and everyone.

"And he manages to do that, despite his deformity?" Geoffroy said.

"Appearances are deceptive."

"In fact I see that the other servants seem to be afraid of him."

"Krikor is a man to be afraid of."

"Why?"

Miriam seemed to hesitate. "I will tell you a story. When I opened the tavern, a customer tried to take liberties with me, in a vulgar way. A few days later he disappeared."

"What do you mean?"

"They didn't find him until two months later, but not all in the same spot."

"Not all... *in the same spot?*"

"Well, they found his head on the shores of the Kidron, one arm in the oasis on the caravan road to Bethlehem, his legs on the Via Maris...."

Geoffroy turned pale and looked towards Krikor. The Armenian, standing by the fireplace, returned Geoffroy's look. Using both his hands, he grabbed a heavy iron poker and, still staring at Geoffroy, he bent it in two, as if it were an olive twig. Finally, he withered Geoffroy with a diabolic sneer, showing all his decayed teeth.

"They found something in the mouth of that man," Miriam went on, bringing the wine goblet to her mouth.

Geoffroy dropped his lamb leg. "What?"

Miriam blushed gracefully. "I beg of you, Sir Geoffroy. I am a lady."

Instinctively, Geoffroy put his hand under the table and covered his groin.

"We Armenians are like that."

"Leave me the hope that there is at least one exception, by my faith."

"We're capable of terrible hatred, but when we love someone, we love deeply — and forever." Miriam stared at Geoffroy. "A love that goes on even after death."

Geoffroy brought his hand near Miriam's. "I would like to do something, as I have never wished to do in all my life long," Geoffroy said. Then he threw a nervous glance at Krikor, who kept his eyes pointed in their direction.

A mischievous gleam flashed from Miriam's eyes. "Exactly one year ago, when you first met me, you said: '*When I see something so beautiful, I make it mine; it's as simple as that.*'" Her eyes brightened. "Am I to think that you don't like me any more?"

Geoffroy took her hand and held it tightly. Miriam returned his grasp, the reflection of the candlelight flickering in her eyes.

By the dragon of St. George, what a woman! Holding her hand and staring into her eyes was like flying on Pegasus's back.

❖

Guichard walked along the *quais* of the Ile Saint Louis. It was a quiet stretch: the gulls circled above the bridges, people were sitting outside in sidewalk cafés, and the sunset painted the waters of the Seine orange. Guichard stopped outside a telephone booth on the Quai aux Fleurs. He took out Accardo's business card and dialed the number.

A blue Citroën drew up a short distance away.

"Allied will pay you in two installments," Guichard said.

"What is that supposed to mean?" the prime minister said.

"Thirty percent when the CIP board resolves on the deal, and the balance when CIP pays in the $500 million. Everything by the end of October."

"But—"

"No buts," Guichard said. "It would be too easy, don't you think?"

A long pause followed.

"Send the official proposal to the chairman of CIP," Accardo said. "He will take care of everything."

Click.

Guichard leaned on the wall overlooking the Seine. The notes of "La vie en rose" drifted up from under a bridge. A *bateau-mouche* emerged, its lights reflecting in the water in a kaleidoscope of silvery sparkles. Guichard's gaze was attracted by an odd gray-green reflection. It suddenly seemed to spin around faster and faster.

Through the ripples of the water, the features of a face began to take shape. Blurred at first, then ever more distinct. The notes of "La vie en rose" faded away, and music from a rebec spread along the quais.... *Her!* That was where he'd seen her before. What did it matter how and why?

Where are thy steps leading thee? asked the Voice in a suspicious tone.

I don't need to account to you, Guichard said.

She hath come back.

Guichard said nothing.

Thief!

Silence.

When thou art in her arms, and enjoyest her kisses, I will delve into thy mind. Take heed! Dare not cross the boundary between thy lands and mine.

And now you expect to check my thoughts as well?

Feigning will not be of use to thee. Remember: the wrath of a Norman knight can be more ill fated than the seven heads of the hydra.

Guichard went back into the phone booth and dialed a number.

When he came out, he hailed a taxi.

As the taxi left, the blue Citroën drew away from the sidewalk.

♣

Geoffroy was about to go down the ladder, but he had to stop. Down below, the men who had the job of removing the rubble were carrying buckets full of earth out of the underground passage. They tied them to the ropes hanging from the pulleys, and the two men standing next to him started to pull them up. The pulleys whined.

Waiting for the men to finish, Geoffroy sat on a rock and frowned. Four years had already gone by since the first blow of the pick, and yet they'd covered just a hundred and sixty feet. They were not even halfway. Geoffroy shook his head and thought back to when they'd started.

When they had initially reached a depth of twenty-three feet, they hadn't found any sign of a tunnel. Just to make sure, they dug down another three feet, but in vain. Then they started to dig horizontally towards the west wall. At first they had hoped that each swing of the pick would be the right one, but soon their optimism faded. Time was going by, but the tunnel went ahead much more slowly than they had anticipated. Archambaud, who had taken charge, had to re-adjust the original project more than once. He tried to make up for this by arranging extra shifts, bringing them to a total of twelve hours a day, but to no avail.

They dug an underground passage six feet three inches high and five feet three inches wide. They came up against several disparate layers of material, and the roof caved in three times on top of the men, killing two of them. First they had to resort to threats, then brought in King Baldwin himself to get the men to go back to work. Archambaud had to reduce the distance between successive props to twenty inches, and he had to use trunks of Lebanese cedar one foot in diameter.

As the underground passage progressed, they gradually had to reduce the length of the shifts down to just two hours. The men couldn't take more than that, because there was little air in the tunnel. Besides, many of them couldn't stand being buried in that rat-trap for long. He'd experienced it himself, that closed-in feeling that grabbed at your heart and forced you to rush back up.

After seven months, they began to lose hope. They had almost reached the west wall, which meant they had covered that distance of fifty-nine feet, but still no sign of a tunnel. He remembered the date clearly: February 14, in the year of our Lord 1119.

The bells of the Church of the Holy Sepulcher had just rung the eight strokes of the vespers. It had snowed that day, and the snow seemed to sharpen not only the silence, but also a creeping feeling of intolerance mingled with depression. They held their cloaks tightly around them, and moved the oak table closer to the fireplace, where a comforting fire was burning. The table was lit by tallow candles stuck on iron tripods.

They hardly spoke to each other: not so much out of exhaustion as out of discouragement, even if no one would ever admit it. Not even the fact that it was Wednesday managed to raise their spirits, for on Wednesdays King Baldwin's cook sought forgiveness for the other six days of the week. That day he'd prepared beef stew with boiled vegetables and, as dessert, figs soaked in spiced wine and crustless "Sienese" tarts.

Instead of eating with his hands like all good Christians, Victor was the only one who made use of a new-fangled invention from Italy known as a "fork" — a two-pronged tool with which he speared the meat, after cutting it into small pieces. Victor had adopted a mangy-looking dog with a reddish coat and only half a tail, which he insisted on calling Baldwin, despite his companions' objections, and every so often he tossed the creature a bone over his shoulder.

The crackling of the fire in the grate and the crunching that Baldwin produced as he gnawed on his bone echoed in the silence hanging over the room.

A large napkin draped over his shoulder, Archambaud was seated across from Geoffroy, absorbed in picking a bone clean. His bearded face was lit by the firelight, and his expression seemed bewildered. A serf went around the table with an acquamanile [a gryphon-shaped pitcher] and poured water into their earthenware finger bowls. He and Archambaud washed their fingers. Suddenly the noise of tramping feet and excited cries came from the corridor. Their fingers still in the bowls, he and Archambaud turned their heads.

"We've made it! We're there at last!" Gondemare de Saint-Omer burst into the room, gasping for breath. His face was plastered with mud, and he was brandishing a rolled up map. "Confounded tunnel! We've found it at last! Exactly in the corner between the north and west walls."

With a crash of overturned benches, they all raced down the stairs.

By the light of the torches, they stared at the point where a laborer's pick had struck a void. What awaited them on the other side of the wall?

Geoffroy was the first to enter the tunnel. He moved forward with caution, holding his torch high in front of him, breathing in the musty air, his shadow flickering on the walls. This gallery had been dug nearly two thousand years before, during King Solomon's reign, and he was quite likely the first man to enter it since then.

After a few yards Geoffroy had to stop. The roof had caved in, and a great pile of rubble blocked the passage. He held the flame of his torch close to one of the props and scraped it with his fingernail.

"Rotten, completely rotten. Damnation!" he shouted. He kicked the wall and grunted with pain. A shower of earth fell from the roof.

Archambaud grabbed Geoffroy's arm and pulled him back. "Out, quick, unless we want to be buried alive!"

They had to resign themselves, and it was like having to dig the tunnel all over again. After a further eight months they had advanced only sixty-five feet. It was then that they had a second nasty surprise. A huge boulder appeared blocking the tunnel, and they realized it would be impossible to break it up. Archambaud decided the only solution was to go around it. But that diversion, an additional twenty feet, took another five months of work.

Geoffroy lost count of the many problems that occurred and recurred in the next two years. Since then, no one dared make any further forecasts, and Archambaud himself stopped making plans.

The whining of the pulleys was over. The men had finished bringing out the rubble. As Geoffroy started to go down the ladder, he wondered if they would ever finish. Give up? Never. He'd carry on digging with his bare hands, if necessary.

He grabbed the torch. That cursed fist of his went on opening and closing of its own accord. He entered the underground passage and banged his head against a beam. "*Damnation!*" he cried.

§

"Ouch!" cried Guichard, clutching his forehead.

The taxi driver, caught unawares, looked at him in the rear-mirror. "*Qu'est-ce que c'est, Monsieur?* — What's the matter, Monsieur?"

"*Rien, je suis désolé.* Nothing, sorry, just lost in thought."

The driver gave Guichard another glance in the mirror, muttered something and shook his head.

17

The envelope was marked Confidential and the sender was Igor Svensson from Stockholm. Ackerman opened the envelope, put aside the videocassette he found inside, and proceeded to read the report.

When he had finished reading, he glanced at the other two reports he'd received earlier in the day from Louisville and Berlin. He reached for the phone and dialed Hübner's number in Berlin.

Dr. Meiner, one hand in the pocket of his white coat, gave Ackerman a condescending look. "As I told you on the phone, Herr Collins, I'm very busy. One of my assistants will look after you."

In response, Ackerman laid his business card on Meiner's desk; Meiner was about to press the intercom button when his eyes fell on the business card. He stopped, picked it up, and gave Ackerman a look bristling with suspicion.

"*Ackerman*?" Meiner said. "But isn't Collins your name? What is International Security?"

Ackerman took a sheet of paper out of his breast pocket and unfolded it. "I see that your contract with the Kohl Institut contains an exclusiveness clause," he said in an amiable tone. "Right?"

"*My contract*?" Meiner said. "Who the hell are you?"

"I see that over the past three years you've carried out an enviable number of private consultations, using Kohl Institut labs and their staff," Ackerman continued remorselessly.

Meiner's hands gripped the armrests of the chair.

"You've made DM 198,500 in this year alone. My congratulations. I see that business is flourishing."

"*You filthy blackmailer!* I'll make sure you rot in jail for the rest of your life."

"Look, *Herr Doktor,* you're making a mistake. I'm not here to ask you for money. Quite on the contrary."

"What the hell are you talking about?"

"I need your services, and I'm ready to pay you handsomely for them." Ackerman opened his briefcase and shoved some sheets of paper towards Meiner. "Read this. It'll make it all much clearer."

As Meiner went through the pages, his face darkened. "If you think I'm going to put my signature on this crap, you belong in an insane asylum," he said, throwing them back at Ackerman.

"I'm afraid you're missing the point."

"What point?"

"It could be embarrassing, for you if the chairman of the Kohl Institut were to receive a copy of this information. Your embarrassment would be even greater if the tax offices in Bonn—the *Steueramt*—were to receive a copy too. 'Steueramt' is a word that makes people break out in a cold sweat here in Germany, isn't it?"

The purple hue in Meiner's face turned to deathly pallor.

"Copy this text on headed notepaper and make two original copies, sign them and send them back to me by courier in Washington," Ackerman said, shoving the papers across the desk again. "If I don't receive them within forty-eight hours, I'll know what to do."

Without waiting for Meiner to reply, Ackerman went to the door. He already had a hand on the door knob, when he suddenly stopped and turned around.

"Oh, I forgot something. Send me the details of your overseas bank account, too."

Meiner gave Ackerman a bewildered look.

"We'll be paying you 50,000 dollars for your professional services. Aren't we nice guys?"

"What else is it you want?"

"If one day, *Herr Doktor*, you were to try to get clever, you'd have a bit of a problem justifying those 50,000 dollars, don't you think?"

Without another word, Ackerman left the office. Meiner remained seated, motionless, staring blankly at the door.

On the afternoon of Thursday, September 18, a DHL van drew up in front of the brownstone International Security building in Georgetown. The driver got out with a package and delivered it to the reception desk.

A few minutes later, Ackerman's secretary opened it. The envelope inside was marked Highly Confidential. She knocked on Ackerman's door.

Ackerman opened the envelope. As he examined the contents, his lips curled in a scornful smile. He reached for the phone and dialed Kovacs's direct number.

It was 10:30 p.m. by the hall clock in de Santis's house when the phone rang.

Tancredi picked up the phone. "… It's me. Who's speaking, please?"

"Good evening, Mr. de Santis. My name's not important. You received an anonymous letter a few days ago, didn't you?"

The letter. "Yes. Is it—"

"Give me a safe number and tell me when I can get back to you."

Tancredi gave him the number of Annibale's bar and suggested a telephone appointment for 11:00 p.m.

"Okay. I have 10:38. I'll call you at eleven o'clock sharp."

The line went dead.

"Who was it?" Carla said.

"He didn't say. Some people just want to remain anonymous."

She sighed, staring at him.

"You've been watching too many spy films," Tancredi said.

"I can't get used to things like this. I just can't help it."

Tancredi hugged her hard. "I've got to go now, but I don't think it'll take long." He whispered in her ear: "If you're still awake when I get back, I promise you won't regret it."

"Silly billy. Don't be long."

The bar was almost empty. Annibale was behind the bar drying some glasses, his bald head glistening with sweat. The CD player was playing the *Radetzky March*, and Annibale seemed to be doing the drying to the rhythm of the music. He flaunted a pair of flaming-red suspenders that stood out even more against a short-sleeved, canary-yellow shirt. He waved to Tancredi, looking at him as if they were two "brethren" belonging to the same secret sect that schemed to turn the destiny of the world upside down.

Tancredi stepped to the counter and told Annibale he was expecting an important phone call. He ordered a bourbon, and went into the billiard room to sip it. The room was empty.

He put his glass down on the edge of the table. He got hold of a ball from the center of the table, concentrated, and nudged it down the table, aiming for a pocket. But the ball seemed to have other ideas and bounced back, coming to rest in the center. Within minutes Annibale called him to the phone.

"I was the one who sent you that anonymous letter," said a voice on the other end of the line.

The man told him that his organization was determined to take action very soon and that they were prepared to help the newspaper. They wanted *La Voce Indipendente* to launch a press campaign based on the information found in Zergas's files. They would do the rest. The man then asked Tancredi what he'd done since receiving the letter. Tancredi told him about Carlomagno.

"D'you need money?"

Tancredi told him what Carlomagno had quoted. "For a newspaper like ours it's a hell of a lot. If we fail, the newspaper will have to close."

"I realize the risk you're taking," the voice said after a pause. "As a sign of our appreciation, I'll send you our contribution in the next few days. Two hundred and fifty million lire."

For a moment, Tancredi didn't know what to say. At the same time, though, he wondered what lay behind that man's generosity.

"All I'm asking you is to keep me informed about your progress," the voice said.

"How?"

"Make a note of this," he said, and gave Tancredi a number. "It's a PO box at the main post office in Rome. You can send me a weekly report there.

"Agreed. And... thanks."

When Tancredi left the phone booth, he went to the counter and ordered another bourbon. Radetzky was raging. While he was pouring the whiskey, Annibale leaned forward his big, bald head close to Tancredi's.

"Hey, Boss, we're nearly there, aren't we?"

Tancredi looked at him. Annibale seemed to have read the doubt in his eyes, because he reached for the glass cabinet containing his miniature soldiers and pointed at a mounted Roman soldier, the figure's silver helmet shining and red cloak flapping in the wind. From Annibale's look, Tancredi could tell that this soldier was his hero: Julius Caesar.

Annibale's jaw contracted, his body becoming erect. "In moments of doubt, I always ask myself the same question."

"What?"

"What would *he* have done, in my place?"

"And...?"

"I try to listen through the din of battle," Annibale said, his hand to his ear, "and the answer I get is always the same. *Attack!*"

On the wall behind Annibale hung a large mirror. It was slightly tilted to show the reflection of the customers standing near the bar. Apart from the name of a brand of a popular liquor, the mirror had a scene of dancers on it from a painting by Toulouse-Lautrec: Moulin Rouge lights, tall, skinny men in top hats, red garters flashing amidst a whirling mass of frothy, white petticoats. Everything seemed to be whirling together to the frenzied rhythm of the can-can.

"So?" Annibale said, snapping one of his suspenders.

"We shall win." Tancredi knocked back his bourbon.

"*Now* you're talking," said Annibale, his jaw sticking out even more. "Let's have another one. It's on the house."

"To Julius," Annibale said, raising his glass.

"To Toulouse-Lautrec," Tancredi said.

Tancredi shut the front door behind him. For a moment the silence in the house seemed more deafening than the printing press at the newspaper office. He missed the feeling of confidence he got at the bar, confidence born of green pool tables, circles of light drowned in the darkness, and inviting can-can dancers.

"Who was it, Tancredi? What did he want?" Carla asked.

"Just some nut insisting on making a donation of 250 million lire to the newspaper."

Tancredi took her in his arms, buried his head in her hair, and started to undo her blouse.

"When you asked me to marry you, couldn't you have told me I was marrying James Bond?" Carla whispered in his ear.

"Would it have made any difference?" said Tancredi, taking her blouse off.

"*Au Louvre s'il vous plait,*" Françoise said to the taxi driver.

She rested her head on the back of the seat. *A ghost had entered her life.* There were moments, at home, when she would remain motionless, trying to perceive its presence. Yet the worst moments by far were at night, when she tossed and turned in bed trying to get to sleep.

Who was that being? The rebec and that music made her think of Jerusalem at the time of the Crusades. The words of the song and the tone of the music told her it must be a woman. Someone known to one of Guichard's ancestors? Who? The Crusades spanned a period of two hundred years, and many de Saint Clairs had fought in the Holy Land during all those years. The master lutanist, though, had said that the song had become popular in the Holy Land after the first Crusade. From the information she'd gathered, a de Saint Clair had lived in Jerusalem at that time: Geoffroy de Saint Clair. A woman related to Geoffroy?

What did she want from her? First the music, then the heraldry book open at that very page, and finally the medallion.... What did those clues aim at? What was the link between the being and the mystery hiding behind Guichard?

She thought of her last meeting with Jules. The tomb in Scotland, Poussin, the Church... and that phrase, *Et in Arcadia ego*, which seemed to crop up everywhere. A copy of the second Poussin in her uncle's study, in the heart of the Vatican, then another in Guichard's house.... A village in Normandy.... A de Saint Clair among the first Templars in Jerusalem. It all seemed like an infernal puzzle.

Whichever way she looked at it, she always found herself faced with Poussin and *Les Bergers d'Arcadie II*. Poussin and his allegories! The muse's expression haunted her day and night, but one thing she was certain of: Poussin had entrusted his secret to that expression. Maybe by looking directly at the original she'd manage to understand. Sometimes it took next to nothing: shading, a brush stroke, a seemingly meaningless detail.

"Here you are, Madam." The taxi driver pointed to the glass pyramid in the center of the main square of the Louvre and the usual never-ending waiting line. "*Bonne chance.*"

When she finally entered hall 42 of the Richelieu wing, she looked around but couldn't see the painting anywhere. Was she in the wrong hall? She turned around.

Les Bergers d'Arcadie II! An incomparable purity of color, a timeless setting, an enigmatic gaze...

Françoise drew closer to the painting.

§

A damned nuisance, Guichard thought, as he walked briskly towards the Pavilion Mollien in the Louvre. And, of course, it just had to happen at a moment like that. But when Wesenheim, the curator of the Louvre's department of paintings, had phoned him, he couldn't really say no. The museum had just bought two sketches by Van Gogh, Wesenheim told him, and he would be "honored" to show them to him personally. Guichard knew it was just an excuse. Wesenheim would surely once again insist on giving that damned exhibition of the de Saint Clair collection. Still, Wesenheim had done him favors in the past, and so it would have been rude to refuse.

On reaching the entrance, Guichard glanced at his watch. He was early. He turned left and set off towards the entrance to the Richelieu wing.

Climbing the stairs to the second floor, he looked up... *Françoise*. He was on the point of racing up the stairs, but then he stopped. Why should she be going up to the second floor? She was responsible for Impressionism at the gallery, and the works of the Impressionists were not on display in that wing of the Louvre.

Guichard saw her hesitate in front of the signboards on the second floor, then she turned right. Taking care to keep out of sight among the crowd, he followed her along the corridor. At the entrance to hall 42, she stopped a moment, then went in. Guichard went after her.

He stopped at the entrance and stepped aside to let a group of Japanese tourists through. Hmm, no. They were too short. That fair-haired bunch was a better bet: probably Scandinavians. Guichard wormed his way into their midst, keeping his face hidden. A few yards further on, he left the group, strolled casually to the end of the room, and turned round.

Françoise was standing immobile in front of the painting. Guichard stepped to one side the better to see her profile. She was so concentrated on the painting that she seemed unaware of anybody else's presence.

"Women aren't happy until they've found out everything down to a man's last secret..." André had said.

"Thou must not see her again, dost thou hear me?" the Voice had said.

Guichard couldn't tell how, but he found himself going down the staircase to the ground floor. He bumped into someone, who blurted out an irritated *"Monsieur, faites attention!"* to him, but he didn't even turn around.

As he walked past the glass pyramid, a couple strolled by hand in hand.

Guichard's eyes followed them.

18

"Tancredi, there's a parcel for you," said the receptionist, poking her head around the office door. "The courier insists on giving it to you personally."

Tancredi raised his eyes from the typewriter and sighed. "Do me a favor, will you? Tell him to bring it in."

Shortly afterwards the courier came into the office, chewing gum. He was a teenager, his face covered with spots and with a teasing sneer. He dropped the parcel on the desk and held out a receipt pad.

"Birthday present coming up, Mister. I bet you were just writing to complain about the delay, weren't you?"

Tancredi read the company name on the boy's cloth jacket. "No, I was writing to the Rapid people, to compliment them on their employees' sense of humor."

"Ha, ha, ha! That's a good one, Mister. I'll have to jot that down." The boy slapped Tancredi hard on the shoulder. "Witty customers. Wow! That's what I like."

Hell! Why did all the raving idiots in the world have to end up on his doorstep? Tancredi rubbed his shoulder and ignored the parcel. He checked the time. He had only half an hour left. He turned the platen, and read the article through for the last time. He shook his head. He looked at his watch again, swore, and hurried off, holding the typed pages. As usual, the idiot in charge of typesetting would come out with his dime-a-dozen jokes, grumbling about having to scan his articles. "For Chrissake! When will you start using a computer?" he would say for the umpteenth time. "All the others have used our paging software for years now. Is it technology you hold a grudge against, or is it *me*?"

When Tancredi got back to his office, he remembered the parcel. He picked it up and turned it over, but the sender's name was nowhere to be seen. He cut the string, and took off the brown paper. Inside there was a cardboard box, the lid fixed on with tape. He cut the tape all around the edge. He was about to lift the lid when the phone rang.

He swore between his teeth and lifted the receiver... oh, no! The typesetting department again. They asked him to confirm the layout for the following day's article. He raised his eyes heavenwards and explained once again how he wanted it set out, forcing himself to stay calm. He then turned back to the box and lifted the lid.

Tancredi stood flabbergasted, the lid in his hand. Caravaggio's face looked up at him from a whirl of 100,000 lire notes. He lifted the top packs: the box was full of them. He picked up a pack and counted ten notes of 100,000 lire each. All of a sudden he remembered the voice on the phone, two evenings earlier. No need to count the bills: the box undoubtedly contained 250 packs of a million lire each.

A shaggy black head of hair appeared in the doorway: Quilici. He was about to say something when his eyes fell on the money. He stood stunned for a moment, then let out a long, low whistle.

"I can see that drug trafficking is doing well," said Quilici with a grin of complicity.

At 9:00 a.m. on Thursday, a black limousine drew up outside 1600 Pennsylvania Avenue in Washington. One of the guards looked through a side window, touched his hat in a military salute, and ordered the gates to be opened. The car drove on through the grounds towards the White House. The Secretary of State Barry Andrews's assistant was waiting on the front porch.

Abramson got out of the car, responded to her formal greeting with a grunt, and marched towards Andrews' office with the assistant trotting behind him, her high heels clicking on the concrete path.

"It's too early to discuss the Palermo list," Abramson said after updating Andrews on his meeting with Cardinal Wolfenberg at the US embassy in Rome.

"What do you mean?" Andrews said.

"They seem a bit too self-confident, for my taste, both in Rome and Palermo."

"Does that surprise you?"

"The Church and the Mafia have been in business together for ages. Something tells me they're thinking of exploiting us."

"That's a risk we've got to take," Andrews said.

"Well, we at Joint Affairs don't like this kind of risk."

"There isn't much else we can do, for the time being."

Abramson grinned. "What about your friends in the CIA?"

Andrews's right eye twitched. "Don't tell me you intend..."

Abramson nodded repeatedly.

"Why resort to extreme measures? What for?"

"Fear can be a great advisor. And *you* should know that."

"But why, in a case like this?"

"A bit of noise will help make them realize they might arrive late."

Andrews sighed. "The Red Brigades are history. What are we supposed to make up, this time?"

"You are asking *me*? The CIA is a master of this kind of hocus-pocus. Make up a 'Communist Fighters for Freedom Movement,' or any other damn nonsense along those lines."

"I'll have to call a meeting, and then discuss the matter with the president."

"Whenever you guys in Washington are at a loss—which is the case nine times out of ten—you either call a meeting or form a committee. Call Langley, and I'll take care of the president."

Andrews's eye twitched again. "What about the Palermo list?"

Abramson opened his briefcase, took out some papers, and shoved them across the desk. "The list is okay, as far as we're concerned."

Andrews leafed through them. "To tell you the truth, I have some doubts. Linking up like this with the Mafia could be costly."

"Why? You and the CIA have been bedfellows with Palermo whenever it's suited you. Isn't it too late to play the shy virgins?"

"*Cosa Nostra* is long-armed. An agreement like this could bounce back at us right here in the States."

"Can you think of a better solution?"

"Not at the moment, but—"

"Don't start iffing and butting with me. I need something solid to move on!" Abramson said. "We'll pay their price. At least, thanks to that list, all the rotten apples will be in one basket."

Andrews adjusted his bow tie. "That's certainly a peculiar way of looking at things."

"If you behave, next time I'm in Washington I'll take you along for a game of golf. I'll give you a nine handicap, as a sign of my appreciation." Abramson vigorously slapped the secretary of state on the back. "Oh, before I forget. You'd do well to give the CIA a kick in the pants once in a while, to let them know who's the boss."

A disconcerted look appeared on Andrews's face. "Why?"

"You and I don't know, but they always do."

Andrews started playing with his bow tie again. Then he pressed the button on the intercom. "Jane, get me Threader at Langley. It's urgent."

The bomb went off in Rome at 3:15 a.m. on Saturday. The sticks of dynamite had been placed in a phone box in Piazza del Viminale, less than three hundred feet away from the entrance to the Ministry of the Interior. The explosion killed a young couple who happened to be passing nearby.

At around 9:00 a.m. on Saturday, someone phoned the editorial desk of *Corriere della Sera* and, immediately after, that of the newsreel of RAI 1, a state-owned TV station. A voice claimed responsibility for the attack in the name of a hitherto unheard of group, the 'Unit of Communist Fighters for Freedom.'

The news was announced on the radio and television in a series of extra editions that continued throughout Saturday. The first photographs appeared in the afternoon papers: one of them showed a lipstick and an address book lying in a pool of blood.

The incident provoked a wave of fear and violent protest all over the country. People feared that this might be the first sign of a return of the terrorist attacks that had plagued the country in the 60s and 70s.

"What do you think of it?" the interviewer asked a bulky woman wedged among the crowd heaving behind the barrier in Piazza del Viminale.

"It's disgusting. We've had a bellyful."

"What do you mean?"

"Those bombs should have been put in Parliament, not among decent people. It's all the politicians' fault. What've we got to do to get rid of this bunch of crooks?"

"Bravo!" shouted someone in the crowd.

Monsignor Feliciani ushered Ambassador Fox into the cardinal's study. When the cardinal walked in, Fox was admiring a Madonna by Cellini at close range. The ambassador waved his hand towards the frescoes covering the walls and the ceiling.

"I envy Your Eminence the privilege of working in the midst of so many beautiful things."

"In the Vatican palaces we breathe history, but we end up taking it all for granted." The cardinal became serious and pointed to a chair. "Shall we get down to business?"

"By all means, Your Eminence."

"Just a question, before we start." The cardinal looked Fox straight in the eyes. "What do you think about the explosions on Saturday night?"

"All I know is what I've read in the press."

"Do you know what Cicero would have asked himself two thousand years ago, under similar circumstances?"

"I must admit, Your Eminence, that I haven't thought of asking myself this question."

"*Cui bono* — Who benefits from all this?" The cardinal's eyes seemed to X-ray the ambassador. "Doesn't the CIA know anything about it?"

"The *CIA*? They were as surprised as we were. Why do you ask?"

"It's a fact that since Saturday night these phantom 'Communist Fighters for Freedom' might rank first among Manus Domini's priorities, and—why not admit it—those of Palermo as well. Which could suit someone all too well."

"Eminence, I don't see what you're driving at."

"To someone who happens to share your same address in Via Veneto, that's what I am driving at," the cardinal said, his jowls quivering. "And this puts everyone under pressure, beginning with us, to reach an agreement with Joint Affairs: on their conditions, needless to say. Isn't that so?"

Fox turned pale and jumped to his feet. "Your insinuations are offensive! Your Eminence has no proof."

"I have no proof, but Saturday night's bombing was in true CIA style: strike in the dark, making sure that someone else gets blamed. We're not idiots on this side of the Tiber, keep that in mind."

"I can only repeat that the CIA was in no way involved! Is there any point in arguing over mere suspicions?"

The cardinal gave Fox a long look. Was he telling the truth? No, the man was just an accomplished actor. Moreover he was a diplomat, and hence an institutional liar. However, as matters stood, pushing things too far would be counterproductive. The message for Abramson, now, was clear.

The cardinal signaled Fox to sit down again, in a conciliatory manner. Albeit reluctantly, the ambassador obeyed.

Fox opened his briefcase and took out the Palermo list. "You may be interested to know that Joint Affairs has approved the Palermo list."

"I'm glad to hear that. Now, though, it's time to talk about another list, Mr. Ambassador."

Fox frowned. "What other list?"

"Manus Domini's."

"I thought our agreement was implicit."

"That was just your impression. Joint Affairs will propose the prime minister and the technical ministers, but our *initiati* will occupy all the administrative posts."

"*All of them*? Isn't that pushing things too far, Your Eminence?"

"If you think Manus Domini is on the ropes because of Saturday night's bombing, you should think again."

"Is that a threat?"

"Just a warning. We're ready to join forces with Palermo only and cut you out of the running, if necessary."

Fox stared at the cardinal's impassive face, then gave a ghost of a tight smile. "I'm sure we'll reach an agreement."

"I have no doubt about that, Mr. Ambassador. No doubt at all." The cardinal slapped the palms of his hands down on the arms of his chair. "Within two weeks I shall let you have Manus Domini's list."

Fox held out his hand. "Your Eminence, we're in business."

The cardinal shook Fox's hand, fully aware it was a diplomatic handshake on both sides. His sixth sense told him that, of the two, Palermo remained the more trustworthy ally.

Guichard sat up, put a pillow behind his back and leaned against the headboard. The alarm clock read 3:00 a.m. Silence sharpened the images of the day before, when he'd seen Françoise at the Louvre. He pictured her profile and the way she stared at the Poussin.

He felt the warmth of her body and the things he saw and heard whenever he held her in his arms: the scent of resin wafting from the woods, surf effacing the imprints of feet on the seashore, moonlight shining on the undulating sand dunes, and an echo of voices endlessly chasing each other—voices now muffled and shrill a moment later, then fading away in a cloud of sand.

Thou shalt leave her, said the Voice. *The curiosity of that female will be the ruin of us.*

Guichard kept silent.

I am cognizant of thy thoughts, but thou deceivest thyself. What thou watchest is only the reverberation of a dream.

It's you who are mistaken. You yourself said it. She has come back.

And even if that were true? said the Voice. *Dost thou hope that she hath come back for thee?*

You were already mistaken once. You could be again.

What meanest thou?

You seem to forget what she said.

The wings of my memory span over nine centuries, thou mortal.

On the evening you dined at the tavern, she said: *"We're capable of implacable hatred, but when we love someone, we love deeply, and forever.... A love that goes on even after death."*

What knowest thou of what happeneth beyond the "tunnel of the great light"?

Enough to realize that she didn't come back by chance.

Thou persistest in yearning for the impossible. No mortal has ever gone back in time.

Who says so? You, only because you haven't done it? Nothing is written.

Thou dolt! Such is thy arrogance, that thou darest challenge the laws of celestial spheres.

The prison of this body will not prevent me from realizing my dream.

Enough! To chase a winged horse, thou forgettest what must be done. If thou dost not keep thy word and leave her, Arno's spirit will persecute thee throughout eternity. Remember thou Porte St. Antoine!

Amid a swirl of flashing chiaroscuros, elongated cross-shaped shadows stood out against the walls. Guichard closed his eyes, grimaced with pain and pressed his hands over his ears. With a stifled cry he fell to his knees.

I'll do it, damn you, but stop. Go away!

Then shalt thou do it this very instant.

It's three o'clock in the morning!

This very instant!

Guichard grabbed a pillow and hurled it across the room. The lamp on the night table shattered to the floor. He sat on the side of the bed and reached for the phone with a leaden hand.

§

Françoise awoke and for a moment wondered whether she was dreaming. It was the phone. The phosphorescent hands of the alarm clock showed 3:20. She groped for the light switch.

"I don't know how to apologize for waking you at this hour, but I absolutely must speak to you," Guichard said, his tone grave.

"What's the matter? Why that voice?"

There was a pause laden with uncertainty. "I could say I have to go away, or invent a hundred other excuses, each one sillier than the one before. But not with you."

Françoise said nothing.

"I think it's better if we don't see each other for a while, just for a few months."

"I see."

"No, I doubt it. My feelings for you haven't changed."

"If that were true you wouldn't be making this phone call."

"Please. Try to understand. How many times have I told you? I've got a very important thing to take care of, but soon it'll all be over and —"

"No, Guichard, it'll never be over."

"What do you mean?"

"You're lying to yourself, as well as to me. And this from the very first moment."

Guichard remained silent.

"No one likes to be the mirror of a dream," Françoise said.

Silence.

"Goodbye Guichard." Françoise hung up.

Françoise lay down on her back and covered her face with an arm. Her mind took her back to that summer spent in the Austrian mountains.

Wearing *lederhosen* held up with colorful suspenders, she ran to her father in the meadow around the chalet her parents had rented for the summer near Seefeld, in Tyrol. The meadow was a palette of wild flowers, and the windowsills an exultation of red geraniums. The air was laden with the scents of summer and with certainties glowing like sunrays. Her father opened his arms, lifted her above his head, and whirled her around in an endless merry-go-round, their laughs blending. Then he hugged her, and his sandpaper moustache stung her face, its odor of cigar mingling with the scent of his after-shave. Time seemed to have stopped that summer.

She couldn't tell how long she'd been lying there, lost in that sort of drowsiness. She forced herself to get up, went into the bathroom, and turned on the hot-water tap. She sat on the edge of the bathtub, swathed in the cloud of warm steam. She slipped off her nightgown, lay down in the tub, and closed her eyes.

A slight draught of cold air brushed her left shoulder and she turned to see if the door was open.

Françoise suddenly straightened: her eyes froze on the steamed mirror above the vanity. Some words were being written across it, drawn in an ancient style of handwriting.

"Discover thou his secret, and he will discover himself."

19

"I have Zergas on the red line, Prime Minister," said Accardo's secretary over the intercom.

"Put him through."

"We've just received the official proposal from de Saint Clair," Zergas said.

"Call a board meeting of CIP right away," Accardo said.

"It'll be held next Monday."

"Good. Any problems?"

"That damn Ricci of the Renovation Party again."

"What does he want, this time?"

"A top position in the joint venture with the Americans."

"Give him what he wants and let's get it over with."

"That's easy to say."

"Where is the problem?"

"The problem is Ricci. A downright incompetent, to say the least."

"You surprise me, Antigono. Have you forgotten the Peter Principle? If Ricci were not incompetent, he wouldn't be where he is."

"Leo, this is no time for jokes. If Ricci ends up at the top of that joint venture, believe you me, we won't be helping either the Americans or ourselves. Furthermore, we'll stink to high heaven from Rome to Hawaii."

"All I care about is the political side. You should know that."

"But—"

"I have a dossier on Ricci. He's a cold-blooded cutthroat. With what he knows—think of the plants down south—he is capable of raising a question in the House, and then talking the minority parties into withdrawing their vote of confidence. Is the picture clear?"

Dusk was falling on Paris, and the lights from the *quais* of the Seine cast silver blades on the water.

Guichard went down the steps leading to the embankment of the Seine, stopped a moment to glance at the river, then walked towards Notre Dame. The sounds of the city came through muffled, smothered by the squawks of the seagulls hovering over the river…. Feelings of a bygone Paris, which seemed to jump out of an Utrillo painting.

"You are lying to yourself, as well as to me…"

"What do you mean?"

"No one likes to be the mirror of a dream."

Silence.

Her words resounded in his mind over and over again, like a gramophone needle stuck in the groove of an old record. Why had he kept silent? Because of the inner admission that Françoise's words had revealed something he wasn't ready to admit even to himself? Or maybe because his rational side had decided that that was the way things should go? That final *"Good bye, Guichard"* had frozen him and words had failed him.

Françoise had given him the inebriating illusion of finding something again that he'd lost in another world, a long time ago, and now he felt adrift, like a survivor from a wreck. Emptiness had a bitter taste, even more so because, deep down, he'd grown used to thinking he was self-sufficient, and had built an invisible screen around himself. That way pain, like the one he'd suffered as a boy, wouldn't touch him any more. If you gave people little of yourself, you didn't risk being hurt. Perhaps you missed out on life, but this was the price you had to pay.

Guichard sat down on a bench. His eyes followed a *bateau-mouche* gliding leisurely past on the Seine, its lights winking in the darkness. A load of light-heartedness carried away by the songs of Edith Piaf and by dreams cut out of a travel brochure.

There was something magical about being a tourist: getting away. You had the illusion of leaving behind your everyday world, and setting off to discover a fantasy world full of expectation, a world whose colored paper promises seemed like Eden only because, even if you didn't want to admit it, you had a return ticket in your pocket. The certainty you'd soon be returning to your humdrum everyday life was like a safe harbor, and so getting away for a few days took on a magic touch.

A burst of laughter mingled with the squawks of the seagulls. A one-way ticket and they wouldn't be laughing quite so much. One-way trips were frightening — to other people.

Clouds of hydrogen and interstellar gas exploded in space in a silent phantasmagoria of primordial flames. Whole galaxies rolled around him. They expanded and contracted, then moved away faster than the speed of light, in a universe in continuous expansion. Worlds that even the most powerful radio telescopes couldn't have discovered because light would never have caught up with them. Space and time, taken individually, no longer made sense, and they merged into a four-dimensional space-time impossible to see from down here on Earth, where one was prisoner of his own senses. Worlds where there was no yesterday, no today, and no tomorrow, where you only perceived the awe-inspiring immutability of an everlasting present.... Worlds that for the first time appeared to you as they really were, and not through the distorting lenses of subjective thought.

In that cosmic dance, it wasn't only space and time that vanished, though, but your identity, too. You looked at the world from a superior state of consciousness, completely detached from things human, for you became one with the consciousness of the universe. The infinite faces of Françoise no longer brought him pain. Nothing touched him anymore, up there. In each of the worlds that flashed past him, enormous black rings spun at a frightening speed in their orbits around galaxies. They orbited in pairs, linked together by a sort of floating tunnel.... *Black holes.*

"*Monsieur, vous ne vous sentez pas bien?*—Sir, don't you feel well?"

Guichard looked up in the direction of the voice. "*No, merci, Monsieur l'agent.—Tout va bien.* I'm fine, officer, thank you."

The *flic* looked at him doubtfully, then raised his baton to his kepi and walked off.

Now the thought of Françoise started to hurt again. Guichard stroked his arm. Feeling pain made you feel human, though, even if defenseless. Up there, in that cosmic dimension, one didn't feel pain, but one couldn't feel hope either, or hate, or love.

The conclusion? A nasty trick. Pain, both physical and moral, was inseparable from the human condition. Throughout his life Man struggled to escape pain. Yet he remained the unconscious victim of an insoluble inner contradiction: even if he managed to achieve his aim, not only would he stop appreciating it, but he would also miss his former ability to feel pain.

Maybe there was a way out, though. Jumping into one of those black holes and reversing the hands of time, so making what "could have been" become reality. Yet no one could travel back in time taking the future with them, science said. But what if someone managed to do it? *A paradox.*

An impossible undertaking, yet with all the appeal of impossible undertakings. Certainly, the return ticket would take you back to a parallel world, different from the one you'd left: no home, no job, no familiar faces.... This would be the price of the return ticket.

But who said that one had to come back?

In the afternoon sun, the Jardin de Luxembourg glowed with the warm hues of late summer. Couples drifted in rowboats on the ponds, elderly people played chess in the shade of striped awnings, and children played hide-and-seek among the plane trees, their cries mingling with the babbling of the Renaissance-style Fontaine Médicis.

Françoise's gaze rested for a moment on the central niche of the fountain. A huge bronze Polyphemus, kneeling on a rock, was staring down with a threatening frown, caught on the verge of flinging a stone at the shepherd Aci, his rival in love, who was holding Galatea in his arms.

"No one likes to be the mirror of a dream."

Silence.

"Goodbye, Guichard."

Why had she reacted like that? Was it pride? Or was it because she'd never before been dropped like that? Or because she'd been afraid of hearing the truth? If she'd mastered her feelings better, maybe things would have gone differently.

"Discover thou his secret, and he will discover himself."

She could see the letters again, as they were being drawn on the steamed-up mirror in that handwriting both childlike and ancient. Her hand clutched a railing. Suddenly she turned and walked away.

Françoise sat down on the grass in the shadow of a tree. Her eyes followed a bird skimming over a nearby pond.

Maybe Guichard had been telling the truth, but it was *his* truth, the one he'd fabricated for himself, for he himself lacked the courage to face reality. *"No one likes to be the mirror of a dream,"* she had said, and now she was convinced more than ever that those words summarized the mystery. What was his dream? And what was the being looking for? Why did she seem so interested in having Françoise discover Guichard's secret?

Françoise opened her handbag, took out the small chain, and stared at the rearing unicorn on the blackened medallion. Her heart felt heavy.

With that *"Goodbye, Guichard,"* she'd purposely made him face a choice, taking the risk. But the silence that had followed had disconcerted her. What was the point, now, in continuing to ponder what might have been? His silence showed that in him reason was stronger than emotion. It was nothing but the everlasting conflict between opposites: reason and feelings, yin and yang, sun and moon, black and white....

Françoise assumed the lotus position, fixed her eyes on a stone and concentrated on her breathing. "Reality" experienced through the subjective ego was just an illusion, an illusion caused by senses that distort the outside world the very moment we look at something. Her mind began to drift in a succession of disconnected thoughts. In the end, all that remained was the awareness of her breathing, and she was one with it.

Like a feather floating in the sky, blown this way and that by the breeze... her body was down there, sitting in the grass, and she was drifting farther away. It was like expanding in space and inhaling infinity: higher and higher, reaching out to a new dimension of space and time.

And finally there was the Void, where she became part of Absolute Reality, an infinite series of universes where time and space existed no longer, and where she was pure consciousness.

"*Ouch!*"

Françoise rubbed her head and looked around dazed.... The gardens! The red ball that had hit her was lying on the grass just in front of her.

"*Excusez moi, Madame,*" said the child—he might have been around four or five. He was watching her from a few yards away, his forefinger stuck in his mouth.

"*Pas de problèmes. Tiens, petit,*" Françoise said, getting up and tossing him the ball.

She breathed in the colors, the scents of the flowers, the shouting of the children. The thought of Guichard aroused in her the same feeling of emptiness as before, but now she felt alive again. An expression of resignation flickered in her eyes.

No, the solution to the problem couldn't be found in a Zen monastery. If so, why not stick a big signpost on Earth, saying: Sorry—Closed for Meditation Until Further Notice? The nirvana of the senses could be useful for numbing occasional pain, but could it provide a stable solution to her problems? She was a human being, and, whether she liked it or not, she had to learn to live with the limits imposed on her by her senses. Pain was part of our humanity; what kind of world would this be, without pain?

Françoise put the medallion back in her handbag. Guichard would follow his logic, which would certainly lead him into doing the wrong thing. On the contrary, luckily for him, she'd go ahead availing herself of her intuition.

She got up, headed for the gate, and mingled with the crowd in Boulevard Saint Michel.

In spite of the lack of wind and of the stillness pervading the Jardin de Luxembourg, the leafy fronds of the plane trees around the Fontaine Médicis rustled and bent.

A ray of sunlight filtered through the leaves and illuminated the face of the marble statue of Galatea.

"Mr. Astarita on line one," Marie Claire said on the intercom.

Guichard picked up the phone.

"… And so this makes a hundred and fifty-one banks," Astarita said. "The total amount is the equivalent of 70,000 billion lire."

Guichard looked at the calendar: barely ten days had gone by since his trip to Sicily.

"Whose names are the accounts in?" he said.

"All dummy companies."

"How about the options?"

"I'm pooling some sixty banks."

"Remember that I need a ratio of one to ten."

"I haven't forgotten. The credit line amounts to 3,000 billion lire, but it will enable you to buy options for 30,000 billion." Astarita paused: "All together that makes 100,000 billion lire. How long will you need to invest all that money?"

"Options can cause problems. First, I've got to see how the market reacts."

"How long will it take?"

"No less than two months."

"Why so long?"

"If you buy six-month lira/dollar options, it means you're selling lire and buying dollars for that deadline, fixing the exchange rate against the payment of a 'premium.' Do you follow me?"

"Franzese is a good school," Astarita said.

"Then you understand that if we were to flood the market with a purchase order of 30,000 billion lire, we'd risk sinking the lira. And we certainly don't want that—at least not now."

"Yeah, I doubt if Tano would be very pleased with that."
Then, after a pause, Astarita said: "Guichard...?"

"What?"

"Make sure nothing goes wrong." The line went dead.

Guichard remained motionless, the receiver still in his hand,
listening to the dial tone. He hung up.

No, there wouldn't be any mistakes. For the Voice's sake,
then for the Lodge's — and *lastly* for Franzese's.

Guichard went over to a globe that stood in a corner of his
study, and slowly turned it around. The Isle of Man, Jersey and
Guernsey would do for Europe. He moved his finger on to the
Caribbean: St Kitts and Nevis, the Turks and Caicos Islands. He
traced a line northward off Central America, towards Florida.
No doubt: Barbados, the Bahamas, Bermuda and the Cayman
Islands. In the end, he turned the globe a bit further east and
stopped at the South Pacific: the Vanuatus.

Guichard went back to his desk and dialed Paulette's number. "Paulette, can you join me in my office?"

"Ten firms are no small number," Paulette said when
Guichard finished outlining his plan.

"It's nothing but the usual dummy companies operating
from tax havens," Guichard said dismissively. He handed
Paulette a business card. "It's a firm of tax accountants based in
Douglas, Isle of Man. They always have a few hundred brand
new companies in store, complete with directors and trustee
shareholders."

"I see. So one buys the full package. How long will it take?"

"Oh, just a few days. They'll take care of everything directly
from Man."

"Which countries should those companies be registered in?"

Guichard gave Paulette a sheet. "I've jotted down a list of
ten offshore centers."

Paulette read the list. "Quite a program indeed."

"Neither our name, nor our client's, will ever appear anywhere."

"We'll have to set up a trust for each company, then."

"Sure, but that won't be enough. From the very beginning, we will need the letters—not dated and already signed— proffering the directors' resignations. Oh, and don't forget. The share transfer certificates must already be signed as well."

"What are those companies up to?"

Guichard waved a hand vaguely. "A large-scale transaction on behalf of a client who wants to remain incognito. People are strange at times, you know."

Paulette looked Guichard straight in the eye. "They are indeed."

When he was alone again, Guichard went back to the globe, and spun it. He stopped on Brazil, and put his finger on Manaus, in the center of the Amazon forest.

♣

Geoffroy fumed. Why hadn't Archambaud come out yet? He glanced at an hourglass. He'd already been waiting half an hour for him to appear to change shifts, since the bells of the Church of the Holy Sepulcher had rung the none. Perhaps something had happened. He grabbed a torch and went into the passage. When he reached the end, he turned into the tunnel. In the flickering light of his torch, his grotesque shadow was dancing on the walls.

Geoffroy thought of the flooding three years earlier. A real disaster. Thank God, Archambaud hadn't given in. Geoffroy had watched him working together with the men, the water rushing into his face from a crack in the wall, until they'd managed to stop the leak. But that deviation had cost them two years of extra work. Would this wretched tunnel ever be finished?

That was a special day: July the fifteenth in the year of our Lord 1127, nine years to the day since they'd arrived in Jerusalem. But still nothing. Damnation! And yet, just one week earlier, Archambaud had confirmed that they'd covered the three hundred and ninety-four feet to the Al Kas fountain, and without taking the deviations into account.

As soon as Geoffroy turned round the last bend, the tunnel got brighter and the picks' dull thuds reached his ears. At the

end of the tunnel, seated on a boulder, Archambaud was studying a map by torchlight, while two men were swinging their
picks at the walls.

"Have you decided to do my shift too, by any chance?"
Geoffroy said.

The two laborers went on digging. They didn't understand
French. Nineteen different languages were spoken in Jerusalem;
worse than in Babylon.

Archambaud turned his sandglass upside down, laid his
map on a rock, and made a helpless gesture. "I just don't understand."

"What?"

"There aren't any more props, which means that the tunnel
ends here." He banged his pick against the wall at the end of
the tunnel. "We've tapped everywhere. And yet nothing."

"Are you sure this is the end? The roof might have caved in
again."

"No, I've just told you, the props end here. Besides, this wall
can hardly be the result of a ceiling collapsing." Archambaud
scraped the wall in several spots with the tip of the pick. "Just
look at it. It's all rock."

Geoffroy pointed upwards. "Have you tried on the roof?"

"On the *roof*? Are you mad? I hope you've read the Bible,
Geoffroy de Saint Clair."

"Of course I've read it, but I just don't see what that has to
do with it."

"Well, you should know one thing, then: whoever touches
the Ark dies."

"What are you blathering about? You continue to speak like
someone who's just seen St. George's dragon."

"You impertinent whoreson! Just why do you think King
Solomon dug this tunnel?"

"To ensure a way to get the Ark out, of course, in case of
danger."

"And how would they have lowered the Ark, if they'd built
a trap door in the floor of the Holy of Holies?"

Geoffroy scratched his beard. "Hmm, I see what you mean."

"The Ark can only be transported by passing the two staves through the four corner rings," Archambaud said. Then he pointed heavenwards. "God was very exacting—Exodus 25: 8-10—when he gave Moses His instructions."

A gleam flashed through Geoffroy's eyes. "Tell me something. If you were to hide a treasure in a room, where would you build a secret way out? In one of the side walls?"

"All right, you crafty bastard, I'd say 'in the floor,' but then how would you lower the Ark?"

Geoffroy shrugged. "Supported by its staves. How else?"

"Oh, really? And what would support the staves?"

"Ropes around the four corners. There's no mention either in Exodus or any of the other books of the Old Testament that this can't be done."

Archambaud looked at Geoffroy in silence. "All right. Let's suppose for a moment that things are as you say." He pointed his finger at the roof. "Then why haven't we found a trap-door? The roof's made of limestone, which means that no one's ever been through here."

Archambaud tapped the roof over his head with his pick. Then he did the same for a couple of yards in front of him and behind. It was solid rock.

"Is it clear now?" Archambaud said.

"What of it? Obviously no one's ever had to use the secret passage."

"But that's absurd! Even if no one's ever used it, nevertheless I have no doubt that King Solomon still had to provide a trap door somewhere."

"But the trap door has always been there, don't you see? We know from the Bible that the Holy of Holies is completely lined with sheets of gold. All King Solomon and the High Priest needed to know was that access to the passage was hidden under certain sheets on the floor."

"But if someone had lifted them, they'd only have found earth and limestone rock," Archambaud said. "Unless—"

"Unless what?"

"Unless King Solomon had built the tunnel starting from the stables, stopping exactly under the Holy of Holies, and deliberately keeping a certain depth under the floor."

"*Exactly,*" replied Geoffroy with a triumphant look. He raised a finger. "'And God gave Solomon wisdom and exceedingly great understanding, and largeness of heart like the sand on the seashore' — Kings I:4-29 — just to show you that I've read the Bible. Would you expect anything less, from such a man?"

Archambaud didn't reply, but started to aim hard blows at the ceiling.

"Wait a minute. Let's move over a little, on my side." Geoffroy took hold of a pick. "The staves for carrying the Ark were ten cubits long, so roughly... fifteen feet."

Geoffroy paced a distance of about eight feet from the end of the tunnel, and pointed to the ceiling. "I say we should try here."

Archambaud and Geoffroy took turns aiming blows at the roof. Half an hour later they stopped. Geoffroy wiped the sweat from his brow. His hand was slimy with mud and his mouth felt gritty. He spat on the ground. Archambaud leaned on the wall, panting. The men were looking at them out of the corner of their eyes. In all those years, it was the first time they'd seen *them* working in the tunnel.

The torch behind them flickered and went out. One of the men fetched another — a bundle of sticks of highly resinous wood — dipped it into a barrel of resin, fat and wax and lit it from another torch burning on the wall a couple of yards further along. Geoffroy gestured to the man to hand him the new torch, and he brought it near the hole. It was twenty inches wide and about eight inches deep.

"Come on, we should get started again," Archambaud said. "We'll do another four inches or so, and then let them take over."

Geoffroy took hold of his pick and aimed a hard blow at the ceiling. The tip hit something hard. A metallic sound came from the roof and resounded along the tunnel.

A painful vibration ran along Geoffroy's arm.

20

Professor Amati was the right man. Françoise's mind went back to her holiday in Crete two years before. Amati, a retired professor of Greek and Latin from Bologna, and his wife had been staying at her hotel. Françoise had struck up a friendship with them. She remembered lazing on the beach in the blazing sun of Elounda, while the professor told stories of Roman and Greek mythology.

She found the number in her address book, then reached for the phone. A few moments later, she heard the professor's friendly voice on the other end....

The following day, Françoise had just got home from the gallery and was taking off her shoes, when the phone rang.

"... Are you sure, Professor?" asked Françoise.

"Absolutely," Amati said. "Virgil never wrote that phrase, nor did any other Latin poet."

"Yet many sources attribute it to him."

"Probably because Virgil wrote bucolics. The theme of an idyllic world is recurrent in his works."

"Couldn't it be that his bucolics contain other verses which are somehow linked with *Et in Arcadia ego*?"

"You never give up, do you? Well, just to leave no stone unturned, I'll check it over again, and I'll call you back in the next couple of days."

Three days went by, and still Amati hadn't rung back. Françoise glanced at her watch, shut her book on the Knights Templar, and through the terrace railings she gazed at the lights of the Café de Flore. Why not call him? She was about to get up when the phone rang. She ran into the living room and picked up the phone: *Amati.*

"None of Virgil's works, including the bucolics, contains that phrase, either as a whole or partially," the professor said.

"I don't know what to do."

"Resign yourself. Your phrase has no classical origin. To find out more, you're going to have to delve into the lives of the two painters."

"Do you think the creator of *Et in Arcadia ego* could have been inspired by those verses?"

"That I don't know, but one thing I do know. Whoever created that phrase wasn't just a learned man, but also a lover of the classics."

"Have you got any ideas?"

"Guercino was the first person to use the phrase. I'd start with him, by trying to find out who commissioned his work. And you know what? I'd look for a man of the Church."

"Why?"

"Guercino's commissions came from men of the Church. He had many friends and patrons among them."

Cardinals and popes behind Guercino's works, cardinals behind Poussin's.... Both Guercino and Poussin had lived in Rome. Françoise thought of the reproduction in Guichard's house and of the way he'd reacted. It must have all started with the first Templars in Jerusalem. Five centuries later, Poussin had come to know the secret in Rome, and had entrusted it to the muse's expression.

The secret must be hidden in that phrase, *Et in Arcadia ego.* Perhaps "ego" didn't refer to Death at all. Françoise remembered something Guichard had said, when he'd shown her his collection.

"*'Ego' refers to Death, doesn't it?*" she had said.

"*Er, yes.... Death exists even in the sort of paradise on earth that Arcadia represented in Greek mythology.... That's what Poussin intended the inscription to mean.*"

Guichard's tone had been too hasty, though, and she'd noticed his hand clenching and unclenching. He'd lied to her.

What, or who, lay behind that "ego"?

"Monsignore, I want today to be a *sine die*, except for the substitute and for Monsignor Petrov," said Cardinal Wolfenberg to Monsignor Feliciani. For the whole day he would receive nobody, with these two exceptions.

"But Your Eminence, I would remind you that—"

"Please don't waste my time, Monsignore. Move everything to some other day."

The monsignor bowed and left the cardinal's study.

The cardinal swirled his cup and gulped the last dregs of coffee down. Then, without getting up, he gave his chair a half-spin, pushed himself towards the middle of the room, and looked up at the triad of frescoes that covered the wall behind his desk. The one on the left showed the young David in the act of picking up one of five stones that lay at his feet. In the center one, David was swinging his sling in the air, preparing to smite Goliath, the Philistine giant. In the third one, David was holding up the giant's head, dripping with blood.

The cardinal recalled his meeting the previous day with Ambassador Fox. A lasting alliance between Manus Domini and Joint Affairs? He snickered. It was like imagining an alliance between David and Goliath.

The Joint Affairs Commission, the modern reincarnation of a Goliath, brainwashed the world with advertising and hammered false myths into people's heads. The purpose of all that? To produce faithful consumers. Their only yardstick was the annual growth of GNP per capita. No wonder. *They* were the GNP!

The myths about progress and prosperity were a devilish trick to undermine Man's spiritual values. Excessive GNP growth brought out people's basic instincts, and the outcome was abortion, homosexuality, debatable ideas regarding equality and other crazy things like that. Progress? Yes, but under strict control. Prosperity? Yes, but with parsimony.

So, the critics insisted that Manus Domini was elitist, feudal, and permeated with pre-Vatican II extremisms. The cardinal slapped his thigh. Thank God those allegations were all true! These were hard times, and Manus Domini needed to stick to its values, like David to his sling. The *initiati* of Manus and the Knights of Malta would take up the sword and charge into battle against this degrading materialism with the spirit of the old Templars.

His plan would mean a battle with Father Cafiero, the father general at the head of Manus Domini, but he already knew how to tackle the problem: His Holiness! How? He chuckled. A little secret. His Holiness loved Manus Domini, but he loved even more a Manus Domini spurred on by the spirit of a crusader knight.

The money necessary to finance the election campaign of the Manus candidates, after Palermo had done their "wiping out," wouldn't be a problem. On paper, Manus Domini appeared poor: in reality it was rich, much richer than even their worst critics could ever imagine. A legal stratagem had settled the matter. Money was collected through various foundations having no legal connection with Manus. However, it was Manus Domini that controlled the foundations' boards of directors, and consequently the flow of money.

The cardinal rolled his chair back behind his desk, pressed down hard on the intercom, and asked Monsignor Feliciani to call Father Cafiero.

The Mercedes was waiting for the cardinal in front of the main door of the palace, Father Emilio holding the rear door open. The cardinal strode out of the palace.

"To Villa Rebecca, Father Emilio."

The Mercedes crossed St. Peter's Square, and drove along Via della Conciliazione. The cardinal looked absent-mindedly at the circular structure of Castel Sant'Angelo as they drove past.

This time the matter wouldn't be solved just by drawing up a list of names, or by splitting a few billion lire: they had come to the final reckoning, with the power within the Church at stake.

The contestants were Manus Domini on one side, and the progressive movements within the Curia led by Cardinal Missiroli, the secretary of state, on the other. The clash between Cardinal Missiroli and himself sprang from a simple question: was it right to take the Church back to a situation prior to the Second Vatican Council? Or should the Church be allowed to carry on towards the abyss opened up by Vatican II?

He could already see the Substitute Dyakonov seated on St. Peter's throne and he himself in the chair of Manus Domini's father general, but with one fundamental difference, when compared with the past: it would be Villa Rebecca that would show the Apostolic Palace the way, and not vice versa.

After Porta Settimiana the road started climbing. Finally they drove through Porta di San Pancrazio and across Parco del Gianicolo dotted with statues. The cardinal caught a glimpse of the familiar tower rising above Villa Rebecca, the patrician villa surrounded by plane trees where Manus Domini had its international headquarters. Every time he approached the villa, he envisaged a flock of vultures hovering over the tower.

They drew up in front of the main gate and Father Emilio sounded the horn.

Father Cafiero was wearing a plain cassock. A large wooden crucifix hung behind him. This narcissistic show of monastic humility always had the effect of enraging the cardinal. But he didn't allow himself to be misled by appearances. The father general's dark eyes revealed a rare inner strength, the pallor of his complexion making them even more intense. The cardinal didn't envy Manus Domini's members, especially the resident *alumni*. He himself, a man used to the rigors of the CDF interrogations, felt uneasy when he found himself face to face with this man.

"Your Eminence, your project is not lacking in basic logic," said Father Cafiero after Cardinal Wolfenberg finished. "Are you sure you've considered all the negative aspects?"

"The skilled chess player doesn't neglect any move, Father."

"Allow me to disagree, Your Eminence — in all humility. Your plan may be valid in the short term, but in the long run Joint Affairs might prevail."

"Quite the opposite. My plan, in the new Italy looming on the horizon, will put Manus Domini in a position of even greater power than it had in Spain with Generalissimo Franco, or in Argentina at the time of Peron."

"You seem not to consider the danger of exposing the Holy See and Manus Domini to accusations, at the very least, of plotting against Italy's internal security."

"Theoretically your observation is quite correct, but it comes just a bit late: by at least half a century."

"Would you care to elaborate, Your Eminence? I beg your pardon, but I am only a modest chess player."

"What is there to explain? Manus Domini's history is a Crusade in favor of power and money."

"It pains me to hear this from you, of all people. Manus Domini's ultimate aim is quite different."

"Is that so?" Cardinal Wolfenberg said with the air of a wolf that has just sighted a lamb. "And just what exactly is the ultimate aim?"

"Need you ask, Your Eminence? It's to ensure that its members purify their spirit through daily work, and help others to do the same."

"Father, keep the official refrains for the outside world and for the many courts of law where Manus Domini has to provide explanations of its work." The cardinal waved his hand in annoyance. "Here we're playing on home ground, and you're talking to someone who has made a career in dialectics. Don't steal my job, please."

"Making converts requires material means. Power and money are merely instruments needed to help us spread the truth."

"Father, why drag the truth into this? The truth lies at the bottom of a bottomless pit."

Referring then to the lay *initiati*, the cardinal asked the father general to tell him just how many peasants, manual workers and simple clerical workers were members of Manus, compared with the number of people in positions of power in finance, industry and politics.

"I don't see the connection," Father Cafiero said.

"You know only too well that we could count the number of *initiati* who don't occupy positions of power on the fingers of one hand."

"With due respect to Your Eminence, the matter is of no relevance," said Father Cafiero in an icy tone. "I have the distinct impression that Your Eminence is here to attack Manus Domini, to which Your Eminence himself belongs."

"I would remind you that the duty of Manus Domini is to bring the Church back to a central position in society, and that calls for a fighting spirit."

"My original criticism was only meant to be constructive. I just wanted to stress the possible dangers in your project."

"Are you telling me you don't intend to back my proposal?" the cardinal said.

"Your Eminence, why enter into an open confrontation? I will only suggest you develop your plan over a longer period of time."

Father Cafiero was the father general, and the cardinal knew only too well that he needed his signature to transfer money from Manus Domini's foreign foundations. The Spaniard's reserve derived from the fear—not-ungrounded—that with this project he, Cardinal Wolfenberg, would become the Holy See's most powerful man, and Manus Domini's too. The dear father general seemed to be forgetting a minor detail, though: Manus Domini had sworn blind obedience to the pope.

"I felt it was my duty to inform you," the cardinal said, casting a withering glance at Father Cafiero. "My plan will be on the agenda of the *Consiglio Generale* next Thursday."

Father Cafiero threw up his hands, palms upward, in a calculated gesture of false resignation. "As chairman of the Manus Domini board, Eminence, it is within your power."

§

Father Cafiero drew the curtain back and watched the cardinal get into the car. His eyes followed the Mercedes moving off along the driveway. He went back to his desk and pressed the button on the intercom.

"Father, please get me Cardinal Missiroli."

21

"No other Renaissance painter quite equaled Mantegna in the art of perspective, wouldn't you agree, Father?" said Cardinal Missiroli, secretary of state of the Holy See, waving his hand toward the frescoes that covered the walls of his study.

Father Cafiero mumbled an unintelligible answer.

"What can I do for you, Father?"

Father Cafiero fidgeted in his chair. "I must ask you to consider this an informal discussion, Your Eminence," he murmured, glancing nervously in the direction of the pope's private apartments.

A shrewd gleam flashed across the cardinal's eyes. "As you wish."

Father Cafiero told the secretary of state about Cardinal Wolfenberg's visit the day before.

"The repercussions of Cardinal Wolfenberg's plan could be disastrous," Father Cafiero said.

"Why didn't you speak with the Holy Father? After all, Manus Domini is directly responsible to His Holiness."

"His Holiness might have believed that my initiative was due to differences of opinion with Cardinal Wolfenberg."

"And is that not the case?"

"Up to now there has never been any disagreement with His Eminence. I'm truly concerned."

"Allow me to express my surprise at this disagreement."

"May I ask why, Your Eminence?"

"Because Cardinal Wolfenberg's plan sounds perfect, from *your* point of view. Not only would it bring the Church back to its state prior to Vatican II, but it would also restore its temporal power."

"Your Eminence, with all due respect, I must disagree with your statement. Many people persist in misinterpreting our aims, perhaps because of the undeniably elitist composition of our lay members."

"Father, you persist in denying the evidence. The secretariat of state has to handle recurrent diplomatic problems in the many countries where Manus Domini has been taken to court."

"Have we not the right to defend our reputation?"

"May I remind you that many of those lawsuits have been promoted by former members of Manus Domini, who left you in circumstances that were, to say the least, highly unpropitious."

Father Cafiero was about to reply, but Cardinal Missiroli raised a hand for silence.

"Father, what's the point of continuing? However, I will mention the matter to His Holiness, but only because I consider it my duty."

"Thank you, Your Eminence. I regret that our views remain so far apart."

"It is the secretariat of state's duty to maintain harmony in today's difficult world. And this implies respecting freedom of thought. It's one of the guidelines that emerged from the Second Vatican Council."

"Manus Domini has always respected those guidelines."

"Father, Father, do not offend my intelligence. I am a statesman and a diplomat: this chair has taught me a thing or two about people."

"You seem hostile to Manus Domini—with all due respect, Your Eminence."

"Just like the rest of the outside world, is that not so?" Cardinal Missiroli said. "Manus Domini is a feudal, elitist sect, deaf to all democratic issues. Father, you are going against history, and against the Church itself."

"Your Eminence, I don't believe anything I could say would make you change your opinion, which is prejudiced."

"Do you know what the real problem is in Manus Domini?"

"I would be happy to hear any suggestion Your Eminence may have," Father Cafiero said with a subtle smile.

"You have not yet realized the fact that Man has urgent need now more than ever before for spirituality and love. Today's world has no use for people like you, people who feel no love or compassion for anyone or anything." The cardinal stood. "I wish you a pleasant evening, Father."

"Your Eminence," Father Cafiero said, bowing his head slightly. Then he turned and left.

§

As soon as Father Cafiero left, the cardinal leaned against the back of his chair and rubbed his eyes slowly. Then he joined the palms of his hands, as if he were praying, and began to drum his fingertips against one another. Finally he sighed and shook his head. His gaze rested on the framed photographs hanging on the walls.

Those photographs had been taken during the 70's and 80's, when the cardinal had been Apostolic Delegate in Lima, Santiago, and São Paulo.

Frozen smiles, diplomatic handshakes, dictators, degrading poverty, the courage of a few Brazilian cardinals—such as Cardinals Arns and Lorscheider—Liberation Theology sweeping throughout South America like a tornado, the clash with the Vatican over the Boff and Gutiérrez affairs....

The cardinal's fists clenched until his knuckles whitened, and his jaw tightened in an expression of intense distress. He jumped to his feet and walked briskly toward the door.

A bowing of heads and murmurs of "Your Eminence" followed him along the corridor of the secretariat of state.

He stopped in front of the office of Monsignor Adami, titular of the *Ufficio Secondo* of the secretariat of state, the office in charge of international relations in the Holy See.

Half an hour later, Monsignor Feliciani transferred a telephone call from Archbishop Dyakonov to Cardinal Wolfenberg.

"... Aha! So the Villa Rebecca's vulture has just paid a visit to our distinguished secretary of state .... Forty minutes, you say? ... No, I believe I already know ... I'll call you back. Thank you, Markus." The cardinal hung up.

It wasn't hard to guess what the two of them had talked about, nor what the secretary of state's next move would be. Missiroli was sure to discuss the matter with the pope the following morning at eight thirty, during their daily meeting.

The cardinal looked up. His gaze rested on the third fresco of David and Goliath, David holding the giant's head aloft. The cardinal's jaw tightened: ever since biblical times, the best defense had always been attack. He picked up the phone and dialed the number of Monsignor Petrov, His Holiness's private secretary.

"Monsignore, I need to see His Holiness right away ... No, I can't tell you over the phone ... Yes, please. It's most urgent."

Monsignor Petrov rang back ten minutes later. The meeting had been arranged for 6:30 p.m.

Cardinal Wolfenberg lit a cigar and blew out a ring of smoke. How should he handle his meeting with the Holy Father? Those four years of fighting side by side against the heresy that plagued the Catholic world had given him a good understanding of the pope's mentality. After all, Sergius I seemed to have fully inherited the Slavic Pope's outlook.

Memories of the Slavic Pope's trips in the eighties and nineties surfaced.

Central America, South America, Holland, the United States.... Chasing endlessly after that tireless man, and never a moment's peace. He remembered the battles with the Sandinist church in Nicaragua, and those with the Brazilian bishops because of Liberation Theology. *Blessed Liberation Theology!* The very thought of the Boff affair set his adrenaline flowing.

He thought of the Hunthausen case in the United States and the split with the American Catholics. He remembered the disastrous visit to Holland and the clash with the Dutch bishops on the application of the Vatican II directives. How many other cases like Boff, Hunthausen, Nicaragua and Holland had there been? He'd lost count even then. Sergius I's intransigence was a good match for the Slavic Pope's, no doubt about that.

He'd realized right away that Sergius was fascinated by a fixed idea: a monolithic society rigidly centered around the

Church. From the very beginning he and Sergius I had got along well together. They had two things in common: a profound hatred for Communism, and the belief that Vatican II had been some sort of Bacchanal from which many bishops hadn't yet recovered.

The cardinal drew deeply on his cigar, and watched the bluish smoke trace lazy whirls round the rim of his desk lamp.

He and the pope were both convinced it was necessary to bring the Church back to how things stood before Vatican II, and sweep away the senseless utopia of democracy spread by Pope John XXIII and Pope Paul VI. Luckily, the Slavic Pope had paved the way for the return journey, and now the Russian Pope was doing the driving. Sergius I had brought with him a Church and a way of life from a country where there had never been any place for dissent. That model had suited Manus Domini's views perfectly.

How to convince him to join forces with Joint Affairs? The cardinal began to fiddle with his ivory beads.

Sergius detested capitalism and its "culture" no less than Marxism; no wonder the Holy See had countless problems with the American Catholics.... The beads stopped swinging as a cunning smile appeared on the cardinal's lips. *That was it.* He would sell the pope the alliance between Manus Domini and Joint Affairs as a necessary evil that would help rid Italy of abortion, divorce, and rampant materialism. A swipe from the Russian bear would be more devastating than an avalanche swamping a Siberian forest.

And in the end he would get rid of Joint Affairs — resorting even to Palermo, if need be.

At 6:20 p.m., Cardinal Wolfenberg left the Palace of the Holy Office and set off toward the Arco delle Campane. When he was under the arch, he stopped near one of the sentry boxes standing on either side of the walk and the two Swiss guards sprang to attention.

Hmm, better avoid the Porta di Bronzo and walk around behind St. Peter's, entering instead by the Corte di San Damaso. In the Vatican City, walls had eyes and ears.

Under the impassive gaze of the guards, the cardinal turned on his heel and went back.

The sexton of St. Sulpice's knelt in front of the main altar and glanced down the deserted aisles. He raised his eyes to the organ clock above the main entrance. He went down the altar steps, crossed the transept, and disappeared through a small side doorway.

Shortly afterwards, the lights in the aisles and in the transept went out, all except for the side chapels and the gallery. Only the flickering of the candles remained to break the darkness of the aisles, designing a play of shadows on the walls, like prayers in search of an answer.

Suddenly the notes of the organ broke the silence. It wasn't an intrusion, for there was nothing demanding or indiscreet about them, but rather a majestic entry, full of power and spaciousness, as if those notes were claiming their rightful place in the House of God.

The sexton looked up towards the gallery and gazed at the organ pipes. He recognized Berlioz's *Te Deum*. That music always stirred alternate feelings of despair and exaltation in him, but in the end he felt closer to God.

Guichard's fingers swept the keyboard of the organ, and the fugue rose to a crescendo. The last notes of *Judex Crederis* swathed him in a blaze of light.... Flashes of infinity.

♣

As soon as Geoffroy felt the vibrations from the blow, he stopped with his arm in mid-air. Archambaud grabbed a torch from the wall and held it up to the hole. They both peered up at the point where Geoffroy's pick had struck, but could see nothing.

"Come on, Geoffroy. Have you seen a gryphon's nest?" Archambaud said.

Geoffroy tightened his hold on the pick and aimed a series of blows. There it was again! He scraped off the last few chips of limestone rock with his fingernails: a golden surface gleamed in the light of the torch! He and Archambaud looked at each other and burst into relieved laughter.

Archambaud dismissed the men for the rest of the day. Geoffroy stayed on guard at the mouth of the tunnel, while Archambaud rushed to call the others.

Soon a pounding of running footsteps came from the underground passage. Geoffroy poked his head around and found himself face to face with Hugues, their other companions right behind him. Archambaud had a coil of rope slung over his shoulder.

They took turns with the pick until the hole was about three feet in diameter. They stopped and gazed as if hypnotized at the shining sheet of gold, which seemed to be made up of two parts joined by gold rivets. Archambaud told the others to stand back. He seized a mallet, and started to swing it round in ever-increasing circles. When the mallet hit the gold, a long metallic vibration resounded throughout the tunnel and faded in the distance.

At the fourth stroke, half of Archambaud's mallet disappeared into the roof. They all gathered below the hole. The blows had forced the joint apart and one of the sheets of gold had lifted a few inches. Archambaud pushed upwards with both hands and the sheet began to move. Geoffroy joined him and the sheet gradually bent along the opposite side, until it remained in a vertical position. They all stood motionless, their heads turned upwards, staring at the dark hole.

Hugues was the first to recover. "Who's going up first?"

They looked around at each other in silence.

"Why don't we draw for it?" Bertrand said.

"Geoffroy should be the one," Archambaud said. "He made the discovery."

Hugues glanced around at the others, but no one protested. He beckoned to Archambaud and they knelt down on one knee on each side of Geoffroy. "Climb onto our knees, then our shoulders," Hugues said. "Go on, Sir Knight."

Geoffroy poked his head inside the hole. It was too dark to see anything, but he noticed a strange odor: it was the smell of his origins, a smell lost in the mists of time. He pulled himself up through the hole, knelt on the edge and laid his hands flat on the floor. He felt dust and a metal surface under his fingers. *He was in the Holy of Holies.*

Still on his knees, Geoffroy looked down. Eight anxious faces gazed up at him. Hugues passed him a torch. Geoffroy choked back a cry.

Two grotesque figures with curved beaks were staring at him from above. Their faces were not human, but those of eagles, covered in gold. Geoffroy raised his torch and only then did he realize that each figure had four wings and that two of these were spread above him and seemed to be fluttering because of the flickering light. The two figures knelt facing each other and instead of talons they had the hooves of oxen. He brought the torch nearer: each figure had more than one face, and on the inside Geoffroy recognized the muzzle of a lion.

For a moment he thought he could hear music, a crescendo that invaded his soul, and his fear vanished. It was powerful music, the likes of which he'd never heard before and which seemed to come from far away. It had always been said that the proportions of Solomon's Temple were magical and that they could reproduce the symphony of the celestial spheres. Was this the reason why the Temple was pervaded by such divine harmony? The notes faded.

Then Geoffroy saw it.

The Ark of the Covenant stood on a golden altar. Two gold-covered staves passed through four rings fixed to the upper corners. It was all overlaid in gold, just as described in the Bible. Cautiously, Geoffroy took a couple of steps forward, looked at the lid of the Ark, and at that moment he understood.

The two figures that had terrified him were exact replicas of the two cherubim in beaten gold that knelt facing each other at each end of the lid. This was the Mercy Seat, described in Exodus and in the Book of Psalms. It was between these two cherubim that God, enveloped in a cloud, had addressed Moses, showing him His mercy for the sins of humankind. It was from there that God had spoken to the High Priest of the Temple when, once a year on the Day of Atonement, the High Priest had gone down into the Holy of Holies carrying the goblet containing the blood of the scapegoat. Geoffroy moved across to look at the outer face of the nearer cherubim. An ox. He knew from the Bible that the fourth face, the one facing the wall, must be human.

A thousand golden reflections danced about Geoffroy in the light of the torch. The Holy of Holies was cube-shaped, each side measuring about thirty-three feet, and was lined with sheets of gold. A blue drape covered the walls about halfway up; a second drape, this time scarlet, overlapped the blue one. Geoffroy turned round. He frowned. A number of wooden chests were piled up against the opposite wall, almost as if they'd been left there by someone in a great hurry.

But those weren't ordinary chests. Coffers! Geoffroy knelt down by the closest one. It was made of reddish wood and inlaid with gold. He brought the torch nearer. The inlay on one side pictured the Flight of the Jews from Egypt. The top picture, on the front, showed Moses hurling the Tables of Testimony in anger at the golden calf. The other inlay work also showed scenes from the Old Testament. He ran his hand over the top of the coffers, and under the dust appeared the outline of the *menorah* [the golden candlestick with seven branches].

Geoffroy took hold of the heavy padlock on one of the strongboxes, and at that moment he remembered what Abbot Bernard had told him: "*...The treasure consisted of twenty-four separate items.*" He began to count the coffers. He had reached fifteen when he heard his name being called insistently. He'd completely forgotten! He rushed over to the hole and knelt down.

"Geoffroy! You son of a dragon! Have you seen it?" Hugues asked.

"Yes, it's here. It's just as it says in the Bible! Bring another torch, but before you come up, pass me some picks and chisels."

It took only a moment for Hugues to be hoisted up, so Geoffroy didn't have time to warn him. When Hugues pulled himself up, he flung out his arms and drew back with a cry.

When all the others had made their way into the Holy of Holies, the nine knights stood in silent awe before the Ark, knowing what lay inside: *the Tables of Testimony*. God Himself had given them to Moses, who had placed them inside the Ark. It was God's hand that had carved out those Tables and now there they were, just a few feet away. The temptation was great to raise the Seat of Mercy, but they all knew that the Wrath of God would be implacable, and would destroy whosoever dared go against the orders He'd given to Moses. It was written in the Book of Samuel that when the men of Bethshemesh had dared to look into the Ark, God had killed fifty thousand of them.

Geoffroy motioned Hugues towards the coffers.

"Someone must have thought they had Cerberus on their heels," Hugues said.

"If they contain what I think they do, the Jews must have piled them up in here to secure them from the Romans," Geoffroy said.

With the aid of a hammer, Geoffroy helped Hugues force the tip of a pick under one of the lids. Hugues pressed down on the handle of the pick with all his strength, until they heard the wood splinter and the lock break open. Hugues raised the lid. The torch crackled in the silence and its flame reflected on a heap of emeralds, rubies and gold. A kaleidoscope of sparkling colors danced on the walls of the Holy of Holies.

"*Pecunia non olet*—Money doesn't stink," murmured Victor.

With Hugues's help, Geoffroy opened four more strong-boxes at random, and in each of them they found a similar treasure... *the treasure of the House of David.*

While the others were busy with the coffers, Geoffroy noticed a wooden chest, hidden away under the strongboxes. It was longer than the coffers, seemed to be made of common wood, and was without decoration. Odd: something so plain hidden amidst such treasures.

Archambaud forced the tip of the pick under the lid of the wooden chest and Geoffroy pressed down on the handle to pry it up. They did the same on all four sides. Then they removed the lid.

Geoffroy stood motionless and broke out in a cold sweat. He didn't need to be told what he was looking at: he knew. And he also knew he couldn't be wrong. He looked at Archambaud. His friend's face was deathly pale.

Geoffroy knelt down near the lid. There were some scrolls nailed to the inside. The nails at the four corners were not tight, and he was able to pull them out by hand. He brought the torch nearer. The characters on the scrolls appeared to be in Aramaic, but it wasn't difficult to guess what was written there.

Meanwhile the others too had gathered around the chest. They looked petrified. A deathly silence had fallen upon the Holy of Holies.

Miriam had drawn the curtains and a warm breeze drifted across the balcony under the beige awning. The moonlight illuminated the silhouette of the minarets and the Dome of the Rock, while dim lantern lights flickered in the windows of the houses. There was something magical in the air of Jerusalem under the stars of a summer night, something that made you raise your eyes to the sky and shout: O Time, stop, because I have found perfection.

"Why have you not eaten your Halvah pudding?" Miriam said, going over to Geoffroy by the railings and taking hold of his arm. "Today I made a special journey to the Malquisinat market to buy what I needed, just to please you."

She was wearing a green bodice laced at the front, a low-necked white blouse with ruffled sleeves tight at the wrist, and a full purple skirt. A red enameled chain necklace lay on her smooth bosom.

"What's the matter?" she asked. "You look as if you've seen a ghost."

"Hold me tight, Miriam. Hold me." Geoffroy clasped her to him. "I want to forget everything."

"What's happened? Tell me!"

Geoffroy didn't answer. He led her inside, undressed her and took her almost with force. He wanted to lose himself inside her and leave everything else behind.

"Geoffroy, please, you're hurting me."

"I'm sorry." He pulled himself away.

"What's tormenting you?"

"Think of something that you've always believed in, something that is really important to you."

"Go on."

"Suppose you suddenly discovered that none of it was true. What would you do?"

Miriam rested her head on his chest. "I'd start to ask myself if it was really so important after all."

"And then?"

There was a moment's silence. "I'd probably end up realizing that it doesn't make any difference whether it's true or not."

Geoffroy stroked her hair and held her tightly. Could she be right?

22

The *Grande Salle des Séances* of the Institut de France was packed full, and under the lofty cupola one could breathe the air of important occasions. Guichard made his way to his chair in the second row.

Followed by a tall man with a mass of white hair, the president of the *Académie des Sciences* went up on the platform, and the murmuring died away. Guichard immediately recognized Professor Gaston Bieri, the atrophysicist he had met at the Seigneurs' dinner party, where he'd first encountered Françoise.

"Ladies and gentlemen, it is with great pleasure that I welcome here today Professor Gaston Bieri, professor emeritus in astrophysics at the Louis Pasteur University in Strasbourg," said the president. "Professor Bieri will be speaking to us today about the extraordinary discovery made a few days ago by astrophysicists from the Max Planck Institute of Extraterrestrial Physics."

The lights dimmed and the screen, which covered the entire wall, lit up.

"Please excuse me for this two-dimensional screen," Professor Bieri said in a mock-serious tone. "It's unforgivable, but the Académie des Sciences has run out of four-dimensional screens."

A chorus of chuckles spread among the audience.

"Scientists from the Max Planck first started to study the galaxy in question—Euridice, thirty million light-years from Earth—almost five years ago, in January 2003. Why all this interest? Well, what aroused the curiosity of the Max Planck astrophysicists was the presence of a strong radio source, Prometheus C, coming from the center of the galaxy. Measuring the orbital speed of the stars in that area of Euridice, they discovered the presence of a large, dark, compact body. Because of the elevated orbital speeds, approaching that of light, they realized there must be something exerting an enormous gravitational force at the center of the galaxy. It didn't take long to obtain confirmation that it was a black hole, with a mass equivalent to 15 million times that of our Sun."

The professor poured himself a glass of water. A new slide appeared on the screen, and a chorus of excited murmurs filled the hall.

"In October 2004, by studying the radio signals from Prometheus C, the Max Planck researchers began to realize they were dealing with more than just a simple black hole. It's taken three years of additional research to reach any definite conclusion." The professor indicated with his pointer a mysterious ring at the center of the slide. "Even if it's only a computer reconstruction, that image is an exact representation based on the data we've received from Max Planck."

The press photographers crowded the area at the foot of the stage, the flashes from their cameras bombarding the screen.

"Up to last week, wormholes were little more than a mathematical abstraction, a possible solution to Einstein's equations. This slide shows that wormholes are very much a reality. You're looking at Alice A, the first natural wormhole. Alice A is not a wormhole with two mouths, but a closed time-like loop. The loop has a diameter of..."

"Professor, I've heard people talk of a *time corridor*," said a journalist sitting in the front row. "Do you agree with this definition?"

"The definition is technically correct. If a spaceship went through the loop, the astronauts would travel back millions of years, at a speed far faster than light."

"But didn't Einstein demonstrate that it's not possible to go faster than light?"

"Yes, and Einstein was right, but only using *his* system of reference, that is, a flat space-time."

"Sorry, Professor, but I'm lost."

"In the theory of relativity nothing can exceed the speed of light, because at the speed of light energy becomes infinite and time stops. So how is it possible to exceed the speed of light if time stops? By warping the space-time. Something that, alas, neither you nor I can do with a mere pair of pliers. Nature, however, has powerful pliers at its disposal, much more powerful than you and I can even for a moment imagine."

"So how was Alice formed, then?"

"A stable quantum tunnel like Alice probably originates from the explosion of a very large star. The enormous amount of energy liberated by the explosion has produced a tear—it's not the right term, but you get the picture—in the fabric of the four-dimensional space-time."

"A sort of shortcut?"

"*Exactly*. It's a shortcut, when compared with the linear route that light would have to follow in a flat space-time. In a tunnel like Alice, nothing can travel at a speed *below* that of light. In that loop, ladies and gentlemen, the space-time is so warped that time becomes negative, which is like getting a passport to the past."

A thrill of excitement ran through the audience.

The professor poured himself something to drink at the buffet. Guichard took advantage of the moment.

"It's nice to see you again, Professor," Guichard said. "Do you remember me? We met at—"

"*Bien sûr, Monsieur le Comte, comment allez-vous*? I'm surprised to see you here. I thought you were already off, space-traveling in the past."

"I only came back—faster than light, of course—when I heard of your conference."

A shrewd look crossed the professor's face. "Someone like you wouldn't come back from the past without having done what he had in mind. Which would make your presence here a paradox."

The professor was referring to the "Granny Paradox" of quantum physics, which posed the hypothesis of a time traveler returning to the past and killing his grandmother.

Guichard pointed to the screen. "Doesn't that loop make the subject of paradoxes particularly current?"

The professor burst out laughing. "Don't tell me you intend traveling back in time to murder your grandmother!"

"You like to joke about it, but we both know that the dream of traveling back in time is as old as humankind. What would you yourself be prepared to sacrifice, in order to accomplish that dream?"

"It's the old refrain of 'if only.' But it's destined to remain a dream for all events belonging to the same space-time."

"Which doesn't preclude, though, the 'if only' story from being one of the events from another universe."

The professor looked at Guichard with curiosity. "True."

"Sticking to the paradox, let's suppose you really did travel into the past and kill your grandmother. What would happen then?"

"Only two possibilities exist. The first is that there's something in nature that prevents it, a sort of law of 'non-interference.' This would prevent you from carrying out, in the past, any action that was incompatible with the principle that the course of history can't be changed. The second is that you can break the rules, but the moment you took your knowledge of the present into the past and used it — allegorically, if you killed your grandmother — you'd be doomed."

"Which means what?" asked Guichard, even though deep down he knew the answer already.

"At that very same moment that world would duplicate itself and you'd return to the present of another quantum world, unknown to you, where, going back to the granny paradox, neither the young grandmother, nor you, had ever existed with your identity." The professor looked at Guichard seriously. "It would be a one-way trip."

One-way trips were frightening to those who didn't know what they were looking for. Guichard was no longer following the professor's words. *All theoretically feasible possibilities are equally real and not just the product of an illusion,* Parmenides had said, and modern physics supported his statement. *If something can physically happen, it* does *happen, in one of the infinite universes surrounding us.*

He thought of when the lightning had struck, of the shock going through his arm and of those images darting in front of his eyes.

There was a third alternative. It had always been there, at his disposal, but stupidly he'd never become aware of it.

"Monsieur le Comte, are you still with me or are you back in space?" the professor said.

The clock in the reading-room of the Bibliothèque Nationale de France read 5:20 p.m. Françoise put the books on Guercino, born Gian Francesco Barbieri, to one side, skimmed through her notes, and sighed. There was nothing to show that Guercino had literary inclinations, so he wasn't likely to have invented that phrase.

"Ssh!"

Françoise looked up and met the frowning eyes of the man sitting opposite her. He pointed to the pen she was holding. She was tapping absent-mindedly on the table, and that drumming resounded in the silence of the room.

She reached for the book with the reproductions of Guercino's paintings, but in doing so she knocked over the pile of books on the table, and the noise echoed through the room.

"Ssh!" said the man again, giving her a withering look.

Françoise moved the table lamp, so that now the lampshade was between her and that man. She went through Guercino's paintings yet again, but she couldn't find anything in them reminiscent of forbidden allegories.

She studied the picture of *Et in Arcadia Ego*, concentrating on the gaze of the two shepherds coming out of the forest. Was it wonder or fear that one could read in their eyes? They were staring at a skull, placed on a stone slab, with a Latin inscription — *Et in Arcadia ego* — carved along the front.

If it wasn't Guercino who invented the motto, who else could it have been? Françoise continued to turn the pages of the art book. The most likely theory had been advanced by Erwin Panofsky, an art historian who had died in 1968. Panofsky taught at Princeton and was the greatest authority in the world on iconography. His theory was that the inventor of the phrase was Cardinal Giulio Rospigliosi, who became pope in 1667 under the name of Clement IX.

What kind of man was this Rospigliosi? Françoise turned the page. There he was. Rospigliosi was a lover of philosophy, art, and poetry, and also a well-known playwright. He spent much of his life in Rome, in the same period as Poussin. If Cardinal Rospigliosi had really been the one to inspire the motto, just what mystery could he have known?

Françoise went back to her notes and checked all the dates. There was no evidence of direct contact between the two painters. Guercino had lived in Rome between 1621 and 1623, but the painter had left Rome before the end of 1623. Poussin, on the other hand, arrived in Rome in 1624, so obviously the two artists hadn't met there. One thing was certain, though. When Poussin arrived in Rome, Guercino had already finished his *Et in Arcadia ego*. Françoise slammed the book on Panofsky shut.

"*Ssh!*" repeated the man, who had a horrible crew cut.

Poussin spent the remainder of his life in Rome. Nothing she researched gave her proof that Poussin might have seen Guercino's painting. Yet she was sure he'd seen it, and in Rome. It was unlikely that Poussin had been inspired by a literary source: no such source had ever been discovered.

She'd reached a dead end. She sighed and rested her chin on the palm of her hand, staring at the reproduction of *Et in Arcadia ego*. A draft of cold air blew gently over her arms. Françoise's hand gripped the arm of her chair.

The pages of the book on Guercino started to turn dizzily, first one way and then in the other, as if the book were being swept over by a strong current of air. When the fluttering of the pages ended, Françoise's eyes remained fixed with an astonished expression on the open book … *The reproduction of Les bergers d'Arcadie II*.

The being had just told her she was on the wrong track, but no one else had noticed anything. Only the man sitting in front of her seemed to shiver and cast an annoyed glance at the windows. Everything appeared to be normal in the reading room —

the two librarians' expressionless faces, some sporadic fit of coughing, the humming of the air-circulation system. Yet she *knew* that the being was still there.

As if pushed by an invisible hand, the pile of her books toppled over, right in front of the man.

"*Madame, vous le faites exprès ou quoi?* — Madam, are you doing it on purpose?" he said, flushed with anger.

"I've had just about enough!" She got up and leaned over towards him. "And let me tell you something else."

The man's eyes widened.

"Why don't you get yourself another barber?"

When Françoise left the library, it was pouring. She tried in vain to get a taxi in Rue Richelieu, so she had to hurry to the subway station on the corner. Some illuminated billboards were advertising *La Bohème* at the Opéra. This was the evening she was to have gone with Guichard.

A car drove through a puddle near the sidewalk, soaking her up to the knees.

Murmurs, lights and oak panels seemed to mingle in the boardroom on the sixteenth floor of the CIP skyscraper. All the directors were sitting round the large, oval table with their usual air of boredom. The CIP board chairman checked the time and glanced down at his papers. There was only one item of business on the agenda: "Proposition of Allied Petroleum Inc. for the setting up of a joint venture with CIP."

"Any comments?" asked the chairman at the end of his presentation.

Complete silence followed and no hands were raised. The chairman looked at the drowsy faces around the table. The vultures had had their fill: supply contracts for the firms of party supporters, top positions for men aligned with party politics, money.

"Since nobody has asked to speak," he went on, "I propose to put the motion to the vote. Will those in favor please raise their hands."

All the directors raised their hands, as if obeying a silent order. All but one.

The silence was broken by swinish snoring, in which spasmodic high-pitched squeals alternated with cavernous low grunts, interposed by rattles, whistles, and clogged sink gurgles. The chairman blanched, as if caught in a grip of polar frost, and his eyes rested on a director sprawling at the far end of the table. The man's head was fully bent backwards, his arms dangling, his stomach fighting with the buttons of his shirt against the edge of the table. The chairman grabbed a folder and slammed it hard on the table.

It was as if a rifle shot resounded in the boardroom.

The director gave a start, straightened up and looked around with a stunned expression. "Eh? W-what?...." He waved a fist in the air. "I object! I object!"

"Idiot! *We're not at the Chamber*," whispered the director sitting next to him.

The director looked around once more, and finally his expression suggested he was back on earth again. His hand shot up again. "I approve! I approve!"

The chairman glared at the director in an Antarctic expanse-like silence. "The motion is carried unanimously," he snarled. "The next board meeting is called on Thursday, October 9 at 11:00 a.m., to discuss the terms of the draft agreement. The meeting is adjourned."

He looked at his watch again. Twelve minutes. A real record.

§

"The proposal has been approved unanimously," Zergas said.

"Very good, Antigono," said the prime minister on the other end of the line. "You're always the best."

"Very good my foot! A present worth $230 million to Mr. Kovacs, with the Italian taxpayers' respects."

"Did a milk cow ever complain about being milked?"

As he sat in his car, Prime Minister Accardo told the driver to take him to the Vatican City. The car left Palazzo Chigi between two police cars, their blue lights flashing.

What a nuisance. His usual monthly lunch appointment with Cardinal Missiroli. Accardo took the day's press survey out of his briefcase and skimmed through it, stopping to read the press comments on the Allied-CIP deal. As the car and the police escort crossed St. Peter's Square, he thought of Kovacs's face when he learned of the little surprise he'd set aside for him.

The hint of a smile flickered across his lips as he folded up the press survey.

§

Kovacs fastened the safety belt of his first-class seat on the 11:05 a.m. United flight 478 to Dallas, and he thought of the pig-like face of Owens, the Overseas Chemicals' boss, whom he would meet at Le Meridien later on that day. He opened the *Wall Street Journal*. A grin of satisfaction spread over his face as he read a front-page article. No one had missed the fact that Allied Petroleum had found a sucker ready to put $500 million on one side of the scales, while his company, on their part, contributed only low-quality coal and hopes. In just that morning's session, Allied's shares had risen by 4.5 percent on Wall Street. Now that the CIP deal was in the home stretch, the acquisition of Overseas was only waiting for his signature.

Kovacs thought of the $230 million present that CIP was about to make him. He shook his head. Wall Street, the SEC, the so-called minority shareholders.... It was either shoot or be shot at.

He reached out and squeezed Martha's hand.

"Monsignore, I need to speak to you," Cardinal Missiroli said, sitting down opposite Monsignor Adami.

"Can I be of help, Your Eminence?" said the monsignor in charge of the Ufficio Secondo at the secretariat of state.

"Monsignore, I know I can count on your discretion."

"Your Eminence has known me for many years."

Cardinal Missiroli told Monsignor Adami about the meeting with Father Cafiero. He confirmed his worries regarding the way the Church was drifting ever further away from the Vatican II directives, and the growing influence of extremist factions within the Church itself. Lastly, he told Adami the conclusion he'd reached.

Monsignor Adami stared speechless at the cardinal. "But, Your Eminence, it's an extremely serious decision. Naturally, you are aware of the consequences of such a move."

"As secretary of state of the Holy See I should know, don't you think?"

"Forgive me, Your Eminence, I didn't mean to be rude. It's just that it's the last thing I'd have expected to hear from you, of all people."

"Do you not feel that this is the way to bring Church affairs back where they belong?"

"But, Your Eminence, are you sure you have examined all the alternatives?"

"Alternatives? Name one."

"Well, a new conclave can't be far off. They might elect a pope who'll return to the path of reform."

"Almost forty years in the diplomatic corps has taught me to be realistic. Think of the heritage left by the Slavic Pope and of all the damage this papacy has caused in such a short period. And, last but not least, of the fact that over three-quarters of the *cardinali elettori* have been appointed by the two of them. With such premises, do you really believe that the next conclave could elect a reformist?"

"I see your point, Your Eminence."

"Without even considering—*ad maiora*—the dealings of Manus Domini and the role that men like Cafiero and Wolfenberg, each in his own way, will play in nominating the next pope."

"If I've got it right, Your Eminence, what you're really saying is that yours is an unavoidable decision."

"If we don't intervene now, after the next conclave it will be too late."

"Tell me what you want me to do, Your Eminence."

"I want you to feel free to decide whatever you think is best. If you say no, it won't make the slightest bit of difference to our friendship."

"Your Eminence, I say yes in the interest of the Church."

The cardinal leaned forward and put his hand on Adami's shoulder. "Now listen carefully, Monsignore...."

The time-zone clock of the Communications Room read one o'clock in the morning when Monsignor Adami walked in with a folder under his arm. He sat down, opened it, and took out a coded message. He looked at another sheet and ran his finger down the list of the presidents of the Episcopal Conferences of eighteen Catholic countries.

When the monsignor left, he exchanged a meaningful look with the two priests on duty. No one would find any trace of those messages the following day.

That night, the NSA station of Bad Aibling intercepted eighteen messages coming from the telecommunications center of Santa Maria Galeria.

Two days later Cardinal Missiroli left for a three-week trip abroad, leaving the secretariat of state in Monsignor Adami's hands.

As the VARIG jet took off over Rome on the flight bound for Rio, the NSA analysts were at work at Fort Meade decoding the messages.

The dentist pressed a pedal and the back of the chair lowered. He positioned a light on its flexible arm and switched it on. Then he pushed the suction tube into Guichard's mouth.

"Open, Monsieur le Comte." The dentist leaned over Guichard with his dental mirror.

The hairs sticking out of the dentist's nose reminded Guichard of a walrus.

"Everything looks fine, Monsieur le Comte. If all my patients had teeth like yours, I'd starve to death."

"How many fillings have I got?"

"Open again. Let's see. One... two in your upper molars... five in all."

"What were they done with?"

"Oh, now I see. Amalgam, the mercury scare," the dentist said, putting Guichard's chair upright again. "Do you really think I'd use that muck? Besides, my patients are all far too appearance conscious."

"So?"

"I use composite resin, of course."

"What did they use in the Middle Ages?"

The dentist's eyes widened. "*In the Middle Ages*? Well, they certainly didn't have composite resin fillings then! They slammed you down against a bale of hay on market day, and thrust some rusty tongs into your mouth. If you could afford it, they made you gulp down a goatskin of wine as anesthetic. Though I doubt it was Bordeaux DOC, Monsieur le Comte."

"But by studying skeletons from the period, surely someone must have seen what they used."

"Well, I don't know about the Middle Ages, but all sorts of things have been used over the years. Splinters of stone, turpentine resin, various metals...."

"Metals?"

"Certainly. The Etruscans, five centuries before Christ, were a very advanced people. Skulls have been found with golden bridges and crowns that reveal extraordinary ability. But I'm afraid that in the Middle Ages —"

"Doctor, I want all my fillings replaced in gold," Guichard said, pushing the chair back down.

The dentist leaned over him. "Monsieur le Comte — with all due respect — have you gone mad?"

♣

The odor of fresh hay mingled with horse dung permeated King Solomon's stables. Every so often the neighing of a horse could be heard through the arches.

As he descended the ladder, Geoffroy stopped. This was his last night in Jerusalem. In the light of the torches, the carts cast grotesque shadows onto the vaulted ceiling. The sergeants were standing guard. The strongboxes were already stacked on the carts, and now the time had come to load the Ark—and the wooden chest.

He entered the tunnel. It was five months since the day of the discovery. That day they'd suspended the excavations, saying they were giving up the search. But ever since that day, they and their sergeants at arms had taken turns standing guard at the entrance to the tunnel, on a twenty-four-hour basis.

The day after the discovery, they sent a messenger to France with a message for Abbot Bernard, informing him that the mission had been accomplished. In his reply, the abbot wrote that he had immediately given the news to Pope Honorius II. His Holiness was awaiting them in Rome, to confer on them the honors of the Church. The pope had already arranged for a special Council to be called in Troyes for 31 January of the coming year. In the course of the Council, the Church would give its official approval for the creation of the Order of the Knights of the Temple. The abbot felt certain that all the noble families in Europe would be most eager to enroll their sons in the Army of Christ.

The pope ordered the Ark to be taken to Rome, together with two-thirds of the Treasure of David. The rest would finance the expansion of the Order throughout the Christian world. The abbot wrote that His Holiness had sent a personal message to the Patriarch of Jerusalem and to King Baldwin, asking them to provide the Templars with all the necessary support for their journey to the coast. The discovery was to remain a secret. Geoffroy had often wondered whether the pope might have instructed King Baldwin to do something else too: in fact, ever since that day, he'd had the uneasy feeling they were being spied on.

"Careful, now, careful," Hugues said, holding up a torch.

Archambaud and Bertrand were at one end, with Victor and himself at the other. Tensing their muscles they slowly stood up. The stave dug into Geoffroy's shoulder and the Ark became detached from the altar. For a few endless moments they remained immobile: Geoffroy thought of what the Book of Samuel said, but nothing happened. They turned to their left, advanced into the center of the Holy of Holies and placed the

Ark down on the ground. Geoffroy wiped his forehead with the sleeve of his tunic.

They'd removed five sheets of gold from the center of the floor, making an opening seventeen feet by three. The staves were fifteen feet long. From a safe distance, they'd measured the width of the Ark, which was twenty-seven inches across.

They tied the ropes firmly to the ends of the staves, and while their companions went down into the passage, the four of them wound the ropes round their shoulders and raised the Ark again. They slowly lowered the Ark down through the hole. As the Ark descended, the flames of Hugues' torch reflected on the Mercy Seat. Geoffroy had a sense of foreboding: after more than two thousand years, the Ark of the Covenant was leaving the Holy of Holies.

"The ropes, Christian," said Geoffroy to his sergeant, pointing to the tangled mass that lay on the ground near the Ark.

Christian bent to pick them up, but tripped. Before Geoffroy could do anything, it was too late: Christian fell sideways onto the Mercy Seat, his right arm crossing the space between the two cherubim.

A flash shot between the faces of the cherubim, the Ark gave off a dazzling light, and a clap of thunder shook the stables. Geoffroy raised his arms to shield himself from the snake of light that whirled all around him. The horses reared up in terror, neighing frantically. Christian let out a blood-curdling cry, and his body started to writhe on the Ark. Eventually he fell to the ground, his body still jerking. But his cries had ceased by now. A cloud of smoke enveloped the Ark and the radiance emanating from its interior began to pulsate. The streak of light continued to spark for a few moments between the heads of the cherubim, writhing like a snake. Then the light grew fainter, and eventually vanished. As the smoke lifted, the smell of burning flesh grabbed Geoffroy by the throat. Christian lay immobile on the ground. His body had been ravaged by horrendous burns and his face was disfigured.

For the last time, Geoffroy went back into the Holy of Holies and, in the light of the torch, he stared at the bare altar. He looked upwards. The two cherubim, with their curved beaks, appeared more menacing than ever. How or when he didn't know, but at that moment he knew that one day he and the other knights would pay the price for this profanation. Christian's death was just the beginning.

Geoffroy and his companions were standing around the wooden chest, in the Holy of Holies.

"We have to take this secret with us to the grave," Hugues said.

"Are you sure it's the right thing to do?" asked Geoffroy.

"What do you mean?"

"I believe we should pass this secret on to our descendants."

Hugues flung out his arms. "But why? This secret will be a curse on anyone who finds out about it. We live in dark times, my brethren."

"But times may change." Victor pointed to the chest. "And this chest is what could make things change."

Hugues gave Victor a skeptical look.

"Don't you see, Hugues?" Geoffroy said. "This secret will be a source of enormous power, if not for us, for our descendants. Who knows? Maybe in a thousand years."

"Let the majority decide," Hugues said. "How many of you agree to Geoffroy's proposal?"

Geoffroy and all the others raised their hands. Hugues shook his head repeatedly.

They formed themselves into a circle. Hugues unsheathed his sword, took hold of it with both hands, and rested the tip on the ground. Geoffroy knelt down in front of the sword. He swore he would hand down the secret to his next of kin, telling him to do the same when the time came, and so on, from then to eternity. He invoked on himself and his descendants the wrath of God if he, or any of his lineage, should one day betray the oath. Then he kissed the hilt of the sword. One after another each of the other knights repeated the oath in turn.

"The oath isn't enough," Archambaud said. "We'll need a motto, a sort of password."

They all looked at him questioningly.

"One day we might need to refer to the secret without running the risk of anyone understanding. Our very lives could be at stake."

It was then that Victor came out with that strange motto of his. Geoffroy couldn't see the connection, and he realized that the others didn't understand it either. What did it matter, after all? Any words would do, so long as they served their purpose.

Hugues shrugged his shoulders. "Why not?"

They re-formed a circle, unsheathed their swords, and raised them so that the tips touched. Then, one after the other, they repeated Victor's motto.

Gondemare de Saint-Omer suddenly raised his hand. "Sshhh! Did you hear that?" he whispered. He tiptoed over to the hole, knelt and looked down. Then he slipped into the tunnel.

Geoffroy and the others gathered around the hole, and they heard the sound of running footsteps. After a few minutes, Gondemare reappeared and looked up at them, out of breath.

"What was it?" asked Hugues.

"I think I heard someone hurrying away, but the torches have gone out, so I couldn't see a thing."

"Isn't there anyone at the entrance?" Hugues asked, looking at the others.

"They're all keeping guard over the carts," Geoffroy said.

Hugues stroked his beard, then flung out his arm as if to embrace the Holy of Holies. "It must be this place. We see ghosts everywhere."

But Geoffroy sensed that Hugues' words betrayed uncertainty, and expressed everyone's fears.

In deathly silence, they lowered the chest into the tunnel.

As Archambaud was about to lower himself into the tunnel, Geoffroy grabbed him by the arm. "Wait."

"What?"

Geoffroy passed him the torch. "There's something I've wanted to do ever since I first set foot in here." He took hold of a pick and a mallet.

Geoffroy went over to the wall where they'd found the treasure, and stopped in front of the gold panels that marked the outline of a door frame. It was through there that the High

Priest must have entered the Holy of Holies on the Day of Atonement, carrying a goblet of blood from the sacrificial goat.

Archambaud held the pick steady, while Geoffroy struck it with the mallet. When the tip had gone far enough into the door frame, they pried up with the handle. The door gave under the pressure, and an avalanche of stones cascaded out onto the floor, raising a cloud of dust. The dust settled, and a skull wearing a helmet grinned up at them amidst the rubble.

Archambaud's torch lit up the door frame. *Human bones.* The stones were still holding prisoner the skeleton of a Roman legionary: his right arm was raised and his fist was still clenched round the hilt of his *gladius*.

"Just this door, and Titus would have got here first," Geoffroy said.

23

Bowing, Cardinal Wolfenberg left the pope's private study at 7:30 p.m. He rubbed his hands together; he felt just as he always did when leaving the tribunal of the CDF, after duly chastising one of those arrogant theologians.

He pressed the button of the elevator. He suddenly turned back and strode down the corridor of the secretariat of state, heading straight for the substitute's office. He'd really earned a glass of that special bourbon Markus kept tucked away for his friends.

Midway through the following afternoon, the cardinal received a phone call from Monsignor Petrov, the pope's personal secretary. The monsignor told him that Father Cafiero had just left the pope's office. He didn't know what had passed between them, but before their meeting His Holiness had asked Monsignor Petrov for an updated list of the Italian *initiati* in Manus Domini.

The cardinal hung up, leaned back in his chair, and reached for a cigar. He'd foreseen everything, as always.

Two hours later, Monsignor Petrov called him again. The pope had asked for the cardinal to join him in his private study at 6:00 p.m. the following day. The monsignor said in a conspiratorial voice that the pope had asked Father Cafiero to be there, too. The cardinal tightened his jaw in anticipation: hand-to-hand combat had always been his specialty.

When Cardinal Wolfenberg entered the pope's private study, Father Cafiero was already there. The cardinal leaned over and kissed the Fisherman's ring, then he sat down next to the father general.

The stacks of folders piled on the pope's desk looked like the Siegfried Line.

Pope Sergius I was one of those men who never laugh. He had thin lips and a face that looked like a cross between a lemon and a prune, and which might even have been generously described as "delicate," had it not been for his thick, black eyebrows, more accusatory than a district attorney. His physical presence, combined with his white robes, exerted much the same effect on people as Original Sin: one would feel guilty even before opening one's mouth. As if backing up those eyebrows, an enormous, wooden crucifix hung behind the pope's desk, the impact of which was enhanced by the bareness of the other walls. The rest of his study was furnished cheaply, a far cry from the studied monastic simplicity of Father Cafiero's office. The cardinal had been present the first day Sergius set foot in his study. The pope, with a glare that reminded the cardinal of a Siberian tundra, had had the antique furniture removed right away and had it replaced with a desk and chairs that the Vatican storekeeper had salvaged from a suburban junk dealer.

The pope took a folder from one of the piles, opened it, and put on his glasses with shaky hands. After glancing through the front page, he raised his eyes.

"We wish to express our disappointment in recognizing that the two most important members of Manus Domini are incapable of seeing eye to eye on matters of such vital importance to the Church," the pope said.

Such a direct attack came as a surprise, but the cardinal decided to wait. Father Cafiero had just raised his hand: let him bear the brunt of it.

"I wish to call the attention of Your Holiness to the fact that we're talking about a very serious matter," Father Cafiero said. "Any decision now would be premature."

"Father, there is no need for you to point this out to us," replied His Holiness. "It has not been easy for us, either, to make a decision."

So he'd already decided, thought the cardinal. No wonder. After all, the Catholic Church was not a democracy — and never would be one.

"But Your Holiness, as father general of Manus Domini, I—"

The pope froze Father Cafiero with a wave of his hand. "We understand your fears, but these are times of moral crisis, and crises call for courageous decisions."

"Your Holiness, with this alliance we would interfere with Italy's internal affairs, which could have very serious consequences, not to mention its repercussions abroad."

"Father, are you not of the opinion that Manus Domini and the Church must be united in their battle against the devastating absence of moral values, especially with regard to abortion, divorce, and birth control?"

"Your Holiness knows that Manus Domini has always been on the front line."

"But you will admit that in spite of all our efforts, we are losing the battle in Italy," the pope said. "Whereas Italy is the country that should be setting an example to the rest of Christendom."

"I would respectfully point out to Your Holiness that the Holy See is—"

The pope again interrupted Father Cafiero by raising his hand. The cardinal leaned back in his chair, settling down to enjoy the rest of the show. He knew what was forthcoming. Nothing like issues of sexual ethics to set the pope off.

"Divorce... abortion... birth control!" The pope shook his head and banged his hand on his desk with each word. "The Church cannot tolerate this epidemic of debauchery any longer."

"But Your Holiness, we face the same problems in many other Catholic countries," said Father Cafiero, wiping his brow. "However, this doesn't mean linking up with Joint Affairs every time we face a crisis."

"Do you really believe we are enamored of the materialistic values held by that Joint Affairs Commission? This alliance is a necessary evil, if Italy is to become an example to the Catholic world once again."

"Does the secretariat of state know about this project, Your Holiness?" asked Father Cafiero pointedly.

The pope waved a menacing finger in the air. "From now on *we* take direct responsibility for this project!"

The cardinal had not enjoyed himself quite so much for a long time, but the moment had come to intervene.

"How do you want us to proceed regarding the list we will present to the Joint Affairs Commission, Your Holiness?" he asked.

"We wish Your Eminence and Father Cafiero to let Monsignor Petrov have your proposals by 6:00 p.m. tomorrow. We will let you have our decision on Monday morning."

"Does Your Holiness think it will be necessary to put the matter before the General Council of Manus Domini?" asked the cardinal.

"Manus Domini answers to us," replied the pope in a tone that did not allow contradiction. "This meeting replaces the General Council."

Ubi major, minor cessat—When the powerful steps in, the lesser man must get out of the way. The cardinal glanced sideways at Father Cafiero. The father general seemed to have sunk into his chair.

At that moment the pope got up, but he staggered and had to hold on to the desk for support.

By late afternoon on Saturday, the ashtray on the cardinal's desk was overflowing with cigar butts. Although the window overlooking St. Peter's Square was wide open, a haze of bluish smoke hung in the room.

The cardinal looked at Monsignor Dyakonov and Monsignor Petrov, sitting in front of him; the substitute's hair was tousled, and the pope's secretary had his clerical collar undone.

The cardinal thumbed through the ten pages closely packed with names: ministries, state-controlled banks, state-run industries.... There was no corner they hadn't filled with at least one of Manus Domini's men.

"Well, I think that's it." The cardinal gathered his papers together and handed them to the pope's secretary.

Ten minutes later, Monsignor Petrov knocked on the door of the pope's private study, a red folder under his arm.

On Monday morning the cardinal's phone rang.

"Your Eminence, His Holiness has just handed me the list," Monsignor Petrov said in an excited voice.

"Well?"

"A real triumph, Your Eminence! Only some twenty changes, and none that really matter."

At 3:00 p.m. on Monday, Monsignor Feliciani, Cardinal Wolfenberg's private secretary, walked through the gates of the American embassy in Via Veneto. A few minutes later, he was handing an envelope marked Private and Confidential to a smiling Fox.

Guichard glanced through the last folder, closed it, then added it to the pile on his desk. When it was all over, those offshore companies would sink without leaving any trace, and no one would ever find out where the final order had come from.

He clicked the mouse and the balances of the offshore accounts appeared on the screen. Then he typed in a code on the Reuters keyboard, and the figures of the separate balances blinked. At the current exchange rates, the overall balance amounted to 70,289 billion Italian lire.

Guichard reached for the contract that had just arrived from London. The title on the front page read:

Credit facility of Lire 3,000 billion between the London Cranfield Bank, representing a syndicate of sixty banks, and Janus Holding SA of Luxembourg.

He skimmed through the document, and stopped at the page with the parties' signatures. His eyes rested on the name of Janus's chairman: *Signor* Mirko Prandi. Certainly a respectable businessman from Milan — alias Rosario Astarita.

Guichard ran his finger down the clauses and stopped on one of them. "… The credit facility can be used at a ratio of one to ten for the purchase of financial derivatives: swaps, currency options…" Then he turned to appendix A: Power of attorney. "… Janus Holding SA grants a full power of attorney to Mr. Guichard de Saint Clair…" That would enable him to buy options of up to 30,000 billion lire. In total, he could count on

100,000 billion lire, a figure that would bring most European central banks to their knees.

He turned to the Reuters screen again and typed in the code for Italian Treasury bills. Then he dialed Paulette's number and asked her to join him in his office.

"… An average of 37,000 billion lire a day of Italian treasury bills have changed hands over the past seven days," Paulette said, checking her computer printout.

"What's the trading volume on the stock market?" Guichard asked.

Paulette leafed through the pages. "Just 3,000 billion a day."

"Then forget about the shares and let's just buy treasury bills."

"Over how many brokers shall I spread our purchases?"

"A dozen or so."

"And what about the currency options?" she asked.

"Have you checked Italy's trade balance?"

"The US dollar and the D-mark take the lion's share."

Guichard rubbed the bridge of his nose. He didn't know the precise date when the Organization would launch its attack, but Franzese had told him that D-day would be by the end of the year, at the very latest.

"Then let's buy lira/U.S. dollar and lira/D-mark options expiring at the end of December," Guichard said.

"How much do we start with?"

"I was thinking of 9,000 billion lire, but we'd better sound out the market first."

"Done. The call option market against the lira is very thin. Even small volumes would cause a drop in the lira exchange rate."

"So?"

"Forget the 9,000 billion."

"Paulette, we have to buy options for 30,000 billion lire. Over how many weeks should we spread the purchases, without affecting the lira?"

"Not less than four months."

"Impossible."

Guichard looked at the desk calendar. It was September 26. Franzese would certainly strike before the end of the year. Then it would be the Lodge's turn.

"No more than ten weeks," Guichard said.

"Are you sure?"

"Don't worry. Even the roulette wheel is more reliable than foreign exchange forecasts."

Paulette looked at Guichard, then glanced at the calendar. "Ten weeks takes us up to December 10, which means 3,000 billion options per week."

"Right." Guichard gave Paulette an inquiring look. "Well, what are you waiting for?"

Paulette made a face. "Just waiting for you to come up with something like that. Now I feel better. Thank you."

"Your Eminence, I have His Eminence Cardinal Blanchard on the line from Paris," Monsignor Feliciani said from the intercom.

"Please put him through, Monsignore," said the cardinal, sitting upright in his chair. "... *Bonjour, Roger*. Have you any news for me?"

"*Bien sûr.* But I'm afraid you won't like it."

As Blanchard spoke, the cardinal's face became grimmer and grimmer.

That nightmare once again, and at a moment like this — into the bargain! And this time his own niece was involved, too. The cardinal's face hardened. He wouldn't let anyone get in his way. Not even Françoise.

"I'm coming to Paris tomorrow morning."

"I'll be waiting for you."

Guichard's footsteps echoed in the silence of the castle library. The janitor had covered the furniture with white dustsheets. Bookcases stacked full and fronted by stained-glass doors covered the walls. Two windows framed a stone fireplace, large enough to roast an ox in ancient times. The carpets had been rolled up, exposing a rough, stone floor beneath. The slabs in the center of the library had been chiseled with the coat of arms of the de Saint Clairs: a unicorn prancing in the center of a shield. Solid oak beams crossed the ceiling.

Guichard lifted a corner of the cover from the armchair by the desk, and ran his hand over the cracked leather. Specks of dust danced in the narrow shaft of light filtering through the shutters and striking the desk, lighting up the things that had been there ever since he could remember. He passed his hand over the dragon-shaped silver inkwell, then the bronze pendulum clock, cast to form a single block with a reclining Bacchus holding a bunch of grapes above his mouth.

From the top of the hill, the castle of the de Saint Clairs dominated Les Andelys. Standing on the parapet-walk of the tower, Guichard leaned against one of the merlons and gazed across the Norman countryside. On the top of the hill across the Seine, the ruins of Château Gaillard recalled an ancient past. Passing over the old roofs of the village nestled on the right bank of the river, his eyes followed the majestic loop of the Seine, overlooked by the chalk hillsides of Craies.

The leaves were turning red, the air was crisper, and the days growing shorter.

People described Normandy as a place where the air smelled of cider, a place full of promises that seemed to rise from its pine forests and its windswept coasts. Promises of what? Of a world where each corner would force you to remember a past you only wanted to forget?

From the pine wood came Véronique's silvery laughter, and the blurred figures of two children darted among the trees.

"You'll never find me, Guichard, you'll never find me," Véronique said.

"That so? And whose ribbon is that, the red one, sticking out from behind the fountain?"

"'Just like you to cheat, like all boys! You were spying! I'll never play with you again...."

All that was left, now, was an empty swing creaking to and fro in the wind.

A sound of music rose from the river. An old barge, now refitted as a pleasure boat, was making its way along the Seine. Two tourist couples stood on deck staring at Château Gaillard.

A dark-gray Renault appeared at the end of the tree-lined drive leading to the castle. Still standing on the parapet, Guichard watched the car stop in the courtyard, in front of the main entrance. A bald man in a striped shirt stretched over a barrel-sized stomach got out. He reached in the back seat for his jacket and briefcase.

Monsieur Barbouillet looked up and surveyed the battlements with an expert eye.

"Hmm, I don't think we've got much choice. It'll have to be on one of the towers, Monsieur le Comte." He bent down and retrieved a catalog out of his bulging bag. "As you can see, the lightning rod is really still a simple device, not much different from when Franklin invented it."

"I'm afraid you've misunderstood me," Guichard said. "It's not on the castle that I want it."

"Not on the castle?" Barbouillet looked around, disconcerted. "Where do you want it then? I can't see any other buildings in the vicinity."

"Come with me."

The skeletons of the oak trees looked just like they had right after the lightning had struck. Time had only lightened their blackness.

"Here," Guichard said.

"Here? I'm afraid I'm not with you, Monsieur le Comte. Where exactly?"

"Between those two oak trees."

Barbouillet gave Guichard a long look, the serious expression on his face contrasting with his jovial manner.

"What is this, Monsieur le Comte, a joke?" Barbouillet laughed slyly. "Go on, tell me. You're one of those people who like to make fools of people like me, aren't you?"

"Do I give you that impression?"

"No, not at all, and that's what drives me crazy!" He wiped his upper lip and forehead with a handkerchief. "Why, then?"

"I want to attract the lightning between the two oaks."

"You want to attract the lightning? Oh my goodness, I thought I'd heard just about everything in the thirty years I've been doing this job, but this beats everything." Barbouillet collapsed on a nearby tree stump. "Monsieur le Comte, lightning is a small, delightful electrical shock that in a few millionths of a second reaches something like 30,000 degrees and over 150 million volts. Not to mention the electromagnetic field it generates. A triviality, you'll probably say. Would it be too much to ask what you intend doing with the lightning?"

"I'm sorry, I can't tell you anything else. Only that it's very important to me. Help me, Barbouillet, and I'll make it worth your while."

"But, Monsieur le Comte, I'm not a lightning trapper. For nearly a century now, my company has been constructing alarm systems to *prevent* thunderbolts, not *attract* them. We play for the opposing team, do you see?"

"As soon as I saw you, I realized right away that you would do the impossible to please a customer." Reproachfulness and disappointment merged in Guichard's eyes. "Do you intend now to disappoint me?"

Barbouillet raised his hand in a gesture of discomfort, then got up. "I'll call the head office in Paris and let you know if it's possible." He looked up at the towers. "If they give me the go-ahead, I don't think I'd be far out in saying we'll have to install a copper rod at least ninety feet high, anchored to a platform in reinforced concrete, with a bomb-proof grounding system."

"Done." Guichard snapped his fingers.

"Mon Dieu."

By the dragon of St. George! said the Voice. *Only a madman can dream of turning a thunderbolt into a winged horse.*

You persist in being a prisoner of your time, Guichard said. And of the memory of your senses. Nine centuries divide us.

No one ever ventured to challenge the celestial spheres.

Don't you understand? I *must* know.

What murky design impels thee?

Guichard did not answer.

Thy silence betrays thee! If thou doest this for her, thou shalt find me on thy path, and thou wilt not be able to shield thyself behind our common blood.

24

On Tuesday morning, a black limousine drew up in the court-yard of the archbishop's palace in Paris. The stone flooring, the white-plastered walls, and the eighteenth-century wrought-iron lamps seemed to testify that the French Revolution had washed over the Church like the backwash of a wave against the cliffs.

Cardinal Wolfenberg, his expression as dark as a soul from hell, got out of the car. He strode briskly towards a glass-paneled door, which opened as if by magic. Passing be-tween the bowing figures of two priests, he ascended the mar-ble staircase in a swish of scarlet robes. Cardinal Blanchard was waiting for him at the top of the stairs. With that aquiline nose and distinctive goatee, Cardinal Wolfenberg would have recog-nized him anywhere.

"What do you think of it?" asked Cardinal Blanchard e-ventually.

"Are we really sure it's him?"

"Absolutely. One of the detectives even took some photographs and compared them with the photos in *Le Figaro*'s archives."

"So it really is *that* de Saint Clair." Cardinal Wolfenberg drummed his fingers on the arm of his Louis XVI chair.

"From the questions your niece asked you, I'm afraid there's not much doubt about that. That blessed story has cropped up again."

"With one difference, though."

"What's that?"

"This time we're not just faced with a writer playing Sher-lock Holmes."

"Then we have to do something," Cardinal Blanchard said. "And quickly."

"Do you think I have any doubts about that?"

"Well, let's be frank. Your niece is involved."

The cardinal glared at Blanchard. "And do you really think that personal considerations could make me hesitate?"

"I didn't mean that."

"In that case, please keep any such thoughts to yourself."

After an embarrassed silence, Cardinal Blanchard said: "What can this de Saint Clair be hiding?"

"With the name he bears, I wouldn't be surprised if he had the scrolls that the Essenes hid under the Temple."

"No one knows what's written in them, though," Blanchard said with a shadow of hope in his voice.

"Nothing exhilarating, that's for sure. Those Essenes were ascetics, and had nothing better to do than write for posterity."

"But in the Dead Sea Scrolls they concentrated on the Old Testament."

"Probably because they decided to leave the best chapter — the one on the New Testament — under the Temple, as a little surprise for us," Cardinal Wolfenberg said. "If the scrolls contain what I fear they do, we might as well close down shop and hang a For Sale sign in St. Peter's Square."

Cardinal Blanchard swallowed hard. "Please don't joke about it."

"Tell me, Roger, if you had those scrolls, where would you hide them?"

"I certainly wouldn't let them out of my sight, not even if it meant taking certain risks."

"Which means?"

"I'd hide them at home. That way I could even get up in the middle of the night to look at them."

A shrewd smile crossed Cardinal Wolfenberg's face. "That's exactly what I would do, too."

"What have you got in mind?"

"Can you not hazard a guess?"

"I daren't think about it."

Cardinal Wolfenberg took out one of his cigars and lit it leisurely. He then leaned towards Cardinal Blanchard and whispered his plan to him. Blanchard's face grew pale, but Cardinal

Wolfenberg soon put a stop to his doubts. Blanchard promised he would call Cardinal Wolfenberg the following evening in Rome.

When the cardinal got into the car, he leaned forward and asked the priest to take him back to Orly-CDG. He wouldn't tell the pope—not right away, at any rate. The matter might well have some interesting developments. He settled back in his seat and thought about Françoise. It was a shame, but from this moment on they would have to go their separate ways.

The yellow and white Vatican flags fluttering from either fender, the sleek limousine headed towards the freeway.

Guichard turned from the windows and sat down on the couch. Professor Bieri's words at the Institut de France rang in his memory: "… *but the moment you took your knowledge of the present into the past and used it – allegorically, if you killed your grandmother – you'd be doomed.*" The professor meant that one can't get away with changing the course of history, but his words made him think now about a more prosaic matter: clothing. Guichard ran his hand over his sleeve: synthetic fabrics, buttons, a watch…. All things incompatible with Geoffroy's time. He remembered that the professor had given him his business card with his private phone number.

"I apologize for calling you this late, Professor, but I really need to ask you a question," Guichard said. He explained his doubt to Professor Bieri.

"Yours is a most legitimate doubt, Monsieur le Comte. None of the objects and materials you just mentioned could exist in a space-time in which they hadn't yet been invented. It would be a physical absurdity."

"Take a hypothetical time-traveler, traveling back to the Middle Ages and wearing a wrist watch and clothes made of synthetic fibers. What would happen?"

"Hmm…"

"Would wearing those things prevent him from traveling back in time?"

"No, I don't think so. He would get there, but the moment he set foot in that space-time, those objects would disintegrate."

"Literally?"

"Yes, I think so. The poor man would remain naked and, quite likely, with burns all over his body."

"That's what I thought."

"Monsieur le Comte? "

"Yes?"

"You mean it, don't you?"

"Whatever are you thinking of? I'm only a lover of quantum physics. A mere dilettante."

"Don't hesitate to call me, if you need me," Bieri said in a serious voice. "And allow me one last comment, Monsieur le Comte: quantum physics can be a dangerous pastime."

Guichard remained seated on the edge of the desk, tapping the business card on it and staring into the distance. Then he strode out of the library and looked for André.

Guichard and André were sitting at the desk in the library, its top cluttered with large volumes. Stacks of books were also piled on the floor. Julius was watching them, crouched on an overhead bookshelf.

"I already know all there is to know about armor and chain mail, André. Let's just concentrate on the clothing they wore underneath," Guichard said. "Especially on the lower torso."

"Poor knights," André said, studying an illustration. "Getting dressed called for a blacksmith."

The pendulum clock in the hall struck two when Guichard and André closed the last books. Yellow Post-its protruded from many volumes and densely written sheets of paper lay on the desk.

"In my opinion, it was the *chausses* [tight fitting stocking-like individual coverings for the legs and feet] and *braies* [large, baggy drawers, with the inside of each leg slit up to the crotch] that, together, functioned as modern pants," André said.

"Hmm, I don't know. It seems to me that only the *chausses* are the equivalent of today's pants," Guichard said. "*Braies* must necessarily serve as underpants."

"Maybe towards the 15th century, Monsieur le Comte, when *braies* began to become fairly short." André looked at an illustration from the Maciejowski Bible. "But not at Geoffroy's time."

"Then what did they wear as underpants?"

"They didn't wear any."

The next morning, André summoned Guichard's personal tailor, owner of a *maison de couture* in Rue St. Honoré, for 11:00 a.m. Then he went into the office adjoining the library, took a book from a pile, opened it at the page from which a yellow Post-it stuck out and laid it on the glass of the photocopier. He pressed the button....

Guichard invited the tailor to sit down in front of him in the library and told him what he needed. As he was speaking, he showed him several illustrations from the photocopies that André had made that morning.

The tailor was a lanky man, wearing an impeccable pin-striped suit. He wore a monocle and a thin handlebar moustache.

"I realize that my request may seem somewhat unusual," Guichard said.

"I can't deny it, Monsieur le Comte," the tailor said, looking hard at Guichard.

"The main thing is that the garments shouldn't contain any synthetic fiber, and no buttons or pockets. The *chausses* should be made of wool and the *braies* of linen."

"It's for a masked ball, isn't it?"

"Um, yes, that's just what it's for. A masked ball."

"Monsieur le Comte, allow me to express my profound gratitude." The tailor half-rose from his armchair and shook Guichard warmly by the hand.

Guichard looked at him in astonishment.

"You see, it's from requests like yours that I have the confirmation that mine remains an important mission. As long as men like you are around, I will know that the brutal devastation of our planet brought about by the vandals of *prêt-à-porter* will always find brave opponents. Monsieur le Comte, you are for me like the ancient lighthouse of Alexandria."

"Thank you, but—"

The tailor took out his monocle and puffed out his chest. "Monsieur le Comte, a man who attends a masked ball in medieval costume and who worries that even his underpants should comply with the dictates of fashion and with the materials of the time, proves one point: style is not dead."

The Bentley drew up in the courtyard of the castle at Les Andelys. Guichard and André got out, and André opened the trunk and unloaded several boxes wrapped in refined beige paper bearing the gilded label of the Maison de Couture Apollinaire Fauberger. Guichard and André picked up the boxes and went up the outside steps of the castle.

They went down the spiral stone steps leading to the cellars. The odor of wine-must hung heavy in the air. Once they reached the bottom, they walked down a corridor lined on both sides with a series of arched cavities, hollowed out of the same rock that supported the castle foundations. The arches rested on large stone columns, with rusty rings hanging from them. Wine racks filled with dusty bottles were leaning against the walls. They stopped at the end of the cellars in front of a heavy oak door. Guichard put his boxes on the floor, ran his hand along the stone beam supporting the doorway and withdrew a key.

They entered a long room with a vaulted ceiling and placed the boxes on a bench. The walls were covered with weapons dating back to the time of the Norman Conquest of England: maces, axes, shields, swords. As if on guard, suits of armor were lined up along one wall.

"Well, Monsieur le Comte, I'm going to discuss with the supervisor the problem of the barrels," André said. "Are you really sure you don't need any help?"

"No, thank you, André. I'll see you later."

After André had gone, Guichard opened all the boxes. Then he stepped up to a suit of armor, raised the visor and put a hand inside. He took out a key, went to the end of the room and stopped in front of a side wall built of large square stones. He pushed one of the stones, which turned on its own axis to reveal a lock behind it. Guichard inserted the key and turned it.

The end wall began to slide silently aside, uncovering a double wall.

The white unicorn of the de Saint Clairs and the red Templar cross seemed to chase one another on the suits of armor and chain mail, the shields, the cloaks and the *surcottes* hanging on the inner wall. Swords, daggers, maces and battle-axes called to mind bloody clashes, but also a past when men believed in honor and unicorns.

Guichard took off his jacket, unbuttoned his shirt, took off his shoes…. When he was completely naked, he took a pair of white linen *braies* out of a box and put them on. They were baggy drawers extending to the mid calf, with the inside of each thigh slit vertically almost up to the crotch. The belt was a green ribbon slotted through a tubular hem with vertical slits, one in the front and the other two over the hips. Guichard tied the ribbon in front. Then he took a bright blue *chausse*, put his right leg in it and pulled it up to his crotch. At the top, on the outside, the *chausse* had a drawstring, which Guichard took hold of. He studied it with a puzzled expression.

Ha! Ha! Ha! By a thousand gryphons, what a great booby thou art, said the Voice, gasping with Homeric guffaws.

What the hell do you want? Guichard said, holding the drawstring of the *chausse* in his hand.

Alas, I laugh when I should rather weep. And whole generations of de Saint Clairs laugh with me. Canst thou not hear them? Strain thine ears, thou dormouse.

I can't hear anything. What's so funny, anyway?

And thou darest ask? They have discovered that we have taken as our avenger a nincompoop not even capable of donning a pair of chausses. *What ignominy!*

Oh, shut up, you blasted chatterbox. I'd like to see you struggling with a tuxedo! What's this wretched string for?

Thou numskull, canst not see there are slits in the sides of the braies *at belt level? Make fast the string to the green ribbon that runs within. Or is the undertaking too challenging?*

Guichard did the job and gave a satisfied nod. Then he put on the other *chausse*. When he had finished, he looked at himself. He still seemed to be doubtful.

What further metaphysical dilemma tormenteth thy mind? asked the Voice.

Er, tell me something... How did you... as it were... Well, how did you pee?

HA! HA! HA! By the dragon of St. George, I believe not mine ears. HA! HA! HA!

Guichard's face darkened. He clenched his fists and ground his teeth.

Guichard de Saint Clair, thy query meriteth to be engraved in letters of gold in the Great Book of Chivalry.

Why don't you shut up? How did you manage to pull him out?

Pull out... what?

Your imagination soars like an eagle over the highest peaks, Guichard said with a withering glare at the ceiling. *What do you think I'm talking about?* He pointed to his groin. *Him!* What else?

Droll, i'faith, passing droll, said the Voice wonderingly. *Never have I heard a knight speak thus of his instrument.*

Guichard fumed. *Well?*

Do those slits inside the thighs suggest naught to thee, my nimble-witted descendant?

Guichard muttered. He undid the *chausses,* which he pulled halfway down his legs. He bent down, put a hand into one of the slits and rummaged around for a while, grumbling. Finally, he snorted and straightened up, shaking his head.

Nothing doing. I can't manage it, he said. And nobody will ever get *me* to pee squatting down like a woman.

Hosanna! I commend thee for thy noble creed, said the Voice. *I will disclose an arcanum to thee:* all dependeth on the crotch, it whispered. *In order that the manoeuvre be crowned with success, it is of paramount importance that the inside slits reach right up to the crotch. Inform thy taillour, and give him ten lashes.*

Guichard put on the *cuisses* [thigh coverings, padded and quilted], that he fixed to a leather belt, a linen shirt with a circular collar, and over the shirt a wine-red *gambeson* [a padded, quilted coat reaching to the knees]. He detached a chain mail from the hidden wall and, tensing his arm muscles, he slipped it on over his head. It extended to his knees and covered his arms to the wrists. Over it, he put on a white linen sleeveless *surcotte* [a loose, short cloak worn over armor], with the coat of arms of the de Saint Clairs embroidered on the front.

That chain mail was my preferred, said the Voice wistfully. *It took five years to make, and 220,000 metal links to fashion it.*

Comfortable as a leaden blanket, Guichard said, trying to move his arms.

And now? said the Voice. *Dost thou believe it sufficeth to gird thyself with a chain mail suit to become a knight?*

Guichard said nothing.

Even shouldst thou succeed in thy insane dream, on arrival in my world thou wouldst not see the first sinking of the sun.

That remains to be seen.

Ho, ho! Let us see, then, whether thy mastery of arms may be likened unto thy haughtiness. Seest thou yon battle-axe near the three hooks?

I see it.

Take it.

Guichard grasped the haft of the huge axe and pulled it off the wall.

Seest thou the wooden shield hanging from the hook near the door?

I see it.

The distance is two roods. Try to pierce the shield with the axe — if thou canst. *Certes I do not expect thee to strike the center.*

Guichard concentrated on the shield that was a good twelve yards away. He swung the axe slowly and repeatedly in ever-increasing arcs, raised his arm, then his body arched backwards and his arm shot forwards.

Turning on its trajectory, the axe hissed though the air and with a sharp thud stuck in the center of the shield.

By the dragon of St. George! said the Voice.

And now for a display of swordsmanship? Guichard said slashing the air.

♣

It was the middle of the night when Geoffroy knocked on Miriam's door. She was awake, waiting for him.

"Miriam, when the bells ring the Prime, I have to leave."

"Say no more. Please, just don't say anything."

After making love, Geoffroy put his arms round her and held her close, stroking her hair. In the silence of the night, Geoffroy sensed a question hanging in the air, a question that Miriam tried hard not to ask, and to which he would have had no easy answer. He wished she could find the strength to speak, because he couldn't.

"Martouni, the village where I was born, lies on the shores of Lake Sevan, a mountain lake with beaches of white sand," she said eventually. "Up there it's always sunny, and the breeze carries the perfume of pine woods. The water is a deep turquoise; it's like a piece of sky fallen to earth. When I was a young girl, I used to sit on the beach and gaze for hours at the waters of the lake, dreaming of what I would be when I grew up."

Miriam got out of bed, and the moonlight filtering through the shutters illuminated the curves of her body. She opened her jewel box, searched inside, then lay down next to Geoffroy again and took his hand.

"I want you to keep this."

Geoffroy felt something like a rough pebble. "What is it?" He raised his hand to look at it, but the room was too dark.

"It's the head of a very old tufa statuette. I found it while I was walking on the beach of my lake."

"Is it your lucky charm? I don't want you to give it away."

"Keep it, please." Miriam closed his hand over it. "One of the old villagers told me a story. He told me that the people who inhabited our mountains in ancient times used to carve statuettes like this, to worship nature. He said that this is the head of a statuette that symbolized the continuity of life after death."

"What do you mean?"

"He spoke of reincarnation, but I have always thought of my statuette as symbolizing a god of lost opportunities."

"A god of lost opportunities?"

"A god that will make everything that hasn't come true in this life come true in the next."

Geoffroy was on the point of replying, but Miriam pressed her hand to his lips. He embraced her, and felt her cheeks all wet with tears. Then he took off the chain he wore round his neck, with the medallion on which the coat of arms of the de Saint Clairs was engraved, and put it in her hand without saying anything.

An arm emerged from the dark at the bottom of the staircase and Geoffroy felt an iron grip seize his arm. *Krikor.*

"May you be cursed for eternity, you dog of a Norman! I have known from the beginning that you would make her suffer."

Geoffroy tried to pull himself free, but in vain. "This is none of your business."

"Oh yes, it is, because to me she is like the very air I breathe." Krikor pointed to his hump, and his voice grew less steady. "I know I'll never be able to have her, but you don't know what it's like to love someone, in the shadow, every minute of one's life, to the point of sacrificing oneself for the beloved's own good."

"I… I couldn't know." Geoffroy restrained from putting his hand on Krikor's shoulder. "I don't know what to say…."

"How can you let go of something so beautiful? *How?*"

"Krikor, stab me to the heart. It will hurt less than your words."

"I won't touch you, but only for her sake. You may go now, but I wish that regret may tear your heart apart for the rest of your days." Krikor freed Geoffroy from his grip and disappeared into the darkness.

When Geoffroy left the inn, he looked up at Miriam's windows, where a dim light filtered through. He looked at her lucky charm in the light of a wall torch, near the inn sign: the head of a statuette. It was a long oval shape carved from orange-colored stone. The head wore an odd triangular hat and had two tiny, black pebbles for eyes. It seemed to be smiling. Geoffroy clutched it.

His feet carried him away, but his heart went back and climbed the staircase of the inn.

Geoffroy, the other Templars, and a hundred crusaders in full armor left Solomon's stables with the four carts. As the bells of the Church of the Holy Sepulchre rang the first canonical hour, the pounding of the horses' hooves echoed through the alleys of the Old City.

Geoffroy turned back for a last look at Jerusalem and its hills. A blanket of dark clouds had gathered over the city. As the rain started to pelt down, a streak of lightning shot across the sky and a clap of thunder shook the earth. Geoffroy shivered and pulled his cloak tightly around his shoulders.

Halfway between Jerusalem and the coast, the column split into two. Bertrand and Gondemare de Saint-Omer took with them two sergeants and an escort of thirty crusaders. As the sergeants unhitched the cart with the wooden chest, Bertrand spurred his horse and rode over to Geoffroy and Hugues.

"It seems our paths part here," Bertrand said.

Hugues raised his hand, dripping with rain. "You know what you have to do. See you in Troyes. Good luck."

"Good luck to you. You may well need it in Rome."

Bertrand galloped back, his horse's hooves splashing mud along the path. Geoffroy watched the column move off in the direction of Jaffa. Bertrand and Gondemare's ship was due to arrive at Jaffa that same day to take them back to France. Their final destination was Blanchefort, in the south. They would hide the wooden chest in the underground chambers of the Castle of the Blancheforts, Bertrand's family. Geoffroy turned his horse and galloped to join his column.

From the top of the hill Geoffroy watched the galley dock in the Port of Tyre. The sails marked with the papal emblem were lowered and the sailors cast anchor. The following day the ship would set sail back to Brindisi, where they would be met by the pope's soldiers sent to escort them to Rome.

Geoffroy dug his spurs in, but his horse refused to go down the slope. The animal wanted to obey, but it was as if some mysterious force were holding it back. The horse shook its mane, neighed, and pawed the ground. It was no use. Geoffroy had the feeling he wasn't alone.

He turned his horse and looked towards the crest of the hill. No one in sight, and yet he felt the presence of some unknown force, a force beyond his comprehension.

He unsheathed his sword. "Who's there? Show yourself!"
Nothing, only the whistling of the wind.
"Were it Lucifer himself, I would have no fear! Show yourself, you coward!" he cried, brandishing his sword towards the hill.
The wind blew harder.
Geoffroy dug his spurs in hard forcing his horse to the top. On the other side, the hill sloped down to a thick forest, beyond which lay a strip of lowland that stretched as far as the coast.
The wind whipped up a cloud of dust, forming a whirlwind that rose into the sky and traced a rust-colored trail above the canopy of trees.

Seated at his desk, Cardinal Wolfenberg finished sipping his coffee. He checked the time. Still half an hour, and *senhor* Ignacio Escobar would be sitting in front of him.
After receiving Escobar's initial letter from Manaus, the cardinal had sent him a fax confirming that the Holy See was interested in examining the project more thoroughly. Just two days later, Escobar had sent him a detailed memorandum: the eighty-page document now lying on the cardinal's desk.
He resumed going through Escobar's report.

"Recursos Naturais is proposing a conservative exploitation of the natural resources of the Amazon rain forests. Our project is based on two considerations.
The first is the fact that twelve percent of the Amazon Forest has already been destroyed. This destruction has occurred as a result of the illegal speculation of big landowners, cattle-rearing enterprises, timber merchants and *garimpieros*—gold-diggers. The destruction of the tropical forests causes a significant drop in the oxygen levels in the atmosphere and the emission of a quantity of carbon dioxide equal to half that of the whole of Europe. The growing concentration of carbon dioxide in the atmosphere is the main cause of the 'greenhouse effect.'....
The second consideration involves the Amazon Indians. The Indian population, estimated at five million in the sixteenth century, has dropped to 220,000. Exploita-

tion and violence committed against the Amazon Indians—suffice it to mention the Yanomami tribes—have
been widely covered in the international press. Brasilia
discourages foreign aid, considering it an attempt to interfere in their internal affairs....

Recursos Naturais is persuaded that the only way to
obtain a truly conservative exploitation of the Amazonian
forest is to involve the Indians economically. Our plan
consists in organizing the Amazon Indians into cooperatives, making them an active part of the project...."

"Dr. Escobar has just arrived, Your Eminence," said Monsignor Feliciani from the intercom.

"Show him in, Monsignore."

Ignacio Escobar was hardly someone who'd pass unnoticed.
He was very tall, corpulent, tanned and, with obvious pride, he
sported a large Souvaroff-type reddish moustache which
curved round to meet his sideburns. He wore a light-colored
linen suit with a vest, and a pin with a sparkling stone sprouted
from his silk tie. He leaned his walking stick against the cardinal's desk—the kind of stick used in the old days, made of reddish wood, with a finely chiseled dolphin-shaped ivory
handle—and laid his creamy panama on the desk.

Escobar seemed the last surviving specimen of late nine-
teenth-century colonial splendor, produced from mixing in a
shaker three parts Robert Louis Stevenson, two parts James Mi-
chener and, for the connoisseur, one part Graham Greene.

The Brazilian knocked back his coffee in one go and
smacked his lips.

"I've read your memorandum with interest," Cardinal
Wolfenberg said. "I have a number of questions—"

"Before talking business, *Eminência*, in my country we like
to create the right atmosphere." Escobar threw the cardinal a
winning smile.

He fished about in the pocket of his vest and took out two
aluminum cigar tubes. His eyes shone with complicity. The
cardinal recognized the unmistakable seal of his favorite Romeo
y Julieta.

"I bet you smoke Cuban cigars, *Eminência*. Am I not right?"

"I must admit it's a weakness of mine. And I, too, smoke only Romeo y Julieta."

"You don't know how happy you make me." Escobar leaned forward to grasp the cardinal's hands. "And you know why?"

"I'd be curious to know."

"I have a theory that has never let me down yet, *Eminência*, either in business or in everyday life."

"Indeed? And what theory might that be, pray?"

"I'm convinced you can judge a man's character by the cigars he smokes. And a man who smokes Romeo y Julieta is a man one can trust," declared Escobar with Solomonic gravity.

The cardinal had never thought about it in those terms, but the idea did not displease him.

"However, your theory fails to take into account all those who do not smoke cigars," said the cardinal.

"But *Eminência*, do you really consider *them* to be men?"

There was some truth in that, too. The cardinal lit the tip of his cigar from the long match that Escobar held out to him.

"A rich and powerful flavor," stated Escobar, taking a deep drag.

The cardinal put his glasses on and looked through his notes. "Why did you think of the Holy See as a possible subscriber?"

"The international controversies over the Indian affair have upset the Brazilian Government so much that Brasilia now tends to see any international offer of help as interference."

"You mean to say that Brasilia would give its blessing to the Holy See's intervention?"

"Precisely, *Eminência*. Besides, isn't Brazil the biggest Catholic country in the world?" Escobar frowned. "However, one mustn't forget that in recent years relations between the Vatican and the Brazilian Church have not been without controversy."

The cardinal stiffened. "What do you mean?"

"Let's face it, *Eminência*. The Boff affair didn't help the Church's image, either in Brazil or the rest of Latin America."

"Is that a criticism?"

"I'm merely stating a fact, *Eminência*."

"I see." The novelty of receiving a frank reply eased the cardinal's irritation. "And tell me, Dr Escobar—and I would ask you to be frank. What exactly *is* our image in Brazil?"

"Do you really want the truth?"

"Absolutely. I promise you I shall not become incensed."

"I am sorry to have to tell you this, *Eminência*, but your image in Brazil, or rather in the whole of Latin America, really stinks."

The cardinal's jowls quivered. No one had ever dared speak to him like that. Escobar's expression, though, was regretful, as if the Brazilian felt sad at having to tell him such a painful truth. The cardinal burst out laughing.

"You know, people are afraid of me. And here you are, a complete stranger, telling me something like that, and I start laughing like an idiot."

"I told you before, *Eminência*. A man who smokes these cigars cannot be bad." Escobar leaned towards the cardinal and looked him in the eyes with a vexed expression. "So why then, *Eminência*, did the Holy Office continue to beat that poor Boff on the *cabeça* for years on end?"

"The situation got out of hand."

"Doesn't Matthew in his Gospel say: '*Pulsate, et aperietur vobis*'—Knock, and it shall be opened unto you?"

The cardinal stared at Escobar with renewed respect.

"Now this project gives you the chance to make up for that big mistake," said Escobar.

"But are you certain Brasilia is prepared to guarantee the Recursos Naturais loan?"

"I went to see Herberto Mendez, the Treasury minister in Brasilia, myself, and he gave me his personal assurance," Escobar replied. Once again, he leaned towards the cardinal. "And do you know why I believe what the minister told me?"

The cardinal gave Escobar a questioning look.

"The minister smokes Romeo y Julieta cigars too," whispered Escobar, his eyes gleaming.

"In your memorandum you mention a huge investment, the equivalent of 10,000 billion lire. Why so much?"

"We want to do something that will leave its mark!"

"The shareholders will have to underwrite a capital stock increase from 230 to 2,310 million reais...."

Escobar clinched his fist as if to reassure the cardinal. "Recursos Naturais's shareholders have broad shoulders."

The cardinal rose and told Escobar he would let him know the Holy See's line of thought within two weeks. Before leaving, Escobar bent over and kissed the cardinal's ring. Then he straightened himself up to his full height of six feet two and looked the cardinal straight in the eyes.

"You and I will do big things together, *Eminência*," said Escobar raising his walking stick. "We'll show the whole world just what the Catholic Church is capable of!"

Then he went out, grasping his stick firmly, with the same prophetic look Moses must have had when he came down from Mount Sinai carrying the Tables of Testimony.

The cardinal stood motionless in front of the door, his gaze lost in space. He turned abruptly and went back to his desk. First he called Archbishop Dyakonov, then Vallanco-Torres. He asked to see them at three o'clock that same afternoon in his office. Then he sank back into his chair.

True. You could trust a man who smoked Romeo y Julieta.

§

After he had left the Palace of the Holy Office, Ignacio Escobar set off towards St. Peter's Square. The colored façade of the Basilica shone in the sunlight and Escobar looked up at the dome. He breathed in deeply, took off his panama and surveyed the scene. His gaze took in the Bernini colonnade, then the Apostolic Palace and finally the Caligula obelisk in the center of the square.

Followed by some curious glances, he replaced his hat and continued on his way towards Via della Conciliazione, swinging his stick with consummate elegance.

He stopped in front of a telephone booth and looked inside. It took credit cards. He had to stoop to get inside, then managed to get out his little address book and checked a number, running his finger across the page.

"Hello? ... Hi Guichard, it's Philippe ... Yes, I've just finished," Escobar said with a perfidious smile. "You were right. I believe we've found a client for our bonds ... Precisely. See you in Paris this afternoon."

Leaving the phone booth, Escobar took off his panama, fanned himself with it, and burst out laughing. He a Brazilian? His real name was not Ignacio Escobar, but Philippe de Mauriac — *Comte* Philippe de Mauriac, to be precise. A pure-blooded Frenchman. And a descendant of Victor de Mauriac, one of the nine Templars of Jerusalem.

Cardinal Wolfenberg was sitting in his private study, puffing away at his cigar. The clock struck the half-hour. It was 9:30 p.m. and Blanchard still hadn't called. He was about to reach out for the phone when it rang.

"*Allô Rolf, c'est toi ?* I have good news," Cardinal Blanchard said.

"Good news at last. Tell me."

The cardinal listened, nodding from time to time. "So when will it be?"

"They've got to wait for him to be away."

"Do they know what it is they have to look for? What did you tell them?"

"Don't worry. They haven't a clue about the contents."

"Will they be able to do it in just one night?"

"There'll be three of them. They're all professionals."

"Keep me informed."

The cardinal went over to the window. Another few days and he would know the truth at last, after two thousand years.

Michelangelo's dome seemed brighter than usual. But now that brightness frightened him.

25

"Hmm, that expression doesn't convince me," Jules said, sitting down in front of Françoise.

"It's all Guercino's fault," Françoise said.

"That's just what I wanted to talk to you about. Today I went to see Alain."

Alain Wesenheim, an old friend of Jules's, was the curator of the Louvre's department of paintings.

"What did he tell you?"

"The key to the problem probably lies in a catalog that was printed in Bologna in 1968 for a Guercino exhibition. The catalog's text was written by Sir Denis Mahon, the British collector."

"What did Mahon say?"

"He wrote that the Vatican Apostolic Library holds an inventory of the Barberini mansion. And guess what? That inventory shows that in 1644 the Guercino painting belonged to Cardinal Antonio Barberini the Younger."

"That's certainly something," Françoise said. "But I still can't see the connection with Poussin."

"I'm getting there. Alain told me that in 1628 Poussin sold a painting, *Death of Germanicus*, to Cardinal Francesco Barberini, Antonio's brother."

"And so?"

"Does the name Cassiano del Pozzo mean anything to you?"

"Of course. Cassiano was a close friend of Poussin's, besides being one of his main clients."

"Well, perhaps you're not aware of something. Cassiano was quite at home in the Barberini household. No wonder: he was Cardinal Barberini's secretary."

"Now I see. So, thanks to Cassiano, Poussin had the chance of visiting the Barberini mansion."

"When the commission for *Death of Germanicus* arrived, Poussin became a regular visitor at the Barberinis' and certainly had many opportunities to see their paintings."

"But that inventory speaks of 1644 and attributes the ownership of the painting to Francesco, not to Antonio Barberini."

Jules shrugged. "It's quite possible that the two of them lived under the same roof, which was quite common among the aristocratic families of the time."

"There's still that difference of sixteen years between 1628, the year *Death of Germanicus* was delivered, and 1644, the year we know for certain that the Guercino painting was in the possession of one of the Barberinis."

"I wouldn't worry about that. When was it that Poussin painted the first version of *Les Bergers d'Arcadie*?"

"Between 1628 and 1630."

"Don't you see?" said Jules. "In 1628 Poussin sells *Death of Germanicus* to Francesco Barberini and sees the Guercino painting at the Barberinis' home. He's so taken with it that he immediately starts work on the first version of *Les Bergers d'Arcadie*."

"Although there's no proof, it all seems to fit." Françoise thought of Panowsky, the Princeton iconography expert. "Panowsky was right, then. Cardinal Rospigliosi!"

"What are you talking about?"

Françoise told Jules about her research on Guercino. "You see? Cardinal Rospigliosi was a friend of the Barberinis. So it looks as if it was he who suggested the phrase to the Barberinis, when they commissioned Guercino's painting."

"Which confirms that the first version of *Les Bergers d'Arcadie* doesn't hide any mystery," Jules said. "Poussin wouldn't have known the secret at that time."

Françoise sighed. "All that useless research on Guercino...."

"If you hadn't done it, you'd have been left with the doubt that it was Guercino who revealed the secret to Poussin. Now everything is clear. If you want to find out what lies behind it all, you've got to discover what happened to Poussin between 1630 and 1640, the year he finished *Les Bergers d'Arcadie II*."

Françoise recalled the reproductions of the painting in Guichard's house and in her uncle's study. They were reproductions of the second Poussin, not the first. There must be a reason for that.

The oak paneling and carpeting in the conference-room of the Financière d'Arcadie failed to muffle the sound of the voices. Papers were piled up everywhere on the large oval table, together with crumpled sheets from legal pads and paper cups. Guichard glanced at the ten executives of Allied and CIP, sitting half on one side and half on the opposite side of the table. They were all in their shirtsleeves, and several of them had loosened their ties: drawn faces, suspicious looks, sharp voices.

Guichard reached for the coffeepot. As he poured himself a cup, he glanced at the resentful face of the head of CIP's legal department.

The previous Friday, Kovacs had sent a copy of the contract draft to both CIP and to Guichard in Paris. A flood of paper overflowing with legal jargon, but it was clear that the deal would revolve around only a few points. Allied and CIP board meetings had already been called for October 9, the following Thursday, to pass the final resolutions, and so there was no time to lose. Guichard knew he had to come up with a final draft by the following Monday, the 6th, which meant making all these people work right through the weekend.

As everyone began to leave for the lunch break, Guichard eyed Phil O'Neill, the lean manager of Allied's financial and legal departments, who was gathering his papers together. He told O'Neill he needed to have a word with him, and led the way to his office.

"I just don't understand," O'Neill said when Guichard was through. "What are you getting at with a clause like that?"

"I'm afraid CIP is up to something. A dirty trick, at the last minute."

"A dirty trick?"

"Uh-huh. Under the direction of the prime minister himself."

Guichard told O'Neill of his suspicions, arisen after his second meeting with Accardo and after reading Paulette's report about CIP's plants in the South of Italy. He knew that O'Neill was likely to call Kovacs in San Francisco right away. Let him. At that point, Kovacs would have no choice but to play CIP's game, hoping he would end up on his feet.

"Are you quite sure?" asked O'Neill. "If you were wrong about the value of those plants, we'd be cutting our own throats."

"Wrong? On a matter like this?"

O'Neill's cold gaze studied Guichard. "I know Kovacs trusts you, but this is pushing things too far. I'm not going to take on a responsibility like this."

"And what if I am right? Kovacs doesn't seem to be the kind of man who forgives easily, but you don't need to be reminded of that."

O'Neill's lips tightened. "All you've got are suspicions."

"Think of the consequences. The pros of doing as I say far outweigh the cons."

O'Neill started pressing and releasing the button on his ballpoint pen, and for a few moments that was the only noise that broke the silence.

"OK," said O'Neill, "but I'm going to call Kovacs right away."

Guichard pointed to the telephone.

As O'Neill was about to dial, he stopped and grinned at Guichard. "If you *are* right, I can just picture the faces of the Italians when the surprise comes to light."

Guichard screwed up the sheet of paper he was holding into a tight ball and hurled it into the waste-paper basket.

"Mr. Abramson on the red line," said Secretary of State Andrews's secretary.

Andrews sighed. "Put him through."

"Why the hell have the NSA taken more than a week to send me those messages?" Abramson said. "Are we paying them to sit around on their asses?"

"The coding system of the Vatican secretariat of state is different from Manus Domini's. The NSA had a tough time with the decoding."

"It looks as if the Vatican secretary of state is suddenly in a hell of a hurry to arrange secret meetings with the presidents of the Episcopal Conferences of half the Catholic countries. Missiroli's up to something."

"What?"

"The Vatican can't keep its empire together any longer and — between you and me — that's no surprise, with this Russian Pope who's been breaking everyone's balls even more than the one before him. I wouldn't be surprised if Missiroli had finally decided to do something about it."

"A rift within the Catholic Church? I can hardly believe it."

"Rule number one: always be prepared for the worst," Abramson said. "We can't let anything happen in the Vatican that could mess up our plans, right? In order for the alliance to work, we need all their strength."

"Are you plotting something against Missiroli?"

"There's no need. Just think of what happened to John Paul I, the last in a long list. I'd rather have dinner with Lucrezia Borgia than have coffee at the Vatican."

"What do we do, then? Do we tell Fox to inform Cardinal Wolfenberg?"

"Mm, better not. Wolfenberg wasn't born yesterday. If Fox tells him, he'll understand right away that we're keeping an eye on them."

"What, then?"

"Our cardinal has a boss in Manus Domini. His name is Father Cafiero. Manus Domini is a moneymaking machine, which requires a united Church. Missiroli's too much of a risk for him. I leave the conclusion to you."

"I see," Andrews said. "Through the CIA?"

"Of course."

"OK, I'll call Langley."

§

On the top floor of the Main Building of the Agency's Head-quarters in Langley, Virginia, the colors of the CIA seal gleamed on the dark marble floor in the deserted hallway. The clock in the lobby read midnight, but the lights were still on in the office of Clive Threader, the director. Two men sat at the table.

"That's about all," Threader said. "We've got to stop Cardinal Missiroli."

The head of Operations, which included all the CIA's undercover activities, nodded. "What do you have in mind?"

"Why dirty our hands, if there's someone else willing to do the job for us? After all, this time it's not just a matter of planting bombs."

"What about dropping Cafiero a few lines, telling him what Missiroli's up to?"

Threader rocked his pen back and forth between his forefinger and middle finger for a few moments. "Okay. You take care of it."

"I'll contact our people in Rome right away."

The door burst open and the whining of a vacuum cleaner filled the room.

"Sorry, gentlemen, I didn't know... Sorry." The cleaner backed out and closed the door.

Man, look at them vultures, he thought, turning off the vacuum. Praise the Lord, I ain't done nuttin' to stand in the way o' them two.

§

Sitting in his office at the US embassy in Rome, Zaslow reread the coded message that had arrived overnight from Langley.

"It's something we could deal with ourselves in a matter of days," said his deputy. "Why involve that guy Cafiero?"

"Langley is right. Why dirty our own hands?"

"When I was a kid, my granny always told me not to trust Catholics, starting with priests," the deputy said. "What kinda' folk are they? Where are we gonna end up, for Chrissake?"

"I'm going to draft an anonymous letter. I want you to take care of the delivery. Today."

§

Father Cafiero reread the letter several times, then looked at the envelope, both front and back.

He crossed his legs and began drumming on his knee, as his foot swung up and down. He shook his head smugly and reached for the intercom.

"Father, I need the phone number of the US embassy."

The following morning, a black Alfa Romeo drew up in front of the US embassy, and a military policeman went over to the car. Father Cafiero leaned his head out of the back window.

§

In the envelope that Monsignor Feliciani had delivered to Ambassador Fox three days before, a page was missing. Sitting in the driver's seat of the cardinal's Mercedes, Father Emilio was driving the monsignor to the US embassy to deliver the missing page.

The car was almost at the embassy when the monsignor suddenly told Father Emilio to stop, pointing in front of him. They watched Father Cafiero talking to the MP.

As soon as the monsignor went back to the Palace of the Holy Office, he knocked at the cardinal's door.

"Are you really sure it was he, Monsignore?" Cardinal Wolfenberg said.

"We were just across Via Veneto, Your Eminence. We saw him distinctly."

"'Verily, verily, I say unto thee, O Abramson,'" said the cardinal in a biblical voice, "'before the cock crows twice, thou shalt deny me thrice.'" (Mark 14:72)

"How disheartening, the predictability of human comedy," the monsignor said with a disgusted expression.

"Well said, Monsignore! A quotation worthy of Schopenhauer himself. I must make a note of this one."

But why should Abramson want to hoodwink him? The alliance of Joint Affairs and Manus Domini needed Palermo, and he was the key for Palermo — not the father general.

Why Father Cafiero, then?

While one of the Frangipanes' servants held the reins, Geoffroy vaulted on to the back of his horse. He flicked the reins, and his horse's hooves clattered over the cobblestones.

Rome lay at the foot of the hill. Geoffroy's gaze took in the clumps of Mediterranean pines and the stretch of brown roofs, then came to rest finally on the ruins of the Roman Forum. His thoughts went back to moonlit Jerusalem, as he used to see it from a house in the Armenian quarter, while holding her in his arms. He reached for his leather pouch, took out the head of the statuette and clutched it.

Geoffroy couldn't understand the reason for that unexpected summons, and from the pope himself. Leo Frangipane had told him personally, only that morning. The Roman patrician had said he didn't know the reason for the summons, but his face was the portrait of a lie. The Frangipanes knew everything that went on behind the scenes at the Lateran. They were the ones who established the Church's policies: they, and Cardinal Aimeric, the pope's chancellor.

Geoffroy spurred his horse on up San Cristoforo's Hill, and from there he trotted towards Vicolo degli Armaioli.

Loud cries and a threatening clatter of horses' hooves filled the air. A squad of the pope's soldiers, halberds at the ready, charged onto the road at full gallop right in front of Geoffroy, cutting across his path. Geoffroy's horse neighed, reared up, and almost unsaddled him. As they galloped by, the *papalini* [papal guards] knocked over a baker's cart, and the baker's boy pulling it barely managed to save himself by leaping to the side of the road. A half-crushed loaf of bread rolled across the road and stopped at Geoffroy's feet.

One of the cart wheels was still spinning, and its squeaking accompanied the fading echo of the horses' hooves. A commoner shook his fist at the soldiers and yelled something that Geoffroy didn't catch, but his face was a picture of age-old hatred.

Since he'd arrived in Rome, Geoffroy had sensed only conspiracy and violence. How could one reconcile one's faith with such a place? He'd never seen the Saracens — the "infidels" — acting like this.

Everything in Rome seemed to revolve round the conflict between the Frangipane clan and the Pierleonis, the two leading patrician families. They were the ones who dominated everything, starting with the popes themselves. The election of each new pope was always marked by plots, corruption, and betrayal, and every time a pope died, Rome was plunged into terror. It was currently the Frangipanes who were in favor. Their power was the consequence of a sudden attack whereby Leo Frangipane and a squad of henchmen had broken into the Lateran, swords in hand, and had installed Lamberto, Cardinal of Ostia, as the new pope, with the name of Honorius II.

The stream of carts and the shouting and bustle around the stalls in front of the Lateran Palace reminded Geoffroy of market day in Les Andelys. Only one thing was missing: the songs of the jongleurs who, going from village to village, sang of fearless knights in quest of heroic exploits and unattainable love.

A country maid crossed the road carrying a basket of apples on her shoulder. She looked up at Geoffroy, took an apple, rubbed it against her shirt stretched over her provoking breasts, and tossed it to him.

"For you, valiant knight, because you're as handsome as a god," she said, with an inviting smile.

Geoffroy waved his hand in a gesture of thanks and bit into the apple.

He reined up in front of the equestrian statue of Marcus Aurelius, between the Basilica of the Lateran and the palace, and dismounted. As he was hitching his horse to a pole, a gaggle of geese crossed the square to drink at the fountain below the statue.

"Before His Holiness receives you, there's something I want to discuss, Sir Geoffroy," said the razor-faced Cardinal Aimeric.

"At your service, Your Eminence."

"Retrieving the Ark was a great feat," he began, his eyes never leaving Geoffroy's face. "It's a pity, though, that strange rumors are going around."

"Rumors?"

"People are saying that the Ark and the Treasure of David are not all you found."

"What are they implying?" Geoffroy tried to make his voice sound normal.

"It's not up to me to tell you."

"Has Your Eminence called me here to discuss the fantasies of some visionary?"

"The fantasies of a visionary, you say? King Baldwin would hardly appreciate such wit."

The cardinal said the rumors had started with the crusaders who'd traveled to Jaffa with Bertrand and Gondemare. The crusaders insisted that they'd seen something else being loaded onto the ship, in addition to the eight coffers. They'd mentioned a strange, wooden chest that looked unusually old. They'd become suspicious when the Templars had tried to send the soldiers away before loading the contents of the last cart. On their return to Jerusalem, the crusaders had referred the matter to King Baldwin.

Geoffroy did not lose his composure. They'd foreseen that something like this might happen. So, before leaving the Holy Land, they'd agreed on what to say to explain the presence of the chest.

"An old wooden chest?" Geoffroy burst out laughing. "But the crusaders were telling the simple truth."

"What was in the chest?" the cardinal asked after a moment's bewilderment.

"Old books, war souvenirs, arms.... Things we'd collected during our years in Jerusalem. Do you find that strange, Your Eminence?"

The cardinal still gazed at Geoffroy. "What seems strange is the type of container you chose to use. The crusaders insisted it looked old — very old."

"Yes, it probably was. We found it in our quarters, in the Al Aqsa Mosque."

The cardinal rose with a swish of violet robes. "I'll be back in a minute, Sir Geoffroy. Please excuse me."

When Cardinal Aimeric reappeared in the doorway, as silently as he had left, he told Geoffroy that His Holiness was ready to receive him.

Honorius II was a thin man. He was completely bald, but that was compensated for by a long beard that met with a moustache it at the corners of his mouth. He was seated on a canopied throne covered in red satin that seemed a size too big for him. Cardinal Aimeric, as sinister as a vulture, stood to one side of the throne.

"Get up, my good Knight," the pope said in a cavernous voice that contrasted with his thin body. He looked Geoffroy over from head to foot. "You Templars are enough to strike fear into anyone. Real warriors."

"Speaking of warriors, on my way to the palace I met up with a squad of yours, Your Holiness. They seemed to be in quite a hurry."

"*Them*? They love spreading terror through the streets of Rome, but are all too ready to run off with their tail between their legs when they have to face a man of character, like Roger of Sicily. However, I didn't summon you here to discuss such things. I have a proposal for you...."

The pope said he was not only afflicted with threats from outside the Church—the Germans in the north and the Normans in the south—but from within the Church as well. He spoke of Roman patricians who plotted in secret, even with the enemies of the Church, and he complained of the unruliness of many monasteries and orders of the Church. The pope said he was favorable to the creation of the Order of the Templars; the Church, he said, needed a "strong arm" to defend it from its many enemies.

"Abbot Bernard, a good friend of our chancellor, has already arranged the rule of the Order," the pope said. "The Council of Troyes will officially sanctify its creation at the end of the month. There's only one thing missing now."

Geoffroy felt forced to break the silence. "What's that, Your Holiness?"

"The name of the first Grand Master."

"We all thought that Hugues de Payens would be appointed Grand Master, Your Holiness."

"You thought? I would remind you that the Order is sworn to blind obedience to us and that *we* are the ones who make all decisions."

"I didn't mean to—"

"We had thought of you, Sir Geoffroy, for this position," cut in the pope. "It only now needs a word from us to Cardinal Matteo, who will chair the Council of Troyes."

The pope looked at Geoffroy, as if expecting a reaction, but Geoffroy remained silent.

"Naturally we shall expect something in return."

Geoffroy had no doubt about that. He pretended to be taken in. "May I know what that something is, Your Holiness?"

"We want the truth about the chest."

"I've already told your chancellor, Your Holiness."

The pope exchanged a quick look with the cardinal. "Evidently Cardinal Aimeric is not convinced."

"I trust Your Holiness will assure the chancellor that there's nothing to be discovered."

"Then perhaps you can enlighten us on the meaning of this phrase," the pope said harshly.

In a voice more cavernous than ever, Honorius II articulated each word of the Latin motto created by Victor.

So Gondemare hadn't heard the footsteps of a ghost, that last day in the Holy of Holies. Someone had been spying on them.

"Why, it's a phrase of Victor de Mauriac's, our Latin scholar. It doesn't mean anything other than what it says."

This time the pope exchanged a longer look with the cardinal. "A pity, a real pity," he said, getting to his feet. "However, if you should reconsider the matter, ask for an audience. Our proposal still holds."

Geoffroy bowed. "Since I shall not be seeing Your Holiness again before I leave, I offer Your Holiness my deepest respects."

As he was about to leave the throne room, Geoffroy overheard the pope "whispering" something to Cardinal Aimeric.

"We're going to have to keep a close eye on these Templars."

As Geoffroy was about to mount his horse, he heard the sound of dull blows coming from inside the basilica. He hitched his horse again, ran up the steps, and went inside. Scaffolding had been erected round the apse and it appeared that they were excavating a crypt underneath the main altar. *The Ark!* Hugues had overheard odd phrases that had made him think that the Ark would end up in the basilica.

Geoffroy thought back to Jerusalem, to the Holy of Holies, and to the empty altar. He thought of the God of Abraham, that God who'd led the people of Israel out of Egypt with the promise of a land flowing with milk and honey. In his mind's eye he saw the contents of the wooden chest again, and his hand began to clench and unclench.... The Church of Rome had never had anything to do with that God. He heard the sound of a rebec, saw the sky-blue waters of a lake on the Armenian highlands, and heard Krikor's words again: *"How can you let go of something so beautiful? How?"*

How blind and stupid! He banged his fist against a column, then strode out, wiping his eyes with the hem of his cloak.

At that moment, the gaggle of geese entered the basilica in single file and waddled towards the apse.

26

"Ricci for *managing director*? Never!" O'Neill said. "That guy can't even tell the difference between a molecule of ethylene and a broom handle. Leave politics out of this."

When the argument broke out, for a moment Guichard feared it meant the end of his plan. However, in the end CIP won the battle and succeeded in getting a certain Ricci appointed as managing director, a man whose only merit was the backing of the secretary of the Renovation Party, an Opposition party.

Guichard could well understand the hostility of O'Neill towards a man like Ricci, who came from an obscure legal firm out in the provinces and had become a state Boyar. Second only to Accardo in the games of Roman politics, this Ricci had gained the reputation of a tireless engraver of his own image. Newspaper photos invariably portrayed him busy gnawing at the earpiece of his glasses. He was known for his rigorous adherence to Schiller's philosophical maxim: "What matters is the appearance, not the substance." Although nicknamed Rasputin by his many detractors, Italian newspapers used to refer to him as the "Czar of the Italian chemical industry."

In exchange, the Allied people wanted Kovacs as chairman, and they got their wish. But that wasn't enough. "Chairmen never count for anything," O'Neill said. Guichard agreed with O'Neill and maneuvered for an Allied choice to get the position of financial manager—a position that, in the events that were to follow, would prove to be of crucial importance. Paulette Janviers was appointed financial manager of Columbus Chemicals AG.

"But I have no intention of quitting my job at Financiére d'Arcadie!" Paulette said, trembling with anger. "Besides, how can you expect CIP to accept *me* as financial manager, knowing that I come from Kovacs's investment bank?"

"You really believe that I would want to get rid of someone as valuable as you?" Guichard said. "Your resignation will take place only on paper, and you'll have my written letter of re-employment starting within three months from today, with a forty-percent salary increase."

"The minor detail of my résumé remains."

"Your CV will be slightly 'retouched,' with references signed by people above any suspicion."

"I don't want to do anything illegal. You know me."

"And you won't. You'll have to establish the value of the petrochemical division of CIP, on the basis of objective data. Allied and I will accept the price you come up with, and without any interference whatsoever."

"Where would my office be?"

"We will negotiate for you to work at Allied's London offices three days a week, and that's where the people of Columbus will find you."

"Three months?"

"Maximum."

"Fine."

When the meeting was resumed on the morning of Sunday, October 5, O'Neill pulled out the new clause Guichard had insisted on.

"I just can't understand," burst out CIP's lawyer and head of the Italian delegation, throwing a suspicious look at O'Neill. "With a clause like that, the joint venture would fall to pieces even if we were to disagree on the color of the toilet paper."

O'Neill made a gesture of impatience. "That's nonsense. It's obvious that the clause would only apply to very special cases."

"Such as?"

"Substantial investments or takeovers, to begin with."

"So an even number of votes in such cases would allow either of the partners to walk out on the other, right?"

"Right, if you want to put it like that. You seem to be forgetting a crucial point, though. In a company where neither partner has a majority, this clause would avoid a stalemate."

"Better a stalemate than this."

"Why?"

"Because it provides too easy a loophole, that's why!" the lawyer said.

"But what loophole? It's limited to just a handful of damned important cases. Besides, it safeguards both partners' interests."

The lawyer slammed his file shut. "Enough of this. We'll never accept a clause like that. And that's final."

Guichard gave O'Neill an almost imperceptible wink.

"In that case the negotiation ends here." O'Neill stood up, gathered his papers together and left the room without saying a word.

One after the other his team followed him, leaving the CIP delegation aghast.

When Guichard went back to his office, Marie Claire told him that the lawyer had just asked the receptionist to call a number in Rome.

Forty minutes later, the lawyer emerged from the boardroom, his face looking like he'd eaten a sour plum. Guichard watched the scene from his office doorway, while talking to Marie Claire. Moving awkwardly, the lawyer went over to O'Neill, who was confabulating with his people in the hallway, and drew him aside. The lawyer's face beamed.

At long last, at six p.m. on Sunday, O'Neill and the lawyer agreed on the final draft. The company would be called Columbus Chemicals AG and would have its headquarters in Zurich. At that point, the only matter left was to get the approval of the respective boards. O'Neill and the lawyer shook hands, but neither they nor any of their people even attempted to fake a smile.

As Marie Claire went round the table filling the champagne glasses, Guichard looked at the drawn faces of the people around him. No one there knew it yet, but the joint venture wouldn't see the year out.

Guichard was raising his glass towards O'Neill when Marie Claire approached him and told him the taxi had arrived.

One hour later, Guichard got out of the taxi and walked into Terminal C of Orly-CDG airport. He headed for the VARIG check-in counters.

The VARIG Airlines Flight 721 took off on time at 11.20 p.m. It touched down in Rio International Airport at 7:30 the following morning.

At 6.15 p.m. on Monday October 6, Guichard got on the VASP flight 412 to Brasilia. As the plane taxied along the runway, Guichard stretched his legs and relaxed. He had an appointment at the Ministry of Finance the following morning at nine o'clock with Alonso Ferreira, the minister's executive secretary. For $600,000, the minister's secretary would do what Guichard had asked of him.

A bossa nova was playing on the radio. The taxi passed in front of the futurist building housing the city cathedral, Nossa Senhora Aparecida, and turned onto the wide avenue leading to the *esplanada* of government buildings. In the background, the twin skyscrapers of the Congresso Nacional stood out against the blue waters of Lake Paranoa. The driver lowered the visor. The explosion of yellow flowers in the *ipe* trees edging the lawns of the *esplanada* seemed to have burst out of a painting by Van Gogh.

The taxi stopped in front of a building of glass and concrete. The brass plaque at the main entrance read *Ministério da Fazenda, Bloco P de Esplanada dos Ministerios.*

"*Senhor*, can I tell you something?" the taxi driver said with a smile, turning round.

He was completely bald and olive-skinned, and wore a bright blue shirt dotted with gaudy flowers. As he counted the change, his syncopated movements followed the rhythm of the bossa nova.

"Of course. Go ahead."

"*Senhor*, since I've being doing this job I've become a bit of a psychologist. I've been watching you, you know. *Vòs* is too serious." The taxi driver pointed a finger to his forehead. *"Vòs* think too much."

"Hmm, I see."

"Your thoughts won't change the *mundo, senhor,* and you'll just be more *infeliz* than before."

"What's the remedy, then? To stop thinking?"

The taxi driver winked at Guichard, and gave him a friendly slap on the shoulder. "Watch this, *senhor.*"

The taxi driver turned up the radio, got out of the taxi, and began dancing in the middle of the sidewalk to the rhythm of the bossa nova. Two boys stopped to clap in time to the music, eventually joining the driver in his dance. Within a few minutes, a knot of people had gathered and were standing around the driver and the boys, clapping rhythmically for the dancers. Soon, several office windows overlooking the street were flung open, and many people leaned out singing and clapping their hands.

"Senhor, isto is the remedy," the taxi driver shouted as Guichard got out of the taxi. The driver pointed to his heart. "Feel the rhythm, and let yourself go."

Ferreira was tall and sun-tanned, and smelled strongly of afters-have. He was wearing an electric-blue suit over an open-necked white shirt. The pocket of his jacket was embroidered with a crest, and a yellow silk handkerchief draped from it. On the wall behind him, between two multicolored ponchos, hung an enormous pair of bull's horns. Guichard frowned.

The Brazilian's questions, however, soon revealed a shrewd man attentive to detail, a man who left nothing to chance. Guichard realized that his first impression had been wrong; so much the better.

Ferreira would get going immediately, and Guichard agreed to credit an advance payment of $300,000 to his overseas account the following day. Ferreira took out two Cuban cigars and offered one to Guichard, who declined. Ferreira lit his cigar and Guichard moved his chair away from the desk.

"What's better than a Cuban cigar to seal a pact?" Ferreira took a puff and blew the smoke towards Guichard. "To me Cuban cigars rank immediately after women and before a good bottle of rum, in the order of things."

"I see."

Ferreira stared hard at Guichard, then shook his head. "I doubt it, *senhor* de Saint Clair, *even* if you are a Frenchman. I doubt it very much."

"Tell me, are they by any chance holding a psychiatry conference in Brasilia today?" Guichard said.

§

Eduardo Borges, director of Post and Telecommunications at the Ministry, walked into Ferreira's office. He had a build that would rival Nero Wolfe's. Borges squeezed his bulk into the chair that Guichard had occupied half an hour earlier.

"So, is everything clear?" Ferreira asked. He had pushed his chair back and was sitting with his shoulders against the wall, directly beneath the bull's horns.

Borges scratched his double chin. "How shall we go about it?" he asked with a voice that resembled the croaking of a frog.

"To begin with, you've got to intercept any letter or fax arriving from the Vatican."

"Which office in the Vatican?"

"Probably APSA, but the secretariat of state may also want to poke their nose into it."

"Then, if in doubt, all the Vatican departments."

"No entries in your incoming and outgoing mail registers, though."

"No, it would be too risky."

"How then?"

"I'll give you a photocopy of everything that arrives from the Vatican. I'll hold the originals down at my office, but just for a few hours."

"Say four?"

"Okay. Four," Borges said. "But it's not the faxes or the mail that's worrying me."

"What then?"

"The phone."

Ferreira waved his hands nonchalantly and grinned. "All we need is a phantom. A phantom with his own extension number."

"*A phantom*? Are you crazy?"

"How often do you have the internal phone directory reprinted?"

"Quarterly. Why?"

"When is it next due to be printed?"

"Around October 15. I still —"

Ferreira pulled his chair over to the desk, scribbled something on a scrap of paper and passed it to Borges. "Start by adding this."

"*Luis Roberto de Oliveira Lima*," read Borges. He started to flip his bottom lip. "Hang on, wait a minute. I can't add a name like that, out of the blue. What if someone checks?"

"Checks what?"

"Well, to start with, the forms used by the various department heads when they apply for new entries. Those forms have to be signed."

"And you call that a problem?"

"Oh, really? And using whose signature, if it's not a problem?"

Ferreira made a nonchalant gesture. "You can always pretend there was an accident. Something might have got spilt on the forms, making the signature illegible."

"Hmm. But I still don't see what we can do about the extension number."

"To start with, it's got to be a real number."

"What a brilliant idea! And who do we put on the other end of the line if a phone call arrives from the Vatican? Your phantom?"

"The office next to mine is still empty. Every so often the phone rings and when Norma answers, it's always someone still looking for Alcindo Marques, although it's four months since the guy left."

"But what if the phone rings for this de Oliveira Lima when you're not there?

Ferreira gave Borges a meaningful look. "There's Norma Rocha."

A flash of biological envy crossed Borges's bleary eyes. "*The* Norma Rocha?"

"Uh-huh."

"The girls in the Ministry are right. You *are* a randy swine."

Ferreira raised his eyes to the bull's horns. "Thanks. I try to keep my end up."

During the lunch break, Ferreira picked up the phone and asked Norma Rocha, who was in charge of the Ministry's secretarial pool, to join him in his office.

Norma came in. She had long black hair and was wearing a tight, mauve knee-length skirt and a satin blouse discreetly unbuttoned to allow a glimpse of her white lace bra. Her clip-on earrings matched her pink, coral necklace and her lips were painted a pale mauve. Her stiletto heels and fishnet stockings enhanced her slender legs.

"... But Alonso, it could be very dangerous."

"No one will find out. All you need to do is leave the door open leading to the office where Marques used to sit."

"It's something I find pretty scary."

Ferreira got up and locked the door. Then he went round to Norma, who was standing in front of his desk. "Won't you do it for your Alonso?" he said, taking her in his arms.

"You know I'd like to, but—"

Ferreira pushed Norma against the wall and forced his body against hers. Then he undid her blouse and slid his hand under her bra.

"Please, Norma, don't say no." Ferreira bit her ear lobe.

She started panting and hung on to him. "Wait... wait... yes... all right, *querido*... yes, yes."

♣

What could Bertrand want at such an early hour? Geoffroy went wearily up the tower steps of the preceptory, went out onto the parapet walk, and leaned against a crenel. The Seine wound among the almond trees in blossom, carrying the scents of another spring. A flock of swallows flew over the tower, but their twittering faded in the emptiness of his heart.

Geoffroy looked at the back of his fist furrowed with wrinkles. It was the year of Our Lord 1156, and thirty years had gone by since he'd left Jerusalem. He unclenched his hand, and the eyes of the statuette looked at him with their smile of commiseration. He thought back to the hills of the Holy City, to the breeze of a summer night, to Miriam.

At the Council of Troyes Hugues had been appointed first Grand Master of the Order. His oath in the cathedral echoed in Geoffroy's mind, amidst the serried ranks of cardinals and nobles. Only two years later, in 1130, Hugues returned to Jerusalem at the head of 300 Knights Templar who came from Europe's most powerful families. Following the success of the Jerusalem mission, and thanks to Abbot Bernard's support, the Order spread rapidly all over Europe.

The Templars acquired lands and castles in all the main European countries and in many regions in the East. Their network of preceptories now covered nearly all of Christian Europe, Palestine, and the neighboring countries. The Order was involved in politics, diplomacy, and finance. The Templars developed a flourishing financial activity and lent money to royalty and nobles. Merchants relied on them to transfer sums of money to distant countries. The Grand Master's signature was worth more than a king's.

He heard Honorius II's' cavernous voice again: *"We're going to have to keep a close eye on these Templars."* Honorius died in 1130, but the popes who succeeded him did not forget. In 1139, Pope Innocent III issued a papal bull by which the Templars no longer had to swear obedience to any secular or ecclesiastical authorities other than the pope. But that was a two-edged sword. The bull raised the Templars to the rank of a great international power, but a power increasingly subject to Rome's oppressive control.

Geoffroy had returned to Jerusalem with Hugues in 1130, three years after they had left. He'd gone right away to the inn, but it had been closed for a year and Miriam was no longer there.

"'Fraid you're wasting your time, sir," said a farrier, putting down his hammer and wiping his brow. " *The inn's been closed for nigh on a year now.*"

"You don't happen to know where they've gone?" Geoffroy asked.

"One morning we woke up to find the place closed. Never heard no more. Folks is strange."

He'd searched for her all over Jerusalem, but in vain. After returning to France, he'd kept on searching discreetly for her for many years, both directly and through trusted friends. He'd ventured as far as her native village on the shores of Lake Sevan in Armenia, but there, too, no one had been able to tell him of her whereabouts.

He'd joined the Order, giving up everything, dazzled by the vision of a great exploit. What? The Ark? The dull blows echoed through the naves of the Lateran. The Church had spread everywhere like a rampant weed, leaving behind nothing but blood and hate.

Now he found himself on the verge of old age, alone, tormented by the regret of what might have been. The curse haunting a knight was longing for stars, and not realizing that the true light had always been inside himself. One only needed to stop, clear one's mind of all trivialities, and listen to the voice of one's true self. Geoffroy banged his fist against a merlon, leaned his head against the wall, and felt the back of his hand wet with tears.

"Brother Geoffroy, the Grand Master will see you now," said a voice behind him.

When Geoffroy walked in, Bertrand was standing in front of a window, through which one could see a loop in the river. His white-streaked hair fell on his shoulders covered by a long, white tunic held around his waist by a wide leather belt. The Templar cross embroidered on his back made him look even more imposing. Bertrand's profile was thoughtful. He gestured to Geoffroy to shut the door. An open map lay on his writing desk.

"... But why, after all these years?" Geoffroy asked.

"Soon the castle will pass to another branch of my family. Someone might find it," Bertrand said.

"Have you already thought of another hiding-place?"

Bertrand leaned towards him. "I might have an idea," he whispered.

Bertrand told Geoffroy that de Blanchefort castle was only three miles from the Templar preceptory of Bézu. Ever since Roman times, there had been gold mines on the mountainside at Blanchefort, disused now for centuries. As Grand Master, Bertrand would have no problem in reopening one of these mines, declaring they were going to start searching for gold again. In reality, they would dig a tunnel leading to a crypt, where they would hide the wooden chest. Besides, it would be safer if the Essenes' scrolls were hidden somewhere other than the chest.

"Why?" asked Geoffroy eventually.

"If one day someone were to find the chest, we'd still have the scrolls."

Geoffroy nodded. "I think I know just the right hiding place."

"Where?"

"Les Andelys. The underground chambers of de Saint Clair castle."

Bertrand's eyes gleamed. "Excellent idea."

"Going back to the chest, however, to dig a crypt in the mountain we'll need miners," Geoffroy said.

"I've already considered that," Bertrand said. "I'll bring them in from Germany. I've already been in touch with one of our preceptories up there."

"Hmm. Miners drink and talk."

"In German, though."

"Experience teaches caution—remember the spy in the tunnel. We'll have to prevent them from mixing with the locals."

"You may be right." Bertrand looked pensively at the map lying on his writing desk showing the Templar preceptories in the south of France. A shrewd smile appeared on his lips as he pointed his finger to a small village near the Pyrenees. "We'll house them in our preceptory at Bézu, a quiet place of no strategic significance—and only three miles away from Blanchefort."

§

The first signs of dawn lit up the mountain slopes and, in the background, the rocky spurs of the Pyrenees, whose snow-covered peaks stood out against a clear sky. Geoffroy flicked the reins and the four horses started to climb up the rough track to the old mine, pulling the cart, which began creaking and shaking.

"Cheer up, we're nearly there," Geoffroy said to Bertrand, who sat beside him up on the box.

"All in one piece, I hope," Bertrand said, clutching the handrail with both hands.

Geoffroy turned around and lifted a corner of the tilt. "Everything all right back there?"

Archambaud and Victor sat one in front of the other, separated by the wooden chest, which they were holding steady.

Archambaud grunted. "I'll tell you when it's all over."

"*Audentes fortuna* iuvat—Fortune favors the brave," Victor said, giving Archambaud a shrewd look.

For a moment Geoffroy thought of their other companions: Hugues, Gondemare, Payen, Rosal, André.... All dead, some on the battlefield, others through illness.

They were approaching a fork marked by a centuries-old oak with immense umbrella-shaped foliage, where the path ended. Geoffroy drew rein. A footpath led to the entrance to the old mine, now closed by crossed poles and boards. He'd had it reopened to deceive the nosy people who every now and then had ventured that far to eye the works. He'd had the tunnel dug higher up, behind the crest of the mountain, and away from the second beaten track departing from the fork. It had taken over a year's work on the part of the German miners.

Geoffroy and Bertrand jumped down off the box, went to the back of the cart, and grabbed the end of the wooden chest, which Victor and Archambaud were pushing out. Carrying the chest two in the front and two in the back, the four men climbed up the barren, rocky slope.

A flock of homing pigeons flew over them. Suddenly they began to scatter in all directions. A falcon appeared over the ridge, its broad, blue wings spread in a lofty curve. The bird of prey swerved, glided down, and cruised low over the clearing that stretched in front of the old mine. Then, with swift powerful flaps of its wings, the falcon rose almost vertically higher and higher, until it was above the pigeons. With a rapid whirring of its wings, it hovered for a few moments, as if to have a better look. Aiming at one of the pigeons, it swooped down, and its predatory talons fastened round the neck of its prey. A screech of agony pierced the air, and the two birds, one clinging to the other, hurtled down, tumbling over and over. The falcon soared aloft again, clasping its lifeless prey in its talons, and disappeared from the knights' astonished gaze beyond the ridge. A few pigeon feathers floated in the air, their iridescent colors gleaming in the sun. The feathers fell on the ground around them, but one of them, bloodstained, came to rest on the chest.

The wind rose, and an icy gust swept over the four knights. They climbed onwards, until they too disappeared behind the ridge of the mountain.

The crypt was lined with stones and propped with big tree trunks. Dampness and silence crept into their bones. Geoffroy fixed his torch to the wall, while his companions laid the wooden chest on the ground. Their flickering shadows seemed to want to escape from the sense of anguish that hung in the air.

Geoffroy and Archambaud exchanged glances. They forced the tip of their picks under the lid and began to pry up with the handles, just as they had done thirty years before, in the Holy of Holies.

They looked inside the chest for the last time. The silence hanging in the crypt betrayed a feeling of restlessness, almost of guilt, which none of them had ever dared to admit to the others, but which each one of them, Geoffroy was sure of it, had felt deep down since the day of the discovery.

Geoffroy reached into the chest and picked up a leather tube in which they had put the Essenes' parchment scrolls.

The four knights unsheathed their swords and raised them, crossed the tips over the chest, and one after another repeated the Jerusalem oath and Victor's motto.

Geoffroy took the torch off its holder, looked for the last time at the chest, and followed his companions along the tunnel, unable to rid his mind of the pigeon's death cry.

Darkness descended on the crypt.

Standing on the wooden beams that served as roofing at the entrance to the tunnel, Geoffroy and Archambaud tied the ropes to one end of the tree trunk lying across the beams. Then they dropped the coils of rope to the ground and climbed down along the rock wall.

After winding the ropes around their arms, Geoffroy and his companions formed a line, dug in their heels, and began to pull, their bodies bending back with the effort. Their feet kept sinking and slipping, sweat dripped down their scarlet faces, and stifled grunts and curses wrenched from their throats.

"By a thousand gryphons … Thou shit-pot … Thou cock-sucker … Thou poxy whore …Pull harder…"

The tree trunk started to give. They went on pulling the ropes until the trunk gave way and rolled down. A massive iron grating opened and, with a dull noise that seemed like a clap of thunder, an avalanche of stones rumbled down the mountainside raising a suffocating dust cloud.

When the dust had settled, the entrance to the tunnel had vanished.

Geoffroy slung the tube with the scrolls over his shoulder and mounted the horse that they had unhitched from the cart. Normandy was on the west coast: he had a long ride ahead of him. Standing near the cart, Bertrand, Victor and Archambaud were gazing at him, their dusty faces furrowed with sweat. Geoffroy waved good-bye.

He flicked the reins, dug his heels in the flanks of the horse and galloped off down the mine track, the leather tube shaking behind his back.

The shadow of a falcon darted across the track.

27

On Tuesday afternoon, upon returning from Brazil, Guichard found a message on his desk from Antigono Zergas, financial director of the Coalition Party. Zergas had asked to be called back urgently.

"If you want the board of CIP to pass a favorable resolution on the joint venture contract, Allied has to accept a new clause," Zergas said.

"I'm listening," Guichard said.

When he heard what it was, Guichard knew his sixth sense hadn't failed him, and that Astarita had been right about Accardo.

"... *With him, it's not just a matter of money,*" Astarita had said.

"*If it's not just a matter of money, what else is at stake?*"

"*Power. Accardo must be persuaded that the Allied affair will be politically advantageous.*"

All he needed to do now was to tell Zergas what the prime minister would expect Guichard to say in a situation like this.

"My congratulations to the prime minister. A straight thrust worthy of a real gentleman."

"Knock it off! Business is business. You'd have done exactly the same thing," Zergas said. "I'm going to fax you the text of the new clause. Remember, though, the matter's non-negotiable. Take it or leave it. However, in the latter case, the whole deal falls through. Tell Kovacs, and tell him not to try to be clever."

Ten minutes later, Marie Claire laid Zergas's fax on Guichard's desk.

"Clause 21 - Within four months of the incorpo-
ration date of Columbus Chemicals AG, a board
meeting will be held. The item on the agenda will be
the take-over of CIP's petrochemical division —
thirty-six plants located in Southern Italy. Allied Petroleum agrees to ensure that the board members of
Columbus Chemicals appointed by Allied Petroleum itself vote in favor of this takeover. In the
event of a disagreement on the price, this will be as-
sessed by an arbitration committee..."

Guichard checked his watch. It was 7:00 a.m. on the Pacific
coast of the United States. He dialed Kovacs's private phone
number.

"Goddamn son-of-a-bitch! So three percent wasn't enough,"
Kovacs said when Guichard had finished reading the text of the
new clause. An icy silence followed. "The takeover price of
those plants is still to be decided. Does this leave us any way
out?"

"We've already valued those plants."

"And...?"

"The value should lie somewhere between minus $26 and
minus $33 million."

"What the hell does that 'minus' mean?"

"That the value is negative."

"*Negative*? Does that mean what I think it means?"

"It does. Those plants are losing a lot of money, and will
continue to do so for years. The accounts balance only by plug-
ging a heavy negative goodwill on one side of the equation."

"How come this hasn't crossed Accardo's mind?"

"At first, we ourselves thought we must have made a mistake somewhere when we got that result. I had the calculations
double-checked. They are right."

"Aha! Then things take on a different perspective," Kovacs
said in a voice that suggested hounds moving in for the kill.
"My people sitting on the Columbus board will vote in favor of
the takeover, but for a negative price. Right?"

"Right. If Columbus Chemicals acquires those plants, it'll be CIP that has to pay the joint venture between \$26 and \$33 million, and not vice versa."

"CIP will never do anything of the kind, of course. What'll happen then?"

Guichard reminded Kovacs of the clause that O'Neill had insisted be included in the joint venture contract, under pressure from Guichard himself, and told him what would happen.

First there was silence on the other end, then a guffaw rising in a continuous crescendo.

"You know something? You're a goddam son of a bitch, de Saint Clair. Take it from me."

"I feel flattered."

"Didn't they say themselves that clause twenty-one is non-negotiable?" Kovacs went on laughing till tears came. "At this point, all we poor bastards can do is pull down our pants. Tell them I'm forced to accept. Ha, ha, ha!"

The phone clicked and the line went dead.

When Françoise entered Alain Wesenheim's office on the first floor of the *Pavillion Mollien* in the Louvre, she found him kneeling on the floor, absorbed in examining a large reproduction.

"Dr. Wesenheim?" Françoise said.

The man looked up at her in surprise over round steel-framed glasses. He had thinning white hair, inquisitive eyes, and a friendly face.

"Did Poussin have any friends?" Françoise asked.

"Friends? I believe there was only the one, Cassiano del Pozzo."

"Why Cassiano?"

Wesenheim described Cassiano as an intellectual, well versed in classical literature and the arts. The affinity that linked Cassiano and Poussin probably stemmed from a common intellectual approach related to the discovery of the origins of Christianity and the mysteries of the classical world.

"However, one fact in particular helps us to understand the special relationship linking Cassiano and Poussin," Wesenheim said.

"What's that?"

"It was Cassiano who commissioned the *First Set of Seven Sacraments* from Poussin. Seven paintings! Which took him six years in all to complete."

"Cassiano must have been very religious."

"Not in the way you think, though. Cassiano was almost certainly a Gnostic Christian."

Wesenheim stressed Poussin's decision to set the paintings in classical Rome, which showed that he wanted to represent the theme from the viewpoint of the first Fathers of the Church.

"Why does this classical setting for Christian themes seem so important to you?" she asked.

"*Why*? These paintings convey ideas far removed from seventeenth century Catholicism, ideas much closer to those of the Apologists and the Gnostics from early Christian times. Of little significance, you think? Remember that, at the time, the Church still used to send heretics to the stake."

"But Poussin also painted many Christian subjects, such as the Passion and the Baptism. How do you explain that?"

"The harmony with which Poussin linked Christian and classical themes shows he'd reached a universal outlook on religion."

"When was it that Poussin painted the *First Set of Seven Sacraments*?"

"Between 1636 and 1642," Wesenheim said. "Why?"

"I'm thinking of *Les Bergers d'Arcadie II*. I wonder whether a leitmotiv runs through Poussin's work in those years."

Wesenheim stroked his goatee pensively. "Poussin painted *Les Bergers d'Arcadie II* around 1638-40, hence right in the middle of the *Seven Sacraments*." His eyes gleamed. "*Mais oui!* And in 1638 he painted *The Capture of Jerusalem by Titus*."

"What's so special about that?"

"Its allegory, my dear. *Its allegory.*"

Wesenheim said that, in order to paint this picture, Poussin had read documents written by the Jewish historian Flavius

Josephus regarding the destruction and pillage of Jerusalem by the Romans in A.D. 70. The painting portrayed the scene of the destruction of the Temple in an apocalyptic context. The allegory referred to Titus mounted on his white horse and to his soldiers, all gazing at the sky above the Temple.

"Poussin probably wanted to show the wrath of God at the destruction of the Temple," Françoise said.

"Hmm, not him. An artist as profound and well-informed as Poussin must have been referring to something quite different."

"Such as?"

"The Ark of the Covenant, of course—and perhaps something else. The Book of Exodus is quite clear about this. The Ark was put into the Temple during Solomon's time and, after that, the Old Testament never mentions it again. When Nebuchadnezzar destroyed the First Temple in 587 B.C., the Ark was missing from the inventory of the loot. So it must still have been under the Second Temple, when Titus ransacked it in A.D. 70."

"No one knows for sure what treasure the Romans found in the Temple."

"Not exactly. From the account of Procopius, the Roman historian, and from the *bas-relief*s on the Arch of Titus in Rome, we know that in addition to gold and diamonds, the Romans found the *menorah*, the gold candelabrum with seven branches."

"No reference to the Ark of the Covenant?" Françoise said.

"None, which makes one think that Titus didn't find it."

"Which leads us to the Templars."

"*Exactly.*"

"Then, if Poussin discovered it was the Templars who found the Ark, what's the meaning behind those eyes staring at the heavens, in *The Capture of Jerusalem*? God's warning to the Romans not to go any further?"

"A logical hypothesis, but not the only one."

Wesenheim explained that Poussin had access to the Roman libraries with the most extensive collections on early Christian centuries, those of Cardinals Francesco Barberini and Camillo Massimi. Barberini's librarian was Lukas Holste, an unrivalled expert in the early Christian period. So one couldn't rule out that Poussin might have discovered a spiritual secret in the course of his research.

"Just imagine a trio made up of Poussin, Cassiano, and Holste, free to roam at will in the best libraries of that time," Wesenheim said. "Who knows what the three of them may have found out?"

These words reminded Françoise of what Jules had told her about Abbot Louis Fouquet's letter to his brother Nicolas, and she mentioned it to Wesenheim.

"The letter the abbot sent to his brother from Rome in 1656, telling him of Poussin's secret, is an undeniable fact. We actually have the original," Wesenheim said. "Just as what happened in Rennes-le-Château is undeniable. I mean the inexplicable behavior of Abbot Saunière."

In 1892 the church in Rennes-le-Château, in the south of France, needed some repairs done, Wesenheim said. The parish priest, Abbot Bérenger Saunière, eventually managed to scrape enough money together. During the repair work, Saunière discovered some old scrolls hidden in one of the pillars supporting the altar. Under the floor the bricklayers found a stone slab, but only the abbot saw what lay beneath it. No one was to find out how, but that discovery made the abbot extremely rich and was the start of a mystery that was to capture the interest of numerous writers. The abbot became the center of a series of inexplicable facts. Why did he chip away the epigraph from the tombstone of Marie de Blanchefort, the last descendent of a Grand Master of the Knights Templar? Why did he have that Latin inscription — *Terribilis est locus iste,* This is a terrible place — engraved on the façade of the church? Why did he spend months searching for in the countryside surrounding the village? That same year, the abbot went to Paris to have the scrolls deciphered.

"When Abbot Saunière came to Paris in 1892, he spent most of his time at the Louvre, where he bought the reproductions of three paintings. One of these was *Les Bergers d'Arcadie II.* Why?" Wesenheim said.

It was as if the fog had suddenly lifted.

"So Poussin might have discovered the secret of Rennes-le-Château in Rome, and then he might have gone down to the Midi-Pyrénées and left us a clue, with the iconography of *Les Bergers d'Arcadie II*," Françoise said. "Is that what you're saying?"

"How else would you explain all those coincidences?"

"But what was he trying to tell us?"

"In *Les Bergers d'Arcadie II*, Poussin made a masterly mélange of pagan and Christian symbolism, and he's done it so well that the true meaning has escaped us all," Wesenheim said. "But before going any further, I want to ask you a question. What does Arcadia mean to you?"

"It makes me think of an idyllic place, a place of everlasting happiness."

"Yes, many people, including Virgil, have described it in these terms. But in Greek mythology Arcadia was quite a different place."

"Different? How?"

Wesenheim described Arcadia as a place full of contrasts, populated on the one hand by nymphs, but on the other also by fauns, satyrs, and by demigods such as Pan and Bacchus. Pan, half man and half goat, played his pipes, but when he spoke he emitted inhuman sounds and terrorized the shepherds. Death and unhappiness were an everyday occurrence. In short, Arcadia was a sort of huge rubbish dump into which the gods of Olympus threw all the demigods and intermediate beings who pestered them.

"In *Les Bergers d'Arcadie II*, Poussin used a pagan image, that of Arcadia, to communicate a Christian secret," Wesenheim said. "He made a pagan mystery, the true nature of Arcadia, coexist with a mystery regarding the origins of Christianity, the mystery of Rennes-le-Château. Oh, what a genius!"

"The art critic Anthony Blunt held that the countryside and the tomb depicted in *Les Bergers d'Arcadie II* were imaginary, though."

Wesenheim shook his head. "There's a spot close to Rennes-le-Château where the countryside is identical. And until a few years ago, there was a tomb identical to the one in the painting. Can I make a suggestion?"

Françoise looked at him.

"Take a weekend off and go to Rennes-le-Château."

It was a sunny afternoon in a never-ending summer, and not a sound could be heard anywhere. Grassy glades criss-crossed by streams alternated with steep slopes where the vegetation was so thick that it was almost impenetrable. While the sheep drank from a river, their shepherds were lying on the grass.

Suddenly a sound of pipes broke the silence. The shepherds jumped to their feet and looked towards the woods. First, a pair of horns appeared from behind a tree, and then the figure of Pan—half man, half goat. The god of flocks and forests kicked his hooves and let out an inhuman cry. The shepherds fled, terrified, frantically driving their flocks towards the river. Meanwhile a gigantic Bacchus, with a huge protruding stomach and with bunches of grapes hanging from his ears, waddled out of the woods and followed Pan. He drank from a goatskin, and wine dribbled down his chin and onto his naked stomach.

Fauns and satyrs appeared out of the woods and started running and jumping around Pan and Bacchus. Then, as if by magic, the naiads, the gentle water nymphs, rose out of the river, and their ethereal forms seemed to hover over the surface of the water. The shepherds tried to seek refuge with the water-nymphs, but in vain. Their hands, reaching out desperately, grasped nothing. The shepherds and their flocks could go no further, because the waters of the river had become deep and rough.

Meanwhile the group led by Pan and Bacchus advanced towards the river, accompanied by the sound of the pipes and the rural god's inhuman cries.

A rapid succession of dull thuds drowned the uproar.

Françoise awoke in a start, sat upright and wiped her forehead. It had just been a bad dream.... Yet the thuds coming from the living room were not a dream.

When Françoise arrived at the doorway of the living room, the scene before her eyes was such that she let out a stifled cry.

Books were scattered on the floor everywhere, and an invisible hand dashed other books to the floor from the bookshelves. The pages of many books were being turned over relentlessly. However, the being seemed to be selective, because not all the books ranged on the same shelf were flung down.

Suddenly everything stopped, lamps flickered, and the china and glass knick-knacks on the mantelpiece and the coffee table began chattering and rattling. But nothing was broken: once more, the being proved to be different from the malicious poltergeists people spoke about.

A book, face down, slid swiftly across the floor and stopped exactly in front of Françoise. At that same moment, a draft of cold air swept over her. Françoise knelt and picked up the book. She turned it over. *An aerial photograph of Rennes-le-Château.*

The lights went off, and the air became colder. The curtains, only half-pulled, let the moonlight through, and Françoise could see the vapor of her breath.

A cord of an opaque substance, similar to fog but denser, began to exude from her mouth. This amorphous mist floated in the air, hovering at a height of a few feet above the floor. The cold became even more intense. Françoise felt goose pimples over her arms. Gradually, a figure took form from the mist, and its contour grew translucent: the figure of a veiled woman dressed in medieval clothing silhouetted in the moonlit room.

Françoise stepped forwards and raised her hand. "Speak to me… *please.*"

The being vanished.

Françoise clutched the book. She would go to Rennes-le-Château.

She realized she was exhausted, as if the being had absorbed all her energy. The vision of that cord of vapor flowing out of her mouth flashed through her mind. Did the being really exist, or was it an externalization of her thoughts?

Leaning from time to time against the wall, Françoise managed to get back to her room. She dropped onto the bed.

As he read the message, Guichard de Saint Clair's hands trembled. *It couldn't be true.* Jean de Joinville, seneschal of Champagne, was informing him that at dawn the following day, Friday, October 13 in the year of our Lord 1307, King Philip's seneschals, by order of the king himself, would arrest all the Templars throughout the Kingdom of France. The king had given orders to seize the Order's preceptories and confiscate all their possessions. The list of charges Philip had made against the Order was long, but it really amounted to two: heresy and sodomy.

The king had also ordered the Grand Inquisitor of France—the Dominican Guillaume Imbert, the king's confessor and friend—and William de Nogaret, his chancellor, to go to any lengths to extract rapid confessions from the Templars. Jean's message ended with an exhortation: "… *Escape this very night!*"

"Flee? Never! A Templar does not flee," said Jacques de Molay, the Grand Master of the Order. "These are infamous lies, and fleeing would be like an admission of guilt."

"That's not the point," Guichard said. "The king hates us, and don't tell me I hadn't warned you. He's never forgiven us your refusal to admit him as 'postulant' to the Order."

The Grand Master grimaced with indignation. "The kingdom's debts with the Order have gone beyond all limits, so now that rascal wants to lay his hands on our possessions. That's the real reason!"

Guichard grabbed the Grand Master by the arm. "We're in serious danger, can't you see that? We've got to follow Jean's advice and flee to England. King Edward will help us, and you'll see that King Alphonse of Spain will be on our side too."

"No, never. We'll appeal to the pope, whom we depend on," replied Jacques de Molay, his hand slicing the air. "Not even a king would dare touch a Templar."

"Imbert and de Nogaret have received orders to proceed quickly. They'll resort to torture, if necessary." Then, after a pause, Guichard added: "You know Imbert's reputation, don't you?"

"That villain Philip will never dare challenge the pope's authority."

"Why don't you face reality? Pope Clement was elected thanks to Philip's support. It's all too possible that this plot was part of their agreement from the very beginning."

"My decision is final," the Grand Master said. "I'll summon the Chapter of the Brethren and send messages to all the other preceptories throughout France right away. Everyone will be free to do as he thinks best."

Shouts, neighs, and heavy pounding came from the courtyard. Guichard went to the window. Amidst a frantic coming and going of men, horses, and carts, squires and guards were already loading the documents and possessions of the preceptory on to the wagons. Bulky sacks were being thrown out of the windows of the dormitories, raising clouds of dust when they hit the ground. How could he warn Arno and tell him to join him at La Rochelle? Whom could he trust? *Tristan*: he'd lost an eye rescuing him from the Saracens. Guichard asked his steward to summon his sergeant at arms.

A few minutes later, Tristan walked in, his brown mantel swishing and his sword thudding against his leather boots. A forelock of flaxen hair hung over the black eye patch covering his empty socket.

"Did they tell you?" Guichard said.

Tristan nodded.

"I have a vital mission to entrust to you."

"At your command, Brother Guichard."

"I want you to leave immediately for the preceptory of Besançon and warn my brother Arno of the danger. You will both immediately head for La Rochelle, where I'll be waiting for you aboard the *Beau Séant*."

"*La Rochelle*? And then where?"

"Away from France, to start with. We will decide where later."

Tristan was about to leave when Guichard stopped him. "Don't speak to anyone of your journey to Besançon. *To anyone at all*. Do you understand?"

Tristan's one eye widened. "You cannot be thinking—"

"There is a Judas among us. Within these very walls." Guichard opened a closet, took out a wooden casket, and counted out forty silver deniers, which he put into a leather scrip. "These should cover any eventuality."

It was one o'clock in the morning. Guichard mounted his horse and trotted over to the carts waiting in front of the entrance to the underground chambers, lit by torches. Just then the sergeants started coming out, carrying the coffers from Jerusalem.

When the loading was complete, Guichard signaled to the battlement guards to open the main gate. With a rattling of chains, the drawbridge was lowered over the moat. The light of the torches flickered on Jacques's stony face. Guichard raised his hand to salute him: he sensed he would never see him again. He spurred his horse on, and sixteen Templars and the carts followed him over the clattering boards of the bridge.

The horses' hooves echoed through the deserted streets of Paris.

When they were within sight of La Rochelle, Guichard signaled to his men to stop. He dismounted from his horse and crept cautiously as far as the edge of the hill overlooking an escarpment behind the harbor. He peered out from behind a tree. The eighteen galleys of the Templar fleet were lying at anchor in the port. Activity around the port and aboard the ships looked normal: no sign of the king's men. Philip had thought of everything, but not that.

At dusk, some furtive shadows approached the ships, boarded the flagship, the *Beau Séant*, and disappeared below deck. Shortly afterwards, two men armed with torches came back on deck and began to wave them towards the hill overlooking the port.

A few minutes later, Guichard and the others came down with the carts along the track winding its way down to the harbor. Finally, they stopped on the pier beside the *Beau Séant*, unloaded the coffers from the carts, and carried them aboard.

That same evening, a group of sailors went ashore and approached the dock warehouses warily. One of them spoke to the watchman and he opened the main gate. The sailors disappeared inside. After a while, they came out again, pulling a number of two-wheeled carts chock-a-block with wooden boxes and canvas sacks. This coming and going between the ships and the warehouses went on throughout the night.

By Monday evening, a further five hundred Templars from preceptories all over France had joined them aboard the galleys. But Arno and Tristan were not among them. As preceptor of the Paris preceptory, Guichard had taken command of the fleet.

He went on the upper deck. The deserted alleyways were shrouded in darkness, and fogbanks were wafting in from the sea. He looked up at the top of the hill. His hands clutched the rigging, as his ears waited to hear the pounding of two horses' hooves at any moment.

The boatswain kept his eyes on Guichard, his expression indicating that they couldn't wait any longer, for every minute that went by increased their risk. Many of the men knew about Arno, and Guichard had already overheard some muttering. He scanned the top of the hill once more, then gave the boatswain the order to set sail.

As the boatswain's horn sounded through the fog, dozens of sailors from all the galleys went ashore and proceeded to loosen the mooring-ropes. The rattle of the anchor chains mingled with the creaking of the hulls and the swashing of the waves.

The rustle of hoisted sails reminded Guichard of his voyage to Santander two months before, when Arno had accompanied him. That time too they had set sail in the evening aboard the *Beau Séant*. He heard once more Arno's Gascon-like laugh as he climbed the ratlines and jumped on the main yard, his eyes scanning the Spanish coast. When you are twenty-three, and a Knight Templar, the world has no boundaries.

The breeze filled the sails and the bow of the *Beau Séant* moved away from the pier, the waves lapping the side of the galley. Lightning lit up a cloudy sky. Where was Arno?

Guichard studied his charts. In spite of the morning mists, he recognized the Sound of Jura and ordered the boatswain to sail in. The other galleys followed the *Beau Séant*.

He leaned over the bulwark of the ship and scanned the headland. An icy wind cut into him. At last! Barren and windswept, but that strip of land represented safety, however inhospitable it appeared. Scotland was the only country in Christian Europe where the pope and Philip the Fair could not get their clutches on them. Robert the Bruce had been excommunicated and was at war with England. He needed men and would welcome them with open arms.

The prow of the *Beau Séant* cut through a thick bank of fog. The other ships became dark shadows, and the muffled shouts of the boatswains were redolent of impending threat. When they emerged from the fog, a jagged coastline with a stony beach loomed, not a quarter of a mile away: their landing place. Guichard had a shallop lowered.

At dawn the day after, the galleys raised anchor. Standing on a cliff, Guichard watched them as they put out to sea. The Sound was shrouded in mist, and only the splashing of the waves against the hulls broke the silence. As the galleys set off at full sail for the open sea, he turned to look at the expressionless eyes of the thirty knights who had decided to disembark with him. The other brethren had preferred to face the Great Ocean rather than stay in Christian Europe. The treasure from the House of David was sailing for the unknown.

As the sails of the last of the galleys faded into the distance, with his mind's eye Guichard went back to Temple Mount two hundred years earlier, and he looked at the empty altar in the Holy of Holies again. Jehovah had waited two centuries, but His wrath had struck the Order in the end: the nemesis of history was now accomplished. The epos of the Templars was over.

Guichard pulled his cloak more tightly round his shoulders and, followed by the other Templars, began to climb up the path.

A heron emerged from behind a crag, but a moment later he was swallowed up by the mist.

28

The Council of Ministers was in full session at Palazzo Chigi.

"Gheddafi can't go on behaving like a desert robber!" said the minister of foreign affairs, getting to his feet and slamming his hand on the table. He was about five feet tall, chubby, bald, and he wore a flashy checked vest and a bow tie. "This time I won't let him get away with it!"

"Cirillo, may I remind you of the size of our export flow to Libya?" the minister of foreign trade said. Sprawled out on his chair, his legs stretched out under the table, he was doodling on a notepad.

"I don't give a shit about our export flow to Libya when national dignity is at stake!" The minister of foreign affairs turned his head toward Prime Minister Accardo, sitting at one end of the long table. "Would it be too much to ask for the prime minister's enlightened opinion?"

Accardo was about to reply when a red light began flashing on his telephone.

"What's the matter, Penelope? I'm in full session," Accardo said. He put his pen down and closed his notebook. The figures of the Singapore banks never balanced. Jackals in ambush round each corner. What had happened to the good old days, when business was done on a handshake?

"Prime Minister, Antigono is here and wants to see you at all costs."

"Put him through."

"Leo, I must speak to you right away," Zergas said excitedly.

"Are you crazy? I'm chairing the council," whispered Accardo.

"Fuck the council, Leo. I've got to talk to you about *serious* matters."

Accardo sighed. "All right."

Accardo stood up and silence fell. "Ladies and Gentlemen, if you will excuse me, the Russian prime minister wishes to speak with me urgently. Another crisis at the Chinese border—I'm afraid. The session goes on. I would ask the deputy prime minister to take over."

Accardo left the council room to the accompaniment of the ministers' whispering.

Zergas was sitting in front of Accardo's desk, his leather briefcase resting on his knees, moving his heels up and down on the floor.

"Well, what's so urgent?" asked Accardo walking in and sitting at his desk.

"Something you won't like."

At that very moment, Zergas said, eighty-seven inspectors of the Bank of Italy, split up into twenty teams, were combing the credit office records of as many banks, including Banca Nazionale, all banks controlled by the Coalition Party. They were examining all the credit facilities in course of approval in favor of state-owned companies, starting with the $500 million loan in favor of CIP. The president of Banca Nazionale had called Zergas just half an hour before, saying that the Bank of Italy had ordered to freeze all credit facilities to state companies. The official motivation was that the banks under investigation had already gone beyond the limit between their credit extensions towards state-owned companies and their net equity. CIP's credit lines were already drawn one hundred percent, said Zergas, and without that loan there was no way that CIP could pay the $500 million to the joint venture.

"No doubt we can thank some son of a bitch in the Opposition for this present," Zergas said. "I'll find out, and I swear—"

"Forget it for the time being." Accardo began to tap his pipe bowl on the palm of his hand, with dull rhythmic taps. "How long has CIP got, to pay the $500 million?"

"Sixty days from the date of signing." Zergas took out a small diary and looked at the calendar. "Which means by December 9. The CIP board was ready to resolve on the matter tomorrow morning."

"Why do you talk in the past tense?"

Zergas stared at Accardo. "Are you kidding? With a seven to one debt ratio, the credit capacity of CIP equals zero. With our banks under the heel of the Bank of Italy, you can forget the whole deal."

"Your proposal?"

"I thought it was clear. Let's come up with some excuse and have the CIP board turn down the project. At least this will help us save face vis-à-vis the press."

"And you really believe I would miss a political opportunity like this?

"Leo! We haven't got a cent!"

"Technicalities."

"*Technicalities?*"

"Let's turn to the foreign banks."

"Why? What's the difference?"

"CIP is responsible for the energy supplies to this country."

"So what? CIP is not a sovereign risk, and a loan like this would never be able to get the guarantee of the Republic: I can already imagine the reaction of the Opposition. You want a miracle, but miracles only happen in fairy tales."

Accardo resumed tapping his pipe bowl on his palm, a subtle smile on his lips. "One makes miracles happen."

"For Chrissake, do you mind telling me what's going on in your mind?"

"That Frenchman, de Saint Clair. He'll find the money."

"Leo, have you gone mad? That guy is Kovacs's investment banker!"

"The Frenchman is as interested as we are, if not more, in this deal coming off — even if I never could figure out why."

"Are you really sure?"

Accardo touched the point of his nose. "This never betrayed me."

"Then what should I tell the chairman of CIP? The board meeting is convened for tomorrow at 11:00."

"Tell him to pass the resolution. I'll take care of the Frenchman."

◈

On October 9 the boards of Allied and CIP approved the joint venture. The following afternoon, Kovacs and the chairman of CIP met at Compagnie Financière d'Arcadie in Paris, where they signed the contract, harassed by reporters' flashbulbs.

An hour later Guichard's direct line rang.

"… So two months are left to find the $500 million," Accardo said.

"Do you think you can raise $500 million in two months?"

"*I* can't, but I think *you* can."

This was the very last thing Guichard expected.

"Would the loan carry the guarantee of the state?" Guichard said.

"You must be joking. The Opposition would tear me apart."

"I'm not the saint of lost causes."

"You'd better become one, then—and quickly. If the deal falls through, you're the one who has the most to lose. And I'm not talking just about money."

Losing face? Why not? A believable pretext.

"Okay. Let's get on with it."

Accardo laughed heartily, with the self-assurance of someone who had seen it all. "Zergas will pay you a visit in Paris on Monday morning. You see? After all, sanctity is nothing but a state of mind."

"I'm sure that banks too will share your point of view, Prime Minister."

Guichard rubbed the bridge of his nose. Who would lend $500 million to a company like CIP, and without any collateral? He turned his chair and his gaze rested on Dali's *The Persistence of Memory*. The back of his chair began rocking back and forth. Now his plan resembled the drooping clocks in the painting. The rocking stopped…. Accardo was wrong. If the deal didn't come off, there was someone else who had even more to lose. *Franzese*. Guichard reached for the phone.

"So the only way to get the $500 million together is to underwrite the loan," concluded Guichard.

A long silence followed on the other end. "Do you need the underwriting to reassure the banks, or because you're afraid you might need it?" Franzese asked.

"The market expects the manager of a loan like this to provide a firm underwriting," Guichard replied. Then he added with forced confidence: "I'll manage to syndicate the loan up to the last dollar, if that's what's worrying you."

"By December 9?"

"By December 9."

Another long silence. "If the Organization's money got stuck in a loan to CIP because of the underwriting, my friends wouldn't be too happy about it. You realize that, don't you?"

"Threats won't help me to understand better."

"You know our laws," was Franzese's sharp reply. "If things go wrong, I won't cover for you."

The words exchanged between Franzese and Astarita by the fountain, that evening a month before, flashed though Guichard's mind. Franzese needed that loan even more than he did, but now it served his purpose to find a scapegoat in case things went wrong. What mattered was that Franzese shouldn't wonder about the real reason Guichard was determined to go ahead with the loan, or that, if anything, he thought that Guichard was willing to run a similar risk because of exaggerated professional pride.

"The de Saint Clairs need no protectors," Guichard said.

"So much the better. It's understood you're taking this initiative under your own responsibility. I wash my hands of it."

"Pontius Pilate did it with more style."

"Pontius Pilate had an empire behind him. I don't."

The shadows of twilight were falling on Paris, and the office was lit just by the lights of the *quais*. Guichard's gaze turned toward Notre Dame. The gargoyles of Notre Dame looked like those monsters that he sensed deep down, wandering unceasingly around in the unremitting search for something indefinable. And yet, when a shaft of light broke through the darkness, the monsters promptly retreated into their crannies where, motionless and suspicious, they waited for the return of darkness, as reassuring as amniotic fluid.

The blow from the mace of a quintaine hurts, said the Voice. *Is that not true, Guichard de Saint Clair?*

Silence.

He is not a true knight, he who dares not face the malicious, serpent-like monsters that wander around in the abysses. But to decide whether one should strike with a mace, an axe or a sword, one has first to grab the enemy and raise his visor.

I see that psychoanalysis was fashionable in the Middle Ages too.

Mockery will avail thee little. There is no hope of winning the joust, if thou hast not first tamed the monster hiding in the abyss of thy soul.

It's easy to pose as masters of the art of life when one is a Voice. I would like to see *you* in my place, you who speak with such presumption, having to fight with the Kovacs, the Accardos, the Franzeses, and with the Roman Church.

I had warned thee. Thou didst choose unworthy companions-at-arms.

Was there a different choice?

Strange words for a knight who says that "nothing is written." Thou art turning the point of thy sword against thyself.

Silence.

Thou art a base churl, Guichard de Saint Clair. I have read thy thoughts. Flying back in time to follow an impossible dream means fleeing from facing the enemy in open combat.

You're only speaking out of jealousy.

Yea, I do love her, and I speak the truth i'faith, whereas thou liest, starting with thyself.

Very convenient. You and all the de Saint Clairs stand at the window waiting for me to do your dirty work, and you even dare to pass judgment on me.

I, like all the de Saint Clairs who have come before thee, am convinced that the code of a knight is immutable in time, and that a de

Saint Clair should listen to the voice that reaches him from the depth of his soul.

Voice? *What voice?* All I seem to be hearing is your voice!

Liar! Thou knowest well what voice I am speaking of. It is the voice speaking to thee from beyond the monster, but that thou persistest in not hearing.

Psychoanalysis again.

Hold thy peace! Hast thou not the courage to gallop against the foul beast and run it through with thy lance? Face the monster, Guichard, and hearken unto the voice!

Guichard bent his head.

Françoise parked the car in front of a café in the main square in Couiza. She opened her road map of the Midi-Pyrénées, and laid it on the steering wheel. The place was called Les Pontils.... She sighed. It wasn't shown.

"It's the road here on the left," the bartender said. He put down his mug of beer and wiped some foam off his moustache.

"Where exactly is Les Pontils?" said Françoise.

"Once you've gone past Serres, after a couple of miles you'll see the sign for a pottery, La Poterie des Pontils, on your left. That's the place: just a few decrepit houses dotted about here and there. Have fun."

After passing Serres, a village of old ochre-colored houses with hollow tile roofs tucked away amidst the greenery, Françoise saw the sign for the pottery. She drove on slowly until she came in sight of a small bridge with a stone parapet, where the river formed a series of loops. She scanned the outline of the mountains to her right. Her breath quickened. She stopped the car. This was the place.

Françoise leaned on the parapet of the bridge and gazed at a hillock some thirty yards in front of her. She unrolled a reproduction of *Les Bergers d'Arcadie II*. Although a clump of bushes covered the top of the hillock, a stone base was visible. According to what she'd been reading, the tomb had been lying on that very base until a few years before. People said that the owner of the land had it removed because of the constant stream of prying intruders. Françoise's eyes followed the outline of the mountains rising behind the hillock. The first crest on the left had to be Mount Cardou, the second one the mountain of Blanchefort. In the background, between the two peaks, a tiny village perched on top of a mountain was barely visible: that could only be Rennes-le-Château.

A barbed-wire fence marked the limits of the estate. Françoise looked round: nobody in sight. She slipped her leg through the barbed wire, right underneath a sign saying *Propriété Privé. Defense d'entrée* — Private property. No trespassing.

Françoise rested her foot on the stone base of the tomb. She looked at the reproduction again, then raised her eyes to the outline of the mountains above her. *The two profiles were identical.* A gust of wind made the leaves rustle. She closed her eyes and took a deep breath. Poussin must have stood here three hundred and fifty years earlier, perhaps on a day like this.

Françoise turned the car into a country lane leading to a farmhouse and drew up to the gate. A woman in jeans and Wellingtons was heading for a cowshed, carrying two buckets. The woman turned to look at her, put the buckets down, and took off her straw hat. Wisps of gray hair tumbled down onto her forehead. A big Alsatian dog with an ear missing began to bark. "*Arrète toi!*" ordered the woman.

"So you've come all the way from Paris just to see the tomb?" the woman said.

"You probably think I'm a bit crazy, don't you?" Françoise said.

"You must have your reasons, my dear. What is it you want to know?"

"Have you been living here long?"

"I was born here, and here I've stayed — though not a day goes by that I don't ask myself why."

"Do you remember the tomb of Les Pontils, the one on the top of the hillock?"

"Sure I remember it. As children we used to play hide-and-seek around it. "

Françoise showed the woman the reproduction of Poussin's painting. "Did it look like this?"

"Yes, it was a big stone block with the top corners rounded off, you know. Just like in the picture."

"And the tomb, had it always been there, up on the hill?"

"Yes, as far back as I can remember. And also grandpa Gustave told me it had always been there." The woman laughed and shook her head. "Ah, dear grandpa Gustave.... You won't believe it. He'd become convinced that the hillock was haunted. How he loved to go hunting around there, because of the pheasants, you know. And in the end he began to go hunting somewhere else, because of that fixed idea of his about the ghosts. He used to complain that the ghosts frightened the pheasants."

"My grandfather used to count the apples growing on the apple trees in our orchard," Françoise said, " and he would give me a nasty look every time one single apple was missing."

"Our grandpas would have got along fine."

"Did you ever take any photos of the tomb, by any chance?"

The woman bent down and stroked the Alsatian behind the remaining ear. "Well, yeah.... I should still have a few around." She gestured to Françoise to sit down on a wooden bench leaning against the wall of the cowshed. "I'll be back in a moment."

When she returned, she was holding a photograph album with a dark-brown leather cover tied up with a red ribbon. She sat down next to Françoise, untied the ribbon, and began to turn the pages.

"Oh, at last. Here we are," said the woman, passing Françoise the album and pointing to a photo.

The photograph showed a young woman standing in front of the tomb and holding a poodle. The tomb was identical to the one in the painting.

Rennes-le-Château gave her the impression of a place lost in time. In the distance, beyond the Aude Valley, the spurs of the East Pyrenees rose high against the sky, displaying their snow-covered summits.

Françoise got out of the car. A gust of wind whistled through the cracks of an old tower rising above the valley. She passed in front of a bookshop selling esoteric books and walked up a steep cobblestone alley leading to the church of Sainte Marie Madeleine.

The architrave above the church porch bore the inscription Wesenheim had spoken of: *Terribilis est locus iste* — This is a terrible place. Just past the church entrance, a grotesque statue of the devil Asmodeus held up the holy water stoup. In Jewish legend, Asmodeus had been the guardian of the treasure in Solomon's Temple. The church had been wholly restructured thanks to Abbot Saunière's sudden wealth. What allegoric meaning had the abbot wanted to give to the Latin inscription and to the statue of that particular devil?

After visiting the church, Françoise crossed the garden and headed towards the gate to the graveyard.

"The usual tour, or something in particular?" asked the guide, a lively-looking young man with fair hair.

"I'm interested in the tomb of Marie de Blanchefort," Françoise said.

The guide turned around and pointed to a tomb in the form of a chapel, at the end of the gravel path that started at the gate. "That's it down there."

There was nothing written on the tomb.

"So it's true that someone chipped away the inscription," she said.

The guide confirmed that after discovering the four scrolls in one of the two pillars supporting the altar, Abbot Saunière hastened to get rid of the epitaph on the tomb, the last resting place of Marie de Nègre d'Ablès, Marquise d'Hautpoul de Blanchefort, who died on January 17, 1781.

"I've read that Marie de Blanchefort was the last descendent of Bertrand de Blanchefort, one of the first Grand Masters of the Knights Templar," said Françoise.

"Yes, Bertrand de Blanchefort came from Blanchefort, just a few miles from here."

"What part did Marie de Blanchefort play in the mystery surrounding Abbot Saunière?"

"Well, an important part. Her confessor was Abbot Bigou, who'd been parish priest of Rennes-le-Château during the

French Revolution, so about a hundred years before Abbot Saunière. It was Abbot Bigou who placed the scrolls in the altar pillar, where Abbot Saunière found them."

"Then Abbot Bigou could have learned the secret from Marie de Blanchefort?"

"Quite likely. Perhaps during Confession."

"And who would Marie de Blanchefort have got it from? Her ancestors?"

"It's a theory that holds water, considering who Bertrand was."

"What could the secret be? The treasure of Jerusalem?"

The guide shook his head. "Personally I think more of a spiritual secret, something linked with the Templars."

"Just because Bertrand de Blanchefort was a Grand Master?"

"Not just that." The guide pointed to the mountains. "Did you know that in Bertrand's time there was an important *Commanderie* of the Templars not far from Rennes-le-Château, the Bézu garrison?"

"Did this area have some strategic importance?"

"None. And that's what makes the whole thing so strange."

"So how do you explain the presence of that Templar garrison, then?"

"One of the theories is that the Templars hid something in the area, something they cared a lot about."

Françoise looked at him in silence.

"There are plenty of clues and coincidences in this story," continued the guide. "But two in particular make me think."

"What clues?"

"Did you know that as soon as Bertrand de Blanchefort became Grand Master, in 1156, the Templars arranged for a group of German miners to come here?"

"German miners? What on earth for?"

"At the time, the Templars said that the miners were going to start digging for gold again on Blanchefort mountain. It seemed rather strange, because the mines had been exhausted since the time of the Romans."

"But why bring in *German* miners?" Françoise said.

"The only plausible explanation is that the Templars wanted to avoid any contact between the miners and the local people," the guide replied.

"Does anyone know what work they actually carried out?"

"In the seventeenth century the French government had some prospecting done here in the Rennes area, and the engineers found traces of excavations made by the German miners over five hundred years earlier."

"What did the engineers say?"

"That no mining had been done. The miners had dug a tunnel inside the mountain, but the roof had caved in, so the engineers couldn't find out where it led to."

The wind whistled around the mountainside.

"Before you spoke of two clues," Françoise said.

"Well, the second one is the Latin—excuse me, Greek—epitaph on Marie de Blanchefort's tomb."

"*A Greek inscription?*"

"The words *Et in Arcadia ego* had been chiseled on her tomb, in ancient Greek though. That was the epitaph that Abbot Saunière chiseled away. The same inscription that could be read on the tomb in Les Pontils, even if that one was in Latin."

"This is really too much of a coincidence, don't you think?" The guide looked at his watch and excused himself, saying he was supposed to lead a guided tour of the church.

Françoise went over to the low wall surrounding the cemetery and looked out across the valley.

The same phrase that Poussin had included in *Les Bergers d'Arcadie II* had also appeared on Marie de Blanchefort's headstone. And in Greek! Everything seemed to point to that phrase hiding a sort of password... a password for a secret passed down through the centuries to just a few initiates. A secret that Nicolas Poussin and Abbot Saunière, 250 years later, must have come across most likely by chance. A secret meant only for the initiated, and of which Guichard must be the last trustee.

It was starting to get dark. Violent gusts of wind lashed the mountain slopes. The squat outline of Mount Blanchefort, enveloped in the shadows of dusk, rose before Françoise.

Bertrand de Blanchefort had been one of the nine knights who'd gone to Jerusalem together with Geoffroy de Saint Clair. What had they brought back from the Holy Land? What had they hidden on Mount Blanchefort?

Françoise remembered the anagram sent in by the BBC viewer. *Go, I hide the mysteries of God.*

The wind raised a cloud of dust. A cold breeze swept over her arms.

♣

29

The dull blows of the guards' mauls became less frequent. The outlines of the stakes were lit up by the flickering light of the campfires that the royal guards had kindled during the night. The stakes were lined up in the middle of a field strewn with rubble, just outside the walls of Porte St. Antoine, one of Paris's many points of entry. The fires cast the poles' lengthened shadows on the city walls, and among the merlons one could glimpse the archers' dark figures, their helmets gleaming in the moonlight.

Philip the Fair's thugs were stacking the last bundles of fagots round the poles.

"*Ugh, tout ça pour des salauds sans Dieu!* — Ugh, all this trouble for some godless swine!" said a guard. He raised a goatskin to his mouth and took a long swig. The wine dribbled through his beard down his neck. He wiped his mouth with a filthy hand and belched.

As dawn lit up the bastions, the crowd began to thicken.

Guichard glanced warily around him, pulled the hood of his cloak down over his face, and mingled with the populace.

No one would be able to recognize him dressed this way. He touched his cheeks: it felt strange to be without a beard after all those years. Although it seemed like only yesterday, two years had already gone by since he'd fled to Scotland. All trace had been lost of Arno. A squire who had managed to escape from the preceptory of Besançon had told him he'd seen Arno and Tristan galloping off from Besançon, but since then they seemed to have disappeared.

A clattering of horses' hooves came from Porte St. Antoine. The king's soldiers passed at a trot through the arched gate, holding torches. Two horse-drawn carts packed with prisoners followed them.

The guards turned down the sideboards. Amidst a rattle of chains, they got the prisoners out, pricking them with their spears and hurling insults at them. The convicts were shackled together by their ankles and had iron collars clamped round their necks. Half naked, filthy, dressed in rags, many of them were still wearing the remnants of Templar clothing.

His fingernails cutting into the palms of his hands, Guichard approached cautiously, elbowing his way through the crowd: faces with noses and ears chopped off, lips torn off, eyes gouged out.... Many had had one or more limbs hacked off, leaving just the stumps blackened with pitch. Their faces were expressionless, their eyes blank. Guichard could hardly recognize Marcel de Lisleferme, Roger d'Avignon, Pascal de Tissier.... Ghosts of their former selves. It wasn't hard to realize how the Dominican Imbert—the "Great Inquisitor"—had managed to extort confessions. Guichard lowered his eyes. Anger swept away horror, blazing up quicker than lightning flashing across the sky, and his hand clutched the haft of the dagger hanging from his belt, until his fingers ached.

The guards chained the prisoners to the stakes and heaped bundles of fagots around them up to their thighs. Some among the crowd gestured to attract the executioners' attention, and began throwing them gold coins, which the executioners snatched up. After biting the coins and slipping them into their scrips, the thugs took green twigs from a separate stack and stuck them into the fagots heaped around which ever prisoners the coin throwers went on pointing to, gesticulating and yelling. Guichard understood. It was unseasoned wood, which would smoke while burning. The prisoners would strive to inhale the smoke as quickly as possible in order to die from suffocation before the pain drove them mad. Guichard's hand felt his leather pouch full of coins. He spotted a thug whose appearance was less loathsome than the others' and elbowed his way over to him. He was about to call out to him when his eyes fell on a prisoner: *Arno!*

He looked like a skeleton. He hung bent at the knees, supported by the chains that held him tied to the pole. The right sleeve of his tunic, torn and bloodstained, dangled limp like an inanimate puppet; a black stump stuck out of it. His head was bowed over his chest. He was unconscious. Guichard's first instinct was to shout his name, but the words died in his throat. What use would it be? There was only one thing he could do for his brother: help him die quickly. Guichard raised his arm to attract the thug's attention, told him what he wanted, and passed him a handful of silver coins. The thug approached an executioner and muttered something gesturing towards Arno. The executioner picked up a heap of green twigs and stacked them on the fagots piled round Arno, who remained motionless.

It seemed impossible that that was the same Arno who had drunk and laughed more than everyone else in the harbor tavern in Santander, attracting ill-concealed looks of admiration from the maids. In the afternoon, he and Arno wandered about the old, white houses perched on the cliffs overlooking the sea, and watched the women hanging fishing nets to dry in the sun among multicolored fishing boats. They strolled along the crescent-shaped sandy beach and played with a brindled dog, throwing a stick into the sea and running with him in the surf. Arno took his shirt off and swung it in a circle, shouting and splashing about in the water, foam spraying up all around him. The dazzling light blinded them, the water stung their skin, and the briny breeze brought with it dreams of far-off lands. That day it seemed the sun would never set on Santander beach.

Drawn by six black horses, a carriage with a black tilt came at a trot through Porte St. Antoine. A sergeant of the royal guards sat on the coachman's seat, his breastplate glittering. The murmurs of the crowd died away.

Ten Dominicans got out of the carriage, their faces hidden by the hoods of their cowls. They lined up and, in a silence broken only by the crackling of the campfires, passed in front of the stakes holding a crucifix pressed to their breasts. They stopped an equal distance from one another, so that they covered the full distance from the first pole to the last.

The Dominican standing on the extreme right stepped forward and pointed his arm at the convicts, holding the crucifix upright in front of himself. A name spread among the crowd: *Imbert... Imbert... Imbert.*

Imbert turned to the executioners and nodded three times. The thugs brought their burning torches to the fagots, and soon the smell of burning wood filled the air. Then the moaning and the cries began, growing louder and louder, and within a few minutes inhuman screams pierced the air above the walls of Porte St. Antoine.

Guichard pressed his hands to his ears, but in vain. He lacked the courage to look at Arno.

The stench of burning flesh defiled the air. You could hear the sizzling of flesh, and jets of boiling blood continued to spurt out of the mouths, ears, and noses of the scorching bodies.

Silence fell.

Imbert and the other Dominicans filed slowly past the stakes. Then they climbed back into their carriage and drove off at a gallop through the nauseating smoke screen enveloping the bastions.

Guichard couldn't tell how, but he found himself standing in front of Arno's stake, his head bowed. He raised his eyes.

Joash ben Uri's words echoed in his mind and he thought of the esoteric mysteries Geoffroy had learned from the Christian Gnostics, the Druses, the Ismailites and from the oriental mystics. Enveloped in an unreal silence, he was dazzled by an explosion of light and was pervaded by a radiant energy. The orderly equilibrium of celestial spheres made him understand that each action must be followed by an equal and opposite reaction; everything must balance out eventually — including unsettled accounts.

"O my brother, I swear I will avenge you and our brethren, in the name of the de Saint Clairs," said Guichard, his fist clenching and unclenching. "'*Eye for eye, tooth for tooth, hand for hand, foot for foot.*'" (Exodus 21:24)

He still had four days before he was to meet the group of Templar fugitives he would lead to Scotland: be it only for a few hours, he must return to the castle at Les Andelys.

He turned and set off for Porte St. Antoine. His hooded figure disappeared through the archway of the gate.

30

Staggering under the weight of two black leather suitcases, Zergas came out of the condo gate wearing a multicolor-striped sweater and a sailor-hat. Waddling like a penguin, he headed for his car parked nearby. Giancana and Intini observed him from the Volvo van, parked across the street. After closing the trunk, Zergas went back into the building. He came out again some ten minutes later, festooned with plastic bags and a bulging green canvas bag slung round his neck.

"Just look at the poor devil," Intini said, "loaded down like a pack-horse. Talk of women's lib!"

"C'mon, follow him," Giancana said. "Make sure he leaves town."

"OK. I'll go." Intini got out of the car. "But don't worry: I shall return."

Giancana sighed. "Is that a promise or a threat?"

Zergas shut the trunk again, stretched, and got into the driver's seat. A few minutes later, his wife Giovanna, wearing a silk foulard and impeccably creased green trousers, marched up to the car, hung her duffle coat above the rear seat, and sat down beside her husband. She turned and started wagging her forefinger at him. The car sped away from the condo.

The Volvo van was parked in the dimly lit, deserted street in a line of cars. A street lamp illuminated the figures of three men sitting inside. The clock on the dashboard read 2:30 a.m.

"Have you checked the walkie-talkie?" Giancana said.

"'Need you ask?" Intini turned towards Carlomagno sitting in the back seat. "No bow-tie this evening. How come?"

"How could I strangle you with a bow tie?" Carlomagno said.

Giancana and Carlomagno left the car and crossed the road, each carrying a black bag. It took Giancana just a few minutes to open both the main gate and the inside door to the stairway. Wall lights cast dim cones of light onto the stairway ceiling. When they reached the third floor, they stood motionless on the landing for a few moments. No sound came from the neighbors' apartment. Only the humming of a lamp broke the silence.

Giancana took a bunch of master keys out of his bag. He passed Carlomagno a flashlight, gesturing to him to point it at the lock. He put on surgical gloves and knelt down in front of the door.

A quarter of an hour later, Giancana got up and stretched himself; he put one ear to the door and slowly turned the key: the steel bars slid out of the doorframe.

Giancana put a silk stocking over his head and passed one to Carlomagno, who gave him a questioning look.

"In case there's a video camera hidden somewhere," Giancana whispered.

Giancana took out the key he had had made from the plasticine mould and nodded to Carlomagno to hand him the flashlight. Swiftly he opened the door, went in and pointed the flashlight at the picture hanging near the door. He slid the picture sideways and inserted the key into the lock of the alarm system. The key turned.

Immobile, Giancana looked at his watch and waited a few minutes. Nothing happened. He poked his head out of the door and beckoned to Carlomagno.

Giancana put on a pair of heavy glasses and handed Carlomagno another pair. "They have special quartz lenses that allow you to see infrared rays."

"Haven't you disconnected the alarm system?" Carlomagno said.

"It could be split into sections."

Giancana walked over to the doorway of the living room. His flashlight danced over the walls and the ceiling: everything seemed normal. He went back to the entryway and headed for the hallway followed by Carlomagno.

They froze: halfway down, three beams of red light crossed the hallway diagonally.

"Stay here," Giancana said.

The beam of Giancana's flashlight searched the walls and the doorframes. Nothing. He advanced gingerly along the hallway, moving the pictures sideways one after the other. When he reached the infrared rays, he lay down face upwards and slid slowly under them. He got up, and moved the next picture. He stood still.

There was a keyhole in the wall, identical to the one by the front door. Giancana put his key in the lock: it fit. He turned it halfway. The red beams disappeared.

They entered a small study, its walls lined with books. A desk was placed against the wall, a personal computer on top of it.

Carlomagno sat down at the desk and turned on the PC. The computer gave out a buzzing, and after a few moments a dialogue window appeared on the screen: *Type in user password*. Carlomagno snorted.

"What's the matter?" asked Giancana.

"There's a password. The files must be coded," Carlomagno said. "Let's not waste time. I'll make a copy of the hard disk and we get the hell out of here."

Carlomagno opened his bag and took out a laptop; he placed it on the table and turned it on. He loosened the screws that held the PC casing in place, removed it, and pushed aside a few bundles of colored cables.

"Here it is," Carlomagno said. He rummaged in his bag again and pulled out a long cable and a tool kit. He fit one end of the cable to the drive of the PC and the other end to his laptop. He typed in a few words, and the PC gave out an intermittent buzz.

"What's happening?" Giancana asked.

"It's copying the hard disk. It won't take long."

The bookshelves above the PC were stacked with books, intensely colored rock crystals with name tags, and CD holders.

Carlomagno stood up and admired the crystals. Then he started to read the titles of the CD's.

"Nat King Cole, Frank Sinatra, Yves Montand…. Our friend is not only a naturalist, but also a sentimental fuddy-duddy," Carlomagno said.

"It must be Accardo's influence."

A short time later the whirring noise stopped.

"Done." Carlomagno put everything in order, and put his laptop back in his leather bag. "Let's go."

When they were back in the hallway, Giancana turned the alarm system back on: the infrared beams cut the darkness again. Giancana and Carlomagno slid under them.

When they got back to the car, Intini was listening to light music. He looked at their smiling faces.

"I almost feel sorry for that poor devil," said Intini. "With all those bags—and all that wife."

§

When Carlomagno got back home, he went into his workshop right away and took the laptop out of his bag. He linked it to his PC network and transferred the copy of Zergas's hard disk onto one of his PCs. Zergas's desktop screen appeared, showing files and folders. Carlomagno clicked the mouse several times.

"Damn it!"

Zergas's hard disk contained 2,652 folders and 10,980 files!

Carlomagno shook his head, yawned and scribbled something on a scrap of paper. He began to unbutton his shirt, turned off the light and left.

The hierarchical tree layout of Zergas's hard disk glowed on the screen, like a beacon in the night.

Under the force of the wind, the rain lashed the hillside. The trees in the park bent like saplings and the stream of water spouting from Neptune's mouth splashed against the low wall surrounding the park of the villa.

Miserere… Miserere…

The walls and the ceiling of the billiard room in the villa were covered with frescoes depicting religious themes, in which frowning prophets pointed to the right path with commanding gestures, holding up with brawny arms stone tablets with the words of the Law. An ancient billiard table in Brazilian mahogany and with finely carved legs stood in the center of the room, on a kilim carpet that covered the parquet floor. Allegri's *Miserere* sung by the Sistine Chapel Choir echoed in the room. A waiter dressed in a white tuxedo left a silver tray with a bottle of Corvo di Salaparuta and two glasses on a cupboard.

Franzese was studying his shot, holding his cue resting on the floor; he was in shirtsleeves with gold cuff links and was wearing a dark vest with a watch chain emerging from its pocket. Astarita filled the glasses.

"We could have done without this." Franzese sunk a red ball. "Black ball," he said, and aimed at a corner pocket.

"Do we really need that joint venture?" Astarita chalked the tip of his cue. "With 100,000 billion lire in our pockets, we can get rid of Banca d'Italia when and how we want to."

"That's what *you* think. The EC would come to their aid." Franzese struck the black ball, which dropped into the pocket.

"They still might decide to, even if we set off the scandal."

"No, they won't. A scandal like this will wipe out the whole political system." Franzese shot a red ball, which dropped into a side pocket. "The EC central banks wouldn't take such a risk.... Blue ball."

"Why did you threaten Guichard like that, then? After all, it's in our own interests for him to get the loan together."

"You starting to play soft, now? All our money is at stake here, to say nothing of my skin."

"You know Guichard," Astarita said. "I doubt if threats have any effect on him."

"Everyone always takes care of number one, him included. He'll close the loan, and much faster—now." Franzese leaned over the table and with a neat shot he sank the blue ball.

"What if he doesn't succeed? It's already October 10. December 9 isn't far off."

"In that case our plan has to be shelved. I'm no roulette player." Franzese shot a red ball, which rebounded from a side pocket.

Astarita aimed at a red ball and sank it. "Pink ball.... What about Guichard? What happens, if in order to syndicate the loan he's got to underwrite it using $500 million of our money?"

"What kind of question is that?" Franzese pointed his thumb to his chest. "Should I be the one to take the risk in his place? The rules of the game are clear, my friend, and Guichard's no exception."

"It makes me wonder what it is that drives him on. All he would have to do is say no to CIP. No loan, no joint venture, no personal risk."

"No, he'll never back down. And you know why? He's got the de Saint Clair blood in his veins. And that comes in very handy—for us."

Astarita slammed the pink ball, which rebounded from a corner pocket, hit a side cushion and came to rest in the center of the table.

"Your shots are too hard, Rosario." Franzese sipped his glass of vintage Corvo di Salaparuta. "I'm afraid you are no good in bed with women."

"*What do you mean by that?*" Astarita's face turned violet. "First of all I don't see how that comes into it, but I can assure you that no woman has ever complained. On the contrary: if you really want to know, they complain because they can't keep up with me."

"Tsk, tsk, tsk. You see? Playing pool well is like making love well, or like politics. Gentle thrusts, and correct angles, are far more effective than hard ones. In love and politics, just like in pool, it's all a matter of brain—not of testicles."

Miserere... Miserere...

♣

The first wave of English mounted knights fell into the spear-spiked pitfalls and death cries rent the air. Those who were following at a gallop could not stop in time and fell in their turn on the ones in front. The Scottish pikemen pierced the few knights who managed to break through. The English charged again and again, each time weaker and weaker, until their own dead blocked the path. In disarray and panic-stricken, the English cavalry started to retreat, leaving the vanguard of their infantry to fight a furious battle with the Scottish army on the hilltop. However, the main body of the English infantry did not even succeed in reaching the top, because the front was only two hundred and twenty yards wide and the reinforcements could not pass through.

Lined up at the bottom of the hill, the English archers watched the battle, powerless to help. They could not shoot their arrows because, in the turmoil, they would have risked hitting their own men. Hidden in a clump of bushes on Coxet Hill, Guichard watched the archers climb the two sides of the slope. Their strategy was obvious: they wanted to reach the flank of the combatants so they could shoot cleanly at the Scots.

Hidden in a thicket on the top of Gillies Hill some two hundred yards away, King Robert the Bruce waved a white cloth in Guichard's direction: it was the agreed-upon signal. Bruce turned to his knights, raised his arm and spurred his horse into a gallop down the hill.

The Scottish cavalry, five hundred of them, came out into the open. They set off at a gallop diagonally towards the right side of the hill, heading straight for the English archers who had spread along the slope of the hill. The ground trembled, the Scottish knights' war cries filled the air, and their swords and maces glittered in the sunshine. The English archers, their faces contorted with terror, dropped their bows and began running wildly down the hill. The Scots' armored war-horses cut them off and plunged into the midst of them. Swords and maces slashed the air and finished what the horses' hooves had begun.

Guichard unsheathed his sword, turned to his men and shouted: *"Beau Séant! Beau Séant!"* The Templars' white cloaks flashed among the trees and the pounding of horses' hooves filled the woods. Guichard spurred his horse down the hill aiming for the left side, where some thousand archers had been lining up. Fear followed surprise on the Englishmen's faces. He and his knights plunged into the midst of the archers, knocking them down and trampling them underfoot. The survivors took flight down the hill. Guichard wheeled his horse around.

Just then, loud cries of exultation filled the air: thousands of Scots appeared at the top of the hill and began running madly down. They were not part of King Bruce's regular army, but gillies [highland chief's backers] who had followed the army to help if necessary. To act so boldly, the "irregulars" must have thought that the battle was over. But why? Simply because they'd seen the English archers take flight? And what about the rest of King Edward's army? Guichard looked over to the other side of the brook: the royal standard was leaving the field! The English were falling back, and soon their slow retreat degenerated into a terror-stricken rout.

From below, Edward and his men couldn't see that this shouting horde was armed only with sickles and sticks. The English king must have mistaken those few thousand Scots running down towards the brook for fresh troops. Or perhaps the English had lost their courage when they'd recognized the Templars' red crosses. Guichard didn't know the answer, but one thing was certain: beyond all expectations, the battle was won.

He spurred his horse towards the right flank of the hill, to join Bruce. A stabbing pain pierced his back. He fought for breath and a death rattle came from his throat. Everything started to spin, but he found the strength to twist his hand round behind his back.... *The haft of a battle axe.*

With a clanking of armor plating, Guichard collapsed to the ground, and his two lives, his own and Geoffroy's, flashed before him. The Ark, Miriam's face, the wooden chest, the Essenes of Qumran, that night of October 13, the galleys of the Templar fleet setting sail for the Great Ocean.... Blood spurted from his mouth and a damp warmth spread over his cheek.

His mind's eye focused on Arno's charred body and in his ears echoed the shrieks from the stakes of Porte St. Antoine.

"O my brother, I swear I will avenge you and our brethren, in the name of the de Saint Clairs ... Eye for eye, tooth for tooth; hand for hand, foot for foot."

The world was spinning faster and faster around him. He saw his own body stretched out at his horse's feet, as if it were something unconnected with him: only a cord of light seemed still to link him to it. His body began drifting away and he started losing all awareness of time and space.... Only a few more instants were left.

A bareheaded knight was riding towards him. The horse seemed to gallop in a haze, appearing and disappearing, moving with unreal slowness.... *Geoffroy!* A sign of the celestial spheres!

The first de Saint Clair to bear my very same name shall be the one to avenge Arno and our brethren.... Geoffroy, let him know no peace until justice has been done.

The cord of light was severed and his body drifted further and further away, until it vanished, a speck swallowed up by a whirlpool.

A blinding light enveloped him.

31

Cardinal Wolfenberg took his glasses off, pushed his papers aside and signaled to Monsignor Griffith to sit down.

"What can I do for you, Monsignore?" the cardinal said.

Monsignor Griffith opened a thick folder on his knees. "His Eminence Cardinal Ortega has a meeting with the Holy Father today at 6 p.m., to reach a final decision on the Recursos Naturais matter. Before drawing up my final report, I need to ask you a few questions, Your Eminence."

"I am at your complete disposal. Fire away."

"We at APSA are astonished at an amount of 7,500 billion lire, your Eminence. Why did you not consider underwriting a minor quota of the issue?"

"Monsignore, we intend to launch a message to the world through this deal. And now you come here talking about small change?"

"Mine is only an invitation to prudence."

"There is a time for prudence—and there is a time for boldness."

"There is an additional point, Your Eminence. APSA, as you well know, only invests in blue chips. What does a project like this have to do with our investment criteria?"

"Have you perhaps acquired any unfavorable information about Recursos Naturais?"

"No, Your Eminence."

"About their shareholders?"

Monsignor Griffith leafed through his folder. "I have to admit that the information collected on Recursos Naturais is very positive." Monsignor Griffith sighed. "But that's not the point, Your Eminence."

The cardinal's jowls twitched. "Then what is the point, Monsignore? Supposing that you have one."

"It's a matter of investment policy, Your Eminence. Nothing else."

"May I remind you that the Holy See will finance the investment with Manus Domini funds?"

"The source of funding is of little relevance, given that the actual investment will be made in the name of the Holy See. Furthermore, I am sure your Eminence will agree that the only reason Manus Domini can raise that kind of money is because of the credibility that stems from being part of the Holy See."

"There are moments when investment policies must be set aside."

"With all due respect, Your Eminence, I would remind you that APSA's job consists of managing the Holy See's portfolio of securities following strict investment criteria agreed upon with the Prefettura per gli Affari Economici. Are you asking me not to comply with those guidelines?"

"Of course not. All I am saying is that one would expect a reasonable degree of flexibility from APSA's director."

Monsignor Griffith kept silent.

"A brilliant career, yours, Monsignore, for someone who only twenty years ago was a mere analyst at an unknown Boston investment bank. A brilliant doctorate in theology, a move to Rome requested by the Prefettura per gli Affari Economici itself, an excellent job in restoring credibility in the financial accounts of the Holy See, after the scars left by the Marcinkus and *Banco Ambrosiano* scandal...."

"I thank your Eminence for these compliments, but—"

"Think about your future, Monsignore. And mind: this is not a threat, just a piece of advice from someone who has been sailing these waters much longer than you have."

Monsignor Griffith got up, a small vein throbbing in his right temple. "I thank you for your time, Your Eminence."

§

Monsignor Griffith slammed the folder shut, turned and switched on his computer.

"... In consideration of all of the above, we strongly advise against this investment.

Signed: Mgr. Neil Griffith"

He printed three copies of the report, put them in his briefcase, and went out. He stopped in front of a door across the corridor, and knocked.

Monsignor Griffith stood in front of the entrance to the papal apartments. He looked again at his watch. Two Swiss guards stood at both sides of the door. He approached the two guards and looked down the corridor toward the pope's private study. He started pacing up and down.

The door of the pope's study opened and Cardinal Ortega's frail figure appeared. As the cardinal went by, the two guards sprang to attention and the clicking of their heels on the stone floor echoed through the deserted corridors.

"Monsignore, I'm sorry," Cardinal Ortega said to Griffith. "I tried in every way to get His Holiness to understand the danger of such an initiative."

"And so?"

"There's nothing we can do. His Holiness believes the political advantages of the deal more than outweigh any risks." The cardinal appeared to hesitate.

"Is there something else, Your Eminence?"

"I'm afraid so. His Holiness mentioned a foreign exchange gain, but he was vague about it."

"A foreign exchange gain? Oh, no! Manus Domini."

The cardinal nodded, a resigned expression appearing on his face. "Either Cardinal Wolfenberg or Father Cafiero."

The echo of the two prelates' footsteps faded down the corridor of the secretariat of state.

Annibale gestured Tancredi to the phone booth.

"I've found the files," Carlomagno said, "but they're all coded."

"How many are there?"

"Six."

"How long will you need?"

"It all depends on the code. I told you that a month ago."

"For Chrissake! Don't you realize I've got everything at stake here?

"Okay, take it easy: five weeks, but I don't swear on it."

"So by the last week of November."

"Yes, but don't count too much on it."

When Tancredi got to his office the following morning, he sat down at his typewriter, lit a cigarette, and started hammering at the keys. He read the text again, folded the sheet and put it into an envelope. He left his office and went up the stairs to the floor above.

When he arrived in front of the mailroom, he stopped and looked a few moments at the envelope. He turned, walked briskly down the corridor and called the elevator.

He crossed the street, got into his car, and headed for the central post office.

§

"It's money well spent," said Franzese, skimming through Tancredi's weekly report.

"Our friend seems to be in quite a hurry," said Astarita.

"Let him champ at the bit." Franzese flipped through the loose-leaf calendar on his desk and stopped at November 30. "Five weeks would do us fine."

"I remind you that Guichard has planned to finish investing our money by December 10."

"Tell him to bring things forward to the end of November."

"But—"

"No buts."

Franzese's mind went back to his meeting with Cardinal Wolfenberg at the Vatican one month before.

"You're whetting my curiosity," the cardinal had said.

"I can only tell you that the foreign exchange market will remember it as a master coup..."

"Won't you give an old friend even a hint?"

"What is it?" Astarita said.

"I've got to call the cardinal." Franzese reached for the phone. "He's an ally, after all. We'd better keep on the right side of him if we don't want to be swept away by an avalanche of Latin quotations."

"… One month ago I made you a promise, Your Eminence," Franzese said. "A little toccata and fugue on the foreign exchange market, do you remember?"

"When is the concert going to be, Tano?" said the cardinal.

"Quite likely at the very beginning of December."

"You'll find me sitting in the first row."

The rays of the setting sun cast their orange light on the pope's study, as if trying to smuggle a moment of truce on a front dominated on one side by Sergius I's bristly black eyebrows, and on the other by the massive oak crucifix hanging behind him.

Cardinal Wolfenberg glanced furtively at Father Cafiero who, seated next to him, was fidgeting in his armchair.

The pope was explaining the reasons for his forthcoming pastoral visit to Brazil and the Holy See's decision to underwrite the Recursos Naturais bond issue. He made no reference to the cardinal, nor did he mention the foreign exchange gain. Forgetfulness? An imperceptible smile hovered on the cardinal's lips. No, it was simply emblematic of Sergius I's way of thinking. All that mattered in his world was ideology and the Catholic dogma. So much the better. Why give Father Cafiero this sort of information?

"But Your Holiness, this is an enormous underwriting! Even after liquidating the portfolios of APSA and IOR [the Vatican bank], the Holy See would have nowhere near that amount," Father Cafiero said. "Can I ask how Your Holiness is thinking of finding all that money?"

"We thought the presence of the leaders of Manus Domini here today would make that question unnecessary," replied the pope, poker-faced, his eyebrows thicker and blacker than ever.

Father Cafiero's jaw dropped. He turned towards the cardinal, who did his best to put on a fleeting expression of resignation in his face.

"Your Holiness surely cannot think that Manus Domini would intervene," Father Cafiero said.

"Why not?" asked the pope. "Is this not a great work of charity towards our Indian brothers in the Amazon?"

"Yes, but—"

"And is Manus Domini not the richest body of the Holy See?"

"Yes, but—"

"Then, Father, tell us where the problem lies."

"But Your Holiness, we're talking about *7,500 billion lire*! Where does Your Holiness think Manus Domini can find all that money?"

"From your *initiati*, Father," the pope said. He opened a folder and put on his glasses with a trembling hand. "The figures for the end of September show a total of 42,380 *initiati*." He leafed though the pages. "We see they hold key posts in banks, insurance companies, industrial groups...."

"Your Holiness, even if every one of them accepted, it would still be too high a figure per capita." Father Cafiero rummaged in his pockets. "Unfortunately I haven't got my calculator on me."

"It comes to 177 million lire each." Cardinal Wolfenberg showed the father general the display on his HP pocket calculator.

"But that's a ridiculous amount!"

"Fully tax deductible, though." The cardinal pressed the keys of his calculator. "If we consider an average tax rate of forty-five percent, the actual contribution would not be more than ninety-seven million lire for the companies of our *initiati*."

"Quite apart from the amount, I would remind Your Holiness of the danger of this sort of initiative," said Father Cafiero, swallowing hard.

"Your concern does you honor, Father."

Father Cafiero shifted in his chair again. "As father general of Manus Domini—and with all due respect and devotion to

Your Holiness—I doubt if Manus Domini will be able to intervene."

The pope's eyes narrowed to slits and his lips tightened into a thin line. "We will pretend not to have heard those words, Father. We would remind you that you have sworn blind obedience to us!"

The cardinal judged the moment had come to intervene: there were times when it made no sense to finish off your beaten foe—not right away, at any rate.

"Your Holiness, I'm certain Father Cafiero spoke without thinking." The cardinal gave Father Cafiero's arm a confidential squeeze. "Manus Domini will immediately start raising the money, is that not so, Father Cafiero?"

The father general glared at the cardinal, his eyes glittering with cold anger.

A few more weeks and Franzese would strike. At that point the alliance of Manus Domini with the Organization and Joint Affairs would reap its reward. The Manaus deal would make him the most powerful man in the Vatican—and in Manus Domini. What had he to fear from Father Cafiero?

Guichard got out of the elevator at the second platform of the Eiffel Tower. He shielded his eyes from the sun: the skyscrapers of La Défense broke the skyline through a veil of mist. He leisurely scanned the tourists thronging the platform. He folded the newspaper he was carrying and held it under his arm, with the title *Le Monde* conspicuously in sight. He checked his watch. A few minutes to four. He stood by the coin-operated telescope.

"They say that on a fine afternoon you can see up to forty-two miles," said a man on his right. "Mr. de Saint Clair?"

"Mr. Asher Levy, I presume."

The man was wearing a green T-shirt. His short, dark hair was streaked with gray, his eyes hidden behind a pair of sunglasses. Guichard could see only his profile, because he was leaning on the railings and looking straight ahead. He didn't turn towards Guichard, nor did he make any move to shake hands. His aquiline nose warned you it was better to have him as a friend.

"I heard in Tel Aviv that you could tell me where to find something belonging to us," Levy said in a neutral voice.

"The last time I saw it, they were hiding it in a church crypt."

"What church?"

"The Basilica of San Giovanni in Laterano, in Rome."

"And when was that?"

Guichard hesitated. "In January 1128."

For a moment Levy said nothing. Then he took off his sunglasses and turned to look at Guichard. Curiosity and sarcasm were competing in his eyes.

"So in January 1128 you were wandering the streets of Rome. Is that what you're saying?"

"Have you got time to listen to a story?"

"I hear many stories."

"Nothing like this, though..."

A long silence followed Guichard's tale. Levy had again taken off his sunglasses and was rubbing his eyes, as if lost in thought.

"I don't believe in reincarnation," Levy said.

"Neither do I, but who spoke of reincarnation? Call it what you like." Guichard shrugged. "Genetic memory, atavistic unconscious... whatever."

"Apart from in our own land, we've dug and delved half the world over: from Persia to Egypt, from Ethiopia to Nova Scotia. Why should we believe your story? What proof have you got?"

Guichard took out a pen and flicked through *Le Monde*, looking for a blank space. With deft strokes of the pen he drew a three-dimensional diagram, putting in the measurements and the cardinal points. When he'd finished, he handed the newspaper to Levy.

"Do you know what that is?" Guichard said.

"It looks like Temple Mount," Levy said. "And I think I know what the two dotted lines refer to. What about it?"

"Do you know what infrared mapping is?"

"It's not exactly new to us in Israel."

"Then I don't need to add anything else."

Levy continued to stare at the diagram, but it was obvious that his mind was elsewhere. Guichard believed he knew what Levy was thinking. Temple Mount was under Arab jurisdiction. The Jewish authorities in Israel hadn't been able to dig under Temple Mount Courtyard to look for the exact site of the Temple for fear of a religious war breaking out—not to mention repercussions from the surrounding Muslim countries.

Israeli physicists and archaeologists, however, had used the latest techniques based on electromagnetic and infrared radiation and had produced charts of all that lay under Temple Mount. Guichard was sure they'd have no problem checking that the tunnel dug by King Solomon's men, and reopened by the Templars, was located exactly where his diagram showed.

"Okay. I'll send your sketch to Tel Aviv and see what they have to say." Levy's eyes scrutinized Guichard. "Why are you doing all this? You are not a Jew."

"It's too long a story. I don't want to bore you."

"You *must* bore me. That's what I'm paid for."

"I'm not a Jew, and I'm not a Christian. So I'm not doing it for the God of Israel, but out of a sense of justice."

"Justice, truth, brotherhood... Big words! What is it you're looking for?"

"What I'm looking for is my business. I told you the truth. All the rest is of no concern to Israel. It's personal."

Levy gave him another look but made no comment. He tucked his copy of *Le Monde* under his arm, gave Guichard a nod and headed for the elevator.

Guichard's eyes followed him. Levy could have been just another tourist in the crowd on that sunny afternoon. No one would ever have guessed that that man in the T-shirt was the head of the Paris branch of the Mossad, the Israeli secret service.

Françoise walked out of the elevator and rang a doorbell. Clorinne opened the door and a smile lit her face.

"Well, how did things turn out at Rennes-le-Château?" Clorinne kissed Françoise on both cheeks and led the way into the living room. "Did you find out the abbot's secret?" She chuckled.

"I think I did," Françoise said, seriously.

"Do you mean it?"

Françoise sat in an armchair opposite Corinne and told her everything, from the moment Guichard had walked into the gallery until her visit to the graveyard of the church in Rennes-le-Château.

Corinne listened, her feet resting on the edge of the coffee table. She was wearing a yellow silk shirt and close-fitting black pants. She had bobbed red hair and green eyes in which a suggestive smile seemed to be permanently hovering. The bookshelves behind her were full of books on Buddhism and spiritualism. The photographs hanging on the walls depicted her amid the landscapes and in front of the monasteries of Nepal. Françoise appeared in many of those photos too.

"This is the most incredible story I've ever heard." Corinne lit a match and brought its flame to the tip of a joss stick inserted obliquely into a narrow wooden board. A thin column of smoke rose in the air and a scent of myrrh and incense filled the room.

"You don't believe me?" said Françoise.

"I know you only too well."

"Oh, Corinne, Corinne. I've reached a point where I don't know what to do any more."

"I bet you even went up on that mountain, didn't you?"

"I certainly did. With the guide. We went as far as the entrance to an old mine, but at that point even the guide had to give up."

"Have you got any idea of what may be hidden up there? A treasure?"

"No, it must be a spiritual secret, something having to do with Death. The expression of Poussin's muse must refer to that."

"Death as such?"

"I don't think so, otherwise the Church wouldn't have reacted the way they have. No, it must be someone's death."

"The more I think about it, the less I understand the being's role," Corinne said. "Are you quite sure it's Geoffroy's woman?"

"It can only be her. All the data fits. The rebec, the *chanson*, the time when Geoffroy was in Jerusalem.... The way she was dressed when she materialized in front of me."

"She seems to want something from Guichard.... Or she wants Guichard to do something."

"That's the impression I have. But what? I've lost a lot of sleep pondering it."

"What does a lovesick woman want?" Corinne spread her arms as if saying that the answer was obvious. "The return of the beloved."

"The return of the beloved? But Geoffroy is dead, like her. And nine centuries ago."

"You surprise me, Françoise. You're a Buddhist, like me. Remember what our master Chandra taught us: past and future don't exist. Linear time is only an invention of our senses."

"Are you thinking of a parallel world?"

"Of course I am. The being, Geoffroy and their world exist in another dimension, physically inaccessible. Who knows? Maybe one day science will succeed in overcoming this barrier, and my travel agency around the corner will organize trips back to ancient Rome or to Egypt at the time of the pharaohs." Corinne waved a hand before Françoise's eyes. "Hey! Are you listening?"

Françoise roused herself. "Sorry, but I just remembered something. Guichard's almost maniacal interest in quantum physics... and time traveling. His office and his house overflow with books on this subject. And..."

"And...?"

Françoise blushed. "Well, it's personal."

"Aha! I smell sex. If you don't tell me, I'll never speak to you again."

"Okay. Every time Guichard made love to me, it was as if he were making love to someone else."

"The bastard. Then he *does* have another woman. Men!"

"No, it's not the way you think. His mind was lost in another world. Once he even let a name slip from his lips."

"What name?"

"Something starting with an *M*, but I couldn't understand what."

"Could it be that the being wants Guichard? No, it makes no sense at all. If she plays that rebec of hers the way you told me, then she's still in love with Geoffroy."

"Then what does she want from Guichard?" Françoise said.

"Thinking of what you told me about Guichard, maybe she wants him to travel back in time — don't ask me how. But to do what? She wants Geoffroy.... Maybe she wants Guichard to tell Geoffroy something. Something that will make Geoffroy go back to her. I don't know what, though."

"Wait.... Something that Guichard knows and Geoffroy doesn't.... *The end of the Templars.*"

"But... but this is impossible. It would mean changing the course of history."

"Guichard *is* capable of impossible things."

"I'm afraid we're imagining things. I have an idea." Corinne's eyes gleamed. "How about a séance at Kamilla's?"

"Hmm, I'm afraid it won't work. A medium needs the co-operation of the spirit. If the being's intentions are what we believe them to be, it won't co-operate."

"Maybe things are as you say, but don't underestimate Kamilla's skills — and the object you have."

"What object?"

"The medallion."

32

Guichard got into a taxi and told the driver to take him to Orly-CDG. As the taxi turned into the Quai de Montebello, a blue Citroën drew away from the sidewalk.

Guichard skimmed through the list of banks he'd be meeting in London. The invitations for underwriting the loan in favor of CIP had been sent three days before. CIP's financial accounts flashed before his eyes and Franzese's words rang in his ears: "*You know our laws ... If things went wrong, I couldn't cover for you.*"

At the London branch of Continental Bank, Guichard had just sat down in front of the manager of syndicated loans when there was a knock at the door.

"Excuse me, sir, but there's an urgent phone call for Mr. de Saint Clair from his secretary in Paris," said the secretary standing in the doorway. "Will you take it here, Mr. de Saint Clair?"

"Yes, thank you." Guichard turned to the banker, who was pouring coffee. "Excuse me."

"De Saint Clair speaking."

"It's Marie Claire, Mr. de Saint Clair. Something awful's happened—"

"What's the matter?"

"Someone broke into your apartment during the night. It's full of policemen upstairs. André's in hospital with a head wound. Please come back right away."

Guichard got out of the taxi. Two police cars were parked in front of the building. He strode towards the main gate.

The front door to the penthouse was wide open. A plain-clothes officer was kneeling in front of the door searching for fingerprints. An armed policeman crossed the hallway, holding a walkie-talkie to his ear. Muffled voices came from the reception room.

"Oh, Monsieur le Comte, here you are at last." Josephine, the housekeeper, rushed over to Guichard and took his raincoat. "André took a nasty blow. Poor fellow, he wasn't such a bad soul after all...."

"Le Comte de Saint Clair?" A detective came towards Guichard. The man was short, with a pale face, one of those people who never smile. "Inspector Charvet of the *Police Judiciaire*," he said, stretching out his hand.

"Will you excuse me, Inspector," said Guichard, hurriedly shaking hands. "I'll be right back."

His head was throbbing. Guichard had to steel himself not to start running. He stopped in the doorway of the library and looked up at the gallery. The panel was closed. For a moment he was tempted to run up the spiral staircase. No, he had to wait until the police left. He turned to go back, but the inspector was standing right behind him.

"I'm sorry, Inspector. What happened?" Guichard said.

Inspector Charvet said that the two outside gates of the building and the main door of the penthouse had been forced open. From the way they'd worked, it was obvious the intruders were professional burglars. They probably weren't aware that the butler lived in the penthouse. André must have taken them by surprise and they'd knocked him out with a blow to the head. He was in the hospital with a concussion. The prognosis was still reserved, but the doctors seemed optimistic. The strange thing was that nothing appeared to have been stolen, said the inspector: the paintings, precious objects, everything seemed to be in its place, according to the housekeeper.

"The paintings hanging in this room alone are priceless. Yet nothing's been touched. Odd... very odd," said the inspector, staring at Guichard. "Unless someone broke in here in the middle of the night just to hit your butler on the head, you're the only one who can clear up this mystery."

"I'm not sure I follow you, Inspector."

The inspector gave Guichard a knowing look. "Any objects of value that only you know about? Perhaps in the library, Monsieur le Comte?"

The man was no fool. Better face up to it.

"Very well, Inspector. Please follow me."

Once on the gallery, Guichard turned the wall-bracket of the lamp, then reached out for the light switch. As he switched on the light, he looked towards the desk. The drawer was open: *the scrolls had vanished.*

The room started to spin and a sharp pain pierced him between his shoulder blades. He leaned against a wall.

The inspector seized Guichard's arm. "What's the matter, Monsieur le Comte? Are you all right?"

"Thank you…. It's nothing, really," said Guichard, gasping. "The paintings, as you see, are all here. Nothing's missing."

"Are you quite sure?"

"Absolutely."

"Then how do you explain it all?"

"I can only think someone commissioned the burglary. They were probably looking for one of the paintings hanging in here. Maybe the Van Gogh."

The inspector heaved a sigh of resignation. "If you should change your mind, you know where to find me." He handed Guichard a business card.

As Guichard came out of the elevator on the second floor of the East Wing of the Salpêtrière, a smell of disinfectant stung his nostrils. A stretcher pushed by a nurse passed hurriedly in front of him and disappeared beyond a stainless steel door with the words *Défense d'entrée* on it. He caught a glimpse of two surgeons in their long green coats washing their hands.

"Only five minutes, Mr. de Saint Clair," said the doctor on duty, checking a medical record. "It was a nasty blow. Please don't tire him."

Guichard went over to the bed. André had his head all bandaged up, but his grizzled moustache was unmistakable. He opened his eyes.

"Monsieur le Comte, is it you? I'm sorry… I'm so sorry."

Guichard put a hand on his shoulder. "It wasn't your fault, André. Quite the contrary. How do you feel?"

André hinted at a smile. "I promise you're not going to get rid of me."

"That's what I wanted to hear."

"Did they take the paintings?"

"No, they didn't touch those."

"The... library?" André pointed his thumb upwards.

Guichard nodded.

André sighed. "I... I've never liked to ask, but I know there was something up there that meant far more to you than the paintings."

"Is there anything at all you can tell me, André? Even some seemingly unimportant detail...."

"When I heard the noise, I went over to the staircase to see what was happening."

"And then?"

"I heard them talking. I turned to go and get my gun. But in the dark I bumped into a chair. What a clumsy idiot I was!"

"And it was then they noticed you and hit you on the head?"

André nodded. "I heard one of them say something strange,though."

"What?"

"He mentioned a cardinal. Unfortunately I couldn't catch any other words."

"A cardinal? Are you sure?"

"I heard it with my own ears."

Françoise had an uncle who was a cardinal.

"Monsieur le Comte, are you all right? Should I call for the doctor?"

The pendulum clock struck four as Cardinal Wolfenberg pushed aside his magnifying glass and shut his Aramaic dictionary, his eyes fixed on the scrolls.

He took his glasses off, held his head in his hands and remained motionless in that position. After an immeasurable time, he got up slowly and went over to the window. The lights from the Bernini colonnade lit a deserted St. Peter's Square.

Deep down, he'd often had his doubts, but he'd always suppressed them, taking refuge behind a barrier of ever stricter orthodoxy — not unlike many others within the Church, after all. And now it took only a few scrolls to make his whole world collapse in a flash. It had all been a lie, a gross, vulgar lie lasting over two thousand years.

He could already hear the derisive laughter rising from every corner of the globe. He tried to dispel it with a gesture of his hand, but the laughter grew stronger and stronger, reverberating through his head. He pressed his hands to his ears, but in vain. They were laughing at the Church! They were laughing at him!

His jaw tightened and he slammed his fists against the wall with an angry cry. No, he would never let two thousand years of history be swept away just like that. Nor would he allow his life's work to vanish. He must keep calm: now the main thing was to think of the interests of the Church — and of his own.

He went back to his desk and sat down, gazing once more at the characters in Aramaic. Discuss it with Dyakonov? With His Holiness? A shrewd smile flickered over his lips. But whatever for? *Utere temporibus!* — Take advantage of the right moments, Horace used to say. With those scrolls in his hands he became *ipso facto* the most powerful man within the Church, so powerful that he could influence all its future decisions as he pleased.

Just a few more weeks and Palermo would strike. At the next conclave it would be child's play to get Dyakonov elected pope. At that point Dyakonov would do whatever he told him to. And, if the rarefied air of St. Peter's throne should by any chance make him believe he really was Peter's successor, those scrolls would bring him back to earth. As pope, Dyakonov would ship Father Cafiero back to Spain and he would become Manus Domini's new father general — and the Vatican's *éminence grise*.

Now he had to find a hiding-place for the scrolls. The Chinese vase standing next to his desk attracted his attention. Hmm, no, too obvious. He looked about the study... then made a dismissive gesture. What was he worrying about? This was the Holy Office, in the very heart of the Vatican City, and below the Swiss guards were on watch twenty-four hours a day. Only a lunatic could contemplate breaking in here.

He opened the left-hand door of the bookcase and began to take the books off the top shelf, piling them up in the armchairs. Then, with extreme caution, he rolled up the scrolls. He paused, glanced around and eventually his eyes fell on some black cardboard tubes piled high in a corner. Normally people used them for storing drawings, whereas he used them to hide his top-secret papers. When people at the CDF tribunal saw him coming with one of those tubes slung over his shoulder, they would shit in their pants.

He opened a tube, made sure it was empty, and carefully slid the scrolls inside. He looped the strap round the tube and pushed it to the back of the shelf. He began to put the books back into place.

The cardinal went silently down the stairs and stopped on the second-floor landing. He searched in his cassock and took out a bunch of keys. The door squeaked. He went straight to his office and shut the door behind him. He switched on his desk lamp and directed it at the reproduction of *Les Bergers d'Arcadie, II*. He turned an armchair around to face the wall and sank down into it. His gaze focused on the muse's face. At last he understood what lay behind that expression. That Poussin, what a twisted mind!

He jumped to his feet, took down the picture and began smashing it with all his might against the wall. He swung it again and again, until the frame lay splintered in pieces. Panting, he knelt down, picked up the canvas and started tearing it into strips.

Suddenly the study door was flung open and the cardinal, on all fours, jerked his head up. Two Swiss guards were standing in the doorway, their guns aimed straight at him.

While Françoise was speaking, Kamilla served Chinese green tea in a set of white chinaware and Corinne cut the strudel.

Kamilla might be around fifty, but her long, black hair was barely streaked with gray. She was tall with a ladylike bearing and an intense look—characteristics accentuated by a long, dark skirt, a cream satin blouse and a Gucci scarf casually draped around her shoulders. Kamilla's reputation as a medium had exploded in Paris one year before, when thanks to her help, the *police judiciaire* had finally succeeded in capturing a serial killer who had already murdered seven people. His arrest had been possible thanks to the information Kamilla had been able to "see" as she touched a gold chain belonging to the killer, that his last victim had torn from him.

"No, Françoise, don't tell me anything else, please," Kamilla said. "I don't want to be influenced."

"Then…? Can we start right away?"

"Why not?" said Kamilla, standing up.

Françoise and Corinne sat at a round table covered with a green cloth. Kamilla turned off the lights. Only a small table lamp with a multicolored lampshade remained on. Kamilla covered the lampshade with a blue cloth. The bluish light cast the distorted shadow of the iron frame of the lampshade on the wall, illuminating a colored print of Solacki Park in Poznan, Kamilla's birthplace.

Kamilla sat down at the table. "Did you bring the medallion?"

Françoise opened her handbag and took out the medallion with the chain, which she handed to Kamilla.

"No, put it on the table. For the moment I'd rather not touch it."

Françoise obeyed.

"Why?" Corinne asked.

"I don't want to be influenced by its aura. First I want to try to evoke the spirit."

"Through your spirit guide?" Françoise said.

"As usual."

"This spirit might not want to co-operate."

"Are you telling me that your spirit is hostile?"

"Not so far. Its intentions are not clear, though."

Kamilla nodded thoughtfully. "Then there'll be no deep trance, without the intervention of my spirit guide. This way I'll be the one to retain control. Let's form the circle."

They laid their hands near the center of the table, in such a way that their thumbs and little fingers touched. Kamilla closed her eyes and took a few deep breaths, each time breathing out slowly. Her arms trembled and a moan escaped from her lips.

"Spirit, if you are here, give us a signal."

Silence.

"Spirit, if you are here, give us a signal."

Silence.

"Spirit, if—"

Françoise felt a draft of cold air and the light of the table lamp flickered repeatedly. The table began to wobble, at first slightly, then more and more strongly, until it rose on two legs and began beating hard on the floor with the third. The circle of hands broke. After an incalculable time, the table stood still. Françoise felt all her muscles tensed. Her hand was clutching Corinne's.

"Don't let that upset you," Kamilla said. "Let's form the circle again."

"Spirit, what do you want from Françoise?"

Silence.

"Spirit, what do you want from Françoise?"

Kamilla began to shake, gave a few starts and moaned, as if suffering an intense physical pain.

"*Quant de il fui partiz, je ne peux pas avoir de solaz. Je sans amor ne porroie durer. Je ne veux pas que les cuers de Françoise aient a souffrer comme moi* [Since the moment he left, I can't resign myself. I cannot live without love. I don't want Françoise to suffer the way I have been suffering]" Kamilla said.

But it was not Kamilla who was speaking. The language was medieval French, the accent foreign. The voice was deep and at the same time melancholic and hard. Right afterwards, Françoise felt a cold touch on her cheek and the palm of an icy hand caressed her. She held her breath.

Kamilla gave a start and moaned, her forehead beaded with sweat. She opened her eyes again. "What happened?"

Corinne told her, and Françoise told them of the hand that had touched her. She shivered. Her skin felt as cold as that hand. A deep silence followed.

"What do you think of it?" Françoise said.

"I felt a great despair, but also a great strength.... It's a spirit without peace, wanting something desperately."

"I'm sorry for her," Françoise said, stroking her cheek. She looked at Corinne. "I feel guilty at having thought badly of her."

"Yet, if you think about it, she didn't answer my question," Kamilla said. "She gave a touching speech, but then she vanished before I could continue."

"What do you mean?" Françoise said.

"She could be lying."

"Lying? About what?"

"About her true intentions."

"Why do you think this?" Corinne said.

"I feel something strange... something that doesn't convince me." Kamilla looked at the medallion, picked it up from the table and let it slip though her hands. She frowned. "We'll find out right away. Let's form the circle again."

Their hands formed a circle around the medallion, the chain intertwining around Kamilla's fingers. Kamilla breathed in and out a few times. A long silence followed.... Kamilla trembled.

A bluish halo appeared around the medallion and Kamilla's hands, and a deep odor of ozone wafted in the air.

"I see the head of a small statuette wearing a funny hat, with two black pebbles as eyes... I hear the music of an instrument similar to a fiddle... A deep grief, so deep as to defy time... Whoever wore this medallion believes that a life is due to her, and she wants it back... It's a soul determined to realize its karma... I feel a threat... I see a journey, a very long journey —"

The table began to wobble violently, the table lamp went out and a current of cold air started to whirl around them. The bluish halo vanished.

"Keep calm," said Kamilla in the dark. "I'm going to turn on the lights."

The room was flooded with light. Kamilla came back and sat at the table again, her face strained. The three friends looked at one another without speaking.

Françoise looked at the table. "Where's the medallion? Have you taken it?"

"No," Kamilla said. "When I stood up, I left it on the table."

The medallion had vanished.

Guichard awoke bathed in sweat. He reached for the light switch. The image of the empty drawer struck him like a lash.

"A cardinal? Are you sure?"

"I heard it with my own ears," André had said.

A cardinal! Who, more than the Church, would want to get hold of those scrolls? When Françoise had first told him she had an uncle who was a cardinal, he'd had an uneasy feeling, but he'd tried to ignore it. He'd been wrong.

Although he tried hard to find another explanation, his thoughts kept returning to Françoise and her uncle. In the weeks before his last phone call after seeing her at the Louvre, Françoise had carried out a lot of research on the de Saint Clairs — she herself had admitted it. But what if the reason for her curiosity had been something quite different?

He looked back on their relationship, from when they had first met at the gallery until the day he'd seen her at the Louvre. He tried to find some evidence, or even just a clue, to prove to himself that Françoise knew of the existence of the scrolls.

Suddenly he sat upright. *The dressing gown!* That dressing gown hadn't been there before. When he'd left the bedroom, that blue and white striped gown had been hanging in the bathroom; he was sure of it. However, when he'd come back from the library, he was sure he'd seen it on the chair by the bed. That could mean only one thing: she must have heard him get up and must have followed him into the library. He remembered leaving the panel ajar. If Françoise had spied on him, she must have seen the scrolls. And who could have told the cardinal about the scrolls but Françoise?

Part of him refused to believe that she could have betrayed him. But another part kept on nagging at him. *Everything's against her, don't you see? All is ruined. And she is the one to be blamed!* The voice became louder and louder until Guichard could hear nothing else.

"Guichard, what's the matter?" Françoise asked, getting up from her desk. "On the phone you sounded so strange and now... that expression."

"Are you really sure you don't know?"

"Why are you staring at me like that?"

Guichard told her what had happened, without taking his eyes off her face.

"Oh, poor André. How is he now?"

"He's out of danger."

"André's all right and the burglars didn't take anything. Why are you so upset, then?"

"It's not true nothing was stolen."

"What did they steal?"

"What's your uncle's name — the cardinal?"

Françoise frowned. "What's that got to do with it?"

"Answer my question!"

Françoise started. "Rolf Wolfenberg."

"Wolfenberg? But he's the head of the Holy Office!"

"So? Have you got a grudge against him? And in any case, how do I come into it?"

"Do you remember the night you spent at my apartment?"

"Of course I do, every single detail. It's you who seem to have forgotten. But why are you asking me that now?"

"Do you by any chance remember a blue and white striped dressing gown?"

"What are you... talking about?"

"You see, you remember now? Do you want me to tell you what you did while you were wearing that dressing gown, or will you tell me yourself?"

"No, I'll tell you myself, because I've got nothing to hide."

Françoise admitted she'd gone to look for him and that she'd seen him inside the secret room in the library.

"Why didn't you come in, instead of spying on me?"

"I wasn't spying on you! It's just that I was afraid, that's all."

"Afraid? Afraid of what?"

"Afraid of you, Guichard. Afraid that if you had found me in there, you might have thought I'd followed you in order to spy on you."

"Isn't that exactly what you did?"

"Don't you dare suggest even for one minute that I did anything of the sort!"

"What did you see me doing?"

"You had your back turned to me. But I thought you were looking at... what looked like old scrolls."

"That's exactly what they were—old scrolls. And naturally you didn't know what was in them, did you?"

"How could I? It was the first time I'd ever seen them."

"The scrolls, that's what the housebreakers stole. But you know that already, don't you?"

"Have you gone mad? Are you accusing me of stealing them?"

"Oh no, Françoise, not you personally, but your dear uncle—the Great Inquisitor. And he couldn't have got the information from anyone else but you."

"I see. So my uncle is a despicable thief, and I'm his accomplice. Right?"

"Who else, if not the two of you? Before he was hit on the head, André heard the housebreakers talking about a cardinal. Quite a coincidence, don't you think?"

Françoise got to her feet. "I don't ever want to see you again," she said in a trembling voice. "Please leave."

Guichard's hand was clenching and unclenching.

"After all, I should thank you," Guichard said, his features contorted with anger. "You are the confirmation that my opinion about mankind is well founded."

He turned and left the room.

33

Cardinal Wolfenberg did not dial the extension number Ignacio Escobar had given him. Instead he dialed the number of the switchboard of the Ministry of Finance in Brasilia.

"*Ministério da Fazenda, bom-dia.*"

"Good morning, this is the Holy See from Rome," the cardinal said. "I'd like to speak to Mr. Luis Roberto de Oliveira Lima of the Guarantee Office."

"*Um momento, por favor.*"

The phone rang in the office across from Norma Rocha's. At the second ring, Norma had already crossed the hallway.

"*Secçao do senhor de Oliveira Lima, bom-dia,*" said Norma.

"Good morning. It's Cardinal Wolfenberg speaking, from the Holy See in Rome. Mr. de Oliveira Lima, please."

Norma's knuckles went white. "Good morning, Your Eminence. I'm sorry, but Mr. de Oliveira Lima is in a meeting at the moment. He shouldn't be long. If you'd like to leave me your number, I'll get him to call you back."

Cardinal Wolfenberg gave her the number of his direct line and hung up.

§

Norma entered Ferreira's office and shut the door. Ferreira was on the phone; Norma signaled to him to cut it short.

"Alonso, a cardinal from the Vatican has just phoned," Norma said, with alarm in her eyes.

"Keep calm. What exactly did he say?"

Norma sat down in front of Ferreira and, whispering, told him about the cardinal's phone call. When she had finished, she passed him the scrap of paper with the cardinal's phone number.

"Did you tell him what time de Oliveira Lima would be calling him back?" said Ferreira.

"I just told him I thought it would be quite soon."

Ferreira took her hands. "You've been perfect."

"Do you promise me that we're not going to have any problem?"

"Have I ever given you any?" Ferreira ran his hand through her hair. "Can I see you tonight?"

"I'll be waiting, *querido mio*."

Ferreira shut his office door behind Norma, turned the key, and went back to his desk. He reached out for his box of Cohiba Especiales, took one and sniffed it.

"Cardinal Wolfenberg...?" Ferreira said. "Good morning, Eminence. It's de Oliveira Lima from Brasilia."

"Oh, Mr. de Oliveira Lima, thank you for calling back. I wanted to speak to you about the guarantee for the Recursos Naturais investment. It's you who are dealing with it, I believe?"

"Yes, I'm your man, Eminence. How can I help you?"

"You realize that for the Holy See this is an enormous investment. I would need to know the Ministry's opinion."

"I'm sorry, Eminence, but for the moment I have to weigh my words."

"Can't you give me your personal opinion, at least?"

"Well, as long as it's understood that this is a completely unofficial statement, and in no way binding for the Ministry, I can tell you that we're in favor."

"It's a guarantee of over $4 billion. You in Brasilia must think a lot of Recursos Naturais."

"Apart from the Ministry, also our government has great faith in Recursos Naturais. You know, it's the largest project of its kind ever undertaken anywhere in the world."

"How long do you think it will take for the guarantee to be issued?"

"About two weeks—again, that's only my personal opinion."

"You know about the pope's forthcoming pastoral visit to Manaus, don't you?"

"It's in all the newspapers. Why do you ask, Eminence?"

"The Holy Father intends to announce the Holy See's decision to underwrite the Recursos Naturais loan from Manaus. Do you think His Holiness could make some reference to the guarantee?"

Ferreira's fingers tightened on his cigar. When the shreds of tobacco fell on the desk, it was too late. *A $25 Cohiba Especial!* thought Ferreira.

"I would strongly advise against that, Eminence. That would put our government in an extremely embarrassing position."

"Why?"

"I don't think I need tell you that the Recursos Naturais project will be a kick in the teeth for quite a few people here in Brazil—people who can open many doors in Brasilia, if you know what I mean."

"I think I'm beginning to understand."

"The cattle breeders, the gold-diggers, the timber merchants, and so on, all still have a big say in things. Let's face it, Eminence: this project is all in favor of the Indios."

"I get your point and thank you for your advice. I'll bear it in mind."

Ferreira wiped his brow and reached for his box of cigars. Before lighting one, though, he collected the tobacco shreds from the disintegrated cigar, slid the little heap towards the edge of the desk, and let it drop into an empty aluminum Montecristo tube. He'd smoke it later at home, in his pipe.

With all those people dying of hunger out there, wasting a $25 cigar would be like slapping Saint Peter himself in the face.

Guichard poured himself a glass of Hennessy and drained it in a single gulp. He poured himself another, then stretched his legs on the coffee table. Julius jumped on his lap and began to purr. Guichard stroked him behind the ear.

"I see. So my uncle is a despicable thief, and I'm his accomplice ... I don't ever want to see you again..."

To hell with the evidence! Her expression, as well as her words, had been sincere. Guichard slammed his hand repeatedly on the armrest of the couch.

"Oh, Julius, Julius. I'm a complete moron."

"Meow!"

"Hmm, many thanks. I could have done without such enthusiastic agreement, though."

Somehow the Inquisitor had come to hear of their relationship. No surprise if he'd had her tailed, or maybe the Church had already known of the existence of the scrolls. After all, it was ever since the time of Honorius II that the Church had suspected something, and maybe the Vatican had already known about the existence of the scrolls.

How could he tell the brethren? How much longer could he keep quiet? He drained his glass and stared at Julius, stroking him on the back.

"What do you think, Julius?"

Julius returned Guichard's stare.

"Good. I'm glad to see that for once we agree." Guichard reached for the phone.

"Have you gone mad?" said Astarita on the other end of the line. "The Vatican City is swarming with Swiss guards. Why?"

"Don't ask me why," Guichard said. "Just help me."

"Which building is it?"

"The Palace of the Holy Office."

"*The Palace of the Holy Office*? That's the most closely guarded building of them all. They keep their secret archives in its underground chambers — two thousand years of dirty linen."

"I didn't call you to get a list of the problems."

"Okay, take it easy," Astarita said. "What do you want then?"

"I need someone who knows his way around in there. A professional."

There was a moment's silence. "First I've got to ask you a question."

"What?"

"You know what we're going to do and who with. Whatever it is you have in mind, I want your word it won't interfere with our plans."

"You've got my word."

"All right then. I'll speak to our man in Rome and call you back."

§

The knocker banged the door of the sacristy of St. Sulpice and its dull thud broke the silence of the night. After the second knock, a shuffling of sandals came from inside.

"Who is it?" said an annoyed voice on the other side of the door.

"It's me, Father Pierpont. Guichard de Saint Clair," Guichard said, his face glued to the door.

"Monsieur le Comte, sooner or later we'll have to regulate this night-traffic." The sexton tried to sound grumpy.

"I know, Father, it's two o'clock in the morning, and I apologize. Did I get you out of bed?"

"As you know, I suffer from insomnia. But I see I'm not the only one."

Guichard pointed up at the gallery. "May I, Father?"

"*Trés bien*, you may go. I might as well listen to you playing," said the sexton, standing aside. "After all, it's not every night I get the chance to hear a concert just for me."

As Guichard sat down at the organ, he was reminded of his organ teacher, who had been the head organist at the church of Mont Saint Michel. He used to come to the castle three times a week to give him lessons. He always came by bicycle, wearing a worn-out old-fashioned frock coat of an indefinable color, his hair like Albert Einstein's.

"Why do you like this particular piece so much?" the maestro had asked. In spite of his age, he still had the inquisitive expression of a child.

"When I play it, it's like seeing flashes of infinity," had said Guichard, who was about fifteen at the time.

"*Flashes of infinity?* Whatever do you mean?"

"I find myself in places I feel I've already been to, a long time ago, as if I've got everything I ever dreamed of. It's as if time had stopped."

The maestro had stared at him in silence.

The notes of the *Te Deum* fugue took Guichard back to those infinite horizons, where he'd already been before all this began. Flashes of light crossed the sky in the silence of a starlit night, and time and space no longer existed.

Flashes of infinity.

Françoise pushed her papers to one side and covered her face with her hands. What ridiculous accusations! How could he have thought she was capable of a despicable action like that? Her mouth trembled. She reached for a box of Kleenex, took one and wiped her tears. What really made her angry was not so much the way he had treated her, as that ridiculous feeling of emptiness that she tried in vain to overcome. And that blockhead just didn't deserve it!

What cardinal could it have been other than Uncle Rolf? She thought back to her visit to the Vatican and the things she'd told him. How naïve of her! He must have suspected she was involved with a descendant of the de Saint Clairs. What if he had had her tailed? A cardinal? Another cardinal maybe not, but Uncle Rolf yes.

Crack. Her pencil snapped in half.

She opened her address book, checked a number, then reached for the phone. Maybe she was still in time to catch the early afternoon flight to Rome.

"Françoise, is something wrong?" Cardinal Wolfenberg asked. "When I received your call I didn't know what to think."

"Are you sure you don't know?"

A wary expression appeared on the cardinal's face. "What do you mean?"

Françoise stared hard at her uncle. "Last Wednesday night someone stole some old Hebrew scrolls from a house in Paris. You wouldn't know anything about it, by any chance?"

"Whatever are you talking about? Why should I?"

"I'll tell you why. The scrolls were stolen from the house of a certain Guichard de Saint Clair."

"So...?"

"*So*! Remember our meeting a month ago. It's a bit of a coincidence, don't you think?"

"My memory is still intact. Your conclusions are unjustified. And offensive."

"Don't think I've forgotten your reaction when I spoke to you about the Templars' secret."

"Whatever do you mean?"

"Stop pretending, Uncle Rolf. It was the reaction of someone who's got something to hide."

"That's quite enough of that!" The cardinal jumped to his feet. "The fact that you're my niece doesn't entitle you to talk to me in this manner."

"So you still say you had nothing to do with the theft?"

"Such a question deserves no answer! If someone has stolen some Aramaic scrolls, that's none of my business. And now, if you'll excuse me, I'm very busy."

"*Aramaic?*" Françoise sprang to her feet. "Who said anything about Aramaic? I just said 'Hebrew' scrolls."

"But... um, I just said Aramaic... probably because I automatically associated old Hebrew with Aramaic, that's all."

"Rubbish! I can see when you're lying and at this moment your face has lies written all over it."

The cardinal pointed at the door. "You will leave this room immediately or I'll send for the guards!"

"Don't worry. I wouldn't want to stay a minute longer under the same roof with you. But don't think you'll get away with this."

Françoise turned and headed for the door, but after a couple of steps she stopped, her gaze fixed on the wall. *The reproduction of Poussin's painting had gone.*

She pointed to the wall. "I see you've already been busy destroying all clues."

A dumbfounded expression spread over the cardinal's face, and he remained speechless.

Françoise slammed the door, walked out and marched off across Monsignor Feliciani's office. Some sheets of paper flew off the monsignor's desk.

The monsignor froze with his pen in mid-air, stole a look at the cardinal's door and crossed himself furtively.

Guichard stopped in front of a period building in Boulevard Hausmann. The immaculate cream façade and the wrought-iron balcony railings oozed tradition and money. Guichard disappeared inside.

The brass plate read Uriah Trading Ltd. Guichard pressed the doorbell. He raised his eyes. A surveillance camera was trained on him. After a few moments the door clicked open.

"Mr. Levy's expecting you," said the woman at the reception desk in a military tone and without so much as a hint of a smile.

Guichard followed her along a corridor lit by discreet wall lighting and adorned with old English seascapes. The atmosphere reminded him of certain private Swiss banks.

Levy was finishing a phone call in Hebrew. He gestured towards an armchair.

The man of Mossad hung up and took a folder from the top of his pile of papers. "The data match," he said without much enthusiasm. "So we've got to believe your story."

Lost in thought, Levy flipped through a report.

"That basilica has seen a lot of changes," Levy said. "What you—that is, Geoffroy de Saint Clair—saw in January 1128, must have been very different from what you can see today."

In 1291, Pope Nicholas IV completely rebuilt the apse and the transept, Levy said. Seventeen years later, in 1308, a fire destroyed the basilica. Another fire destroyed the roof and the chapels in 1361. Reconstruction began during the Renaissance and went on until halfway through the eighteenth century.

"Even admitting that Honorius II had the Ark hidden under the floor of the basilica, no one can be sure that it's still there. The Church could have moved it, especially after the fire in 1308."

"I'd be surprised if they had," Guichard said.

"Why?"

"At each side of the entrance there's a big column. On the base of the columns there's a Latin inscription that says the basilica is 'the Mother and Prince of all the churches of Rome and of the World.'"

Levy shrugged. "So what?"

"For the Church, the Basilica of the Lateran has always been the Mother of all the Churches, ever since the time of Constantine. You only have to remember that the pope's church—the church of the Bishop of Rome—isn't St Peter's, but San Giovanni in Laterano."

Levy nodded thoughtfully. "Let's suppose that the Ark is still under there. But where, with all the alterations that have been made?" He leafed through the report again. "Was the layout of the church like this, when Geoffroy... or you, or whoever it was, went inside?"

Guichard looked closely at the diagram. "It's hard to say if there were five aisles then. Geoffroy stopped at the entrance to the Church, here, at the beginning of the center aisle."

"What did he see exactly?"

"A large scaffolding covering the whole of the end part of the central aisle, that's to say the apse."

"So you're in no doubt that the work was being done in the apse?"

"None at all."

"What did Hugues de Payens say to Geoffroy about the Ark's hiding place?"

"He told him it looked as if the Ark were going to be hidden in a crypt under the main altar. It was only hearsay from the palace, but reliable hearsay, in Hugues' opinion. Naturally, with all those alterations one can't rule out that the main altar may now be in a different place altogether."

"We've thought of that, but it's something we can overcome, thanks to image technology," Levy said. "Two portable radar units have already been sent by diplomatic bag to our embassy in Rome. In a few days' time two of our agents will be saying lengthy *Ave Marias* in the basilica."

"How long will they need?"

"Not more than a couple of days. They will check out the floor of the whole basilica, if necessary. The tracings will be interpreted by a computer. We know the Ark's measurements: if it's under there, we'll find it. "

"Finding it is one thing. Getting it out is another."

Levy shrugged his shoulders. "The Mossad has dealt with far harder things than that in its time. Besides, in this case, we have no doubts about our success."

"Why not?"

"Because God is on our side," Levy said, as if he were mentioning a fact taken for granted.

"I see. You've made a personal pact with the Creator Himself."

"If you had read the Old Testament, you would know what I'm talking about."

"I have read it, but I don't believe a single word of it. The Old Testament is just a fictionalized distortion of history put together by a people—yours—wanting at all costs to cut out a special place for themselves in a world they populated with false prophets and a false god."

"I remind you that it wasn't we who asked to be the chosen people. It was the God of Abraham who wanted it."

"But this is precisely the point. Since the escape from Egypt onwards—admitting but not granting that things went as narrated in Exodus—Israel has gone from one disaster to the next, and this thanks to the very covenant entered into by your Jehovah and your Moses." Guichard pointed a finger at Levy. "Do you want to know what should be the invocation rising from every Jew on earth?"

"I crave to listen to the words of the prophet."

"Jehovah, couldn't you get yourself a different chosen people?" Guichard raised his arms to heaven in prophetic posture. "*Why us?* What have we done to you?"

Levy shook his head with a pitying look. "You blasphemer! You understand the meaning of the Torah and the Kabbalah to us Jews as I understand the dialect of Kazakistan."

"On the contrary, given that I learnt them from a rabbi. And that's why either you Jews have an atavistic calling for mass masochism, or the Moses of the Torah — had he ever existed, instead of being the High Priest of Heliopolis under Pharaoh Akhenaten — would only have deserved one thing."

Levy gave Guichard an inquiring look.

"A kick such as to pulverize his ass."

"Get out!"

Half a million Brazilians, many of them Indios, were crowded together on the north bank of the Rio Negro, around a white awning under which the white-robed pope was saying Mass. The cranes and the cargo ships anchored in the port of Manaus loomed in the background. An Indian woman standing near the platform opened a colorful parasol, then resumed eating her *farofa* pastries from a paper bag.

The pope blessed the crowd and then, supported by a prelate, he sat down in an armchair in the middle of the platform, where he began reading his speech from a sheet he held with trembling hands.

Three cardinals were sitting behind the pope.

Cardinal Wolfenberg fidgeted in his center chair and, with a sigh, he raised his eyes to the white awning on which a scorching sun was beating. His robes were sticking to his back and drops of sweat ran down his neck. He ran a handkerchief over his forehead and neck.

When the pope announced the underwriting of the four-billion-dollar loan in favor of the Amazonian project on the part of the Holy See, initially a moment of silence followed, as if the audience had not understood. Then, thunderous applause broke out and the reporters' flash bulbs lit up the awning. A TV camera swung around and pointed at the pope.

The following morning, the cardinal was sipping his coffee on the balcony overlooking the tropical garden that surrounded the archbishop's palace, when the archbishop's secretary approached, addressed the cardinal with a *"bom-dia, Eminência"* accompanied by a bow, and left a selection of cuttings from the main international daily papers on the table.

Cardinal Wolfenberg leafed through the press survey. The dailies were unanimous in praising the "historic decision" of the Holy See. A shrewd smile curved his mouth as he took out his pocket calculator. That "historic decision" would bring the Vatican a foreign exchange gain of at least one and a half billion dollars, if what Franzese had told him a week earlier were to happen, which the cardinal didn't doubt at all, knowing Franzese.

He blew out a perfect ring of smoke, and his eyes watched it wafting upwards and dispersing through the vines of the pergola laden with red and orange flowers.

The alliance with Joint Affairs and the Organization was settled and the scrolls were safely hidden in his apartment. Now all he needed was the money from the *initiati* of Manus Domini, but this was only a matter of time. He took his diary out of his cassock and made a note in it. Before flying back to Rome, he must call Dyakonov and remind him that all the donations had to be made in lire.

"Good morning, Rolf. Did you sleep well?" said Cardinal Jorge Zacarias, archbishop of Manaus, tapping the cardinal on the shoulder and sitting down at his table. Zacarias had an easy-going look and a bulk that betrayed his love of good food.

"Magnificently, Jorge. And this park of yours makes me think of the Garden of Eden."

"May I bother you a moment?"

"No bother at all."

Cardinal Zacarias confirmed to Cardinal Wolfenberg that Secretary of State Missiroli had recently met quite a few cardinals and archbishops in several countries of Latin America, yet avoided any meeting with members of Manus Domini. Disturbing rumors had been going around regarding the subject matter of those meetings. Veiled rumors of a schism had reached Manaus.

"A schism? With Cardinal Missiroli involved?" Cardinal Wolfenberg burst into laughter. "Impossible."

"That's what I thought myself. However, I thought you should know."

After Cardinal Zacarias left, Cardinal Wolfenberg ate the last slice of papaya and finished his coffee. Then he retrieved his cigar from the edge of the ashtray and went down the steps of the external staircase leading into the garden, humming the initial notes of *Dies irae, dies illa* in an inspired voice.

34

Françoise stopped in front of a boutique in Boulevard Saint Germain; an Armani dress caught her eye. The first raindrops began to fall. She opened her purse and tied a scarf around her head.

Shouldn't she warn him? The information she had was vital. Françoise turned abruptly and crossed the boulevard at a traffic light. On the other side, a man wearing a beret, a baguette under his arm and with the air of a Bohemian painter, left a phone booth. Françoise was on the point of going inside, then she stopped. "*He couldn't have got the information from anyone else but you...*" With her mind's eye she saw Guichard's face contorted with anger. Call him? After that the way he'd treated her? She walked on.

It was raining harder now and the streetlights cast multi-colored streaks on the glistening asphalt. She stopped at a small bistrot, the kind with lace curtains at the windows and polished brass everywhere. She went inside, sat down, and ordered a calvados.

She took a sip, but the taste of the calvados only made her think of Normandy, and Guichard. She found herself listening to the tapping of her ring on the marble table. She let out a deep sigh, then clenched her teeth. She got up, left a few coins on the table near the half-empty glass, and walked out under the pelting rain. She ran to a nearby phone booth, went in, and dialed a number.

"Hello, Françoise here. I'm—"

"Françoise—"Guichard said.

"Please don't interrupt," she said. "I'm calling you against my better judgment, only because I feel it's my duty to do so...."

Françoise told Guichard of her meeting with her uncle in the Vatican. She made it plain that she had known nothing whatsoever about the cardinal's machinations and that, at any rate, she judged it superfluous to defend herself from such accusations that were as unjust as they were humiliating. Guichard asked her where her uncle could have hidden the scrolls. She said that, knowing the cardinal, the most likely hiding place must be his apartment, even if one couldn't discount the fact that the scrolls might have already been sealed in the Vatican archives.

"The only reason I've phoned you was because I felt you ought to know," she continued. "But I want you to know that it's taken a big effort on my part to make this call."

"Françoise, I—"

"Ciao."

Standing in the rain, Françoise hailed a taxi and gave the driver her home address. She huddled in a corner of the back seat and took off her drenched scarf. Guichard's voice resounded in her mind. Now he was sorry and would have been ready to make it up to her. So why had she hung up? Just out of wounded pride?

She started sobbing.

Guichard went on tossing and turning in bed. André had heard correctly: the cardinal was guilty. Why should he feel like this, then?

"I'm calling you against my better judgment, only because I feel it's my duty to do so...." He saw himself back at the gallery, his voice contorted with anger.... He sat up, slid out of bed and drew back the curtains. In the light of the street lamps, a water truck was moving slowly along the Quai de Montebello sprinkling the deserted street. Guichard went over to the bedside table and dialed her number. The phone went on ringing—unanswered.

He hung up and got dressed.

Standing on the opposite side of the street, Guichard looked up at the windows on the third floor. The shutters were all closed. It was 5:30 a.m., so she must be in bed. He crossed the road and a car had to brake sharply, its horn sounding. Guichard ran a finger down the names listed on the entry phone. He pressed the button again and again....There was no answer. He looked up once more, then walked away, his head down and his hands in his raincoat pockets.

The siren of a police car rent the air.

At 9:00 a.m., Guichard dialed the number of the gallery. "Madame Mikaelian, please."

"I'm sorry. Madame Mikaelian is away at the moment. Can I help you, Mr....?"

"De Saint Clair. Can you tell me where I can find her?"

"I'm sorry, but I'm not allowed to give out that sort of information."

"Can you at least tell me when she'll be back?"

"Next Tuesday."

He seemed to hear the creaking of a chain and the whistling of the wind.

♣

Geoffroy lifted the knocker again and banged it hard against the door of the inn. There was no answer. The shutters were closed and no light filtered through from inside. Heavy clangs resounded through the alley and Geoffroy turned. A little further down, a farrier enveloped in a cloud of sparks stood in front of his forge hammering a horseshoe.

"'Fraid you're wasting your time, sir," said the farrier, putting his hammer down on the anvil and wiping his brow. "The inn's been closed for nigh on a year now."

"You don't happen to know where they've gone?" Geoffroy asked.

"One morning we woke up to find the place closed. Never heard no more. Folks is strange."

The farrier turned, picked up the horseshoe with his tongs and tossed it into a barrel of blackish water. The water bubbled and a cloud of dark smoke rose in the air, a choking smell of charcoal filling the alley.

A gust of wind blew and a creaking sound came from the inn. Geoffroy raised his head. The inn sign, an eye over a sea horizon, was swinging in the wind. Only then did he realize that he'd never asked Miriam what that sign meant.

Geoffroy slowly made his way towards the old town, but that creaking followed him as far as the mosque.

He tossed and turned in bed all night, haunted by a gigantic eye staring at him from above a sea horizon.

Guichard finished reading the report he had received from Paulette half an hour before. He frowned, and looked at his diary. It was November 5, already three weeks since the launching of the loan. He leafed through the diary. It was still slightly over a month until December 9, the contractual deadline by which CIP must credit $500 million to the joint venture account. Guichard's eyes rested on the last lines of the report: "... Out of one hundred and twenty banks invited, as of today sixty banks have declined our proposal and no bank has accepted it. Unless a substantial change takes place in our syndication strategy — but I can't realistically see what — the likelihood of placing the loan in favor of CIP is marginal."

"A sententious conclusion, yours, Paulette," Guichard said, pointing to the report.

"The phrase 'I told you so' is obnoxious, but this time you really deserve it. How did we get ourselves into a mess like this? Without the guarantee of the Italian republic, that loan has the same chance of success as one in favor of penguin colonies at the North Pole, and you should have known it from the outset. Why, then?"

"I had no other choice."

"I've heard better answers."

"Finance is not made of numbers alone. At times we have to do things that clash with any apparent logic, and yet we've got to do them, even if this means holding our noses."

"I'm not a little girl any more, Mr. de Saint Clair, so don't treat me like one. Here we're talking about an underwriting commitment of $500 million! A commitment binding us directly, as Compagnie Financière d'Arcadie. And I don't need to remind you that we don't have credit lines for $500 million."

"Are you willing to help me?"

"What kind of question is that? Of course I want to help you. What do you want me to do?"

"Get yourself all the help you need, but call the sixty missing banks—today. Try to figure out their intentions. We meet again at 6:00 p.m. Okay?

Paulette sighed. "Okay. Besides, why wait? Bad news should come all together."

"If one day I were to end up in death row, I wouldn't want to have *you* as warden."

At 6:10 p.m. there were a couple of discreet knocks at the door. Paulette, her face drawn and a stray lock hanging over her cheek, walked in and sat down in front of Guichard's desk. She crossed her legs and opened her notepad.

"Shall I read?" she said.

"Ready," said Guichard.

"We have managed to contact forty-six banks out of sixty. Thirty-six said they're likely to decline, which brings the overall no's to ninety-six. A further eight have given a vague reply and only two said they would present the proposal to their credit committee."

Guichard looked at Paulette in silence, stroking the bridge of his nose.

"Fourteen banks are left to be contacted, but they're of marginal weight," said Paulette.

"What do you suggest?"

"Let's withdraw the deal from the market-place and renegotiate its terms with CIP. No guarantee from the republic? No money. It's as simple as that."

"We're already contractually committed to issue our underwriting commitment. If we tried to back out, CIP would take us to court, and they would win."

Paulette closed her notepad. "Then I'm afraid you've got a problem."

"You may be right."

Guichard stood up, went over to the French windows, and turned around. He gazed at Dalí's clocks drooping from the trees like withered leaves. First the scrolls, then Françoise, and now the loan: a succession of failures was like the singularity of a black hole. One felt swallowed up by a superhuman force and realized it was useless to resist; so, over the few minutes one had left, despair changed into resignation and crept into one's body like a poison paralyzing any will left.

Guichard leaned against the wall, his head down.

Raise that head of thine, thou craven! said the Voice.

Leave me alone, Guichard said.

Knowest thou the secret of a victorious knight?

My memory is not what it used to be.

The victorious knight is like the Arabian phoenix rising from its ashes. Unhorsed, he finds the strength to remount and ride towards the Promised Land, where victory is concealed.

And where would this Garden of Eden be?

Beyond the uttermost bounds of despair, a land meant for none but the chosen few.

Oh, I see. A land not shown on any map. But what does it matter? The stars will certainly show your knight the way, won't they?

Hold thy spiteful tongue. Suffice it to see the sign. I saw it.

Guichard raised his head. What sign?

I first set eyes upon it the night before my dubbing. I was but twenty. I kept vigil all night in prayer and meditation, as was the custom. A voice spake within me, enjoining me to hie me hence from the castle to the first loop of the river, beneath the hills of Craies. It was a moonlit night, and I ventured forth on foot thro' the wood without squire and without torch. When I came to the river, I found nobody there. My sole companions the hooting of owls and the croaking of frogs, mingling with the murmur of the river. And anon there fell a great silence, forthwith broken by a neigh. I raised my eyes. A destrier reared up beneath the crags of Craies, above the wood, its white coat shimmering in the moonlight, its mane streaming in the wind. It galloped like an arrow thro' the wood, its white pelt flashing twixt tree and tree, its hooves thudding in rapid drumming. It stopped a few yards from me, pawed the round and shook its mane. The spiral horn issuing from its forehead glittered in the moonlight. A unicorn! It stared at me with eyes of a blue brighter than a sapphire thro' a sun-

beam, and it was as if in those eyes I saw the sublimest of what a knight may crave: freedom, courage, honour, the unconquerable strength to rise up from defeat.... I approached it and was about to stroke it, but its eyes flashed and it stamped back, with nostrils a-quiver. Only then did I recall that the unicorn is indomitable, the freest among all creatures, more so even than the proud eagle. None but those knights that are pure in heart and spirit may discern it — none may touch it.

And then what happened?

It came nigh the river, lowered its head, and lastly dipped the tip of its horn in the water.

And then?

At first, nothing. Then the water seethed, a whirlpool formed, becoming as clear as a summer sky, and images took shape in the bottom.

What images?

I cannot tell thee, because no words may describe them. Just this may I tell thee: I saw myself, but not in the flesh. Pure spirit I was, free from the constriction of body and mind, free from the false myths and all the phantoms of this world. Never had I felt thus: time and space had stopped, and around me was naught but the silent pulsating of the celestial spheres.

Guichard said nothing.

Hast thou ever seen the unicorn? said the Voice.

Oh, sure. The streets of Paris are so full of them they've had to make special tracks for them.

Thou dolt! Each man sees the unicorn in his own way, scrutinizing within himself. However, there are knights who will never see it, since they were born blind. Take heed lest thou be like them.

And if I should see it, could I too see what you saw in the river?

Thou shouldst reply to a question.

What question?

Will the unicorn be willing to serve thee? (Job 39:9)

Who can reply to that — if it's not asking too much?

Thou alone, Guichard de Saint Clair.

The following morning, Guichard was tempted to call his banking contacts in Kuwait City and Tokyo. He went as far as lifting the phone, but stopped. It was too soon. The market would interpret a phone call from him at this stage as a sign of weakness. He hung up.

He would wait until Monday afternoon. And then...? *"You know our laws,"* Franzese had said. *"If things go wrong, I won't cover for you."*

Sitting in an armchair in the library, Guichard examined the list of paintings he was holding in his hand. He jotted down some figures. Even at a conservative estimate, he must already have reached $420 million. He raised his eyes and looked at the long neck in Modigliani's *Portrait of a Woman* hanging on the wall opposite. How much could it be worth?

André, his head still bandaged, approached Guichard carrying a silver tray. "Your Hennessy, Monsieur le Comte."

"Thank you, André."

Julius padded over to Guichard's armchair. He sat with his back to Guichard and André, forming a perfect triangle.

André gave a discreet glance at Guichard's list. "Any problems, Monsieur le Comte?"

"I'm afraid so. We may have to say goodbye to our paintings, at least for a while."

"It grieves me to hear you say that. Monsieur is an astute businessman. How did it happen?"

"How did it happen?" Guichard shook his head. "It's the result of my own folly. Reaching for impossible goals, just to prove they're not impossible. All the de Saint Clairs have suffered from it."

André frowned. "Monsieur le Comte, if it were not for that yearning after the impossible, would life be worth living?"

Guichard looked up at André. "It would be like going to sea for life on Eisenstein's *Battleship Potemkin*."

"Dreaming of the impossible is what makes it all possible," André said, his eyes gleaming. "Besides, is it not Monsieur who always says that 'fortune favors the brave'? If it worked for the ancient Romans, why not for us too?"

Guichard got up, filled a second glass of Hennessy, and handed it to André. "André, have a drink with me."

"With pleasure, Monsieur le Comte."

"Meow," said Julius, without turning round.

Julius jumped onto the desk in the library, glanced cursorily at the map of the Vatican City on which Guichard, a ruler in his hand, was drawing some lines, then crouched down right in the middle of St. Peter's Square.

"Well-behaved cats don't hang around places like St. Peter's Square," Guichard said, pushing Julius aside. "Now, I understand that you, as a Siamese cat, feel entitled to do things that normal cats—"

The phone rang.

"He's the very man you're looking for," said Astarita. "His uncle worked for thirty years as a lay employee of the Vatican, three of which were spent on the first floor of the Palace of the Holy Office."

"When can I meet him?" Guichard asked.

"As soon as tomorrow, if you want."

"Perfect. Tell me where and at what time."

"At 2:00 p.m., by Caligula's obelisk in St. Peter's Square."

"How am I going to recognize him?"

"He'll be the one to recognize you. By the way, his name's Sante Gardenia, but everyone calls him 'the Doctor.'"

Guichard walked within the borders of a spoke of the eight-spoked wheel drawn on the pavement of St. Peter's Square and reached the foot of the Egyptian obelisk. He was ten minutes early. His eyes wandered over the people standing around the two imposing fountains on each side of the obelisk, but he didn't see anyone who could possibly be Gardenia. Sunrays shone through one of the fountain jets and the rainbow colors dazzled Guichard. Not far off, a priest holding an open map was telling a group of black nuns the story of the obelisk. "...*It was Sixtus V who, in 1585, decided to position it in front of the Basilica*..." A column of Japanese tourists marched by, following their guide.

"Mr. de Saint Clair?"

Guichard turned. The man addressing him was well built, with a determined jaw and wearing a camelhair coat. His gold-rimmed glasses and neatly combed silver hair gave him a distinguished look. If he'd bumped into him in the street, he'd have imagined him to be a banker, or a doctor. The nickname was well chosen.

"Yes," said Guichard. "And you must be Mr. Gardenia."

"In person." Gardenia smiled, showing a gold crown, and held out his hand. "My friend Astarita told me you might be needing my services."

As they strolled under the Bernini colonnade, Guichard confided his plan to Gardenia. The Doctor was listening, chewing a black cigarette holder with an unlit cigarette in it, his hands clasped behind his back.

"So, to reach the fourth floor of the Palace of the Holy Office, I don't see any other route than the main gate. What do you think? Is there another way?" Guichard said.

"Hmm... the building next door is the *Salone delle Udienze*, and the roofs of the two palaces are joined. I'll have to study the plans."

"How can we get rid of the Swiss guards?"

"Consider it done," Gardenia said with a reassuring gesture.

"You seem very confident."

"My confidence wears the three stripes of a captain of the Swiss Guard. Is that enough?"

"It is."

"As long as the cardinal won't be at home that night, and you'll be the one to take care of that. D'you think you can handle it?"

Guichard clutched the ends of his silk scarf pensively. "I don't know how as yet, but the answer is yes. You can count on it."

"*Perfetto*. Then—"

"On one condition," Guichard said.

Gardenia stopped. "What condition?"

"I want to come, too."

"This isn't exactly a stroll in the gardens of Villa Borghese, you know."

"I *must* come. Don't ask me why."

Gardenia took the cigarette holder from his mouth and pointed it at Guichard. "Listen, de Saint Clair, we've got to get one thing clear from the start. Either we do things my way, or it's all off."

"Then it's all off."

Gardenia stared at Guichard. He sighed. "First, I'll have to discuss the matter with Astarita."

"How does Astarita come into it?"

"He certainly comes into it. For reasons I don't know — and which I don't want to know — if something were to happen to you, I wouldn't even have the time to make my will."

After Gardenia had gone, Guichard walked across the long, thin shadow the obelisk cast over St. Peter's Square. He passed under the Arco delle Campane and a few minutes later he was standing in front of the Palace of the Holy Office. His eyes slid over the massive iron bars at the windows, the closed-circuit camera above the main gate, and the halberds of the two Swiss guards mounting guard at both sides of the gate.

Guichard glanced up at the windows on the fourth floor. How could he get the Inquisitor out of there, just for one night?

A black Mercedes stopped in front of the main gate. A tall, fair-haired priest got out of the car, hurried around and opened the rear door by the sidewalk. A cardinal walked briskly through the gate.... *The Inquisitor!*

Guichard crossed the street and walked the few yards to the car. The cardinal had already disappeared inside. Guichard bent in front of the rear window. The spear of a halberd flashed in front of his eyes, stopping between his face and the car.

"*Bleiben Sie still!* — Stay where you are!" said a guard, while the second one positioned himself behind Guichard, his halberd pointed at Guichard's back.

"But... but I only wanted to ask His Eminence for an autograph," Guichard said, putting on an idiotic smile. He took out a pen and rummaged in his pockets until he found a business card, which he hastened to turn on the blank side.

The window was lowered, revealing Cardinal Wolfenberg's amused face.

"*Es gibt keine Gefahr*—There is no danger," the cardinal said to the guards, signaling to them to raise their halberds again. He took the pen and the card from Guichard, signed, and gave them back to him. "Next time try to be more careful. You were close to having the tip of your nose chopped off."

"Thank you, Your Eminence. I'm at a loss for words," Guichard said, his voice trembling. "When I recognized you, I just couldn't restrain myself, thinking of all the fine things you do for the Holy Church."

"Such devotion does you honor," said the cardinal, visibly pleased.

Guichard stared at the card bearing the cardinal's signature. "I just can't wait to tell my wife."

"Oh, you're married, are you. Any children?"

"Six, Your Eminence," Guichard said proudly. Then, with an embarrassed smile: "Um... The seventh is on the way."

"Oh, very, very good. Did you hear, Father Emilio? And there are people stating that Catholic values are in decline! Well done, my son. You are a rock, like Saint Peter. A large and healthy Catholic family: what more can one expect from life?" The cardinal leaned over to Father Emilio and whispered: "Father, hand me one of your holy images."

Father Emilio searched in his cassock, took out a packet of paper slips held together with a rubber band, and handed one to the cardinal.

"For you, my son, in memory of this fortunate encounter." The cardinal handed the holy image to Guichard, who looked at it reverently.

"Saint Nicholas of Myra," Guichard read aloud. "I'll treasure it for the rest of my days. Um, excuse me, Your Eminence. Whose protector is Saint Nicholas?"

The cardinal hesitated. "Um, of thieves."

A surprised expression spread on Guichard's face. "A saint protector of thieves?"

The cardinal chuckled. "Whatever are you thinking of! Saint Nicholas's patronage of thieves simply means that he is helping them to repent and change."

"Oh, I see." Guichard gave the cardinal a subtle look, his forefinger pointed heavenwards. "Poor Saint Nicholas must be fairly busy up there. Don't you think so, Your Eminence?"

The cardinal stared at Guichard and curled his lips pensively. "You know what? I have the impression I've already met you somewhere...."

"Oh, mine is a common face, Your Eminence."

"Well, good bye, my son. And don't forget: take care."

"Oh, I will, Your Eminence, I most certainly will. These days you never know who you may run across."

With his head towering above the two guards' red plumes, Guichard waved Saint Nicholas's holy image at the car driving away, the idiotic smile still imprinted on his face.

§

Gardenia arrived in Via di Porta Angelica shortly before six p.m. He stopped on the sidewalk across from the entrance to the Swiss guards' barracks, at Porta di Sant'Anna. He lit the cigarette already stuck into his cigarette holder, went over to a newsstand, and bought the latest issue of the magazine *Giardini*—Gardens. He began leafing through it, keeping an eye on the gate to the barracks.

A fair-haired man of athletic build emerged from the barracks. He was wearing civilian clothes—a blue blazer and green pants. The man's name was Alois Kunzelmann and he was a captain in the Swiss Guard.

Gardenia's and Kunzelmann's eyes met for a split second.

Kunzelman set off towards Piazza del Risorgimento. Gardenia waited a minute, closed his magazine and headed in the same direction.

35

The pigeons fluttered around the statue of St. Francis, in St. John Lateran's Square in Rome. Two men were sitting on a nearby bench, two black leather cases lying at their feet. One of them threw a handful of nuts to the pigeons.

"As if we didn't have better things to do," Habib said, shooing the pigeons away from the bench.

Habib laid one of the cases on his lap, opened the lid and pulled up two antennas about five inches long.

"Okay then," he said, fiddling with a knob. "We work on 150 MHz, so the antennas shouldn't be too conspicuous. We should have a range of about 120 degrees. I'm afraid the resolution won't be too good with that frequency, though."

"In Tel Aviv, they say the new software is much better," said Gideon, leaning over and picking up his case.

"Let's hope so. Time to go." Habib got up and slung the case over his shoulder. He straightened his tie and adjusted the strap of the camera slung round his neck. Then he looked at Gideon's ponytail and shook his head.

As they set off towards the Basilica of St. John Lateran, Habib looked up. Sixteen statues of Apostles and saints, each seven yards tall, towered above the façade of the basilica. The gigantic statues seemed to be eyeing them with surly faces.

"Saints never laugh," he said.

"Yeah, it must be the eleventh commandment of the Catholic Church," Gideon said.

Habib and Gideon walked in front of Emperor Constantine's imposing statue standing in the atrium and passed through the two bronze portals. At that time of day, the basilica was almost empty. The two men walked up the center aisle as far as the beginning of the apse. Two long rows of wooden stalls ran down each side of the apse, and the area was closed off with a low, marble balustrade, a sign saying No Entry hanging from it. Above them, a large mosaic of Christ and the Virgin Mary with Saints covered the lower part of the dome. They sat down in the front pew by the balustrade. Habib nudged Gideon and jerked his head to a sexton busy fixing some candles on a candelabrum standing at one end of the transept.

"You stay here," murmured Habib. "I'd better go and speak to him alone. And next time cut off that ponytail! D'you want them to think we're drug addicts or something?"

"Hark at Beau Brummell!"

"Can I bother you for a moment, Father?" Habib said.

The sexton muttered something without turning round. Habib explained that he and Gideon were professional photographers and were working on an illustrated book on the great places of worship in the world. The Basilica of San Giovanni in Laterano was one of the churches they'd chosen for Catholicism. Since they needed to take some photos, were they allowed to go into the apse? It was only from there that they could get the best angle on the mosaic.

The sexton went on setting up the candles. "It's strictly forbidden to go beyond the balustrade. Can't you see the sign? Besides, you can't use a flash camera in here."

"Can't you make an exception, Father? We've come all the way to Rome for this purpose. It's a book that'll be sold everywhere. After all, for you it would be free advertising."

"God has no need of advertising!" The sexton glared at Habib with a sour face.

"We'd thought of making a donation."

The sexton finished pushing a large candle into its stand, then looked round at Habib. "How much?"

"A million lire."

"Wait right here," said the sexton, who scuttled off through a side door.

He reappeared a few minutes later, accompanied by a priest so fat that he could hardly squeeze through the doorway. The two of them stood muttering in the semi-darkness, glancing across every so often at Habib and Gideon. In the end the sexton came over.

"All right," the sexton said, holding out his hand.

Habib counted out the notes, which vanished in a flash into the sexton's cassock.

"What's in those bags?" said the sexton, throwing a suspicious glance towards Gideon, still sitting in the front pew.

"Nowadays, you need a computer even to get a photo," Habib said.

"Let's have a look."

Habib opened his bag, signaling to Gideon to do the same.

The sexton bent over. "Well, I guess it's all right," he said, not fully convinced.

Habib and Gideon split the apse into two halves. Gideon started at the front and Habib at the back. They examined the floor inch by inch, moving sideways towards the altar, two antennas sticking out of each of the leather cases.

Pretending to study the light and perspective, every so often they took a photo for the benefit of the sexton, who kept turning to look at them.

When Gideon reached the center of the apse, some ten yards in front of the altar, he suddenly stopped. He glanced sideways at the sexton and beckoned to Habib.

When Habib was at his side, Gideon pointed to the luminous green dial between the two antennas. He took a tentative step towards the altar and the needle shot up to the top of the graded scale.

"Well, are you through with it at last?" said the sexton's grumpy voice behind them.

Carrying a plate with a ham sandwich and a glass of pineapple juice, Carlomagno went back to his lab. He pushed aside a bundle of cables, put the plate down on his workbench and sat down. He was on the point of biting into the sandwich, when he suddenly stopped and turned his head to the computer screen. *The image was still.* The program had stopped running and the cypher was flashing on the screen.... Zergas's birth date! He slapped his forehead.

He dropped the sandwich, grabbed the mouse and clicked on the first of the coded files.

§

From his corner table, Tancredi glanced at the bar door every time someone walked in. Even though there was no music, every so often his foot tapped rhythmically on the floor. Loud shouting and a burst of laughter rose from a nearby table where people were playing cards.

Carlomagno walked in shortly after eleven p.m. carrying a black briefcase, his face serious. With his professorial air and his bow tie, he looked out of place. He sat down, put his briefcase on the table, took out a manila envelope and opened it. Without speaking, he handed Tancredi a few sheets of paper.

Tancredi ran his finger down the columns of figures. On the same line beside each of the amounts, were the name of a company, a date, a bank and a country. The banks were all offshore and the countries were all tax havens: Jersey, the Cook Islands, the Turks and the Caicos Islands.... The figures varied from half a billion lire to around ten billion. Tancredi's finger rested on a figure of nine million dollars. *Allied Petroleum!* Allied had made two payments on October 10, exactly a month earlier: one of eight million and the other of one million dollars.

"Have you had a good look at the last page?" Carlomagno asked.

Tancredi leafed through to the last page. Carlomagno was right: it was different from the others. It was a list of bank accounts. The name of the account holder and the account number appeared beside each bank. The account holders were companies bearing Anglo-Saxon names, and next to each was the name of a trustee.

Tancredi grumbled. "All the accounts are in the name of trusts."

"And so?"

"Getting to know who hides behind a trust is as easy as winning first prize at the national lottery."

"Don't despair." Carlomagno opened the briefcase and took out another sheet of paper. "A surprise for you."

This time the column of figures referred to the same payments as before, but with a difference: it showed who the beneficiaries were. Tancredi's eyes darted down the figures and stopped on the line with the nine million figure. The Coalition had cashed eight million, while one million had ended up in Accardo's pockets. A sadistic smile appeared on Tancredi's face.

"I knew it! I knew it!" said Tancredi, banging his fists on the table repeatedly. "Now, not even all the prayers in the world will save that son of a bitch."

"I wouldn't want to be in your place."

Tancredi looked at Carlomagno, dismayed.

"Pull that thread and you might hear the last trump," said Carlomagno.

"Isn't it precisely what we've been working so hard for? As to that trump, I *want* to hear it, I'm *itching* to hear it, I *long* to hear it. Need I go on?"

"There are lots of people out there who're far more interested in making sure things stay *precisely* the way they've always been. It would be like trying to pull a bone away from an angry mastiff."

"Well, the supply of bones has run out." Tancredi took the sheets of paper and slapped them against the palm of his hand.

"You're an incurable idealist, Tancredi. Once this Accardo is gone, another one will turn up. Do you really think they'll let you change all this?"

"What should I do, then? Remain seated, like you?"

"Haven't you thought about yourself? About your family?"

"After that list comes out on the front page of my newspaper, they won't dare touch my family or the paper or me," said Tancredi, but with the voice of someone who needed to convince himself.

"Playing the devil's advocate is never much fun, but someone has to do it," Carlomagno said. "How are you going to justify being in possession of that list at all? And even if you managed to do it without collecting a series of indictments from the usual corrupt judge, how will you prove that the files really come from Zergas's computer?"

Tancredi did not answer.

"Working for the Ministry of the Interior, I've learned to be afraid of the state. Having the proof to catch a bastard like Accardo means one thing only: being alone."

"What are you driving at?"

"Don't ever trust either the judges or the police. *Never.* Otherwise, before you know it, you'll suddenly find yourself in the murderers' wing at Regina Coeli. Then, after a few weeks, someone will find your body hanging from a water pipe. Suicide, they'll say. End of the investigation."

"Blast you! You want to scare me at all costs, don't you? Well, you'll be happy to know that you've succeeded." Tancredi leaned toward Carlomagno. "But this doesn't mean I'm backing out. Quite the contrary."

Tancredi stood up, gathered his papers and strode to the door.

Guichard looked at his watch once again. It was 11:10 a.m. and the phone remained silent. None of the missing banks had called yet.

"The victorious knight is like the Arabian phoenix rising from its own ashes…"

"And where would this Garden of Eden be?"

"Beyond the uttermost bounds of despair, a land meant for none but the chosen few."

Guichard grabbed Paulette's report, crumpled it up and tossed it in the waste paper basket. Then he dialed her extension and asked her into his office.

"Paulette, send a fax to those fourteen missing banks and to the eight that are still uncertain. Tell them that half the CIP loan has already been underwritten."

Paulette's eyes widened and a smile of relief lit up her face. "Really? When did that happen?"

Guichard's expression betrayed him, because her smile vanished. "What if they ask for a list of the underwriting banks?"

"We'll worry about that if and when the time comes."

A reproachful look appeared on Paulette's face.

At 11:30 a.m. Guichard's intercom buzzed.

"There's a call from Mr. Al Jhaffyr, of Kuwait International Bank," said Marie Claire.

"Put him through."

"... So KIB might be interested in taking a large portion of the loan," Al Jhaffyr said.

"What do you mean by 'a large portion'?"

"The $250 million that's left—but on one condition."

"And what might that be?"

"How much is your underwriting fee?

"It's 1.75 percent. Why?"

"We want to take over half of the underwriting commitment from you, with you turning over to us the underwriting fee for that share."

"I'll have to discuss it with my partners," said Guichard indifferently.

"Our offer's only valid until 5.00 p.m. today, your time."

"Hold that rod tight! Now pay out a bit of line.... Like that, that's good, tire it out," the steward running the castle used to tell him when he took him fishing on the river. Kneeling in the boat, Guichard still felt the tugs of the trout jumping out and back into the water, its scales glistening in the sun. And meanwhile his heart would beat faster and faster.

He was still left with $250 million to place. What now?

I forgot to confide a secret to thee, said the Voice.

What?

Dost thou remember I told thee that in 1548 Audric de Saint Clair, disguised as a brigand, attacked and robbed a king's courier?

What of it?

Well, Audric engaged in the same venture again in 1549. And he was never caught.

Thanks, ancestor.

Not at all, descendant. Men of honor ever understand one another.

Guichard picked up the phone and asked Paulette to join him again.

"Send another fax to the twenty-one missing banks and tell them that a bank—no names, of course—has offered to take the $250 million, but that they're asking for fifty percent of our underwriting fee, and that—"

"I don't understand," Paulette broke in. "After the fax we sent this morning, this additional fax will make the banks think that the $500 million has all been placed."

"I haven't finished. Tell them we're reluctant to accept that offer and that we're prepared to accept any further underwritings by 4:00 p.m. today."

"I see," Paulette said, icicles forming around her words.

At 3:45 p.m., Marie Claire put through a phone call from the London branch of the Credit Bank of Japan.

"We might be interested in taking those $250 million," said Kimura, the branch manager.

"On what condition?"

"The whole $250 million is too much for our books. We would keep only $100 million, but we would like to syndicate the remaining $150 million to other Japanese banks. So we want exclusivity on all the Japanese banks."

Guichard paused. "First I have to consult my partners. Can you fax me your proposal?"

"Okay, but my proposal will only hold until 6 p.m. today."

Guichard turned round, reached for a bottle of Hennessy, and filled a glass.

À la santé, said Guichard, raising his glass high.

À la santé, said the Voice. *I know not what sinuous machinations thou hast contrived, but on one thing I am not mistaken, Guichard de Saint Clair: in my world thou wouldst have been a base horsethief.*

Tancredi went on tossing and turning all night. *"Don't ever trust either the judges or the police ... Then, after a few weeks, someone will find your body hanging from a water pipe ..."* He listened to Carla's breathing. He felt guilty for having already canceled twice the vacation to Egypt that she and Simona wanted so badly. But this time would be it. It was only a matter of a few more weeks now. At the end of that story, he would make it up to them by giving them a surprise.

He passed a hand over his neck and felt his skin wet with cold sweat. He sat up. The prospects of the day ahead of him allured him as much as a tête-à-tête with the moustached virago heading the accounting department. He slipped out of bed and groped for his slippers.

In the kitchen he fixed himself some coffee. He filled a cup and went to the window. The strong brew washed away the shadows of the night. Dawn was lighting up the sky. In the apartment opposite, the old lady with the hairnet was feeding her two cats. On the floor below hers, the retired colonel came out on the terrace and started doing his deep knee-bends, wearing a T-shirt and flashy red gym shorts.

Tancredi finished his coffee, went over to the phone and dialed a number.

Tancredi and Sergio met at their usual corner table over two cappuccinos.

"Since when do you wake people up at crack of dawn, you rotten sod?" Sergio said, sitting down.

Tancredi told Sergio about Zergas's files.

"I'm really afraid I'll have to involve a judge," concluded Tancredi.

"To cover your ass?"

"It's not just that. I've got to get proof—before Zergas removes the files from his computer."

"Are you thinking of a search warrant?"

"Of course."

"That shouldn't be too difficult," Sergio said.

"That's easy to say. How will I justify having those files?"

"You're a journalist, for Chrissake. You could have gotten them anonymously through the post. The judge will turn a blind eye."

"Maybe an honest judge. A pity, though, that it's a rare commodity from what I hear."

"A few phone calls to the Ministry of Justice and someone will be able to direct me to the right man."

"I hope so. The thought of ending up in Regina Coeli and finding myself 'suicided' isn't exactly thrilling."

"Do you really intend to go on?"

"First Carlomagno, and now you too?" Tancredi said.

"Well, that should tell you something. But I know it's useless trying to make you change your mind. I'll tell you one thing only: be careful."

"This is really a conspiracy. What's that supposed to mean?"

"Maybe a list will clarify the picture. It means limiting the use of your phone to the minimum, it means changing your usual schedules and itineraries, it means not going out in the evening, it means—"

"Hell, that's enough!"

"No, that's not enough, and you know it. I'll draw up the full list, and if I happen to find you hanging around your bar after 8:00 p.m., I'll kick your butt. Is that clear?"

Tancredi walked into Quilici's office, shut the door and sat down.

"I've got Zergas's files," Tancredi said. He opened his briefcase and placed the printout of Zergas's files in front of Quilici.

When Quilici was through reading, his smile would have aroused Long John Silver's envy.

"When do we go to press?" Quilici said, rubbing his hands together.

Tancredi told him of his doubts.

"Have you turned into a sissy, or what?"

"Accardo might try to stop us. Or take revenge."

"But it wouldn't make sense. It would be like signing a confession."

"Maybe you're right."

Quilici flipped through the printout. "I'd like to know just where the fiddle is."

"It must be something to do with the coal-mines. Otherwise how d'you explain that payment to the professor of mineralogy?"

"What are you talking about?"

Tancredi leaned over and turned the page. "Look there at the bottom, and look at the date. Just a week after the initial Allied payments."

Advance of Lit. 200 million to Prof. Paolo Serrano, Istituto Superiore di Mineralogia di Roma. Balance of Lit. 800 million on delivery of report, by end November. Payment through KBS in Zurich.

Quilici grinned. "What little scamps! They've overvalued the mines."

"For the moment, though, all we've got is this piece of paper."

Quilici's expression turned dreamy. "If only we could bring to light all the sleaze hidden underneath...."

"We don't have the time. We're facing banking secrecy and Trust laws. Besides, you seem to be forgetting a minor detail."

"What?"

"If we don't break even by December, the two of us will have to pack our bags." Tancredi pointed to the calendar. "And it's already November 11."

"Hmm." Quilici was deep in thought. "The distinguished professor of mineralogy has to deliver his report within three weeks...."

"And so?"

Quilici told Tancredi what he had in mind.

"I've always thought you were a goddamned son-of-a-bitch," Tancredi said.

Visibly pleased, Quilici grinned and reached for the phone.

As soon as she entered her apartment, Françoise smelled an unusual odor. She went to the kitchen, checked the gas stove and looked around: everything seemed normal. She stopped. It was the same odor she had smelled during the séance at Kamilla's. Her heart pounding, she walked slowly towards the living room.

She turned on the light switch, but the power went off, as if there were a short circuit. Now the odor of ozone was strong. A bluish luminescence appeared over the coffee table and a thin column of smoke rose from it. Françoise went over to the couch and sat down.

The luminescence grew stronger and a splash of whitish, wax-like substance materialized on the glass of the coffee table. The smoke thickened, the splash took on a darker shade and an outline began to show through.... *The medallion with the coat of arms of the de Saint Clairs.*

The medallion shone with an unreal bluish brightness that seemed to radiate from inside it. Françoise's hand hovered above the medallion, lowered and clutched it. The brightness spread to her hand and grew so intense that the veins and bones showed through. A cloud of ethereal ectoplasm emanated from her hand, spread until it reached her face and was sucked in through her nostrils.

Françoise picked up the rebec from the couch, tucked it under her chin and drew the bow across the strings. A slow melody arose, high-pitched and piercing, and a song sung in a deep and melancholy voice came out of Françoise's mouth.

A vous, Amors, plus qu'a nule autre gent, est bien raisons que ma dolour conplaigne. Quant il m'estuet partir outrement et dessevrer de ma leaul compaigne...

The lights came back on, the music stopped and the medallion began to fade, its outline more and more blurred. The unicorn engraved on it leapt into space and started spinning in a circle round on itself, as if chasing its own horn. It spun round faster and faster, until it formed a whirlwind that sucked it up.

Françoise stared at the rebec in bewilderment. She tried to remember when she had picked it up, and why.

What was that unicorn supposed to mean?

36

"Françoise, it's me," said Guichard, speaking on the outside entry phone.

"What do you want?" she said.

"I need to speak with you. Please."

The street door clicked open.

As Guichard went up in the elevator, he thought once again of what he was going to say to her. He looked in the mirror. His hands were moving in agreement with his inner monologue. As soon as the door of the elevator opened, Françoise's eyes froze him. She was standing in the doorway of her apartment, facing the elevator. Her hair was tied back; she was wearing a pink blouse and jeans and was barefoot. Soft piano music came from inside.

"I need to talk to you. Please," Guichard said.

"Don't you think you've already told me everything you wanted to tell me — and in no uncertain terms?"

"Can't I come in — just for a minute?"

Françoise stood aside.

Guichard sat down in an armchair. Françoise huddled on the couch, in the corner furthest away from Guichard.

"I know, I know," said Guichard. "I should have realized right away that you didn't know anything about it, but try to understand: appearances were all against you."

"Don't you dare talk to me about appearances!"

"I beg your forgiveness."

Françoise made a dismissive gesture. "It's much too easy." She turned her face away.

There was one way only to open a passage: tell her something, just the bare minimum.

Guichard told Françoise about his reminiscences, from the day the lightning had struck and he'd felt that shock run up his arm, and of the scrolls his father had found buried in the under-vault cellars of the castle. He told her about the promise of re-venge Guichard de Saint Clair had made in front of Arno's charred body, which his ancestor had added to the scrolls on October 20, 1308, but he didn't tell her anything about Guichard de Saint Clair's invocation before dying at Bannockburn.

"Now do you see why those scrolls are so impor-tant?" Guichard said.

"Why didn't you tell me all this before?"

"You make it all sound so simple, don't you? There's a plan to avenge the Templars, and I've sworn not to talk to anyone about it." Guichard went over and sat down on the sofa. "I've already told you too much."

Françoise asked Guichard once more what lay behind Pous-sin's picture and what was hidden inside the mountain of Blanchefort. With self-assurance, Guichard answered that all that was only the imagination of some writers turned archae-ologists. Françoise said it couldn't be just a coincidence that a country abbot had chiseled away the epigraph from a head-stone in the graveyard of Rennes-le-Château and that the epi-graph had included the phrase *Et in Arcadia ego* — the very same phrase in Poussin's painting. Guichard said that it was just a fact embroidered by folklore.

"Oh, is that so?" Françoise said. "So it's also folklore that the grave belonged to Marie de Blanchefort, a descendant of Bertrand de Blanchefort — a well-known name to a de Saint Clair, right?"

"Unbelievable as it may seem, it's only a chain of coinci-dences."

"Oh, Guichard, Guichard. When will this story be over?"

"Sooner than you think."

Guichard moved close to Françoise and embraced her. He began to kiss her passionately and to stroke her body. Françoise remained passive.

"Maybe we're not talking about the same story," Françoise said. "Mine is a story with two overlapping plots."

Guichard stopped.

"What do you want from me, Guichard?"

"An answer like 'It seems obvious' might sound vulgar, and I'm not a vulgar man. On the other hand, something like 'I can't live without you', despite being close to the truth, would sound dull and melodramatic, and I'm neither one nor the other." Guichard sighed and leaned back. "Your Honor, after careful consideration I've decided to avail myself of the Fifth Amendment. Thank you for spoiling a magical moment."

"Your subconscious is a judge who doesn't accept the Fifth Amendment. Refusing to look inside yourself means refusing to face reality."

"Shall I lie down on the couch, doctor?"

"There are people who are afraid of what they can see, and they end up becoming estranged from themselves. Be careful not to become like one of them, Guichard."

Thou dolt! Each man sees the unicorn in his own way, scrutinizing within himself. However, there are knights who will never see it, since they were born blind. Take heed lest thou be like them.

"So *I* would be afraid of reality? Ugh! You don't even know what reality is about. You're like one of those slaves chained in Plato's cave, who have only seen shadows cast on the walls for their whole life and end up mistaking them for reality."

"Maybe I'm like one of Plato's slaves, but *I* don't need to travel back in time in search of a dream. And it doesn't matter that the dream be either an idealized love or a place, because it's always only an escape."

"Oh, doctor, compared with you Freud himself was a shrink good only for a suburban madhouse." Guichard joined his hands and assumed a pleading expression. "Please, tell me doctor, what am I escaping from? Maybe a lascivious love for my great-grandmother?"

"From a reality that you persist in not accepting. I've read that there are people who hear voices or have recurrent dreams. Some people go as far as suffering a real splitting of their personality." Françoise stroked Guichard's head with a deliberately motherly attitude. "Do you hear voices, Guichard?"

Guichard jumped to his feet, a vein throbbing in his neck. "I see and hear things you wouldn't even conceive of in your wildest dreams. And I have no intention of wasting my time explaining to you why they are real!"

"Is jumping back in time a dream to find a lost love again?"

"Time doesn't exist! 'Jumping back in time', as you call it, is no dream, but rather traveling into a parallel world. And the goal goes far beyond meeting a lost love again, since it aims at changing…"

Guichard froze.

"You drove me so mad that I'm saying meaningless things. You did it on purpose, didn't you?"

Françoise put her arms round Guichard's neck. "You're right, poor dear. I'm unforgivable. But perhaps there is a way I can make myself forgiven." She loosened his tie, then whispered to him: "Do you still remember that flesh-pink nightgown you used to like so much?"

What a strange woman. He'd never known the likes of her before.

Geoffroy had been right.

When Habib reached St. John Lateran Square, the first rays of dawn were lighting up the statues of the saints above the basilica. A hobo wrapped in a ragged army blanket was sleeping on a bench. A bicycle with its lights on emerged from a corner of the square. The cyclist looked a real card, a derby on his head and dressed all in black with leather boots. He pedaled at high speed around the Thutmose III obelisk. Then, as he passed Habib, he raised his arm in a fascist salute and yelled: "When He [Mussolini] was in charge, trains always ran on time." Habib shook his head, turned up his coat collar and walked round the basilica.

When he reached the back of the basilica, Habib found Gideon sitting on a low wall, playing a sad song on a harmonica. He was still sporting his ponytail.

They could hear a coffee machine hissing steam. They went into the bar. The fragrance of freshly baked croissants wafted in the air. They ordered cappuccinos and croissants, and sat down in front of the window, away from the counter. Habib spread a plan out on the table.

"There are twenty canons and three sextons living in there," murmured Habib, pointing to a reddish building across the road, next to the basilica. "From now on I want to know exactly who comes in and out of that door and at what time. You'll begin the first shift at six in the morning. Ethan will relieve you at 3:00 p.m. and will stay here until midnight."

Gideon studied the plan. "But that building and the basilica are linked. There's a way through to the basilica inside. The canons are bound to hear the noise."

"Even if they do, they won't be able to call anyone for help." Habib jabbed his finger at the plan. "First we'll cut the phone lines, here. Then ..."

"When do I start?"

"You've started already." Habib stood up. "And now I'm going to meet the others."

Five minutes later, Habib sat down on a bench at the foot of the statue of St. Francis.

When the two agents arrived, they sat down next to him. Habib laid the open plan on his lap and explained what they had to do....

"Is everything clear?" he said.

The two men nodded.

"Good. The men on the second shift will relieve you at 2:00 p.m. The night shift will begin at midnight."

After the two agents had disappeared inside the basilica, Habib looked up at the statues of the saints. It was just a matter of days, then the Ark would be back home.

He turned his back to the basilica, took out an embroidered satin *kippah* from his pocket and put it on his head. "*E-L Sh-add-ai* – God Almighty One," murmured Habib in a singsong. "*Sh-ma Yisroael, adonoi elohaynu, adonoi echud* – Hear, O Israel. The Lord our God, the Lord is one..." (Deut. 6:4)

The corridor on the third floor of the *Ministério da Fazenda* was deserted. The hall clock read 1:10 p.m. The only presence seemed to be that of the sad-eyed and brick-red-skinned Indios represented in the naïve frescoes covering the walls, busy cutting their way with machete strokes through the undergrowth of the Amazonian forest.

Ferreira stood up, locked the door to his office, and sat down again. He pulled a bunch of keys from his pocket and opened the desk drawer and took out a folder. He re-read the letter on Ministry headed paper, whereby Minister Mendez gave official communication to Recursos Naturais of Brazil's guarantee. Examining Minister Mendez's signature, Ferreira gave a satisfied smile. It had been worth the hours of practice. Things must be done professionally. *Absolutamente.*

Ferreira leafed once more through the two bulky enclosures — the text of the guarantee and the description of the Recursos Naturais project — all on Ministry letterhead. He studied the metal stamps of the Ministry and the Guarantee Section with a critical eye, then tested them several times on a piece of blank paper. He would put them back in their place by 2:00 p.m., at the end of the lunch-break, and no one would be any the wiser. Ferreira grinned. When Cardinal Wolfenberg called him in the afternoon, he'd be thrilled to know that the guarantee was ready.

Like a blacksmith's hammer on the anvil, the stamp banged down on the first of the fifty-two pages, making the desk shake.

In mid-afternoon, the door of Ferreira's office was flung open and Norma appeared in the doorway. With an alarmed expression, she gestured repeatedly towards Marques' former office, where a phone was ringing.

Ferreira ran to the door and shot across the corridor.

"Yes, Your Eminence, I'm glad to confirm that the Rt. Hon. Mendez has signed the guarantee and the attachments this very morning ... No, not immediately, Your Eminence ... A couple of days to protocol the guarantee, after which we'll send it to Recursos Naturais in Manaus ... Yes, naturally, to the attention of Dr. Escobar...."

Ferreira came out of the ministry and set out along the Esplanada dos Ministerios towards Lake Paranoa. The twin towers of Congreso Nacional stood out against a fiery sunset. When he was some two hundred yards from the ministry, he stopped near a phone booth, looked around and went inside.

"*Senhor* Escobar? *Boas tardes.* It's Ferreira ... Yes, it's all ready ... In a couple of days ... The cardinal called me this afternoon ... *Mui bem*, the balance into the same account."

As he left the phone booth, he remembered that the following morning he would have to tell Borges to remove Luis Roberto de Oliveira Lima's name from the ministry's internal directory.

A pity. He'd miss Luis Roberto de Oliveira Lima.

Captain Kunzelman was walking along Via di Porta Angelica at a leisurely pace, every so often stopping in front of a shop window and glancing behind him. Gardenia was following him at a distance of some fifty yards, his camelhair coat draped over his shoulders and the smoke from his cigarette wafting away into vanishing wisps.

Kunzelman turned into a winding alley where washing hung out of the windows and the stink of cat-urine mingled with the aroma of vegetable soup. He stopped in front of a protruding rusty sign, with the drawing of a flask of wine on it. *Osteria da Nando*, read the writing on the window of a door that had forgotten what paint was. Kunzelman disappeared inside. After a short time, Gardenia stopped in front of the tavern, threw his cigarette stub away and went in.

Gardenia walked through the semi-deserted tavern permeated with a penetrating odor of stale wine, and headed for Kunzelman's table in the back corner. A radio was transmitting a soccer match and the commentator's excited voice shattered the sleepy atmosphere of the place.

The innkeeper—triple chin, apron up to his armpits and pencil over his ear—was sitting behind an old-time counter, made of massive wood and topped with white marble. He drained his glass of red, then shuffled over to their table. He wiped the red-and-white checked plastic tablecloth with a rag and took their order.

"... Both the main door to the palace and the front door of the cardinal's private apartment are reinforced," whispered Kunzelmann, his eyes as blue as a Swiss alpine lake. He paused for the innkeeper to leave two large mugs of beer on the table and knocked back half of his in a single gulp. "There are two independent alarm systems, which are switched on from midnight until seven in the morning. *Alles klar?*"

Gardenia nodded, gnawing his cigarette holder thoughtfully. "And the keys?"

Kunzelman laid two different-sized keys on the table. "This is the one to the main door and this is the cardinal's."

"What shall I do to break the alarm systems?"

Kunzelmann took a folded sheet of paper from his breast pocket, opened it and laid it on the table. It was the plan of the Palace of the Holy Office.

"The palace alarm system comes into action two minutes after the door's opened." He pointed a golden pen at the plan. "The switch is here, to the right. *Verstehen Sie?* Just two minutes."

Gardenia slid a thick envelope over the table. Kunzelman opened it with feigned indifference and discreetly counted the bills without taking them out.

"*Zum Wohl,*" Kunzelman said, raising his beer mug.

"*Zum Wohl,*" echoed Gardenia, banging his mug against the captain's.

In the distance, church bells rang.

"Mr. de Saint Clair, Paulette here," said the voice over the intercom. "I've just finished updating the investments in the computer file. Would you mind opening it?"

"Just a moment." Guichard reached for his mouse. The date—Wednesday, November 19, 2007—flashed on the screen. "Okay, Paulette, I've opened it."

"As you can see, as of today the off-shore companies have invested 62,238 billion lire in Italian Treasury bills. We've also bought lira-dollar and lira-Deutschmark options for 21,996 billion lire through the Cranfield Bank."

"I see we're ahead of schedule. "

"Things have turned out to be easier than expected. The lira has been holding fairly steady."

Guichard scribbled a few figures. "Around 7,000 billions of T-bills and 8,000 billions of options remain to be bought. When will you be through?"

"Next Thursday, on November 27, if no problems arise."

After which, all he needed was the go-ahead from Franzese.

"Paulette, if you were here I would kiss you."

A long sigh of relief rose from the intercom. "Wow! I got away with it this time."

Just then Marie Claire poked her head around the door and said that a Signor Gardenia was on the line from Rome.

"… I've done my bit. Now it's your turn," Gardenia said. "Have you figured out how to get rid of our man?"

"Just give me another forty-eight hours."

"I'll be waiting to hear from you."

The notes of Chopin's *Nocturnes,* played by Artur Rubinstein, wafted through the library like a summer breeze. André—his shirtsleeves rolled up, but his dark-gray vest rigorously buttoned over a wine-red silk tie with a barely visible pattern— was polishing the frames of the paintings hanging in the library under Julius's watchful eye. Every time André moved to the next painting, Julius moved along with him.

Guichard sat down on the couch and stretched his legs on the coffee table. For a moment he couldn't help noticing the impeccable crease of his pants and the reflection of light on his black leather shoes. Once, he'd put on a pair of jeans and a cowboy shirt, but André's look had lowered the room temperature. When he'd inquired about those garments a few days later, André had said that the dry cleaners had lost them and that he "had thanked them."

Guichard opened his notepad and began to jot down a few notes. The Inquisitor's parents were dead and only a few distant relatives were left: an urgent call from the Innsbruck University Hospital wouldn't work. Guichard picked up a business card from the coffee table and examined the signature that the cardinal had traced on it. He went over his notes once more and reviewed the ways in which he could use it, after forging it. Eventually he shook his head and crossed out three pages of his notes.

Guichard closed the notepad. Only one possibility was left: the wooden chest hidden inside the mountain. However, the Inquisitor must stay away all night....

"André, imagine someone you didn't know phoned you and told you to meet him at ten o'clock the following evening in a London hotel. What would make you decide to go? Give me the first answer that comes into your head."

"Power, money, sex," said André epigrammatically, going on with his polishing. "No doubt about it, Monsieur le Comte."

"In exactly that order?"

André stopped, turned and looked at Guichard quizzically. "But each is a consequence of the other, Monsieur le Comte. Power generates money, and money buys sex. *C'est la vie, n'est-ce pas?*"

Guichard nodded.

In this case, too, everything boiled down to a question of power, as always. *The wooden chest.* Guichard circled a number, pressing hard on the paper. His Eminence the Inquisitor didn't know it yet, but very soon he'd be making a nice little trip to London. Guichard was about to reach for the phone, when he stopped. Why turn to someone else?

"André, how about a trip to London?"

André turned, stared at Guichard for a moment, then his eyes gleamed. "A dirty trick, Monsieur le Comte?"

A sly smile appeared on Guichard's face.

"No, not simply a dirty trick," André said. "A classic Arsène Lupin-type rip-off, *n'est-ce pas*, Monsieur le Comte?"

"I would rather call it a theatrical performance. Yet worthy of Laurence Olivier, I should say."

André's chest swelled. "And the audience?"

"A cardinal."

André stroked his bandaged head and a scoundrel's smile lit up his face. "When do I leave, Monsieur le Comte?"

37

Guichard and Françoise were sitting at the desk in the library, in front of an open map of the Vatican City and the plan of a building. Julius jumped up onto the desk and crouched down on the map.

"I want to come too, Guichard," she said.

"Am I supposed to laugh?" said Guichard.

"Why? Because I'm a woman?"

"Spare me those women's lib litanies. I don't want anything to happen to you."

"I could say the same thing about you."

"What a way to reason! I've *got* to do it."

"So have I. Can't you see I feel responsible for all this?"

"Nonsense. You have nothing to feel responsible about."

"I know my way around that apartment. I could be of help."

Guichard hesitated. "My answer is no."

Françoise looked at him coldly.

"Oh, drop it!" he said.

Françoise's expression didn't change.

"How did I ever get mixed up with someone like you?"

"Well?"

"*All right, all right!* I must have done something to deserve it."

"It's a question of karma, even if you don't believe me. You were a skunk in your previous lives, and now you have to pay for it."

Before Guichard could think of a suitable answer, Françoise sat down in his lap and wrapped her arms round his neck.

"But every so often karma concedes a truce, even to skunks like you," Françoise murmured in his ear.

"Oh, is that so? And what do skunks like me do during the truce?"

"What do you expect...?"

Guichard picked Françoise up and laid her on the couch. He gave her a lingering kiss and began to undo her blouse.

For a while, Julius watched the scene curled up on the desk. Then he got up, sprang onto the back of the couch and from there onto Guichard's back.

"Julius, there is one too many of us here, and it's not me," mumbled Guichard pushing him away.

§

"*Éminence*, my name doesn't matter," said the voice in French at the other end of the line. "What does matter is that I have something to sell you."

"Something to sell me?" said Cardinal Wolfenberg, fingering his pectoral cross. "And why should I be interested in this purchase?"

"Oh, I've no doubt about that, *Éminence*, none at all. It's a wooden chest."

"*A wooden chest*?"

"Not just any wooden chest," whispered the voice. "A chest that was found a long, long time ago in the Holy of Holies of the Temple in Jerusalem. You understand now, *n'est-ce pas*? Those scrolls, without this chest, are like an umbrella as riddled with holes as a colander."

The cardinal felt a cramp in his stomach. "What do you want from me?"

"*Me*? Nothing. I have reason to believe it's *you* who want something from me. The appointment is in London, in the lobby of the Dorchester Hotel, on Friday evening at 9:30 p.m."

"What makes you think I'll be there?"

"Oh, I am positive you will, *Éminence*. Because if you're not there, I shall sell the information to your competition that same evening and the following day you'll be the laughing stock of the whole planet. Think of the newspaper headlines."

The cardinal swallowed hard.

"I'm certain I'll recognize you by your clothes, *Éminence*," said the voice with a chuckle. "*À très bientôt.*"

The line went dead.

§

A few miles south of Rome along the Via Appia Antica, the traffic vanishes as if by magic. The remains of ancient Roman villas and tombs still flank what was the most important consular road in ancient Rome. Mediterranean pines cast their shadows across the roadway made of large hexagonal blocks of basalt lava. Those shadows issue an order: stop and listen. If the traveler hears that order and obeys, above those stones he will hear the rhythmic tramp of a Roman legion pounding in the air and the roll of the drums that accompanied the triumphal return of the legionaries from their wars of conquest in Africa, Asia, and Gaul.

A little after the Fourth Mile of the Appian Way, not far from the two anonymous "tower tombs," stood a stately private house built of venerable stones, surrounded by a high wall and half-hidden by pines and ivy. The nametag on the entry phone at the gate was blank.

"What, *again?*" said Françoise, sitting on a seventeenth-century Venetian couch and looking up at the coffer ceiling. "But we know the whole thing by heart."

"*I* will be the judge of that, *Madame!*" Gardenia said, his face purple and his chalk breaking in half. He was standing in front of a blackboard, a cigarette alight in his cigarette holder. He wore a smoking jacket with a crest embroidered on the pocket. "May I remind you that we're not going to a fashion show."

The phone rang and Guichard picked up the receiver. "Yes, he's here ... Just a minute." He turned to Gardenia. "It's for you."

"Hello ... yes? ... So we weren't mistaken, then ... No, follow him as far as the airport." Gardenia hung up and looked at Guichard. "His Eminence is on his way to Leonardo da Vinci. Your butler must be a born actor."

Guichard smiled. "That, and much more."

Gardenia went back to the blackboard. "Okay, let's start again," he said, looking askance at Françoise. "So, what time do the Swiss guards change shifts?"

"At midnight," she said.

"Where's the button...?"

Four hours later Gardenia put his chalk down. "I think that will do." He looked at a pendulum clock. It was 11.15 p.m. "Above all," he concluded, "don't underestimate the Swiss guards."

"They always made me think of a Viennese operetta army," Françoise said.

"Well, you're wrong, lady. They are karate experts and train daily at the rifle range—while some other people are at fashion shows."

"For *your* information, I never go to fashion shows!"

There was a sharp metallic click and Guichard and the others turned their heads toward a man dressed in black, a six-foot-three individual weighing well over two hundred pounds, sitting on an Empire-style chair. He had just inserted a magazine into his Smith & Wesson .40; with a practiced hand he fixed a silencer to the barrel of the pistol. He had an impassive deeply lined face. Since the meeting had begun, he had said nothing but a few monosyllables.

His name was Pio Santangelo and he was a professional killer.

§

"Taxi, sir?" asked the liveried doorman at the Dorchester Hotel in London as he opened the rear door of a waiting cab.

"*Merci*," said André, in his impeccable, gray double-breasted suit. He got in.

"*Mon cher ami*, I have decided that this evening I deserve a reward," said André to the taxi driver, an Andy Capp type. He leaned forward and slipped him a ten-pound note. "From your spacious forehead and profile *très distingué*, I can tell you are a gentleman with refined tastes, who undoubtedly knows the right place."

The taxi driver pocketed the money and studied André in the rearview mirror. A lecherous leer appeared on his face. "Leave it to me, guv'nor," he said, winking. *"Oh, la France!* There must be something special in the air, down there. I've always thought that you Frenchmen must have an extra gear."

And you are quite right, you son of perfidious Albion, André thought, leaning back and stroking his moustache.

§

After the man had left, Cardinal Wolfenberg lit a cigar and asked the barman of the Dorchester Hotel to bring him another Remy Martin. He sipped his cognac, then took a deep draw on his cigar. There was something in all this that didn't quite fit. That man seemed too ready to sell his merchandise too cheaply — and too fast. His work at the Holy Office tribunal had helped the cardinal develop a sixth sense. Instead of listening to what people said, he watched their eyes and followed their gestures. He could always understand if someone was lying, and now lies were crawling all around him, like vipers in a shady bush.

What had been the real reason for the meeting, then? That Frenchman had got on his nerves from the very beginning.... The cardinal's cheeks twitched. *You fool!* He looked at his watch, jumped up, put out his cigar with a moment's regret and strode over to the reception desk.

"Can I ask you a favor?" the cardinal said.

"At your service, Your Eminence," said the receptionist, visibly overawed by the cardinal's robes.

"Could you call Heathrow for me and ask for the next flight to Rome?"

"Of course, Your Eminence. If you'd like to make yourself comfortable, I'll let you know as soon as possible."

A few minutes later the girl went up to the cardinal's chair. "You're lucky, Your Eminence. The British Airways flight 497 that was due to leave at 11:15 p.m. will be delayed for technical reasons."

"Are there any seats left?"

"Yes, just one. Would you like me to book it for you?"

"Yes, please. Something very urgent has come up."

"I'll do it straight away. I still have BA Reservations on the line."

Cardinal Wolfenberg looked at his watch. It was 10:50 p.m.

The cardinal walked briskly through the International Departures Lounge at Heathrow Airport and stopped at the BA reservations desk.

The clerk checked on his monitor. "The new departure time of flight 497 is at forty minutes after midnight, Your Eminence."

"The flight takes about two hours, doesn't it?"

"One hour and fifty minutes, Your Eminence."

The cardinal worked out the arrival time and thought that at this time of night it shouldn't take him more than forty minutes by taxi to reach the Vatican City. Then he remembered he had to add on an hour and cursed the Greenwich meridian.

§

St. Peter's Square was deserted. Ghostly banks of fog hovered just above the wet pavement. A sound of footsteps echoed under the Bernini Colonnade and four dark figures passed under the Arco delle Campane. They stopped in front of the main door of the Palace of the Holy Office; with a muffled clanking noise, one of them put his black bag down on the ground.

Gardenia took out his keys and opened the door. A wrought-iron lamp radiated a bluish light, leaving the entrance hall in semi-darkness. Gardenia leapt to his right, pointed his flashlight at the wall and pressed a switch. Then he stooped and moved on, followed by Santangelo, Guichard, and Françoise. They advanced close to the wall, as far as the glass panel of the guards' quarters. Gardenia stretched his neck and peered inside. Without turning round, he signaled to them to crouch down. They crept along below the level of the glass panel until they reached the door.

A faint sound of music was coming from inside.

Gardenia crept past the glass door. Guichard peeped inside. A Swiss guard in his shirtsleeves was sitting at a table with his back towards them, busy polishing a halberd. His orange and blue striped jacket was lying on a chair. The entire sidewall was made of glass paneling, so there was no way they could reach the stairs without being seen. Guichard realized what Gardenia was up to: they had to get rid of the guard. Gardenia reached out his hand towards the door handle...

"Make a move and I'll blow your head off!" whispered Gardenia, aiming his gun at the back of the guard's head.

"Wer zum Teufel –"

Santangelo slapped a strip of sticking plaster over the guard's mouth. He was young, probably not much over twenty, but there was no fear in his eyes, just rage. Guichard grabbed a coil of rope and tied his arms tightly behind the back of the chair.

Gardenia gestured towards the door at the end of the room. Santangelo took out a bottle of chloroform and poured some onto the two pads Guichard was holding out. Gardenia tiptoed to the door and signaled to them to be ready.

The clock on the wall read 2:50.

§

Sitting in his first class seat, Cardinal Wolfenberg looked at the time. It was 1:50 a.m. He put his watch forward an hour.

"What time will we be landing in Rome?" he asked a hostess.

"Our arrival time is estimated at approximately three thirty a.m. local time, Your Eminence."

The cardinal tightened his grip on the armrests of his seat. *Hurry, damn you, hurry.*

§

The two guards were lying on their beds, chloroformed and gagged. Under Gardenia's watchful eye, Guichard and Santangelo finished tying their hands and feet. A smell of sweaty socks hung in the air. The walls were plastered with photographs of Swiss alpine landscapes and blue-eyed girls. The photo of a fair-haired girl wearing a traditional dress carried across it the dedication *Zu Hans, Küsse von Greta.*

They left the guards' quarters, the homicidal stare of the young guard tied to the chair following them. Françoise joined them again. They started up the timeworn stone staircase. A mixture of mustiness and incense filled the air.

§

Cardinal Wolfenberg ran out of the arrival lounge at Leonardo da Vinci Airport towards the waiting queue of taxis.

"You've got to fly faster than the Holy Ghost, do you hear me?" he said, leaning towards the taxi-driver—leather jacket, pony tail and a small ring piercing his nostril.

"What if they stop us, Yer Em'nence?"

"Don't worry, my son." The cardinal clutched his pectoral cross. "If they dare, they will be smitten by biblical wrath."

"Righty-ho, Yer Em'nence. You're the boss—and the Holy Ghost." The taxi driver gave him the thumbs up and grinned. He switched on the meter and shot off with a screech of tires.

The cardinal looked at the dashboard. The speedometer was touching 110 mph. The luminous hands of the clock read 3:50.

§

Guichard sank down in the cardinal's chair and shone his flashlight at the wall. The clock read 4:15 a.m. Françoise and Santangelo took down the last paintings, but no sign of a safe. They'd searched everywhere: storerooms, cupboards.... They'd pulled out drawers, looked under the carpets, the mattresses.... Nothing at all. Where could the wretched Inquisitor have hidden them?

"I don't know what to say," Françoise said. "This is his favorite room. I'm sure they must be in here somewhere."

"What do we do now?" Gardenia asked, standing in the doorway and staring at Guichard.

Guichard didn't answer. He jumped up, threw himself at the bookshelves and started to grab the books, flinging them all over the floor. Nothing. And yet they must be there, somewhere. He could feel it in his bones. Only the left hand side of the shelves remained. He swept away the entire contents of the top shelf with one swing of his arm. He froze, his arm still in the air: the circle of light lit up a cardboard tube, of the type used for storing drawings. He pulled it out and opened it. *His scrolls!*

Guichard unrolled them on the desk. Like elves mad with joy, the Aramaic characters seemed to dance in the flashlight.

A sound came from the entrance. Guichard stiffened. *The steel rods of the main door were sliding back.* Gardenia motioned them to switch off their flashlights. Santangelo, his gun at the ready, dashed across the hallway and hid behind the door of the living room, across from the study. Gardenia took out his gun and stood behind the study door.

Someone turned on the lights in the hallway and the sound of footsteps and muffled voices reached the study.

"Drop the gun or I'll shoot!" Gardenia shouted.

A shot exploded in the hallway. Gardenia cried out in pain and dropped his gun. Santangelo fired a return shot and a stifled cry came from the hallway, followed by a dull thud. Guichard grabbed the pistol that Gardenia had dropped and peered out. The cardinal was in the middle of the hallway, his hands held high. A Swiss guard was stretched out on the floor, clutching his shoulder with a bloodstained hand.

While Gardenia was bandaging the surface wound on his arm and Françoise was binding up the guard's shoulder, Guichard motioned with his gun for the cardinal to go into the study, where he made him sit down at the desk.

"Take a seat, *Your Eminence*," said Guichard, sitting on the edge of the desk. "You were quite right, you know. These days one has got to be very careful, with all the scum roaming around."

Cardinal Wolfenberg kept silent.

"I see that you decided not to purchase the chest, after all. A real pity, for you."

The cardinal went on staring straight ahead, his face disdainful.

"Do you know who I am?"

"Someone who'll end up in jail very shortly."

"Not in the Vatican's, though, for when I'm through with you, the Vatican will only exist in the ads of the real estate agencies."

The cardinal sneered. "You haven't learnt anything about people, have you? We stand for something that no army will ever be able to destroy, let alone a nobody like you."

"We'll see about that." Guichard rummaged in his pockets, and took out the holy image of Saint Nicholas of Myra. "I believe you should have it back, Your Eminence." He slipped it through two buttonholes of the cardinal's cassock. "Saint Nicholas being the patron saint of thieves, it will be of more use to you than to me."

"All this rope wasted on a priest," Santangelo muttered, tying the cardinal to the chair. "It would be quicker to hang him."

"Have no doubt, my son. I'll remember you in my prayers," the cardinal said. His eyes, full of irony, met Guichard's. "Do you really think you'll get out of here with those scrolls? How? Flying?"

Before Guichard could reply, Françoise planted herself in front of her uncle. "So you're the one who didn't know anything about the theft of the scrolls, are you? And you even pretended to be offended!"

"Get out of my sight! You are no longer my niece!" the cardinal shouted, his cheeks quivering and his eyes glaring.

"Don't worry. I've already forgotten I once had an uncle."

"Priests!" Santangelo mumbled again, tying one more knot behind the cardinal's back.

Gardenia's cell phone rang.

"Yes?... *What?* ... Are you sure?... We'll be right there." Gardenia looked at Guichard. "It seems half the Porta Sant'Anna squad's downstairs waiting for us. Time to get a move on."

"Where to?" asked Guichard, slinging the tube over his shoulder.

Gardenia didn't answer, but jerked his head towards the cardinal with a meaningful look.

When all four of them were out on the landing, Gardenia pointed upwards. "The only possible escape is by the roof. Someone's coming to meet us up there," he whispered. "The guards will be here any minute now. Quick!"

They flew up the four flights of stairs, but when they reached the top landing, there was no one waiting for them.

Gardenia gave the door two mighty shoves with his shoulder. It was locked. Heavy footsteps sounded on the stairs below. They looked at each other. The guards were on their way up. Santangelo grasped his gun. Françoise gripped Guichard's arm.

A key turned in the lock.

"*Schnell!*" whispered a man in the doorway, beckoning them in. He was wearing a skullcap and his face was smeared with black all over.

"Kunzelman! Thank God," Gardenia said.

Kunzelman, flashlight in hand, led the way through the palace attic, where dust and cobwebs covered all kinds of things: an early Olivetti, gilded frames, a life-size photograph of Pope Pius XII... Eventually he stopped and shone the flashlight upwards. *A trapdoor.* He climbed the iron rungs, raised the trapdoor and pushed it backward with a clang. He disappeared onto the roof. A moment later Guichard, Françoise and Santangelo were dazzled by his flashlight.

"*Schnell!* Come up!"

A gust of icy wind whipped Guichard's face. Michelangelo's dome shone in the dark, so close that one was tempted to stretch out one's arm and touch it. The roof was very steep, plunging into space at the bottom on both sides. Guichard went last, right behind Françoise. They crawled on their stomachs along the top of the roof, clutching at the curved tiles. Guichard held the strap of the tube tightly under his left arm, and used his right to drag himself along. The icy tiles had numbed his fingertips. There was a sharp crack. Françoise gave a stifled cry and slid down the roof. Guichard flung out his left arm and grabbed her by the hand.

"Keep still! Don't move!" said Guichard.

He'd hardly stopped speaking when something rolled down the roof, the sound fading away far below. *The scrolls.*

"Guichard, it's no good. It's too slippery!"

"Put your other arm up."

"I can't, I'm sliding down. It's no good!"

"Put it up!"

Santangelo had turned around. He stretched his free arm downwards, trying to reach Françoise's hand. *"C'mon, catch hold."*

Françoise tried to find a foothold.

"Stick your hand out, dammit!" Guichard cried, fearing he couldn't hold on much longer.

Françoise's fingertips touched Santangelo's.

Guichard — hoping against hope that the tiles would hold — made a superhuman effort to pull Françoise up a few inches. Santangelo's hand clamped Françoise's and a few moments later she was back up with them.

"Guichard! The scrolls!" said Françoise shaking and clutching Guichard's arm. "It's all my fault."

Guichard held her close and didn't say anything. When he'd thought he wasn't going to be able to hold on to her any longer, the scrolls had no longer mattered.

"And now what?" said Gardenia, looking at Guichard over Santangelo's shoulder.

"Is there any rope left?" Guichard looked first at Santangelo, then at a brick chimney protruding behind the roof.

"There's still one coil," Santangelo said.

"Are you mad?" Françoise tugged at Guichard's arm.

"I've got to go down and see."

"See what?"

"A cardboard tube, five floors down, in the middle of a dark street?" Gardenia said. "Not to mention the guards swarming everywhere."

"Verdammter Dummkopf! Crazy fool!" echoed Kunzelman. "D'you want to ruin us? We've got to get out of here."

As for Santangelo, he simply stared at him. Guichard could see that he had understood, maybe because he'd been the one nearest to him when the accident had happened. Santangelo took out the coil of rope and started to loop it round the chimney.

"The tube hasn't fallen in the street," Guichard said.

"How on earth d'you know?" said Françoise amidst the others' impatient protests.

"If it had, we'd have heard it hit the cobbles."

"From up here?"

Guichard grabbed a chip from the broken tile that had caused Françoise's slip, sat astride the rooftop and tossed it out into space on the courtyard side of the building. A few seconds later they heard a sharp crack, as the fragment hit the cobblestones way below.

After winding the rope twice round the chimney, Santangelo looped one end round his chest, and held the remainder of the rope in his hand. Guichard tied the other end of the rope firmly round his waist and chest. They'd calculated thirty-five feet of rope from the chimney to the edge of the sloping roof.

The moonlight and the spotlights on Michelangelo's cupola lit up the roof, making icy patches gleam here and there. Guichard moved a couple of yards back from where Françoise had slipped and started to slither down. When he was about halfway, he moved across a couple of yards, positioning himself on the path along which the tube had rolled down. His fingers were numb and gusts of wind cut into his face. He looked down. There were still some twenty feet to the edge of the roof.

As he ventured down a bit further, he suddenly lost his grip and slithered downwards. He grabbed the rope, but a burning pain in his hands forced him to let go. As he fell, the lashing of the rope against his back took his breath away. He suddenly found himself stuck, his stomach pressing against the gutter and his feet dangling in mid-air. As soon as he got his breath back, he took hold of the rope again, but yelled with the pain in his raw hands. He tried to pull himself up but it was no good. He tried to swing one foot up onto the gutter, but in vain: he had slid too far down. Suddenly he felt himself being hauled upwards. Standing on the ridge of the roof, Santangelo and Gardenia were pulling him up. For a few seconds he reveled in that exulting ride upwards.

Guichard heard a dull knocking and turned his head. The tube was there, dangling from the gutter.

When he reached the edge of the roof, he motioned Santangelo and Gardenia to stop. He reached out his arm, detached the strap, and clutched the tube to his chest.

Eventually they reached the roof of the building next to the Holy Office. Kunzelman stood up, pulled up a trapdoor, and slipped inside. They followed him. A few minutes later they were going down in an elevator.

"Where are we?" Guichard asked.

"In the Palazzo delle Udienze," Kunzelman said.

"But the street'll be swarming with guards."

"We're going right down to the cellars."

The cellars seemed like a maze, but Kunzelman picked his way through with confidence. At the end of a tunnel, they came to a stonewall: it wasn't possible to go any further. Kunzelman knelt down and started lifting up the stone slabs covering the floor and pushing them aside. A moment later a manhole cover appeared. Kunzelman and Santangelo lifted it. Guichard shone his flashlight inside: an underground passage!

"The tunnel goes under St Peter's Square and runs as far as Via della Conciliazione. The exit is in Italian territory, where the Swiss guards cannot circulate. Follow me," Kunzelman said, lowering himself down.

When they were all inside, Kunzelman said that the tunnel had been dug in the sixteenth century as an escape route for the popes, when things took a turn for the worse. Only a handful of people knew of its existence.

Ten minutes later they reached the end of the tunnel. The first lights of dawn filtered into the tunnel through an iron grating over their heads. Kunzelman passed his flashlight to Gardenia and drew back the bolts that secured the grating. He raised it a few inches, peered outside, then he threw it open.

"The way's clear. Out!" Kunzelman said, standing aside.

"Aren't you coming?" Gardenia asked.

"I'm going back this way. *Alles Gute.*"

When they were outside, the bolts clicked back.

"Better if we go separately," said Gardenia, waving goodbye.

He and Santangelo walked off in opposite directions.

"Signor Santangelo!" Françoise said, rushing after him.

Santangelo turned in surprise.

"Thank you." She stood on tiptoe and kissed him on the cheek.

"My pleasure, *madame*," said Santangelo, touching his cheek.

On the other side of Via della Conciliazione, a pink bar sign began to flash on and off. The shutters began creaking upwards.

"What do you intend to do with those scrolls?" Françoise asked.

"Coffee?" Guichard pointed to the bar.

Françoise glared at him.

Cardinal Wolfenberg put his head in his hands and listened to the rain beating against the windows. He thought of the explanations he'd had to cobble together for the pope and the cardinals of the Curia, to try and explain what had happened at the Holy Office during the night. He couldn't mention the scrolls, because it would have meant admitting they had been in his possession, and explaining why. They couldn't be professional thieves, the pope had said, his eyebrows blacker than ever, because they hadn't touched any of the masterpieces stored in the Holy Office. So what had they been looking for? And why in his private rooms? The cardinal had spoken of an attempt at revenge by one of the theologians investigated by the CDF, but he'd read the doubt in many cardinals' eyes, and in the pope's. The guards had said there was a woman among them: if the Curia had known it was his niece! He flushed with rage. He no longer had a niece.

With a grunt of exasperation, he banged his fist on the desk. No good brooding over it; he had to find a solution. That man hated the Church, now more than ever before. What would he do with those scrolls? The cardinal was petrified at the thought of the scrolls falling into the hands of the press. He jumped to his feet and stood there, motionless. He had to stop him, and without delay. But how? He grimaced and drove that thought away with a gesture of his hand. No, he couldn't do that. Besides, it would serve no purpose: the Frenchman couldn't be alone. What, then? *Destroy the scrolls.* That's what he must do. How? De Saint Clair was sure to conceal them in his house again, but how could he get in there a second time?

The cardinal lit a cigar with a long wooden match. He was about to blow out the match when he froze: he stared at the sinuous flickering of the flame and some characters in Aramaic began writhing inside it. A crafty smile twisted his lips.

He was reaching for the phone when a thought struck him like the vision of the Four Horsemen of the Apocalypse across the sky. *The Ark!* He thought back to Honorius II's suspicions and the report of his meeting with Geoffroy de Saint Clair. Curse the de Saint Clairs! Geoffroy was one of the Templars who'd taken the Ark to Rome. Quite likely he'd discovered where the Ark was hidden. And if that was how things stood, then Guichard de Saint Clair must also know the hiding place.... That soul from hell was plotting to steal the Ark!

The cardinal stubbed out his cigar in the ashtray, grabbed his cloak and strode out of the office.

Cardinal Wolfenberg passed through the Porta di Bronzo, entered the elevator and pressed the button for the third floor. The prefects of the Congregations should be there by now. On the phone, the pope had agreed with him: they had to find a new hiding place for the Ark—and right away. Telling the pope he'd recognized one of the de Saint Clair descendants among the men who'd broken into his apartment had been a real stroke of genius. Now everyone was convinced that the burglars had been looking for clues regarding the Ark's hiding place.

Since the time of Honorius II, the hiding place of the Ark had been the most guarded secret of the Church. Only the pope and a handful of cardinals, he being one of them, had access to the documents that disclosed the exploit of the Templars and the removal of the Ark to Rome. Only the prefects [the cardinals heading the nine Congregations of the Curia] knew the secret. The cardinal thought for a moment of the day when he'd been appointed head of the CDF, when the pope had revealed the secret to him. On bended knee in front of Sergius, he had had to swear on the Gospels that he would carry that secret with him to his grave. The evening of his appointment, the pope had taken him to the Basilica of San Giovanni, and the pope himself had unlocked the crypt under the apse. At the sight of the Ark, he had felt what Moses must have felt in front of the Burning Bush.

The elevator opened and he made his way along the hall leading to the pope's private study. One could sense that something important was in the air: greetings were somehow more deferential, secretaries walked along the corridors more fleetingly, voices were more muffled.

Monsignor Petrov opened the door of the pope's study. The prefects were seated in a circle around the pope's desk, like initiates waiting for the high priest to disclose the Word.

The plan of the Sistine Chapel was spread out on an easel.

§

Habib rubbed his hands together. While waiting for the agents on the night shift, he sat down on the steps of the fountain at the foot of the Thutmose III obelisk. Everything was ready for the following evening. The Mossad had mobilized twenty agents and all the equipment was already at the Israeli embassy in Rome. A special El Al plane was due to land at Leonardo da Vinci airport in just a few hours. They'd take the Ark straight to the airport and send it to Tel Aviv by diplomatic bag.

Three blue vans stopped in front of the basilica. Three priests and two cardinals got out. Four more priests jumped out of the back of the middle van. Habib got to his feet. The priests hurried across the parvis and disappeared inside the basilica. It wasn't possible! He pulled out his cell phone. No, it was just tension playing tricks on him.

He'd just returned the mobile to his pocket when three priests came out of the basilica and stood beside the bronze portals. The other four priests followed close behind, carrying what looked like a wooden packing crate. Judging from the care they were taking, the contents of the crate must be very precious. The two cardinals were walking next to them, giving orders. The priests were carrying the crate on their shoulders by means of two staves. The light of the street-lamps reflected on the staves and a golden gleam dazzled Habib. A flash of lightning lit up the basilica and the statues of the saints shone like ghosts in the darkness. A clap of thunder reverberated in the square.

The Ark!

Habib thought of calling in one of the Mossad commandos to intercept them, but then he shook his head: there was no time. He knew only too well where they were going, and at that time of night it wouldn't take more than a quarter of an hour. There was nothing he could do but follow them. Walking with feigned indifference, Habib made his way to his car, parked some one hundred and fifty yards away from the parvis.

The three priests strode toward the middle van, one opened the back door and two of them disappeared inside. The priests carrying the crate stopped behind the van and pushed the crate inside. Another flash of lightning lit the square and torrential rain started to fall.

There was still some traffic about and Habib was able to keep one car between him and the three vans: the pelting rain helped. When they arrived in sight of St. Peter's, he slowed down and parked at the end of Via della Conciliazione.

He climbed out of the car, his eyes on the three vans driving by the Egyptian obelisk. His hair clung to his head and his overcoat was drenched. He shielded his eyes with his hand.

The three vans stopped in front of the steps leading to St. Peter's. They must have been expected because the doors of the cathedral opened. The priests carried the crate across the parvis and disappeared inside the basilica. The doors shut behind them.

Lightning shot across the sky above Michelangelo's dome and a deafening clap of thunder shook St. Peter's Square. *The wrath of Jehovah!*

Habib pounded his fists again and again on the roof of his car. Then he took out his cell phone and dialed a number.

38

Trill... Trill... Trill...

Guichard groped about in the dark until he found the light switch: a quarter past three. He lifted the receiver.

"... If I find out who talked, I'll strangle him with my bare hands," Levy said. Then, after a meaningful pause, he added: "I'm ready to swear by my agents."

"Oh, give it a rest. It means as much to us as it does to you for the Ark to return to Jerusalem. Why else d'you think we came to you?"

"Who then?"

"The point now is not who, but where. You need a bike to move around in St. Peter's."

"The answer is in the Old Testament."

"Levy, I'm in no mood for biblical riddles at three o'clock in the morning."

"The Sistine Chapel is exactly the same size as King Solomon's Temple: one hundred and thirty-four feet long and forty-four feet wide. Convert that into cubits and you get the measurements given in the Old Testament."

Guichard was speechless. Levy must be right. There was a way to get confirmation, though. "I must make a call to Rome. I'll get back to you in a few hours."

He dialed Gardenia's number. The Doctor answered with a yawn. Guichard told him what had happened. Gardenia promised he would contact Kunzelman right away and that he would call back.

He called back at nine.

"I've just come off the phone with Kunzelman," Gardenia said. "This morning the Vatican closed the Sistine Chapel until further notice. Officially it's for repairs, but there's something odd about the whole matter."

"In what way?"

"Kunzelman says it's different from usual. Too much secrecy. People talking under their breath, furtive glances.... Not to mention the fact that neither he nor the other Swiss Guard officers were informed, nor did anyone ask them to organize extra shifts."

"Let's suppose they have hidden it in the Sistine Chapel. But where?"

"Kunzelman has his spies," Gardenia said. "It's the area round the main altar."

No one could have said for sure, but Guichard would have bet anything that the main altar in the Sistine Chapel was in exactly the same position as the Holy of Holies had been in King Solomon's Temple.

He dialed Levy's number.

"... That d-d-declaration's ready," said the first voice.

"Good. Give me a time and a place," replied the second voice. "Better a crowded place."

"How long will you need to cr-cr-credit the b-b-balance?"

"It'll be through tomorrow morning."

"Let's make it t-t-tomorrow afternoon, then," the first voice said. "In Via P-P-Piemonte, about halfway up, there's an alehouse c-c-called Keller. How about meeting there at 5.00 p.m.?"

Giancana yawned and stretched. He pushed the rewind button and listened to the tape. Why wonder? Everyone cheated in this world, even stammerers.

He keyed in a number on his cell phone. "Alfio? It's me. I think we're getting there ... Yes, tomorrow afternoon, in an alehouse ... Okay, I'm coming."

Giancana took off his headphones and got out of the back of the van. He climbed into the driver's seat and started the engine.

The Keller alehouse looked like a Bavarian *Bierhalle*, with the jukebox playing operetta nonstop, polished brass and waiters wearing white aprons and always on the go carrying big mugs of beer and platters of Tyrolean smoked ham. Sitting at a table on a balcony, Giancana focused the zoom on a corner table on the ground floor.

The professor of mineralogy—a wart on the nose, full lips like those of a Penthouse model and stumpy, hairy fingers— swallowed half a platter of smoked ham in one mouthful and gulped down a long draft of beer. He wiped off the foam with the back of his hand and produced an envelope, which he passed to Zergas... *click*... Zergas took out a sheet of paper from the envelope and read it... *click*... He slipped his hand into his breast pocket... *click* ... He held out an envelope to the professor... *click*... The professor peeped inside and passed his tongue over his lips... *click*... He nodded, then swallowed the remainder of the smoked ham and drained his mug of beer.

Look at that greedy son of a bitch, thought Giancana. He's pocketing 800 million lire and acts as if he couldn't care less. I bet he's even stopped stammering.

A few minutes later the two of them shook hands... *click*... The professor stood up and left, busy picking his teeth with his little finger. Zergas finished his coffee. He put the sugar wrappers in the ashtray, wiped a coffee stain off the table and, with a grimace of disgust, put the professor's knife and fork back on the platter. He stood up and made his way to the exit.

§

"Yes? ... When will the photos be ready? ... Well done Tincani," Tancredi said.

He dialed the number in Sicily. While the phone was ringing at the other end, he thought of what was due to happen in the next few days.

§

At 11:30 the same evening the phone rang in Guichard's house.

"Sell off all the T-bills and transfer the money to the offshore accounts," Astarita said. "How long will it take?"

So it was just a matter of days.

"Three banking days," Guichard said. "Next Monday, December 1, the lire will be in the accounts."

Franzese must have already told the cardinal. Guichard had no doubt that the Vatican would buy a fair amount of dollars over the following two days—$4,250 million, to be precise—A stifled laugh came from the other end of the phone.

"Can I be in on the joke too?" Guichard said.

"Tell me, what were you up to Saturday night in the Palace of the Holy Office?"

"I repossessed something that belongs to me. Why do you ask?"

"Oh, nothing. Just know that your friend the cardinal called Franzese and asked him to set fire to your house."

The following morning Guichard signed the coded faxes instructing the Milan brokers to sell 70,000 billion lire of Treasury bills and to transfer the proceeds to the offshore accounts.

As Archbishop Dyakonov dictated the figures, Cardinal Wolfenberg tapped them out on his calculator.

"This is the situation as of yesterday, November 25," said the substitute, handing a few sheets to the cardinal. "As you can see, we've already raised the equivalent of $3,610 million—$280 million from Brazil alone—And all in lire, as you requested."

The cardinal tore off the strip from the calculator and checked the figures against the sheets. "Hmm, less than I thought."

"But much more than *I* expected. There's still $640 million missing, though."

"Who's to say more isn't on its way?"

"Nothing's come through for several days now. Rolf, I'm worried."

The intercom buzzed.

"What is it, Monsignore? How many times—"

"I have Mr. Franzese on the line, Your Eminence. He says it's urgent."

"I'm keeping my promise, Your Eminence," Franzese said. "Tell APSA to sell lire and buy dollars. Starting from tomorrow morning and no later than next Tuesday. Remember: *not* a day later."

"*Next Tuesday?* Listen, Tano, I need another ten days at the very least."

"That's impossible."

Franzese's tone left no room for argument. The line went dead.

Cardinal Wolfenberg hung up and looked at the substitute. "That's it."

"... But it's too soon!" the substitute said. "What are we going to do about the $640 million missing?"

"We'll make the sum up ourselves."

"*Us?* Have you gone mad?"

"Franzese's plan can't fail. Believe me, it's a safe investment. Besides, it's only for a few days."

"But what if something went wrong?"

"Leave it to me."

The substitute stared at the cardinal in silence.

As soon as the substitute had shut the door behind him, the cardinal called Monsignor Petrov and told him he had to meet His Holiness straight away.

Half an hour later, Cardinal Wolfenberg was hurrying across St. Peter's Square, his cloak wrapped round him and his hand raised to protect his face against the icy wind.

Paulette hurried along through the reception area of the Hotel Krone in Zurich. She stopped in front of a notice board. Board meeting of Columbus Chemicals AG, Conference Room C, she read. She went to the reception desk and asked for directions.

Paulette walked briskly into Conference Room C, her high heels clicking on the parquet. Twenty-two pairs of eyes looked in her direction. She was wearing a pin-striped blue suit with a skirt extending to just above the knee, which enhanced her slender figure and perfect legs. She sat down on the only vacant chair at one end of the horseshoe-shaped table, opened her briefcase and delicately took out a pack of transparencies. She put on a pair of stylish, transparent-framed glasses.

"And now that *everyone's* here," said Kovacs, sitting at the center of the table next to *Avvocato* Ricci—aka Rasputin—the managing director of Columbus, "we can finally get on with the item on the agenda, that's to say the acquisition of the petro-chemical plants of CIP in southern Italy." He turned to Paulette. "Miss Janviers, the floor is yours."

Paulette stood up, went over to the slide projector and laid the first transparency on the glass…. Muttering rippled through the conference room.

The last transparency appeared on the screen. Amidst a background of stifled muttering and exclamations of disbelief, Paulette directed her luminous pointer at the figures.

"… and so we arrive at a final value of *minus* $27 million," she said. "Which is what CIP will have to pay Columbus Chemicals—and not vice versa—if Columbus is to take over these plants. Any questions?"

A silence charged with tension descended on the conference room. Ricci's eyes had narrowed to slits. Rasputin was slowly gnawing at the earpiece of his glasses.

"Allied Petroleum always sticks to its contracts." Kovacs got to his feet. "In accordance with our commitments, I hereby in-vite the Columbus Chemicals board directors appointed by Al-lied Petroleum to vote in favor of this takeover. On condition that CIP pay Columbus Chemicals $27 million, naturally."

The eleven Allied board directors raised their hands, whereas none of the CIP directors made a move. Rasputin had stopped gnawing at the earpiece of his glasses and sat still.

Kovacs turned to Ricci. "Clause 21 of the contract speaks clearly," he said, stony-faced. "Do you realize the consequences of a vote of eleven-to-eleven on a take-over proposal?"

"And *we* should vote for nonsense like this?" Ricci said.

"CIP can always go to arbitration."

"Arbitration will only be the beginning!" Ricci jumped to his feet and pointed his forefinger at Kovacs. "You bunch of crooks!"

Totally unruffled, Kovacs looked at Ricci. "Gentlemen, may I remind you that, in cases like this, the contract provides for unilateral withdrawal." He looked around the table. "I'm sorry to inform you that Allied Petroleum intends to exercise this right, and so we hereby withdraw from Columbus Chemicals. The meeting is adjourned. Good luck, everyone."

As Kovacs turned to leave, the directors of the two sides jumped to their feet and started shouting at each other.

Paulette gathered her papers together and headed for the exit. When she came out of the Krone Hotel, the fog was lifting. She paused in front of Greider in Bahnhofstrasse to look at a Valentino dress, then she went into a Kaffeehaus and ordered a *Kaffee mit Sahne*. She took her cell phone out of her handbag and dialed a number.

"... At this moment, they're still inside paying one another compliments," she said.

"Business life: what a thrill," Guichard said. "*Bravo*, Paulette."

"Bravo to me? Bravo to that son of a bitch who had the idea of Clause 21. For a contract that lasted just six weeks, Kovacs has cashed in $500 million from CIP in exchange for tons of coal full of sulfur. You don't know who that could have been, by any chance?"

"Um, the usual fog in Zurich?"

At Sergius I's request, on the morning of Thursday November 27 a grim-faced Father Cafiero called the directors of the Manus Domini foundations and ordered them to transfer the *initiati*'s contributions to the currency accounts of IOR, the Vatican bank, at KBS in Zurich.

By 5:00 p.m. on Friday, the foundations credited a total of 6,137 billion lire to the currency accounts of IOR, instructing KBS to convert the whole amount into US dollars when the market opened the following Monday.

§

"But... Your Holiness, $640 million corresponds to eighty percent of our lire-denominated securities," said Cardinal Ortega, head of APSA, standing up as soon as he heard the pope's voice on the phone. "Has Your Holiness considered the risk of such a divestment? ... I see ... But ... Naturally I'll do what Your Holiness orders ... By Tuesday December 2? ... Of course, Your Holiness."

At ten o'clock on Thursday, November 27, Monsignor Griffith signed the faxes addressed to the banks managing APSA's securities portfolio. The faxes ordered the banks to sell off the equivalent of $640 million worth of lire-denominated bonds and convert the proceeds into US dollars, to be credited to the IOR currency accounts in Zurich.

On the morning of Tuesday December 2, Monsignor Griffith received the last fax from the KBS in Zurich, informing him that the accounts showed an overall balance of $4,250 million. Monsignor Griffith went to the safe, took out the coding instructions, and sat down in front of his computer.

> "We hereby order you to credit $4,250 million to Sociedad Amazonica do Recursos Naturais at Banco do Brasil, in Manaus, checking account number 400-3864-700892... "

A few minutes later, he was knocking at Cardinal Ortega's door.

Cardinal Ortega read the fax, shook his head and heaved a deep sigh. He signed it with an unsteady hand.

"I don't envy that signature," Monsignor Griffith said. "Your Eminence, I have to tell you something you won't like." He paused. "I've decided to leave the Church."

"What? But... but why?"

"For what that fax stands for. I've reached the conclusion that one can serve God better by staying out of the Church."

"I see. However, the men of the Church remain men, Monsignore, and their errors cannot touch the Church per se. Have you thought of this?"

"Your Eminence, with all the respect I owe you, I'm no longer willing to listen to this kind of reasoning. Society is no longer what it was at the time of the Sea of Galilee. Of what use is the Church if it's incapable of finding the strength to change with society? Here we're facing two thousand years of errors, and the volte-face of the Slavic Pope and of this pope to the guidelines of Vatican II proves what I'm saying. The Church is *also* made of men, Your Eminence, and men like these haven't got anything more to say to anyone."

"Monsignore, I would like to remind you that this is also the Church that produced men like Cardinals Arns, Lorscheider, Landázuri.... You know I'm a close friend of Cardinal Missiroli, don't you?"

"Yes, I do...."

"Thanks to Cardinal Missiroli, we're on the eve of facts that will gravely upset the Church, but facts that will greatly benefit Her too. Monsignore, we need men like you at our side."

"What do you mean, Your Eminence? What facts?"

"Do I have your word that you won't mention it to anyone?"

"Of course you have my word."

The cardinal disclosed to Monsignor Griffith the facts he had referred to.

"Your Eminence... it's unbelievable. I don't know what to say."

"Will you stay now?"

"I will."

Tancredi looked around in the office of the deputy prosecutor of Rome. A stuffy smell hung in the air. The green linoleum flooring was ripped off in several places. Heaps of papers with orange covers were piled up everywhere, even on the metal filing cabinets — all rigorously mouse-gray. Rolls of toilet paper and plastic bottles of mineral water were lined up on the windowsill.

The deputy prosecutor finished reading Zergas's files, then studied the photos of the meeting between Zergas and the professor of mineralogy. The double chin, the large, watery eyes, and the egg-shaped head with a few surviving hairs clinging to the top gave the prosecutor a bovine air, enhanced by the candy he was sucking noisily. He scratched his cheek with a black chipped ruler.

"Hmm, it's already six p.m.," the deputy prosecutor said, glancing at his watch.

"You only have to make one phone call to block Zergas," Tancredi said.

"Don't worry. A rude awakening awaits Zergas tomorrow at the crack of dawn. But I have to withdraw lots of passports and issue dozens of notices of criminal proceedings. You've got to stop the paper from going to press. I need time."

The way the deputy prosecutor had said those last words worried Tancredi. His evasive expression and bulging eyes told him not to trust him.

"Even if I wanted to, I couldn't stop it," Tancredi said. "We've taken special precautions, and the paper's being printed at this very moment. You'll never find out where."

"Legally, Mr. de Santis, I can stop you any time I want to," said the deputy prosecutor with a squelchy suck.

"You're mistaken. We're doing the printing elsewhere."

"Why do you persist in not collaborating?"

"Who with? Should I stop everything just to allow you to hit whoever you want?"

"Remember who you're talking to. I'm a judge, not a politician.

"What's the difference?"

"I don't like you, De Santis. You journalists are a dangerous breed."

"The feeling's mutual," said Tancredi, standing up. "You judges are as much to blame as the politicians and the Church for all this shit."

As soon as Tancredi left, the deputy prosecutor dialed a number.

"... So I can nail Accardo down, but there's no way to stop the journalist," he said.

"If tomorrow morning he prints his paper, tomorrow afternoon trains and airplanes will be taken by storm," said a voice.

"I'll have the passports of the top men of the Coalition withdrawn straight away.

"It's not just them. We need evidence to put all those filthy Communists out of circulation."

"A night in Regina Coeli—in a cell with a couple of nasty homosexuals—and they'll be reciting the Gospels by heart."

§

Wearing a dressing gown and sunk in an armchair, Accardo opened a rack of audiocassettes: Federico Garcia Lorca's Selected Poems. He inserted a cassette into a tape recorder, then resumed flipping through the papers his secretary gave him each day to take home.

> "A las cinco de la
> tarde. Eran las cinco en
> punto de la tarde..."
> [At five in the after-
> noon. It was exactly
> five in the afternoon...]

The phone rang, a blue light flashing. Accardo grunted and reached for it.

"Leo, we've got a problem," said the minister of the interior. "The general prosecutor of Rome called me here at home half an hour ago. You know what? Tomorrow, he's going to file a request for authorization at the House to start legal proceedings against you and against a number of—"

"Legal proceedings against *me*?" Accardo laughed. "It's like Samson shouting *'Let me die with all the Philistines!'* But the last Samson I heard about is the one in the Bible—and, from what I hear, his health can't be too good."

"Leo, it's a serious matter."

"And the charges?"

"Corruption and private interest in office. He wouldn't tell me anything more. No wonder: that gowned swine sides with the opposition...."

> "Ay que terribles cinco
> de la tarde! Eran las
> cinco en todos los relo-

jes !" [Horrifying five
in the afternoon ! The
stroke of five on every
clock!]

The minister told Accardo he had called an informer of his right away at the public prosecutor's office in Rome. In the afternoon, the journalist Tancredi de Santis — "Do you remember ? That pain in the ass at the *Voce Indipendente*" — had called on a deputy prosecutor and he had been sitting in his office for over two hours. Right after De Santis had left, the bar had suddenly emptied and the offices on the top floors had started to work with their doors shut tight. All the informer had managed to learn so far was that the general prosecutor was going to issue notices of investigation against some eighty politicians and business people, and that the prime minister and his party were at the top of the list.

"Yo quiero ver aqui los
hombres de voz dura.
Los que doman caball-
los y dominan los
rios... A qui quiero yo
verlos. Delante de la
piedra..." [I want to
see here the men with
harsh voices. Tamers of
horses, subduers of
rivers... I want to see
them here. Here at the
stone...]

"What proof can they have?" said Accardo.
"This I don't know, but they must have something."
"If you were a journalist, and you had found out something important, would you tell a judge about it?"
"Not before publishing the news."
"And neither would I."

"However, I doubt whether that journalist called at the deputy prosecutor's office just to have a five-o'clock tea. What are we going to do, Leo?"

"Let me think about it."

"Well, think fast. Remember: you're not the only one involved."

"I'll call you back in a while."

Accardo took his glasses off and cleaned the lenses with the edge of his dressing gown. He took hold of his pipe and began rhythmically tapping its bowl against the palm of his hand.... He reached for the phone.

> "Dite a la luna che venga, que no quiero ver la sangre de Ignacio sobre la arena. Que no quiero verla!..."
> [Tell the moon to come, I refuse to see the blood of Ignacio on the sand. No, I refuse to see it!...]

§

At first Zergas didn't know what had awakened him. He was about to reach out for the phone when he realized it was the doorbell ringing. He turned on his bedside light. Five o'clock. Who the devil could it be at such an unearthly hour! Giovanna muttered something and turned over in bed.

He threw on his dressing gown and hurried to the front door, just as someone started hammering on it. He looked through the peephole. *Jesus!*

"Signor Antigono Zergas?" said one of the three police officers in blue and gray uniform, holding out two sheets of paper full of official stamps. "We have a warrant for your arrest and a permit to search the premises."

§

On the morning of Monday, December 1, *La Voce Indipendente* distributed a special edition of 100,000 copies, compared with its usual circulation of 35,000. By ten o'clock they had all sold out and the newspaper was bombarded with requests for further copies. In the space of a few hours, Tancredi de Santis became one of the most reputable names in world journalism.

Tancredi went into Quilici's office and leaned over his shoulder to read the Reuters news appearing on the screen.

> "Antigono Zergas was arrested in his house at dawn today ... The public prosecutors in Rome and Milan have so far issued eighty-nine notices of proceedings to top names in the business world and in politics, including Prime Minister Accardo ... The law courts are seeking authorization to proceed against forty-three Members of Parliament ... Unnamed sources in the offices of the law courts in Milan say that the public prosecutor has already requested the Swiss authorities to investigate some suspicious bank accounts...."

Quilici raised his eyes from the screen and beat his chest repeatedly like a gorilla. Then he began pirouetting nimbly around the room, singing in a tenor voice: "*Oh, what a beautiful morning, oh what a beautiful day... Everything's going my way.*" He went over to a filing cabinet with an ice bucket on it containing a bottle of Dom Perignon. He uncorked the bottle, filled two glasses and handed one to Tancredi.

"We've really strung them up by the balls," Quilici said, raising his glass.

"Rodolfo, you should have been a poet," Tancredi said, clinking glasses.

When Tancredi went back to his office, he sat down at his desk and dialed a number.

"Stella? Hi, this is Tancredi. I'm calling to confirm those three reservations on the Egypt Air flight from Rome to Cairo leaving this Saturday morning...."

Tancredi tilted his chair back and stretched out his legs on the desk. Basking in southern sunshine, he leaned his head against Carla's legs, while the felucca glided silently over the Nile off Luxor.

§

Sitting at his desk, Franzese was looking at the front page of *La Voce Indipendente* that showed a picture of Zergas and Serrano exchanging envelopes. Astarita was on his feet, leaning over a computer screen, his gaze fixed on the text scrolling on it. He clicked a mouse and the whirring of a printer wafted through the room.

"Look at this." Astarita handed the printed sheet to Franzese.

> "The US Department of Justice and Wall Street authorities have opened an inquiry into Allied Petroleum in San Francisco, in connection with the Italian bribes scandal ... On Wall Street, Allied shares have lost nine percent. The Italian lira has dropped by six percent against the main currencies...."

"Call Guichard," Franzese said.

Françoise lit an incense stick, crouched on the sofa and tried to concentrate on her report for the Louvre concerning a forged Modigliani. But that unicorn kept whirling on the pages. She let her thoughts wander with the coils of smoke.

First the rebec, then the medallion, and in the end the photograph of Rennes-le-Château.... She thought back to the disappearance of the medallion during the séance at Kamilla's and to its mysterious materialization in that bluish halo, with the unicorn spinning in a circle around on itself and eventually sucked up in a whirlwind....

"Discover thou his secret, and he will discover himself," the being had written across the steamed-up mirror.... *"What does a lovesick woman want?"* Corinne had said. *"The return of the beloved."* ... *"Spirit, what do you want from Françoise?"* Kamilla had said, then adding: *"She gave a touching speech ... but she didn't answer my question."*

Françoise thought back to that voice, melancholic and hard, that had spoken in medieval French—the voice of a woman who didn't give up. But how did Guichard come into it? *"...I see and hear things you wouldn't even conceive of in your wildest dreams."*

Her thoughts kept whirling incessantly, like that unicorn. *The unicorn.* She'd always thought of the medallion as an object, without ever dwelling on the unicorn. In the Middle Ages, when people believed in its existence, the unicorn had represented an ideal of purity and perfection.... *Discover thou his secret....* But perhaps she'd been wrong from the very beginning, and the real secret was not the chest hidden inside the mountain, but a secret of Guichard's that had to do with the unicorn. What was the unicorn hiding?.... She thought of the straight horn of the unicorn.... The Third Eye Chakra!

A rustle came from the bedroom.

"Oh, no!" Françoise stood up, turned on the lights in the hallway and made her way to the bedroom. She stood in the doorway, motionless, but couldn't hear the faintest noise. She turned on the light.

The bed was strewn with several of her clothes, and the doors of the closet were wide open. The veins of her temples began throbbing wildly. She went closer to the bed and crossed a cold spot. She stopped and thought of the being, when it had appeared in front of her.... *And now the clothes.*

Forcing herself not to run, Françoise went back to the living room and dialed a number.

"Corinne? Can you put me up for a few days? ... No, but I can't explain at the moment ... Thank you. I'll take just the bare minimum and I'll be with you in half an hour."

She hung up. She knew she wasn't alone.

39

Tancredi opened his car door. Carla hadn't seemed surprised when he'd phoned to tell her that the three of them were going out to dinner to celebrate.

"Mr. De Santis?" said a voice from behind him.

Tancredi turned round, but by the time he realized what was happening it was already too late. The gun looked like a toy. The muffled sound of the shot reminded him of the pop of the champagne bottle that Quilici had uncorked shortly before. He felt a sharp pain in his chest and his legs buckled. As he fell, Carla's and Simona's faces drifted away from him, until they disappeared into a white mist.

He slipped down into emptiness.

Cardinal Wolfenberg woke up with a start. He had the impression the night had been shorter than usual. The phone was ringing. His alarm clock said 5:40.

"Who is it?" He yawned.

"Rolf, it's Markus. Something awful has happened."

"Tell me! What is it?"

"It's Cardinal Missiroli.... He's dead. They found him half an hour ago."

"*Dead?* How? Have you called Dr. Veronelli?"

"Veronelli says the whole thing is rather odd."

"Get to the point, for God's sake! What do you mean 'odd'?"

"Veronelli suspects that... well... that he was poisoned."

"*Poisoned?*"

"The symptoms are quite suspicious: bluish lips, pinpoint pupils, vomit...." the substitute said.

"Did he rule out a heart attack?"

"Absolutely."

"Whoever would want to see him dead?" the cardinal said, almost to himself.

"Even the two of us, for that matter."

"Let's reflect a moment. Who knew what Missiroli was up to?"

"You know who. Besides you and me... His Holiness, Monsignor Petrov and... maybe Father Cafiero—if those rumors Cardinal Zacarias told you about in Manaus reached him too, which is likely to be the case."

"Don't forget the Via Veneto boys," the cardinal said.

"What are you getting at?"

"Have you really got no suspicions?"

"What do you mean? You *surely don't think...* and anyway, what would have been his motive?"

"Money is everything to him. A split in the Church would have meant a drastic cut in Manus Domini's revenues. Is that not a valid motive?"

"Couldn't it have been the CIA?"

"It may well have been their hand that cast the stone, but they were quick to withdraw it, as befits their style. Who could have told Father Cafiero? Think about it! Joint Affairs must have found out about Missiroli's plan, and at a moment like this, with our alliance practically concluded, they needed a strong Church."

A long silence followed at the other end of the line.

§

A press conference called at just two hours' notice by Dr. Vallanco-Torres, head of the Press Office of the Vatican, was an unmistakable sign: something serious must have happened at the Vatican.

When Vallanco-Torres announced the death of the secretary of state—from a heart attack—there was a moment of consternation in the packed Vatican pressroom. Then the pope's spokesman was bombarded with questions. When one of the journalists asked if a post-mortem would be carried out, Vallanco-Torres' reply was a sharp "No." There were no doubts whatsoever about the circumstances of His Eminence's death, he declared. Besides, Canon law did not allow post-mortems. Then Vallanco-Torres rushed out of the pressroom, unruffled, ignoring the barrage of questions shouted at him by the journalists.

The next day, the following headline appeared in *La Repubblica*:

"Death of Cardinal Missiroli: Remember John Paul I in 1978? The List of Vatican Mysteries Lengthens"

France 2 broadcast some pictures received by satellite from the United States. Kovacs answered with a curt "No comment" to the journalists' barrage of questions, turning his face away. Then it was the Rome correspondent's turn, with an update on the bribery scandal and the killing of the journalist Tancredi de Santis. The reporter said the police had no doubts about the link between the scandal and the murder. How had the Italian reporter managed to find out? Or had someone put him on to it?

Guichard stopped listening. He remembered that cigarette stub glowing in the dark, and Franzese's words: "*The Allied-CIP affair will explode in his hands and set off our plan. What's important is that he should never learn who lit the fuse.*" If things were as Guichard suspected, it wouldn't be long before someone called him, which would enable him to find out the truth.

Just as pictures of Carla De Santis leaving the morgue in Rome appeared on the screen, the phone rang.

"We're there at last," Astarita said. "Start buying the day after tomorrow. How many days will it take?"

"Five will be enough," Guichard said. "This is rather a coincidence, isn't it?"

"What do you mean?"

"I'm referring to what happened in Italy today. Most convenient."

There was a long pause on the other end of the phone.

"When you needed help at the Vatican, you told me not to ask any questions," Astarita said. "Now it's my turn."

"But still you asked me one, just the same."

Silence.

"Did you have anything to do with the death of that journalist?"

"Nothing whatsoever. Believe me."

Astarita sounded sincere.

"I want you to do me a favor," Guichard said.

"It depends on the favor."

"From my fees, deduct ...."

"I've always thought that deep down you were an idealist," Astarita said when Guichard was through.

"Me an idealist? Idealists are fanatics who always end up leaving a trail of blood behind them."

"What does this gesture mean, then?"

"I just follow my instincts, and let others pontificate about great ideals."

Geoffroy and Guichard had believed strongly in honor, glorious deeds, in leaving something behind them, although it couldn't be said they had been repaid for their deeds. There'd been a time when Guichard's father had firmly believed in things like the state and the Church, but he, too, had been badly repaid for it. And now that journalist. Guichard thought of the Kovacs, the Accardos, the Wolfenbergs, the Franzeses.... Where did the Lodge place itself, with reference to those two extremes? And he himself?

Dost thou mingle the sacred with the profane? said the Voice.

Is revenge something you can call "sacred"? Guichard said.

Canst thou think of a more noble deed?

An exploit, to be called noble, has to spring from a deep sense of justice. Is our revenge the product of *that* sense of justice?

Wouldst thou dare insinuate the contrary? thundered the Voice.

I'm only wondering if this is not just a revenge of the de Saint Clairs.

Traitor! Thou art denying the blood of the de Saint Clairs! Apart from Arno, thou art forgetting the torture and death of thousands of innocent people.

Revenge at any cost? Even if innocent persons suffer the consequences? It's an endless spiral.

Is not the wickedness of men also an endless spiral? said the Voice. *Every epoch hath its Inquisition, but let each Inquisition know that every epoch hath its avenger too. If we were to turn the other cheek, every epoch would have ten, one hundred, one thousand Inquisitions.*

With his mind's eye, Guichard continued to see the pictures of Carla de Santis leaving the morgue. Didn't letting people like that journalist get involved make him all too similar to the Kovacs, the Accardos, the Wolfenbergs and the Franzeses?

One after another, Guichard signed the coded faxes with instructions to sell the first 14,000 billion lire. He checked them again one last time. The faxes were addressed to the London branches of the offshore banks, advised two days before. Thanks to the concentration of the transaction in London, sales would be simultaneous, thus avoiding the lags due to the different time zones involved.

Guichard left his office and strode along the corridor into Paulette's office. "Off we go, Paulette," he said, handing her the faxes. He checked the time: it was 8:15 a.m. GMT.

Half an hour later, the London dealing rooms of the banks started to buy dollars and D-marks against lire in a ratio of two to one. Lira sales hit a foreign exchange market already bearish on the currency. Since 9:00 a.m., the Bank of Italy had started to draw on their own currency reserves, selling D-marks and dollars up to an equivalent of 10,000 billion lire; notwithstanding this, that day the lira fell seven percent against the main currencies, and the dollar closed at 1,819 lire. By Wednesday afternoon, the market had perceived that the attack on the lira was unprecedented. "The run on the lira is going far beyond the usual speculation triggered off by a political crisis," reported an Associated Press release at 5:20 p.m.

On Wednesday evening, the lights in the dealing rooms of the main financial centers, from Frankfurt to London, from Zurich to New York, stayed on late. The dealers were planning their strategies for a Thursday that promised to be hot.

At 8:30 a.m. the following day, Guichard ordered his banks to sell a further 14,000 billion lire. Then he went straight to the foreign exchange room, glanced at the clocks displaying the time around the world and sat down in front of a Reuters screen next to Jean-Paul, the head dealer.

"Have they realized what's going on?" Guichard said, pointing to the dealers.

"They would have to be blind not to."

"Jean-Paul, I need to know what the Bank of Italy's up to."

Jean-Paul stood up and walked from one desk to another, exchanging a few words with the traders. Shortly afterwards, they were all on the phone staring at their screens.

"The Bank of Italy is selling dollars and D-marks," said Jean-Paul, sitting back next to Guichard.

"Yet the 'bid-ask' spread for dollar-lire has already risen to 400 basis points." Guichard pointed at his screen. It was 11:10. "The Bank of Italy doesn't seem inclined to bleed itself dry. What will it do now?"

"It will seek help."

"From the Bundesbank?"

"I'm afraid so."

Guichard stared silently at his screen.

At lunchtime, the governor of the Bank of Italy called first the governor of the Bundesbank, and then the governors of the other main European central banks. Starting at 1:10 p.m., the Bundesbank and the Banque de France joined forces with the Bank of Italy to sell dollars and D-marks against lire. At 5:00 p.m. the 'bid-ask' spread for dollar-lire had fallen to 200 basis points.

"Now we're playing against the Bundesbank," Jean-Paul said, giving Guichard a meaningful look. "Today the lira only lost three percent."

Guichard didn't say anything.

On Friday morning, Guichard entered the dealing room at 7 a.m. Jean-Paul and Paulette were already there, their heads bent over a screen. Guichard joined them. It was an AFP release. The impact of the Italian bribery scandals was rapidly worsening, and public opinion and the opposition were not only demanding the immediate resignation of the government, but also the dissolution of the parties involved in the scandals. The Italian crisis had filled the day's editorials in *Le Figarò*, the *Financial Times* and *Die Frankfurter Allgemeine Zeitung*. However, according to the *Financial Times*, the main European banks, starting with the Bundesbank, seemed determined to support the lira.

"What shall we do?" Paulette raised her head towards Guichard.

"We'll sell another 14,000 billion lire," he said.

Jean-Paul and Paulette stared at him in silence.

Guichard sat down next to Jean-Paul. At 10:30, the spread had risen to 900 basis points. The Bundesbank and the Bank of Italy started selling dollars and D-marks against lire, and at 11:45 the spread dropped to 500 points.

"They're not budging," Jean-Paul said. "Sure you want to go on?"

The phone rang.

"... Yes, it's me," said Jean-Paul. "... Yes, just a moment." He looked at Guichard. "It's United Commercial from Jersey, on behalf of all the banks. They're asking if they should go on selling."

"Down to the last cent."

"That makes 42,000 billion in just three days."

"Thanks, Jean-Paul, but I can count."

The exchange rates started to flash across Guichard's screen. The spread began to climb again... 590 at 12:20 p.m... 680 at 1:40 p.m... 850 at 2:50 p.m. From 2:50 p.m. to 3:40 p.m. it fluctuated at around 850, as if unsure which way to go. In the meantime, the conviction that there would be a strong intervention by the Bundesbank began spreading around the dealing room. Indeed, at 3:46 p.m. the spread started to slip back again.... Down to 720 at 4:00 p.m... 570 at 4:40 p.m... 405 at 5:05 p.m... 180 at 5:30 p.m., when the dollar was worth 1,911 lire.

Guichard pressed the keys on his calculator. That day the lira had eased only two percent, and for a two-percent drop he'd thrown another 14,000 billion lire out of the window. He still had 28,000 billion, but was it any use continuing? The Bundesbank seemed determined to keep hanging on.... His phone rang.

"I've got the entire Organization against me," Franzese said. "Let's stop."

"Stop *now*?" Guichard said.

"Accardo doesn't seem to have any intention of resigning."

"Accardo is bluffing. We've got to go on."

"If you fail, you know what awaits us."

"Why, if we were to stop now — with 42,000 billion lire in the red — do you think that the treatment would be any different?"

Franzese remained silent.

"You see? The choice isn't that difficult, after all. There's only one way we can go: forward."

When the market reopened on Monday December 8, Guichard ordered another 14,000 billion lire to be sold. The spread swung between 200 and 500 points until, towards the end of the morning, the Bundesbank appeared to slow down, then started to back off. Its support ceased altogether by 12:40 p.m., when Prime Minister Accardo was forced to hand in his government's resignation during a rowdy session at parliament. In the early afternoon, the press agencies reported that a number of Italian politicians and business people had already fled abroad, and the spread soared higher and higher until it reached 1,500 points at 5:30 p.m. The lira lost eight percent and the US dollar was now worth 2,064 lire.

The tension subsided in the dealing room, and all the dealers gave Guichard a standing ovation.

"You know something?" Jean-Paul said.

Guichard went on looking at the numbers flashing across his screen. "What?"

"I was sure I would have to look for another job."

"Me too."

The next day, the last wave of sales hit a market already in free fall for the lira. The spread stopped the zigzagging of the previous days, and it moved only in one direction: upwards.

The Bank of Italy withdrew altogether from the market. It had already burnt up reserves equivalent to 40,000 billion lire, half its total.

On Tuesday, the lira lost a further twelve percent.

On Wednesday, international speculation caused the lira to lose an additional eight percent. At 4:00 p.m., the US dollar was quoted at 2,380 lire and the D-mark at 1,288. In five days the lira had plummeted by forty percent.

Guichard flipped through the 30,000-billion option contract entered into between the banking syndicate headed by the Cranfield Bank and Janus Holding, alias the Organization. The contract allowed him to buy dollars at a *striking price* of 1,750 lire, making a profit of 630 lire/dollar. The striking price for the lira/D-mark options was 920 lire, which meant a profit of 368 lire/D-mark.

At 4:10 p.m., Guichard signed a coded fax to Cranfield Bank, exercising his right to purchase dollars and D-marks against the entire 30,000 billion lire at the agreed-upon striking prices.

At 5:15 p.m., Guichard looked at the exchange rates on the Reuters screen once again. He keyed in some data on his calculator. That day the Organization had made a foreign exchange profit of 10,057 billion lire, and ten percent of that, 1,005.7 billion, had gone to Compagnie Financière d'Arcadie.

Guichard dialed Philippe's number in Manaus.

Carla de Santis walked slowly towards the cemetery exit. She was in mourning and her head was bowed.

"Mrs. Carla de Santis?"

She turned. The voice with a Sicilian accent belonged to a tall man wearing a gray felt hat and horn-rimmed glasses.

"Yes... do I know you?"

"My name's not important," Astarita said. He handed her an envelope. "This is something for you, from someone who thought highly of your husband."

For a moment she had the feeling she'd already heard that voice somewhere, then she dismissed the thought. What did it matter? Before she could say something, the man touched the brim of his hat and walked away.

Carla opened the envelope, her hands trembling. She took out a folded slip of paper.

It was a check in her name for $5 million.

"Make sure you don't leave any traces," Guichard said.

"It'll be as if we never existed," said Philippe, sitting in his office in Manaus.

The desk was the only piece of furniture left in the office. Some crates were piled up against a wall. Two men in blue overalls came in and said they had to load the desk on the truck. Philippe got up and picked up his panama; he went out on the balcony and looked at the waters of the Rio Negro, disappearing into the forest in the distance. He lit a Romeo y Julieta — the last one, he thought, as president of Sociedade Amazonica do Recursos Naturais.

"So long, Dr. Ignazio Escobar," said Philippe wistfully, looking at his creamy panama. "Maybe we'll meet again in another life."

Philippe grabbed the hat and flung it as far as he could out over the river. The hat circled skywards in a long curve, then floated downwards until it landed on the surface of the water. Shielding his eyes from the dazzling sunlight, Philippe watched the panama bob up and down as it drifted away with the current, until it was no more than a tiny white speck.

When he heard the recorded message, Monsignor Griffith assumed there must be some mistake. He opened his address book: the number was right, and it was the very number Cardinal Wolfenberg had given him. He redialed, but heard the same message as before. How could Recursos Naturais' telephone line possibly have been disconnected? He called the international information service: the number had been disconnected the previous day. Doubt started to creep into his mind. Although he tried to ignore it, that doubt kept gnawing at him until in the end he decided to call de Oliveira Lima, at the Ministry of Finance in Brasilia.

"Luis Roberto de Oliveira Lima? *Un momento, por favor,*" said the voice on the switchboard. After a long wait: "I'm sorry, *senhor,* but there's no one here by that name."

"But... are you sure?"

"Absolutely, *senhor.*"

"Who's the director of the Guarantee Office?"

"*Senhor* Alvaro Gomez."

Monsignor Griffith managed to get his voice back. "Would you put me through to him, please?"

"*Un momento, por favor.*"

"... But Cardinal Wolfenberg has always been in contact with Mr. Luis Roberto de Oliveira Lima!" said Monsignor Griffith.

"*Monsenhor,* I repeat, there's no one here by that name," Mr. Gomez said. "Do you think I wouldn't know? I've been in charge of the Guarantee Office for the past seven years."

"I don't understand... I just don't understand. Can I ask you a favor?"

"Of course, *Monsenhor.*"

"Could you check the registration number and date of the guarantee issued on behalf of Sociedade Amazonica do Recursos Naturais?"

"A guarantee on behalf of *Sociedade Amazonica do Recursos Naturais?* It's the first time I've ever heard of it. The Ministry of Finance has never issued a guarantee on behalf of this company."

"But... but... *are you sure?*"

"*Monsenhor,* do you think I wouldn't know? All guarantees must be approved by me. Even more so for a guarantee for $4,250 million!"

Monsignor Griffith put his head in his hands.

A swindle. A swindle worth over four billion dollars!

Overturning his chair, the monsignor jumped to his feet, ran out in the corridor and knocked at Cardinal Ortega's door.

§

Cardinal Wolfenberg passed a cigar back and forth under his nose and inhaled deeply. He reached for his box of long, wooden matches. Escobar was right; they made all the difference.

"There's nothing like a Romeo y Julieta to celebrate a great victory," the cardinal said to Archbishop Dyakonov, taking a long draw and blowing some lazy smoke rings in the air. "You don't know what you're missing."

"So, how much?" said Dyakonov with a grin.

"When we transferred the funds to Zurich on November 27, the dollar was worth 1,700 lire," said the cardinal, taking out his pocket calculator. "Today it's closed at 2,380. Do you really want to know how much we've made on this little deal, my dear Markus?"

"If I know you well, you sly old fox, you're more eager to tell me than I am to hear it."

"Just 2,890 billion lire. Or $1.7 billion, if you prefer. The Holy See shouldn't have any problem paying us our salaries this month."

The phone rang on the cardinal's direct line.

"Your Eminence, His Holiness wants to see you immediately," said Monsignor Petrov. "Something really serious must have happened. Everyone seems to have gone crazy here on the third floor."

"What's all this about?" the cardinal said.

"I believe it's got something to do with Recursos Naturais. Over the thirty years I've known him, I've never seen His Holiness so furious."

The cardinal broke out into a cold sweat.

"Your Eminence?... Hello... Your Eminence? Are you still there?" Monsignor Petrov said.

Dyakonov leaped to his feet. "Rolf, are you all right? You're as white as a Host."

It was since the clash over the Boff case that there hadn't been so many journalists at the archbishop's palace in São Paulo. The pressroom was so packed there wasn't any standing room. That mysterious press conference had aroused the curiosity not only of the Brazilian journalists, but also of the foreign correspondents.

When His Eminence Cardinal Carlos Montoya, archbishop of São Paulo and president of the Episcopal Conference of the Latin-American Churches, entered the room, the hum of voices stopped. Cardinal Montoya was a tall, energetic prelate, whose jaw seemed to say "no nonsense, please."

> "These facts show that the differences between the Catholic Church and ourselves are insuperable. We are no longer willing to accept humiliating compromises between the guidelines of the Second Vatican Council and the increasingly conservative policies of the Church of Rome. It is therefore with great consternation, but also with the joy that comes from hard decisions, that I hereby announce to the world the birth of the Conciliar Catholic Church, which unites 480 million Catholics from thirty-eight countries and their bishops. The Conciliar Catholic Church will be separate in all effects and purposes from the Roman Catholic Church—"

With shouts and cameras flashing away, the journalists descended on the cardinal and chaos broke out in the pressroom.

Within a few minutes, the international press agencies were conveying the news to the rest of the world. The Reuters agency wrote:

> "After the Western Schism and the Protestant Reform, the announcement made by Cardinal Montoya today in São Paulo is the third split in the history of the Catholic Church, but by far the most dramatic. The Church of Rome has lost half its followers...."

At midday on Sunday, the last window but one on the third floor of the Apostolic Palace remained closed. The Holy Father did not appear as usual to say *Angelus* with the crowds. The note prepared by Dr. Vallanco-Torres referred to "a slight indisposition."

That Sunday, a flock of pigeons hovered at length over Caligula's Obelisk.

◈

"A letter for you, Monsieur le Baron," said the postman, jumping off his bicycle. "I've heard the news, and I'd like you to know how sorry I am."

"Thank you, Antoine." Baron Armand de Tissier patted the postman on the shoulder.

The baron put the letter in his pocket without opening it and walked on along the tree-lined pathway leading to the castle. The ground was strewn with leaves and the warm autumn hues had vanished, replaced by bare branches, gnarled like an old man's hands. The baron counted the days to December 20, the date fixed for the court auction.

Once upon a time, many centuries before, the barons de Tissier had owned a third of all the land in the region. But when Pascal had entered the Order of the Knights Templar, the family fortunes had begun to decline. Poor Pascal, what a horrible death.

The baron reached the main gate when he remembered the letter. He opened it without bothering to read the sender's name — it must be just another solicitor.

"Monsieur le Baron de Tissier,

Please consider the enclosed check as compensation for the assassination of Pascal de Tissier by the Inquisition. The spirit of the Templars is not dead.

'Beau Séant!'
The Templar Lodge"

The baron read the amount on the check several times over, his heart pounding: $10,925,450!

So somewhere out there justice did exist, after all.

§

Guichard went through the fax from the Jersey bank. It confirmed the debit of $4,250 million for the 389 checks issued.

The Lodge had used two companies that specialized in heraldry, but it had still taken three years to track down all those people. All traces had been lost of any other descendants.

Guichard knocked on the door of the darkroom. "André, have you finished?"

"One minute, Monsieur le Comte," shouted André from inside.

"Meow," said Julius, pacing the floor.

The door opened and André emerged in a black plastic apron, his forearms in black over-sleeves; he held a pack of slides in his hand.

"Well? How have they turned out?" Guichard said.

"They are perfect."

"Let's go down to the library. The slide projector is ready," said Guichard, making his way towards the staircase, closely followed by André and Julius.

André inserted the slides into the carousel and turned on the projector. A beam of light hit the rectangular screen, cutting through the darkness of the library. André turned a knob until the image was perfectly in focus. A handwritten Aramaic text made of backward sloping and elongated characters appeared on the screen. The writing appeared to be full of *t*'s, the *t*'s crossed with long, upward-slanting strokes.

André slowly showed the slides of the reproductions of the original scrolls.

"What do you think, Monsieur le Comte?"

"You did an outstanding job, André. Let's see the translation, now."

André positioned the carousel on the slide with the beginning of the translation.

> "My name is Lot ben Maimon of Bethany and I begin to write on the fifth day of Nisan in the year 3828, praised be the Lord. With the inner freedom of a man whose moons are counted, I shall write the truth for all those Gentiles who have eyes to see and ears to hear. We live in an age of wickedness, sur-

rounded by hate and destruction. The Via Maris is paved with bodies of the dead, caravan traffic has ceased, and animals no longer come to drink at the springs of Jericho and Nazareth. Anon the pounding of the Romans' horses will shatter the silence of these shores, the sand will obscure the sun and the Day of Judgment will dawn also for the Essenes of Qumran.

This is the story of one of us, a man y-clept Jesus, a disciple of John, Teacher of Righteousness. And the day came when our brother Jesus returned among the people to preach the Word..."

As soon as they had viewed the last slide, Guichard turned towards André. "Are the copies ready?"

"Yes, Monsieur le Comte. The packages are all sealed, ready for the courier."

"Let's check the list of newspapers again." Guichard pointed at the packs of letters piled up in the middle of the table.

André took a sheet from the top of the pile. *"Washington Post, The Times, Le Monde...."*

As André went through the newspapers listed, Guichard checked the corresponding envelopes and set them aside.

"And with the *Sydney Morning Herald* that's it," André said. His expression turned thoughtful. "One thing is certain, though: life is really unpredictable." He repressed a laugh.

Guichard looked at him inquiringly.

"Lot ben Maimon would have never guessed that one day his writing would become famous all over the world."

40

Standing by the cocktail cabinet in the library, Guichard poured a glass of Hennessy for himself and one of port, which he passed to Françoise who was talking to Julius curled up on her lap. He sat down in the armchair in front of her.

"Tomorrow it will all be over," he said.

Françoise put her glass on the table and stared at him. "Why tomorrow?"

Guichard explained that that night in Scotland he had made a promise and he was now ready to keep it. He had a story to tell her: the story had begun when he was nine and lightning struck near de Saint Clair castle at Les Andelys ....

"I had a premonition, but I hoped I was wrong. I don't know why," Françoise said when Guichard finished speaking. "How did His body end up in the Temple?"

"The Essenes took it there," Guichard said. "After bribing the Roman guards, they entered Joseph of Arimathea's garden during the night and removed the body from the tomb. They embalmed it in Qumran."

"Why the Essenes?"

"Jesus was one of them."

"But why did they put the body in the Temple? And when?"

"It was Joash ben Uri who told Geoffroy and Hugues de Payens the whole story," Guichard said. "In A.D. 68 — the year 3828 in the Hebrew calendar — in the middle of the Judean revolt, the Essenes realized that the Romans were approaching Qumran and that the end was near. They decided to take Christ's body to the Holy of Holies. They put it in a wooden chest, together with the scrolls on which Lot ben Maimon had described how things had actually gone."

"Why did Victor de Mauriac choose that particular Latin phrase?" Françoise said.

"Geoffroy asked Victor the same thing, after they'd taken the Ark out of the Holy of Holies."

"And what did he say?"

"He said that for him the Holy of Holies was like the pagan Arcadia of the Roman poets."

"But why *Et in Arcadia ego*? — I too in Arcadia."

"The phrase came to him instinctively, to express how he felt on discovering the death of the Son of God in God's dwelling place. The words *Et* and *ego* expressed all of Victor's desolation."

"The muse's expression in Poussin's painting means just that, doesn't it?"

"How did you find out?"

"I just felt it, deep down. There's one thing I haven't been able to fathom, though."

"What's that?"

"How did Poussin find out?"

"Does the name Lukas Holste mean anything to you?"

"Certainly. Holste was Cardinal Francesco Barberini's librarian. Poussin and Cassiano del Pozzo did a lot of research with him."

"Cardinal Barberini was the Vatican's official librarian in the period 1627–36," Guichard said. "The cardinal put the faithful Holste in charge of the library and the Vatican archives. In February 1636, Holste discovered an old manuscript in the archives and told Poussin and Cassiano about it."

"And then?"

"It all started because of Victor's vanity and his passion for all things classical...."

♣

Geoffroy crossed the courtyard of the preceptory. The bells had just rung the sext and many brethren were heading for the church to say their midday prayers. He entered the tower and began to go up the spiral steps. He was really curious to find out what Victor was up to. Over the past three weeks, his friend had been disappearing more and more often to shut himself away in a room at the top of the tower, a cubbyhole used as a private chapel of the Grand Master, where Bertrand had never set foot. His steward had told him that Victor had had a writing desk carried upstairs. He knocked.

"*Entrez.*"

A goose-quill in his hand and a smudge of ink on his nose, Victor was sitting at a writing desk too small for his bulk. He frowned at Geoffroy and hurriedly covered up a parchment sheet lying in front of him.

"Are you writing your memoirs, by any chance?" said Geoffroy, sitting down on a prie-dieu.

"Um, nothing that could interest you. It's a… poem."

"A poem? What about? What's its title?"

Victor made a wry face. "Pah! Did you come up here to pester me?"

"Aha, you old owl! I see we've got a secret. Now you're starting to put on airs with your best friend?"

Victor hesitated. "Promise you'll keep it to yourself?"

"You should know me by now."

Victor turned to a small wooden altar he used as a bookcase. He reached for a stack of parchment sheets, took the one on top and handed it to Geoffroy.

"*Et in Arcadia Ego?* Have you gone crazy?" Geoffroy looked at Victor in alarm. "You rascal! A fine way indeed to keep our oath."

"But don't you see? I couldn't help writing it. In any case, it's in the form of poetry, as well as being in Latin, and is full of allegories and periphrases."

"What of it?"

"I defy anyone to grasp its meaning."

"Are you going to put the mountain in your poem too? Maybe with a nice map?"

Victor shrugged his shoulders, then his expression turned dreamy. "When my *Et in Arcadia Ego* is finished, Virgil himself will look like an amateur compared with me."

"Virgil managed to die in his own bed, at least."

Victor stood up, tiptoed to the altar, looked warily around and opened the shrine. He took out a laurel wreath and gazed at it as a father would his firstborn who has just seen the light.

"Sh! I got it ready for that day," whispered Victor. He put the wreath on his head, struck a pose in profile and puffed out his chest. "How do I look?"

Geoffroy stared at him speechless.

§

"How did Victor's poem end up in the Vatican archives?" Françoise said.

"It was the Inquisition that found it, when they sorted through the documents of the Templar preceptory in Paris," Guichard said. "They couldn't make any sense out of it, so they sent it to Rome."

"Until Lukas Holste came across it."

"Holste, like Victor, was a lover of the classical world. He, Poussin, and Cassiano studied Victor's poem and in the end they understood its hidden meaning."

"But how do you know all this? At that time, none of your ancestors were in Rome."

Guichard reached his hand out towards a faded booklet lying on the coffee table.

"The answer is in here," he said, carefully turning the pages yellowed with age.

"What is it?"

"It's the diary of Guy de Saint Clair, an ancestor of mine. He writes about a visit he received at Les Andelys castle on May 23, 1637. Can you guess who his visitor was?"

"Incredible. *Poussin?*"

"In person."

"What did he want with Guy?"

"Guy agreed to receive Poussin, partly because he was so well-known and partly because the painter came from Les Andelys. Poussin knew everything. The only thing he hadn't been able to find out was which of the Aude mountains the body was hidden in. When Poussin mentioned mount

Blanchefort, Guy didn't dare to deny it. He said nothing, and Poussin got the confirmation he needed."

"Why did Guy help him? Wasn't he bound by the Templar oath, too?"

"When you've read this, you'll understand. Guy realized that Poussin was a man of great depth, someone who had reached a universal outlook on life and religion."

"But that still doesn't explain why."

"Poussin had been fascinated by the classical esotericism of Victor's poem. He wanted at all costs to paint a picture in which he could pour the emotions he had felt on reading the poem, thus immortalizing the meaning of *Et in Arcadia ego*. That's why Guy decided to help him. He didn't feel he was betraying the oath: on the contrary."

"Is the body still hidden in the mountain?" Françoise said.

Guichard nodded.

"And now?"

"Tomorrow the Lodge will send a copy of the scrolls, with the translation, to sixty-two newspapers all over the world. Moreover, we'll ask the French government to authorize excavations on the mountain of Blanchefort to recover the body."

Françoise widened her eyes. "I can't believe you mean it."

"I've never been more serious: the Church will never pay enough for all the evil they've done."

"But haven't you thought of the people?"

"What do you mean?"

"Over a billion people believe in Christ's resurrection. Do you realize what that means?"

"I certainly do. It means that the Catholic Church deserves a platinum Oscar as the most shameless liar that has ever existed."

"But what does it matter if Christ rose from the dead or not? The point is that there are hundreds of millions of people out there who believe it. It's this faith that gives them the strength to bear their daily suffering."

"Reasoning like that, one could justify any shameful action! Your absurdity is unbelievable."

"You and your friends in the Lodge are just blinded by your thirst for revenge. Don't you realize the evil you're about to commit? Wasn't Brazil enough?"

"*Revenge?* This is justice, not revenge. Not to punish the Church would mean condoning those atrocities."

"But the Inquisition, like the Church, was made up of men — human beings with all their faults and weaknesses. Why do you persist in not understanding?"

"There's nothing to understand."

"You don't know how deeply you disappoint me."

"There's someone in Kilmory Chapel who's been waiting seven centuries for this moment. I owe it to him."

"Are you really sure it's him you want to avenge and not yourself? If you think about it, you'll end up realizing that it doesn't make any difference whether it's true or not."

Guichard stared at Françoise, unable to utter a word. He thought of Miriam's words on that night in July 1127, when Geoffroy had returned to the inn from the Holy of Holies, after the discovery.

"*I'd start to ask myself if it was really so important after all.*"

"*And then?*"

"*I'd probably end up realizing that it doesn't make any difference whether it's true or not.*"

That night, Guichard's mind roamed across a desert and voices lost in the sand led him to a campfire by an oasis, where a camel caravan had pitched their tents for the night. The camels were drinking water at the oasis and the campfires glowed before the tents, casting flickering shadows on the sand dunes.

The desert was wrapped in a clear still night.

Men dressed as Bedouins sat in a circle around a large fire. Their *burnous* fluttered in the night breeze. Geoffroy sat among them. A Bedouin stood up, stirred the fire, and dropped some herbs into the water bubbling in a large, long-spouted pot. An aroma of spices wafted in the air.

Enveloped in the awe-inspiring majesty of the star-lit desert, the Bedouins were talking of the great mysteries that man had always been confronted with. Despite their poor attire, their words revealed a great wisdom and the knowledge of distant customs and lands.

"Monotheistic religions," said an oriental mystic, "have brought only pain and spiritual suffering to mankind since the day of creation, stifling man's aspirations."

"What is man's greatest aspiration?" Geoffroy asked.

"To free himself from suffering," said the oriental mystic, the other sages nodding in agreement.

"Physical suffering?"

The mystic smiled. "Any suffering."

"How can we free ourselves from suffering?" Geoffroy asked.

"With the sixth sense," said the Cabbalist.

"Through enlightenment," said the oriental mystic.

"Through Gnosis," said the Christian Gnostic.

"By being one with the harmony of the universe," said the Druse.

"By following the stars," said the head of the caravan, an Egyptian, pointing a finger at the sparkling heavens.

"Why the stars?" asked the Cabbalist.

"Since the dawn of time, stars have guided the caravans, and I have learnt to observe them. By looking at the stars, I've learnt to look inside myself."

"And what have you seen?" said the Cabbalist.

"I've seen that it's not possible to understand the Outer without first understanding the Inner."

The sages discussed the matter at length, eventually recognizing that—in spite of their widely differing cultures, languages, and traditions—they had all given the same answer. In order to free himself from suffering, man had to open his mind to a higher state of consciousness, which the sages called the Ultimate Reality.

"How does one reach the Ultimate Reality?" Geoffroy asked.

"Silence your rationality, empty your mind, and listen to the flow of all things," said the oriental mystic.

"How shall I recognize the Ultimate Reality?"

"You will be dazzled by a light that will make you aware of a new dimension in which space and time no longer exist separately, but merge into a state of higher consciousness. In that moment, you will forget your identity, be one with the universe, and will suffer no more."

The wind rose and a cloud of sand swallowed up the camp.

The light of dawn filtered into Guichard's room. He drew the curtains back and gazed down at the empty streets. As the first rays of sunlight rose above the gargoyles of Notre Dame, Françoise's words echoed through his mind.

"But what does it matter if Christ rose from the dead or not? The point is that there are hundreds of millions of people out there who believe it. It's this faith that gives them the strength to bear their daily suffering."

As children we believed in Santa Claus, and the day we found out it wasn't true, we felt betrayed. That day something died in us. Christmas tree balls lost the twinkle that had made us dream, and the carefree spell of childhood came to an end. As the children grew up, they persisted in believing that a man had been born to a virgin, and that this man was immortal. Man lived on dreams, and religions had known how to exploit those dreams to their own advantage — the Catholic Church more deviously than the others.

What did it matter if such beliefs were merely the result of the inborn, unrestrainable aspiration of man to immortality, if not of the flesh, at least of the spirit? Man had invented God because he needed to legitimate a place called Paradise, in the unconfessed hope that one day he would be able to knock on that door. The revenge of the Lodge would wipe away not only the Church, but also all those hopes.

Guichard banged his fists on the wall, shouting with rage.

The worst evil of a wrong wasn't so much the physical or material violence one suffered from it, as the moral brutalization produced by the creeping thoughts of revenge, which degraded one to the same level as the wrongdoer. Where could one find the strength to forget and look beyond men's wickedness, above all of those who hid a history of blood and machinations behind a mask of self-conferred infallibility, behind dogmas as empty as their dialectics and behind rituals as cold as the expressions of their saints? Forgive? *Never*. Refrain from revenge...?

But would *he* agree? And even so, what sense was there in thinking that the Lodge might renounce their plan?

Why don't you say something? asked Guichard.

But the Voice kept silent.

Julius jumped off the bed, rubbed himself against Guichard's legs and made for the door. On reaching the doorway, he turned back. Guichard followed him.

Julius leapt onto the terrace parapet, walked along it and stopped, with Notre Dame in the background. The sky opened above the cathedral and a cloud of red dust whirled around the tower.

A mounted knight Templar was galloping through a rocky desert, his chain mail glinting in the sun. He began moving as if in slow motion, until he tightened the reins. Even though Guichard could see him only from the rear, he recognized the Voice—Geoffroy. In the distance, the Essenes' tents stood out against the waters of the Dead Sea. All of a sudden, Geoffroy's image seemed to split and another knight, mounting his horse, his face hidden by his helmet, was superimposed on it.

A parallel world.

The knight and his horse were in full armor; the knight's *surcotte* was torn and blood-splattered, and the battlefield around him was strewn with corpses. An English soldier lay on his back, his hands still grasping a spear stuck in his chest and his eyes wide open in the surprise of death. The knight removed his helmet. *Guichard de Saint Clair!* He ran his blood-soiled hand over his face stained with sweat and death, and pointed his arm eastwards. He moved his lips and a word echoed through Guichard's mind: *The Aaaark... The Aaaark... The Aaaark...*

A shining path lined with pomegranate trees streaked the sky, the ground sparkling like crystal, and the gilded Dome of the Rock rose above the horizon. The clattering of horses' hooves filled the sky and a unicorn flashed along the path, galloping towards the dome. The unicorn vanished beyond the horizon, and the path vanished with it.

A whirl of dust blew up, spinning around faster and faster, and the sands of time swallowed up the knight.

§

In the arms room of De Molay castle, a silence charged with tension and bewildered looks followed Guichard's words.

"*Never!* Do you hear me? Never!" Trembling with anger, Gilbert de Molay jumped to his feet. "Do you think we've done all this for nothing?"

"Brasilia was far from nothing," Guichard said.

"Brasilia was merely due compensation and doesn't wipe out the guilt of the Church." Gilbert pointed a finger at Jacques de Molay's portrait. "Neither does it wipe out all the suffering those brutes have inflicted."

"I haven't forgotten it, just as I haven't forgotten Arno de Saint Clair's death."

"Then you are a traitor, and doubly so. You betray their memory, and you betray the oath of the Lodge."

"True betrayal would be to avenge a wrong by causing another. Was this the Templars' code of honor?"

"Remember who you are addressing and spare me your country-parish priest philosophy. The Lodge will go ahead as planned."

"You are forgetting one minor detail."

Gilbert looked at Guichard with suspicion.

"*I* have the scrolls."

"Bastard! The scrolls belong to the Lodge. I would remind you that they were hidden in de Saint Clair castle at Bertrand de Blanchefort's orders. Your family has simply had them in safekeeping on behalf of the Templars. And *now* you must return them to us."

Guichard looked around the table. "I ask that the question be put to the vote."

"So be it." Gilbert addressed the brethren. "Those of you in favor of the restitution of the scrolls raise your hand."

The brethren exchanged uncertain glances. A few hands rose: one… two… three… four… five.

"Anyone else?" Gilbert shot a piercing look at those left.

No one moved.

"Vote not valid," Gilbert said. "According to our statute, we shall vote again. Those in favor?"

Five hands rose again.

"Well, what do we do now? Cry?" Philippe said, looking round.

"I have a suggestion," Guichard said.

The brethren turned their eyes on Guichard.

"The Ark," he said. "To make the accounts balance, the Church must return the Ark."

"But the Ark is hidden under the main altar of the Sistine Chapel," Philippe said. "I defy even the Mossad to break into St. Peter's. Not to mention the political repercussions of such an undertaking."

"Take it as done," Guichard said.

"What do you mean?"

"All the Israeli government has to do is ask the Vatican to return it."

"Are you out of your mind?" Philippe stood up and assumed a theatrical stance. "How do you do, Prime Minister, I'm the pope. I hope you'll forgive us. It was just a small oversight. It was those wicked Templars who took it, you know; we just stumbled on it by chance. Do you want to take it away now? Yes? *Hey, Peter, get a move on! Wrap the chest up.*"

Guichard waited for the laughter to die down. "You're forgetting the scrolls."

"The *scrolls*? How do they come into it?"

"We'll inform Israel of their existence. The Israeli government will only need to hint at the scrolls — pretending to have them — for the Church to return the Ark."

"Hmm, I see. But what if the Church refuses?"

"Very unlikely. But in that case, we'll give Israel a copy of the scrolls — and believe you me, they'll know what to do with them."

A perfidious smile appeared on Philippe's face.

"I ask that my proposal be put to a vote," Guichard said.

Gilbert glared at him. "Those in favor?"

Guichard and Philippe raised their hands. Five more hands followed.

Gilbert remained motionless, saying nothing.

"Seven in favor." Guichard turned to Gilbert. "We will proceed as I have suggested."

Gilbert got up, grabbed his sword, and made his way around the table, followed by the eyes of all the brethren. When he was in front of Guichard, he slapped him hard in the face with the back of his hand. A trickle of blood dribbled down from the corner of Guichard's mouth.

"With Jacques' compliments," said Gilbert pointing to Jacques de Molay's portrait. Then he cleft the air with two strokes. "And now I'm ready to give you satisfaction. *En garde!*"

Guichard grabbed his sword, took a step back and put up his guard, but Philippe jumped to his feet and seized his arm.

"Hold it!"

Guichard freed himself from Philippe's grip and looked menacingly at Gilbert. "I won't soil my hands with your blood, but only out of respect for him," he said, pointing to the portrait.

Guichard stuck his sword into the floorboards and strode out, the vibrations of the blade accompanying his footsteps.

At sunset three weeks later, an El Al plane landed at Ben Gurion Airport in Tel Aviv. The plane taxied to a hangar some distance away from the complex of the main buildings.

A red carpet was unrolled up to the base of the gangway, the door of the plane opened and ten men in dark suits climbed down. On the ground, the Israeli prime minister took a step forward and held out his hand.

(An evening a few months later, in Sicily)

Dim lights flickered down in the valley. The air was full of the scent of limes and the chirping of crickets mingled with the splashing of the Neptune fountain. Sitting on the low wall near the fountain, Guichard turned to Franzese.

"On our way through Rome, Françoise and I went to visit the Vatican Museums," Guichard said. "It looks as if the Church has suddenly decided they need a lot of restoration."

"Don't tell me you don't know why, you scoundrel. Because of the Brasilia rip-off, they had to sell over 600 million dollars worth of works of art. The new pope had no other choice."

"How are things going with him?"

Franzese shrugged. "Just the same as the previous one. In any case, it's Manus Domini that's really in charge in the Vatican these days. Since that poor devil Wolfenberg has been relegated to the archdiocese of Lagos — thanks to you — Cafiero has become the real *éminence grise* behind the Church."

"São Paulo hasn't taught them anything at all."

"Why, do you think that they'll be any better in São Paulo than they are in the Vatican? Eventually, power will go to their heads too: it's the same old story."

"The Church of São Paulo seems to be different."

"It'd be like saying that things have changed since Accardo."

A professor of economics had been made prime minister, Franzese said, but now it was the Joint Affairs Commission and Wall Street pulling the strings, apart from Manus Domini. Only one thing had changed: the pockets the money went into.

"This country will never change," Franzese said. "Corruption, nepotism, and the 'tell them I sent you' attitude have become part of our DNA."

"So that journalist died for nothing."

"De Santis? Like all idealists he was convinced he could change the world."

Guichard didn't say anything.

"You know something?" continued Franzese. "Only one man realized what makes the world go 'round: Accardo. Look at him now, lying in the sun in the Cook Islands, where no warrant of extradition can reach him."

"Accardo left a legacy worthy of him."

"Rosario's right when he says you're an idealist." Franzese gave Guichard a skeptical look. "Have you ever read *The Leopard*?"

"Years ago. Why?"

"Do you remember the pages where the prince refuses the position as senator of the Kingdom of Italy, offered him by Chevalley, the *cavaliere* from Piedmont?"

"Vaguely."

"Well, the Prince of Salina—the Leopard—tells Chevalley he's refusing because the Kingdom of Italy won't be any different from all the earlier foreign governments that oppressed Sicily. He says things will never change."

"But Tomasi di Lampedusa's book is set in Sicily one hundred and sixty years ago."

"You don't understand because you're not Italian. Tomasi di Lampedusa—who was a thoroughbred Sicilian—says something that will always hold true."

"What's that?"

"The prince replies that 'Sicilians never want to improve, for the simple reason that they think themselves perfect. Their vanity's stronger than their misery.'"

"And what does Chevalley say to that?"

"Chevalley says the Sicilians want to improve, and that the Piedmontese administration will change things. The Leopard gives him an answer that still holds: 'We were the Leopards and Lions; those who'll take our place will be little jackals, hyenas; and the whole lot of us, Leopards, jackals and sheep, will go on thinking ourselves the salt of the earth.'"

"The Leopard had forgotten the power of dreams."

"Dreams? Bah!" Franzese made a gesture of contempt. "What Tomasi doesn't say but you can read between the lines, is that there's a Sicilian in every one of us. Every one of us—it doesn't matter whether leopard, jackal or sheep—considers himself the salt of the earth, and that's why nothing will ever change in this world."

While Franzese was walking back to the villa, Guichard took something from his pocket and opened his hand. The head of a statuette carved from orange-colored stone appeared. Its eyes—two tiny, black pebbles—seemed to be smiling…. Flashes of infinity.

Thou wilt never yield, i'faith, said the Voice.

I want to see the unicorn, Guichard said.

The face of Neptune gleamed in the moonlight.

41

When Françoise opened the door of her apartment and was enveloped in silence, she regretted rejecting Corinne's offer to accompany her. She only had to get a few clothes, she'd told Corinne, and it would be just a matter of a few minutes.

Françoise strode down the hallway, turned on the lights of the bedroom and opened the closet. She had just started taking some clothes off the coat hangers when she felt that draft of cold air brushing over her neck. She turned, anger swelling up inside her.

"What do you want from me?" she shouted. *"What?"*

A figure of opaque ectoplasm stood in front of her, its outline revealing a woman. Little by little, starting with the outline, the being began to lose her opacity, gradually becoming translucent, to such an extent that Françoise could see the wall and the curtains through her.

The woman was veiled and dressed in medieval clothing. She was wearing a long, loose robe closely fitted under her breasts. Her hair was covered with a headband secured by a mesh of diadem.

The being raised her hand to her face and let the veil drop. Françoise held her breath, her heart racing: *the resemblance between the two of them was striking.*

Françoise was about to go nearer the being, but its outline became blurred and it went back to a state of opaque ectoplasm. A cord of mist-like substance exuded from it, which began swiftly to penetrate into Françoise's nostrils until the ectoplasm was fully inhaled.

The room began whirling madly around Françoise.

The force of the gale bent the trees and torrential rain lashed the walls of de Saint Clair castle. A thick blanket of clouds of an unusual greenish hue darkened the sky. Lightning lit up the heavens, flashing beyond the ridge of the hills.

"Sit down, André." Guichard pointed to an armchair facing him in the castle library. "I have something to tell you."

"What's the matter, Monsieur le Comte? I have... an uneasy presentiment."

Guichard told André what he was about to do.

"Monsieur le Comte, I... I'm trying to persuade myself this is a nightmare. It can't be true!"

Guichard said nothing.

"But... why? Is there anything wrong in your life, Monsieur le Comte? As far as the scrolls are concerned, everything has turned out well. You're a successful man; you have got all that life has to offer. *Why?*"

"I've got nothing, André. I've always dreamt of escaping and going back to a place where I'm sure I already lived once, a place lost in another dimension. I'm not happy in my own skin, that's all."

"But you might get yourself killed! Have you thought of that?"

"I have."

"I'm not thinking of myself, Monsieur le Comte, but... haven't you thought of Julius? Of Madame Françoise? Of your business?"

Guichard took out an envelope and he handed it to André. "Don't open it sooner than in twenty-four hours. When you do, you'll see you have nothing more to worry about for the rest of your days. As to details, please get in touch with my notary: my will is in order. As far as Julius is concerned, I entrust him to you, because I know you love him as much as I do."

André swallowed hard, his eyes moist.

Guichard stood up and André did likewise. "You've been much more than a butler to me, André. You've been the friend, the confidant, the faithful companion of so many shady escapades. Wherever I go, you'll always be with me."

In silence, Guichard and André exchanged a long handshake.

"And now I must go into the underground vaults and get dressed. Think of how proud Monsieur Fauberger would be if he knew where his garments are going."

Lightning lit up the library. Stretched out on the sofa, Guichard reached out for his watch lying on the coffee table and looked at the phosphorescent second hand. One... two... three.... The battery of sirens installed at the foot of the lightning rod sounded again, but this time with greater frequency. It was the six-minute warning signal set on the counter; at fifteen there was a faint rumble of thunder, and Guichard reckoned that the lightning must have struck about three miles away. The area around the castle was now a high-danger zone and it was highly likely that lightning would strike the lightning rod within the next few minutes.

Absent-mindedly, Guichard slipped his watch onto his wrist. It read 4:39. He pulled down the visor of his helmet.

The sirens started to shrill almost continuously and deafeningly. As if uncertain which way to go, lightning flashed over the castle, tracing a jagged line of dazzling red. This time the rumble of thunder was almost instantaneous and resounded through the library like gunfire. Then lightning struck the top of the ninety-foot lightning rod and snapped most of the insulating clamps round the copper rod; vibrating spasmodically, the steel cables tightened against the reinforced concrete base. But at the very instant it struck the rod, the line of fire split like the forked tongue of a snake, leapt the hundred and twenty feet that separated the lightning rod from the castle, shot up along the drainpipe and writhed into the library through the open window.

The thunderbolt struck the tip of Guichard's sword, shot out of its hilt and began to whirl around the sofa, tracing a tunnel of fire. Retracing the path of the lightning, the tunnel reached the window and spun towards the sky like a tornado.

It was as if space had been torn apart and a vortex of staggering dimensions opened up over Guichard. It seemed to be motionless, but Guichard knew it was spinning at a speed impossible according to the laws of earthly physics; although it was black, it was enveloped in a phosphorescent green halo. Its surface began swaying idly, like a hot-air balloon drifting with the wind. Guichard couldn't tell how far he was from it, but of one thing he was certain: he was about to approach the *event horizon* — the boundary of a black hole, the point of no return. In fact, shortly afterwards, he felt himself being sucked into the center of the vortex by an immense force and the veins of his temples started throbbing. *Singularity!* "*If you were swallowed up in there,*" Professor Bieri had said, "*you'd be literally annihilated, squeezed to infinite density.*"

He was falling into four-dimensional space-time. Distorted, grotesque forms streaked before his eyes like the images of a convex lens or a spatial projection of the surrealist paintings hanging in his study. The time-curve was becoming negative, under the effect of a force unknown on earth. He was racing towards his physical annihilation at a speed faster than light. He shut his eyes waiting for the end.

When he opened his eyes again, he found himself in the middle of the cosmos, immersed in the silence of myriads of stars: yellow, blue, red.... They appeared to be suspended in clouds of luminous dust, now shapeless, now in the form of a ring. He didn't know how fast he was traveling, only that he was moving much faster than the speed of light. Nevertheless, the multicolored worlds that flashed around him were traveling even faster: the universe was expanding and light traveled at too low a speed to reach it. Every so often, blinding flashes of light appeared in the cosmos, only to drop limply out of sight again, like jets of lava penetrating the darkness.

Were those worlds still part of life or what comes after life? And if that was life, was he really traveling through a universe of galaxies, or through the helix of his DNA? Was four-dimensional space-time the meeting point of the infinitely small with the infinitely large?

A whirl of white light spun around him. He was sliding through a giant esophagus, projected forwards by a mysterious force emanating from that white light. The tunnel was reaching a bend, and he felt himself being pushed against the wall: at this speed even collision with a small pebble would mean the end! However, when the contact took place all he seemed to touch was a wall formed of energy resilient to impact, and the only effect was a shower of sparks.

A blazing, reddish light appeared: that must be the end of the tunnel. What was awaiting him out there?

For a moment he couldn't see anything and had the sensation one has when resurfacing after diving into the sea. A barren hill, a glimpse of woodland, and a cliff overhanging the sea flashed before his eyes.... Eventually he felt himself being pushed up towards a leaden sky.

Guichard landed on his back, the impact made even more painful because of the chain mail he was wearing. As soon as he had recovered from the shock, he pulled himself upright into a sitting position. He had ended up on a raised beach of compact, reddish sand, swept by the wind and backed by cliffs sheer above a dark sea. Waves smashed against the rocks lifting sprays of foam, and the roar of the sea deadened the shrill cries of the wild birds that soared high above the cliffs.

He felt a lash on his left wrist, followed by a burning sensation. *His watch.* Idiot! He looked at his wrist, but all he saw was a strip of red skin.

"Rise," said a commanding voice behind him. "Slowly, if thou cherishest thy life."

Guichard started and turned round. The first thing he saw was the glint of a sword pointing straight at his throat. He looked up. *Geoffroy.* But this was a menacing Geoffroy, very different from the one he was used to seeing in his dreams.

"On thy feet, I said! And remove thy helmet."

Guichard stood up and removed his helmet, letting it drop to the ground.

Geoffroy gave a start. "Who art thou? There's something... familiar about thee."

"My name is Guichard de Saint Clair."

Geoffroy's eyes widened. "A de Saint Clair? Where art thou from?"

"I'm from Les Andelys, like you, Geoffroy de Saint Clair. But I come from your future — a future nine centuries away."

Geoffroy stared at Guichard, first in astonishment, then with blazing eyes. "I know not how thou comest to know my name, but beware, Sir Knight: one does not mock a de Saint Clair and live. Thou liest." He pressed his sword against Guichard's throat. "For the last and final time. *Who art thou?*"

Although Guichard tried to control his fear, he could see from Geoffroy's eyes that he would kill him. The instinct of self-preservation took over and he put his hand to his sword. But he had barely touched the hilt than his sword shot out of its sheath of its own accord, swished through the air rotating on its axis and finally joined with Geoffroy's. In the end there was only one sword: Geoffroy's.

Geoffroy dropped his sword as if it were red hot and leaped backwards. "By my faith, I cannot believe my eyes. Thou must be the devil himself."

Guichard's sword had been Geoffroy's, nine hundred years before. How could Guichard explain a physical paradox to Geoffroy, a man of 1127?

"But a devil who speaketh, acteth and dresseth very strangely," said Geoffroy, studying Guichard from head to foot warily.

"Take a good look at me," Guichard said. "Then think of looking at yourself in a mirror, clean shaven, and with shorter hair."

In spite of his thick, black beard, the long hair and tanned skin that made him look like a Saracen, Geoffroy's features were the same as Guichard's.

Geoffroy stroked his beard. "Fortsooth the resemblance is striking. But how canst thou be a de Saint Clair from Les Andelys? I have never set eyes on thee before." Then he added, with a gleam in his eyes: "And believe me, Sir Knight: had I seen thee — and heard thee speak — I would surely remember."

"I too am a de Saint Clair, so watch what you say," Guichard said.

A faint swish came from above and the two knights raised their eyes. A bright-red whirlwind was spinning in the sky, writhing like a gigantic snake.

"I've come a long way to meet you, much further than you could ever imagine. And I've done it for you, or rather for all of us. I bring news of tremendous importance, something that will change your life, the Order, and the course of history."

The whirlwind thrashed frantically, the wind started to blow and thunder rumbled in the distance.

"*The course of history?* Thou makest me doubt my own sanity. And yet in thee I see myself — even though I would slay any barber-surgeon who reduced me to that state — and I know not what to think. Eternal damnation!"

Lightning struck in the middle of the woods and a burst of thunder shook the ground.

"Geoffroy, we have just a few minutes! You've got to believe me when I tell you I come from your future, otherwise you won't believe what I'm about to tell you."

Geoffroy's eyes lit up. "Proof. Give me proof."

Guichard drew closer to him and uttered Victor's motto.

Geoffroy gave him a murderous look, his fist opened and closed and he bent to pick up his sword. "So *thou* wert the varlet spying on us in the tunnel!"

Guichard put his foot on the sword. "Hold it, you dolt."

He told Geoffroy of the meetings with Abbot Bernard and Joash Ben Uri. Then he spoke to him about Miriam, giving details that no one could possibly have known. "... It's the head of a statuette carved from orange-colored stone, wearing a triangular hat, and its eyes are two small, black pebbles." So saying, Guichard untied the opening of the leather scrip hanging from his belt and rummaged in it. His hand felt hot. A black-rimmed hole was on the bottom of the scrip: the head of the statuette had disintegrated.

Lightning streaked across the sky, lighting up the deserted beach. The sea surged and whitened, as huge waves smashed on the rocks. Torrential rain slanted by the wind buffeted Geoffroy and Guichard. The red whirlwind came down above them, its mouth turning into a black vortex.

"Hold! Enow!" shouted Geoffroy, covering his ears. "Dost thou want to render me insane? I must believe thee."

"Geoffroy flee! Don't go to Rome! But first, leave the Order. And tell Hugues and the others to do so as well."

"But why?"

"On October 13, 1307, a terrible tragedy—"

The roar became deafening. The rumble of the thunder and the howling of the wind covered Guichard's words, forcing him to shout. He moved closer to Geoffroy, again trying to yell the future into his ear.

But his words were swept away by the wind.

Suddenly, a second whirlwind of a turquoise color appeared in the sky. It twined around the red whirlwind, like one snake trying to crush another. Then it untwined, and a vortex of the same turquoise color formed at one end, its opening widening.

"… A pope will destroy the Order and the Church will inflict indescribable tortures on the Templars. A de Saint Clair will be burnt at the stake—"

The turquoise vortex was now spinning right over Guichard and Geoffroy. An invisible force began to suck them upwards and Geoffroy started to rise above Guichard.

Geoffroy, not him! His feet were still touching the ground! He went on disclosing the future and, while Geoffroy was hovering in mid air between him and the turquoise vortex, an infinity of blurred worlds flashed around the vortex: cosmic clouds, stardust, whole galaxies. Then the images slowed down, and Guichard caught sight of distorted metaphysical shapes, archetypes of Jungian memory, warped mandalas….

Guichard understood what was about to happen. If he went on speaking, disclosing the future to Geoffroy, it would be like buying a one-way ticket to another world—but for Geoffroy, whereas the red whirlwind would take Guichard back to earth.

A law of cosmic censorship did exist, which prevented you from changing the course of history, and a sort of cosmic police punished anyone attempting to do so with life exile to another world millions of light-years away!

Geoffroy, his face lashed by the rain, remained hovering above Guichard. "Cry louder, damnation! I canst not hear thee from up here."

But Guichard stopped speaking. The turquoise vortex vanished and Geoffroy fell to the ground. Now, Guichard felt he was beginning to be sucked upwards and raised his eyes: the black vortex was whirling over him, enveloped in the same green halo. Geoffroy seized his arm.

No, it wouldn't end like this.

Guichard gave Geoffroy a tremendous punch on the chin, knocking him out. Then he ran towards Geoffroy's horse, hitched at the edge of the glade. At first, he moved as if in slow motion, because of the force exerted on him by the whirlpool, then faster and faster. When he reached the horse, he unhitched it and leaped into the saddle. He looked at Geoffroy, who was getting up, and waved him goodbye.

"Sorry, ancestor! Perhaps one day you'll understand," Guichard cried.

"Thou accursed horse thief!" Geoffroy picked up his sword and ran towards Guichard. "I swear on the dragon of St. George that—"

Geoffroy was spot lit in a flash of lightning, then the vortex came down right over him and he seemed to multiply and become distorted, as if Guichard were looking at him in a hall of mirrors.

Guichard spurred his horse and galloped down the hill. From there, he watched the scene taking place on the harbor wharf. The crusaders and the Templars were loading the coffers on to the pope's ship.

He turned his horse and shortly afterwards reached a fork with no signs. Without hesitating, he took the left road and soon disappeared amid a cloud of rain.

§

(... Back to the castle)

The fall on to the stone floor of the library left the knight breathless. The whirlwind disappeared out of the window. Lightning lit up the room. The desk clock read 4:42 p.m.

The door was flung open and André rushed inside, followed by Julius.

"Monsieur le Comte! Thank God you're safe and sound," said André, bending to help him up.

"By the dragon of St. George! Who art thou? A squire?"

Bewildered, André stared at Geoffroy. "But Monsieur le Comte, what are you saying? What a way to speak! And that beard...."

"But... this is my castle!" Geoffroy stared at André suspiciously. "Is this the manner to attire thyself, squire?" He suddenly seemed to remember something, let out a bellow of rage and grabbed André by the tie. "Where is that horse thief? *Where is he?*"

André's cell phone rang. Geoffroy startled, unsheathed his sword and hurled himself at André, who raised his arms and let the phone drop to the floor. Geoffroy shattered it with two slashes sending the fragments flying in all directions. Julius darted under a couch. Frowning, Geoffroy strode to the window.

"I descry not the archers! And what hath befallen the fosse? And the drawbridge?"

Dumbfounded, André stared at Geoffroy.

"Thou squire, assemble fifty serfs and put them to dig the fosse. I desire to hear the whip cracking. Forthwith!"

"Here trade unions don't allow work in the evening hours. As to the whip — even though the idea is tempting — I'm afraid it would give rise to some objections."

"*Trade unions?* A gang of Viking raiders?"

"Worse."

"Aha! We shall see. I enjoin thee, put the oil to boil in the cauldrons, have the pitch heated and have the catapults taken up on the battlements."

With a sigh, André collapsed on the couch. A clicking of heels came from the hallway.

"The 'trade unions' have betimes gained access into the castle, methinks!" Geoffroy raised his sword and hastened to lie in wait behind the door. "Make haste, squire. Grasp a halberd!"

"Unfortunately we've run out of halberds," André said, walking to the door, "but tomorrow I'll call the Vatican and ask the telephone number of their supplier."

Françoise appeared in the doorway.

"Madame Françoise! Perhaps it's advisable for you—"

"Where is he, André?"

"Madame, I'm afraid Monsieur le Comte is away on a journey and—"

"No, not Monsieur le Comte. *Him.*"

Geoffroy emerged from behind the door and stared long at Françoise. "My lady, I know not who thou art and never I saw a chatelaine attired like thee, but... thine eyes, thy look, thy voice." He paused and grew pale. "*Miriam.*"

Françoise flung herself into Geoffroy's arms. "Do you remember? A love that goes on even after death."

André sank onto the couch again. Julius emerged between his legs from underneath. "Dear Julius, let's not despair. Merlin will be here shortly."

§

Guichard rode into Jerusalem through St. Stephen's Gate. As he was trotting along the Cardo, he breathed in deeply, luxuriating in the sensations he'd spent a lifetime trying to recapture: the odor of spices from the street stalls, people's chattering, the whiteness of stone houses, the dim glow of oil lamps filtering through the shutters.... At the turning into the Street of David, he went right, and a few minutes later arrived at the square tower with rhombic grating where the Armenian quarter began. He rode under the archway of the tower.

When he arrived in front of the inn, Guichard drew rein. His eyes took in the inn sign, the façade, and finally rested on a window on the first floor. A soft light filtered through the shutters. He left Geoffroy's horse with the farrier, asking him to look after it for the night. A curious expression on his face, the man watched him walk away.

Guichard entered the inn and was about to climb the stairs.

"Hold it there, *seignior!* Where do you think you're going?" An iron hand clutched his arm.

Guichard turned. *Krikor.* The Armenian was holding a plucked chicken by the neck in one hand and a butcher's knife in the other. Guichard said nothing.

"*You?* You dog of a Norman, maybe I was wrong to think ill of you, after all. But.... what happened? I can hardly recognize you, clean-shaven as you are."

"You were right, Krikor," Guichard said, using the Provençal French he still remembered from his high-school years. "One cannot let go of something so beautiful."

"Up you go." Krikor watched him going up the stairs. "But think carefully of what you're going to do, Norman."

Guichard turned around.

"If you make her suffer once more..." With a slash of his knife, Krikor lopped off the chicken's head.

The music of a rebec accompanied Guichard's footsteps down the hallway. That music was like the breeze of a summer night, when, smelling the freshly ploughed earth, you hear a voice in the woods and feel a melancholy that gives you a lump in the throat. You dream of someone in a place lost in another world, where once you felt perfect and wished time to stop.

As he stood in front of Miriam's door, his heart was pounding so fast that he had to swallow and heave a deep breath. He knocked. Three times, as Geoffroy always used to do.

The music stopped... the door opened. *Miriam.*

A unicorn leapt out of the water.

Epilogue

(... A summer afternoon, long ago, on the shores of Lake Sevan)

A cart laden with bales of hay lumbered along the road skirting Lake Sevan near the village of Martouni. It was drawn by a pair of oxen goaded by a man stripped to the waist and wielding a pointed reed. Surrounded by pinewoods, the village dozed on the verdant slopes of Mount Murguz; the July sun brought out the glow of the reddish tufa stones of its houses, heightening the contrast with the turquoise blue of the lake. To the west, the snow-covered summit of Mount Ararat stood out against a clear sky.

Miriam stroked Guichard's cheek, stood up, shook the sand off her skirt and set out for the village. Guichard leaned his back against a fishing boat and watched her walk away.

Standing immobile by the shore of the lake, with the water up to his knees, Krikor was clutching a spear with both hands, the tip pointing downwards. With a lightning-swift movement, he plunged the spear into the water and lifted it out at once, a silvery trout wriggling on the point.

Krikor waded out of the water, took the trout off the spear and hurled it into a cauldron in which several dead trout floated in bloody water. The water splashed Guichard. Krikor grinned.

Guichard grunted, ran his hand over his face and sat up. He looked thoughtfully at Krikor.

"Krikor, how about making a pile of money?" Guichard said.

Krikor looked at him with skepticism mixed with interest. "How?"

"I've heard that farmers are worried about the wheat harvest. In the course of a few weeks, the price of wheat has gone up by thirty percent."

"What of it? The sage from the mountain has said that the *vichap* [the dragon in the Armenian mythology] told him it's going to be a wet summer and that the harvest will be poor."

"As far as you know, does it often rain around here?"

"Hardly ever."

"And people really believe in what the sage says, don't they?"

"His word is law."

"Just as I thought. So, this is what we'll do...."

"Are you out of your mind?" Krikor said when Guichard had explained his plan. "How can you sell something you don't have?"

"In my village we do it all the time. We call it *short selling*."

"A fine village of crooks, yours is."

Krikor hired a dozen trustworthy friends who went round all the villages on the high plateau spreading word of a poor harvest, which sent the price of wheat up even higher. Guichard asked the most important landowners to meet at the house of the sheriff of Erevan. The day of the meeting, with the sheriff sitting next to him, Guichard stood up in front of a restless audience of landowners, merchants and nobles.

"When the harvest is over, I undertake to sell you all the wheat you need at 2.4 silver dinars per bushel. As collateral, I've pledged my lands in Normandy to the sheriff," Guichard announced.

"I accept!" said a grain merchant, jumping to his feet. "Two hundred bushels for me."

"Three hundred and fifty for me!" yelled a landowner.

"Three hundred for me!"

Krikor was badgered by the bidders, their hands outstretched to sign the purchase orders.

It was a wonderful hot summer, the harvest was plentiful, and that "dog of a Norman" bought the wheat at 1.4 silver dinars per bushel. In October, Guichard was the wealthiest man in the highlands.

"This is your twenty percent, Krikor." Guichard pushed a bulging pouch towards Krikor.

Krikor untied the pouch, slipped his hand in and pulled it out full of silver coins. "Hm, now I'll have to find a hiding place."

"Money must be invested—not hidden," Guichard said. "I have another idea."

Krikor's eyes gleamed. "What?"

"The Silk Road."

"Forget it, Norman. Those merchants are very cunning. They've learned all conceivable tricks from the Chinese."

"How much is silk per ell?"

"About a silver dinar. Why?"

"Would you like to bet we're going to buy it for less than half a dinar?"

"Pshaw!" Krikor shook his head.

"Listen to me...."

When Guichard had told him what he had in mind, Krikor smiled slyly, put out a big, hairy hand and clapped Guichard on the shoulder, knocking over his chair and bumping his head against the wall.

"Sorry, Norman. It was meant to be a friendly gesture," said Krikor, jumping to his feet.

"Blast you!" Guichard rubbed his shoulder and got to his feet again. "Next time you intend to deal me 'a friendly gesture,' give me a little warning, so that I can wear my chain mail and helmet."

"Ah, so you lose your temper too!" Krikor wagged a finger under Guichard's nose. "And what should *I* say?"

"Oh, some gratitude!"

"Hating you was a pleasure, Norman, but now you've taken *even* that away from me." Krikor blew the pouch off the table, and the silver coins flew in all directions. "You dog of a Norman!"

Guichard glared at him, and Krikor stared him out.

They both burst into uncontrollable laughter.

THE END